Surfing Detective Double Feature Vol. 2

WIPEOUT!

MURDER AT VOLCANO HOUSE

two mysteries in one volume

Other Surfing Detective books by Chip Hughes

MURDER ON MOLOKA'I

KULA

HANGING TEN IN PARIS TRILOGY

Critical Acclaim for *Wipeout!*

"A carefully crafted mystery . . . quick-paced action and wild yet credible plot turns." *Honolulu Advertiser*

"*Wipeout!* is a lot of fun, and doesn't overstay its welcome, leaving you curious about the next volume in the series. It's smart that way." *Honolulu Star-Bulletin*

"*Wipeout!* is a light, easy to read detective book that will keep you smirking while you turn its pages. Another bit of fun fiction for the summer from Chip Hughes." *Waterman's Library*

"[J]ust right for the flight to the islands. Hughes's prose flows easily, slipping into Hawaiian pidgin when needed. His series began with *Murder on Moloka'i* and might remind readers of a charming new *Magnum, P.I.*" *Library Journal*

Critical Acclaim for *Murder at Volcano House*

"Entertaining Hawaiian whodunit. *Murder at Volcano House* . . . glides along at a satisfying clip. The landscape and characters are consistently colorful. [Kai] Cooke appealingly lapses into the indigenous patios when talking to other locals . . . Hughes effectively uses the native Hawaiian language throughout and also provides vivid descriptions of the legendary island scenery." *Kirkus Review*

"Ka Palapala Poʻokela award-winning author . . . Chip Hughes' hard-bitten detective Kai Cooke . . . ventures to Hawaiʻi island to investigate a series of mysterious deaths in Hawaiʻi Volcanoes National Park. Some say it's Pele exercising her wrath . . . But there are human suspects as well." *Honolulu Star-Advertiser*

SLATE RIDGE PRESS

P.O. Box 1886
Kailua, HI 96734

slateridgepress@hawaii.rr.com
ISBN: 0982944497
ISBN-13: 9780982944493

Wipeout! © Chip Hughes 2007
Murder at Volcano House © Chip Hughes 2014

SURFING DETECTIVE
CONFIDENTIAL INVESTIGATIONS : ALL ISLANDS

WIPEOUT!

A Surfing Detective Mystery

CHIP HUGHES

SLATE RIDGE PRESS

For Mark Foo, Todd Chesser,
Donny Solomon, Malik Joyeux,
For Mark Foo, Todd Chesser,
Donny Solomon, Malik Joyeux,
and other big wave riders
who have lost their lives
in the pursuit.

"If you want to experience the ultimate thrill,
you have to be willing to pay the ultimate price."

—*Big-wave rider Mark Foo*

Foreword

By Big-Wave Pioneer Fred Van Dyke

Wipeout! will grasp you from the very beginning. No details have been overlooked. The characters, the events are woven together in an inextricable mystery that unfolds slowly, and it is not until the very end that you realize what has taken place. There is really no second guessing the author. Many times when you are expecting one thing to happen, the opposite occurs.

I am a big-wave surfing legend who lived thirty years adjacent to the famous Pipeline break, having the experience of nearly losing my home on a number of occasions to the huge waves that sweep the beach during winter months. I have wiped out at Waimea and all the other big-wave breaks on Oʻahu. I passed into the other world on a wipeout, but it was not my time to lose my life. I feel deeply what Chip writes and describes.

As I was reading, I totally became a part of the narrative. The scenes out at Waimea Bay happen similarly. The people who live on the North Shore are depicted in a real fashion. I have lost friends to the Waimea ferociousness—closest to me was Mark Foo, who handled Waimea beautifully but lost his life at Mavericks.

Chip was able to fully wrap me into the story by this authenticity of description. I could feel the dry throat, the anxiety of waiting for a closeout set on the horizon, the flushed face, being caught in the riptide and washed seaward after losing your board.

The relationship you feel between the board and yourself is an important part of surfing and Chip caught that, nearly making the board seem like a friend or an extension of body and mind.

Whether you're a surfer, a mystery lover, or both, *Wipeout!* is a read I think you will enjoy.

Fred Van Dyke
April 2006

Acknowledgments

Many thanks once again to my wife, Charlene, whose inspiration guides my writing and my life, to my mother, Kathryn Cooley Hughes, for her unflagging support, and to Stu Hilt for sharing his nearly fifty years' experience as a Honolulu P.I.

Mahalo to big-wave legend Fred Van Dyke for his generous foreword; to my writing group—LaRene Despain, Sue Cowing, and Felix Smith; to Les Peetz, Lorna Hershinow, Ku'ualoha Ho'omanawanui, Ian MacMillan, Steven Goldsberry, and Rodney Morales; and to my invaluable editor, Kirsten Whatley.

one

"Are you the Surfing Detective?" she asked in a voice as soft as trade winds whispering in bamboo.

"Yes …" I wondered if this was yet another crank call.

"Good, because you're the only one who can help."

That got my attention.

She kept details to a minimum, then made an appointment and promised an advance.

A few mornings later I waited for her in a red vinyl booth at the second-floor Denny's in Waikīkī. The aroma of lattes and espressos wafting up from the Starbucks below made me wish I was down there on Kapahulu Avenue, or on my way to a morning surf session.

But she had chosen Denny's. She didn't say why. And she was late.

I sat there in my most flamboyant aloha shirt—*hula* dancers, Diamond Head, swaying coconut palms and, yes, surfers—watching the sun shimmer on glistening Kapi'olani Park and the damp, cocoa-colored sands of Waikīkī Beach. The campy aloha shirt was to help her recognize me, along with the mostly true description of myself I had given:

sun-bleached brown hair, six feet even (a stretch), and a perpetual tan from surfing. I didn't mention my age, thirty-four, nor did I claim Hawaiian ancestry. Though my name, Kai, means "sea" and though I was *hānaied,* or adopted, by a Hawaiian family when I was eight, my Cooke ancestors were about as New England as you can get. Anyway, all my client seemed to care about was that I was both a surfer *and* a detective.

By 10:15 most evidence of the morning showers had vanished, but the pavement on Kapahulu still ran blacker than usual to the beach. There were few surfers out today. This morning's gloomy grey canopy—coupled with small surf on the South Shore—had kept all but the diehards at home. Most had gone up to the North Shore, where a huge winter swell was thundering in from storms in the North Pacific— off Japan, off China, off the Aleutian Islands, off who knows where in that immense, blue, fathomless ocean.

We'd had some enormous days in December and January. Twenty-five feet. Thirty feet. February figured to bring more really big ones.

Today was Monday, February 3. I stared through the steam swirling up from my coffee. If I were a smoker, I would have lit up about now. Instead, from the pocket of my aloha shirt, behind a swaying palm, I slipped a sweet *li hing mui* crack seed onto my tongue and instantly the sweet-sour plum pit exploded with pungent flavor.

Glancing up I saw a woman who was very *hāpai*, very pregnant, at the entrance. She caught my eye and made her way toward me. I ditched the crack seed in my napkin.

"Summer?" I stood and clasped her trembling hand and breathed in the flowery scent of her perfume. She nodded as she slipped her hand from mine and edged slowly into the booth.

"Want some coffee?" I noticed her eyes were violet—not blue, but intensely violet like orchids. Then I gazed at her protruding tummy. "Uh … orange juice? Milk?"

"Nothing, thank you," she replied in that whispering voice I'd heard earlier on the phone. I leaned toward her so I wouldn't miss a word.

Summer's hair was blonde, wheat blonde, turned under in the golden roll of a pageboy. She had a cute cheerleader nose and a dimple in her chin. Back in California, she would have been that knockout in high school every guy had a crush on at least once.

"How difficult this must be for you," I said. "I'm very sorry about your husband."

She tried for a smile that didn't even reach the corners of her mouth. Her delicate hands were folded neatly on the tabletop. Her violet eyes looked misty.

"You said on the phone you wanted me to look into his death?"

She nodded.

"It happened in December at Waimea Bay?" I prompted.

"Yes, on the day before Christmas at sunset, almost Christmas eve."

"Did you see him wipe out?" I recalled the incident from news coverage. Corky McDahl had been pounded by a succession of twenty-foot waves and not seen again.

"No." She glanced down at her tummy. "We thought with the baby due soon and all …"

"So you stayed behind in …where is it you live again in California?"

"Newport Beach."

"And you didn't mind staying home while he surfed in Hawai'i?"

"I'm very independent. So was Corky." She pulled from her purse a snapshot and handed it to me. "My husband." She introduced him as if he were still alive and sitting with us in the booth.

I glanced at the photo of a deeply tanned man in his middle twenties. Under a thatch of straw yellow curls, green eyes dominated. Mirrored sunglasses, the expensive kind some surfers wear, hung from a cord around his neck. His adolescent smile turned downward on one side, revealing a hint of attitude. He looked agitated, like a guy about to throw a punch.

"Corky took out a two-hundred-thousand-dollar life insurance policy before his trip," Summer said. "The time lapse clause, or whatever they call it, matured just a few days before his accident, but the insurance company hasn't paid. Mr. Gold, the adjuster, is very apologetic."

"Surfers do unfortunately sometimes disappear. Your Mr. Gold must know that."

"Oh, he does. It's not just the short time the policy was in effect. Mr. Gold says Corky's case raises several red flags."

"What red flags?"

"Corky withdrew all our savings before he left," she said matter-of-factly.

"Did he tell you he was going to clean out the account?"

"No, not at the time. But he probably needed the money for his trip." She seemed unconcerned by an action some spouses might consider treacherous and disloyal.

"What else?"

"Corky charged our credit cards over the limit. A few charges came through even after he died."

"The card could have been stolen," I conjectured, "or the purchases posted late."

"Well, we have low spending limits, so it's no surprise he went over them. Another thing," Summer went on, "Mr. Gold asked me why Corky would have been seen driving a BMW convertible—an expensive new model."

"What did you tell him?"

"I said Corky didn't own a BMW. We couldn't afford one. But he had an auto detailing business in California. He may have earned extra money in Hawai'i by working on that BMW, and just took it for a ride."

The red flags were adding up. "Anything else?"

She shook her head. "Corky always wanted to be a big name surfer—a sponsored surfer—and he looked at his trips here as investments in his career—and in our future. He dreamed that someday, somehow, a sponsor would discover him. He even changed his name from Charles to Corky after a legendary California surfer..."

"Corky Carroll?"

"Yes, I believe that's the one. Corky... er, Charles ... talked about his idol constantly, though he never actually met him."

I caught myself gazing at her again. I was thinking about her baby. If she were my wife, and in the last months of her pregnancy, would I abandon her to ride the world's biggest, most dangerous waves? Maybe Corky didn't want to be a father after all. Maybe he preferred to go out in a blaze of glory, rather than face his parental responsibilities.

"Summer, I have to ask you this." I hated to say it out loud. "Do you know any reason why your husband would fake his own death?"

She shook her head. "It wasn't like him to do something so desperate."

"Not even to defraud the insurance company of two hundred thousand dollars?"

"Not my Corky."

The waitress came by and refilled my coffee. "Would you like anything?" I asked Summer again.

"Nothing, thanks," she said.

"It won't be easy to prove your husband died." I tried to be realistic with her. "When surfers disappear, a shredded wet suit or torn board shorts may be all that turns up. Some vanish without a trace."

She didn't respond, but kept looking at me hopefully.

"'Course Waimea on a big day is like a huge outdoor arena, with hundreds of onlookers and photographers, so we may come up with something. A bobbing surfer might have been spotted, though maybe not after sunset when your husband wiped out. But even if I find evidence of your husband's …"—I groped for words—"evidence of your husband, I can't guarantee the insurance company will accept it as proof."

Summer's determined look suggested she wasn't fazed by what I'd said.

"How soon can you start?"

"Right away. But about the retainer…" I reminded her of her promise. "In a case like this confined to O'ahu, five hundred would be OK for starters."

She reached into her purse and pulled out a handful of crumpled green bills—all Ben Franklins—setting them on the table. There must have been a dozen hundreds easily, all wadded up and wrinkled.

I separated out five crumpled notes and slid the others across the table to her.

"I wish you would take them all, so I don't have to make another trip here." She slid the bills back my way. "I trust you'll return what you don't use."

I decided not to argue with her. I gathered up all that green and shoved it behind the swaying palm on the pocket of my aloha shirt.

"Where are you staying?" I asked, in a lighter mood now. "Can I give you a lift?"

She pulled a paper from her purse and handed it to me. The phone number on it began with 739-. *Kāhala? Ritzy Kāhala?*

"The Kāhala Resort?" I asked. "That's a posh hotel."

"No, a private home," she said. "You can call me there."

"You have friends in Kāhala?"

She nodded but didn't explain. As she struggled up from the table, I handed her my card. "I'll phone you as soon as I have anything to report."

Summer glanced at the longboard rider on the sand-toned card and slipped it into her purse.

My eyes returned to her bulging middle. "When is your baby due?"

"Early March—so the doctors say." Summer made a cute smirk that almost turned into a smile. "They're never right, you know. My mother tells me I came three weeks early."

"Three weeks early for your baby would mean just a few days from now…"

Summer shrugged. "The baby will wait until you find evidence of my Corky." Her confidence worried me.

She started to walk away. Before she got out of earshot I couldn't help saying, only half joking, "Delivering babies is not in my standard contract."

She turned around, shrugged again, and then duck-stepped past rows of mostly empty booths and out the door. A few minutes later, on the street below, I saw Summer climb awkwardly into a hearse-black Mercedes sedan. A door closed and she disappeared behind darkly tinted glass. The Mercedes turned toward Diamond Head and soon vanished.

Later, when disentangling the green bills Summer had left behind, I counted not twelve, but sixteen. Sixteen hundred dollars. *In cash.* More than I would need, no doubt, since this case was most likely going nowhere.

Better than a month had passed since Corky wiped out. If he had died in the huge surf, by now his bones would be licked clean, if any bones remained at all. I could try to find his board and track down his credit card purchases and maybe even locate the BMW he was allegedly seen driving. But evidence of his body? No way.

Unless, of course, Corky had pulled off one of the most daring skip traces in recorded history. But to play dead in Waimea's massive winter surf would have amounted to suicide. Twenty-foot waves are not make-believe. That Corky would go to such lengths simply to escape paternal responsibilities seemed unlikely—unless he and Summer together were trying to defraud the insurance company to the tune of two hundred grand.

If this was their game, the pregnant blonde was well coached—her trembling hands, her misty eyes. But her story didn't match her bankroll. If Corky had left her broke, how was Summer underwriting her trip to Hawai'i? And what about her friends with the Kāhala phone number and black Mercedes?

I pocketed the cash again and, despite my qualms, found myself sympathizing with the violet-eyed widow.

Whatevahs. I had a case. Or it had me.

two

Located on Maunakea Street above Fujiyama's Lei Shop, my office is about the size and sturdiness of a Cracker Jack box. It boasts one window overlooking the bustle and varied aromas and questionable charm of the storied old ramshackle street. Just one block down, amidst the color and ambience of Chinatown, is notorious Hotel Street. Once the province of pimps, prostitutes, porno palaces, and flop houses, these days you're more likely to find art galleries and ethnic eateries.

I pulled open the bottom drawer of my battleship grey filing cabinet, on which sits a tarnished surf-rider trophy: Classic Longboard . . . Mākaha . . . Third Place. *My faded glory*. Way in the back of the musty bottom drawer where I store personal files, I reached for a manila folder of news clippings labeled Big-Wave Wipeouts.

The first story my eyes fell on eulogized Tahiti surfer Malik Joyeux who died at Banzai Pipeline in December 2005. The lip of a powerful wave had hit him dead on, broken his board in half, and ripped off the leash. Joyeux was found under water, about two hundred yards from where he had wiped out. The treacherous Banzai riptide had carried him away.

The next clipping recalled the drowning of Todd Chesser near Waimea Bay in February 1997. A faded photo showed Chesser—glistening shaved head and seal black wetsuit—shooting a mammoth green tube during the filming of *In God's Hands*. Another photo pictured the memorial service for the wave rider at Ali'i Beach Park in Hale'iwa, attended by hundreds of fellow surfers and family and friends.

Next came a raggedly torn and yellowed *Star-Bulletin* clipping about Mark Foo's wipeout in 1994 at Mavericks in Half Moon Bay near San Francisco. More stories about Foo's drowning lay beneath this clipping and some glossy magazine spreads commemorating his life.

Where did I put that one about Corky? I thumbed through the folder crammed with clippings. Who knows how I got started collecting such sensational and morbid stories? I also collect accounts of surfers attacked by sharks, since it happened to me. But the shark-bite pieces have their own separate folder.

"'The Wave of His Life' Was His Last." There it was. The *Honolulu Advertiser,* December 25, Christmas day. And there was Corky's straw hair, intense eyes, and cocky smile.

The accompanying story told how Corky had wiped out at Waimea on Christmas Eve. The sun had set, but the huge waves kept cranking, enticing surfers to stay out in the crimson afterglow. The waves that got him were twenty feet—a two-story building. Though the irony of big wave tragedies is that typically the unfortunate surfer miraculously survives the biggest wave of the day, only to be pummeled to death by a smaller one.

Corky had just successfully ridden a monster of nearly thirty feet. "He died with a smile on his face," proclaimed a fellow surfer. "He was grinning from ear to ear. Corky wished me 'Merry Christmas' and then paddled out for another one." The next wave would be his last. "It's the way he'd want to go," said the surfer. "Not die in a car wreck or slowly wither of old age. He died happy. I'm glad for him."

The *Advertiser* continued: "The 27-year-old California native could not catch the first wave of the next set and was pounded back by three 20-footers that followed." A lifeguard was quoted: "We figure the big waves pushed him deep underwater and kept him there. His body may never be found. It happens this way sometimes, unfortunately for loved ones left behind."

Three twenty-footers thundering in. Like freight trains. Caught in that boiling soup, tumbling head over heels and struggling to hold his breath, he wouldn't have known which way was up.

What must happen in white water twenty feet high? You probably *whirl*. Like a feather in a gale, only not so gently. It must feel more like the spin cycle of an industrial-strength washer. Or being massaged by a hammer—*jackhammer*. Most likely, Corky turned endlessly in the dark, exploding wave, then was sucked out unconscious to sea in Waimea's powerful riptide. What happened afterwards is anybody's guess.

According to another clipping, more than a month later no trace of his body had been found. Not even a shred of his wetsuit. The tiger sharks that roam these coastal waters—those silent, steel-jawed killers—sometimes leave nothing behind.

The sole known remains of Corky McDahl was his surfboard. The candy cane-striped board had drifted to shore, evidently ripped by coral on its tumultuous ride. The battered board shown in the *Advertiser* photo had no chunks missing, no telltale saw-toothed crescents torn from its rails. I decided to pay a visit to the Honolulu Police Department later that day—they'd have sharper photos than this newsprint image.

I glanced at my answering machine. The red light was flashing like a warning beacon, so I pressed Play.

"Kai? I missed you last night," said the shy, childlike voice. "Weren't we going to see that film?"

Leimomi. Just like her to sound not the least bit angry—just pondering if she had the wrong day or time. She had them right. I forgot. Again. I had promised to take her to a movie remake of *The Merry Widow* that critics touted as "spellbinding" and "hilariously funny." Some woman whose husband is barely in the grave takes up with another man and causes quite an uproar. It didn't interest me in the least. I would have preferred to see a new surfing documentary that was playing. Maybe that's why I forgot about Leimomi's film.

"Are we seeing *The Merry Widow* tonight?" Leimomi asked plaintively. "Not last night, but tonight?"

I imagined her waiting for me last night in her Punchbowl duplex after stringing *lei* all day in Mrs. Fujiyama's shop. Leimomi didn't even phone my apartment with her innocent, slightly hurt questions, but that's not her style. When she called my office the next morning expecting to find me in, I was sitting in a booth at Denny's in Waikīkī gazing into the violet eyes of a pregnant California blonde.

What I had done yesterday instead of showing up for my date with Leimomi was surf. I paddled out to my favorite spot in town, offshore of the Sheraton Waikīkī—the long, hollow, right-breaking walls of Populars. I rode waves until the mango orange sun slipped into the sea. Then in twilight I strolled back to my apartment—a studio penthouse on the forty-fifth floor of the Waikīkī Edgewater—and hopped into a long hot shower. By seven, when I was supposed to be pulling into Leimomi's duplex, I was sipping a beer in front of the Triple Crown of Surfing recap on ESPN.

"Kai, I'm off today so I won't see you at work. Would you call me . . . please?" Leimomi's voice drifted from the answering machine. I sighed.

A second message contained the sardonic voice of my attorney friend, Tommy Woo: "Hey, Kai, how many piano players does it take to change a light bulb?"

Another doozy. The punch line included the names of keyboard legends Bill Evans, Keith Jarrett, and Yanni, and to my tone-deaf ear made absolutely no sense. Though he practiced law, Tommy's true passion was the jazz piano.

"How about dinner?" continued Tommy. "Got a gig on Tuesday, but Wednesday looks good. Same old place at seven?"

Same old place meant Ah Fook Chop Sui House on River Street in Chinatown, where the best thing on the menu was the prices. If Tommy and I have anything in common, it's being cheap.

I erased the messages and returned to my newspaper clipping on the unfortunate Corky McDahl. "The best wave of his life . . . The way he'd want to go . . . He died with a smile on his face . . ." It all sounded so convincing—such a purposeful, happy death. Not something you could easily fake. I scanned the not-yet-yellowed newsprint once again—then realized I was procrastinating. *Call Leimomi.* I picked up the phone and dialed. It rang three times, then her answering machine kicked in.

"Sorry about last night, Leimomi . . ."

As I began to sheepishly explain, there was a barely audible tap on my door.

"Be right with you!" I barked through the solid mahogany. "I'll take you to that film, Lei. How about tomorrow night?"

Tap. Tap. Tap. This time not so faint.

"Look, I'll have to call you back. A customer is knocking. We'll see that movie, I promise."

"Coming!" I reached for the knob and swung open the door. "Leimomi? What are you doing here?"

Startled into abruptness, I gazed down upon her. She stood barely five feet in sandals—waist-length brown hair, mocha-colored skin, eyes glistening like black pearls. She was a Kaua'i girl whose mixed Japanese, Chinese, and Filipino heritages blended together beautifully.

"You don't work today," I said, studying her innocent face for some clue. A simple black shift hanging on her slim frame revealed just a hint of the curves I knew were there. Her expression looked neither anxious nor angry, but bewildered.

"I wondered," she said in her quiet voice, "if anything was wrong."

"No, nothing is wrong. I'm sorry about last night. I know you wanted to see that movie."

"We can see it another time," she said almost apologetically, as if the missed date were *her* fault. I suddenly felt guiltier than if she had given me the verbal thrashing I deserved.

"I know we can see that movie another time," I uttered abjectly, "but today was your day off and all, and we had planned to spend some time together last night . . ."

"So you still love me then?" She peered into my eyes with those glistening pearls.

"Of course."

"And everything is all right between us?"

"Everything is fine."

"Good, because I worried last night . . . I worried that after all we've shared you really didn't love me."

"Why are you so worried?"

"We need to talk, Kai. But . . ." She hesitated.

"Is something wrong?" I was becoming curious.

"Tomorrow night would be better." She lowered her dark eyes. "OK?"

"OK," I agreed, though I didn't like to be left hanging.

"Kiss me, Kai." She puckered her plum red lips. So I did.

Leimomi then turned and glided down the dim hallway, past the offices of my fellow tenants: passport photographer, accountant, freelance editor, and psychic Madame Zenobia. Soon Leimomi disappeared down the orange shag stairs.

I gave her a few minutes to clear the building, imagining she might stop to chat with the other *lei* girls and with Mrs. Fujiyama. Then I grabbed my manila folder with the clippings and headed down the stairs.

As I walked through the shop, I glanced into the back room and saw Chastity and Joon stringing sweet-scented *pīkake*. Another *lei* girl, Blossom, sat nearby tying off a pale yellow plumeria *lei*. Passing the refrigerated cases displaying colorful strands of island flowers, I glimpsed Mrs. Fujiyama at the cash register, bone thin, steel haired, and, as always during business hours, wearing a courteous smile.

"Good morning, Mrs. Fujiyama," I said.

She glanced up at me over half glasses, her smile suddenly bending into a frown. "Good morning, Mr. Cooke."

Strange. Mrs. Fujiyama and I were on the most cordial of terms, though she was a stern mother hen hovering over her *lei* girls.

"Anything wrong, Mrs. Fujiyama?"

"Nothing wrong, Mr. Cooke," she replied in an expressionless tone that suggested otherwise.

I stepped from the flower shop onto Maunakea Street and headed for my parking garage. The sharp competing smells of kim chee, cappuccino, rancid garbage, and screw-cap wine reached my nose. As I turned in, I realized the silent wrath of my landlady was making me feel nearly as guilty as the apologetic behavior of my girlfriend.

three

Cruising toward HPD headquarters on Beretania Street, I spotted a black Mercedes in my rearview mirror. The car was behind three others, so I couldn't swear it was the same black Mercedes Summer had climbed into after our Denny's meeting. But I didn't doubt it either.

I kept my eye on the car as my Impala growled along, turning a few heads. My '69 Chevy is not your nondescript, front-wheel-drive, pale imitation Impala of today, but a genuine V-8, gas-guzzling, glitzy dream machine of the sixties. The real thing.

My surfboard rode beside me inside the teal cockpit, the nine-six's rounded, duckbill nose resting comfortably on the padded dash. That's the beauty of an outsized classic car like this—pop out the backseat and my longboard slides right in. I like to bring my board along even when I'm not heading for the surf. On the spur of the moment, while cruising Oʻahu's streets and highways, I can run my fingers along its glossy surface, reminding me of the white-crested beauties that await the end of my day.

Lucky you live Hawai'i, as we say. I feel sorry for my landlocked friends who can only surf virtual waves on a computer. Sitting on their *'ōkole* in front of a video screen is hardly the same thing. If just once in their lives they could paddle out and catch a real wave—feel the burn in their arms and the salt spray in their faces. Then they'd know that this ride is nothing like the imaginary ones. Corky McDahl would tell them. If he were still alive.

When I finally pulled in front of HPD's art deco headquarters, the Mercedes, behind me now by about eight car lengths, also pulled to the curb. I sat in my Impala and waited a full minute. The Mercedes didn't move. I waited another minute. So did the Mercedes. As I prepared to wait another five, the big black sedan pulled from the curb and slowly drove by, windows so dark that I couldn't make out the driver or passengers. No doubt about it. I had been followed.

Inside HPD's photo lab I caught up with crack police photographer Creighton Lee, whose expert shots often proved a prosecutor's best friend. Creighton could size up a crime scene in seconds and capture just the right views of the crucial evidence.

"Creighton—howzit?" I grabbed his meaty right hand and we shook by hooking thumbs, local-style.

"Kai, brah," he said in a soft-spoken pidgin totally at odds with his thick fire-hydrant frame. "Surprise' you not up on da Nort' Shore. Big swell, brah. *Beeeg!*"

Creighton was not only a prodigy with the camera, but also a dedicated soul surfer. He usually rode his twelve-foot tanker in knee-high fun stuff, having little ambition for anything bigger, let alone the infamous North Shore titans.

"Not surfing today, brah," I told Creighton in my own pidgin. "Working one case. You like help me, or what?"

"Shoots." The crack photographer shrugged in agreement.

"Remembah dat California surfer wen' wipe out Christmas Eve at Waimea?"

"Da big wipeout? Da guy dat die?"

"Yeah, da same one," I said. "Da widow no can collect on da life insurance. Two hundred gran', brah."

"Ho!" Creighton raised his thick black brows.

"She hire me to prove him dead."

"How you goin' do dat? Da guy been gone since Christmas—da sharks eat 'em, bruddah."

"I figgah dat," I explained, "but I need one photo of his board, plus anyt'ing else you got on da case."

Creighton disappeared for a while, then returned with an accident report and photos of Corky's board, recovered near Sunset Beach the morning after his wipeout. The Californian had ridden a "big gun," also called an "elephant gun." Legendary surfer Buzzy Trent coined the term in the late fifties. Trent reportedly told his shaper, Joe Quigg, "You don't go out hunting elephants with a BB gun, you hunt elephants with an elephant gun. Make me an elephant gun to shoot big waves."

Corky's narrow, stiletto-like gun measured nearly eleven feet with a deep rocker, pin tail, pointed nose, and single fin. Its red and white stripes resembled a candy cane—appropriate for Christmas Eve. Pockmarks in Corky's board showed evidence of being ripped by coral and rock. No sign of shark bites. However, the absence of crescent-shaped *puka* didn't necessarily mean he had escaped the tiger sharks himself.

A Sunset Beach woman reportedly had pulled the fallen surfer's board from the water on Christmas morning and then, for whatever reason, waited nearly twenty-four hours to contact police, who examined and photographed it on the day after Christmas. The surfboard evidently still remained in the possession of this woman, since Corky's next of kin—I guess, Summer—had declined to claim it.

The police report told the story of Corky's wipeout much as his wife and the *Advertiser* had told it. After riding "the wave of his life," he was pounded by three successive twenty-footers and not seen again. A several-day search by Coast Guard, fire department, and HPD teams turned up no trace of the missing surfer, except for the battered candy cane-striped board.

After thanking Creighton for his help I wheeled my Impala back to Maunakea Street while pondering Corky's disappearance. His widely reported wipeout had all the earmarks of a big-wave catastrophe. Each winter, unwary *malihini*—newcomers like Corky McDahl—journey to the islands to challenge Hawai'i's fabled waves. Each winter, tragically, one or more may meet his fate. Knowing firsthand the power and massiveness of Waimea's winter surf, I began to sincerely doubt that Summer's husband had skipped out on her and their baby.

From what I had learned about Corky so far, he probably wasn't my favorite kind of surfer—an aggressive upstart pushing to join the pro circuit, and typically a wave hog who believes he *owns* a wave. If you so much as stroke for the same wave, they go ballistic. A wave hog in the lineup can ruin an entire session.

One day on a beautiful hollow curl at Populars, a guy took off next to me and shot within inches of my board. As a courtesy to a fellow surfer already on the wave, I pulled out. Astonishingly, after riding this beauty all to himself, the guy paddled straight for me, cursing and threatening that if I so much as came near him on a wave, he was going to "beat the sh– out of me." I paddled away. He had no concept of community, of the brotherhood and sisterhood of wave riders. His selfish vision of the lineup included no one but himself.

Why Corky reminded me of this experience I'm not sure—his arrogant eyes or snarly smile? You can't tell that much from a photo. Or can you?

four

"A high-surf advisory is in effect for all North- and West-facing shores," said the wrought-up voice on the radio as my Chevy purred through pineapple fields and coffee groves on Kamehameha Highway, heading for Hale'iwa. "On the west side, Mākaha is reporting in at fifteen to eighteen. On the North Shore, Sunset and Pipeline, eighteen to twenty-plus. Waimea is the big story: occasional twenty-five foot sets, or higher . . ." The excited voice paused. "Be careful out there today. Expert surfers only!"

My throat felt suddenly dry. It got even dryer when I crested the ridge overlooking the panorama of the entire North Shore. Across the wide blue horizon, one mammoth wave after another was creaming the turquoise sea. Had I been looking less at the surf and more in my rearview mirror, I might have noticed sooner that black Mercedes behind me again. Even so, it wasn't the Mercedes that was parching my throat. It was the waves.

My cousin Alika had agreed to meet me at a shop called Surf 'n Sea in Hale'iwa, near the old two-lane bridge by the harbor. Corky's hangout during his last days, Hale'iwa town featured an eclectic blend of old and new, of local and cosmopolitan, of traditional and trendy. Tin-roofed Matsumoto's General Store, famous for its shave ice, stood shoulder to shoulder with glitzy eateries, new age art galleries, and designer boutiques. Cruising through town I whiffed roasting garlic, sizzling veggie burgers, freshly brewed Kona coffee, grilling *mahi mahi,* and coconut-scented surfboard wax. And I eyed countless boards for sale. Despite the proliferation of upscale surfing-themed retailers that sell more logo apparel than boards, Hale'iwa still boasts more bona fide surf shops per capita than any other town on earth, living up to its nickname—Surf City.

Inside Surf 'n Sea, a rustic country surf shop with a rambling plank porch, I wandered among the racks of gleaming boards by T & C, Robert August, Stewart, Ben Aipa, Donald Takayama, and lots more. Leaning in to get a closer look at a nine-seven carbon fiber Velzy was cousin Alika, his coffee brown eyes as focused and intent as an airline pilot inspecting his ship before takeoff.

"Eh, *haole* boy!" Alika glanced up from the black surfboard and flashed a roguish grin, his deep, resonant voice filling the surf shop like the thrum of a bass fiddle. He extended his muscular brown arm and we shook local-style.

"Howzit, Alika?" I looked up at my cousin, towering over me in board shorts and a bulging tank top emblazoned with "Hawaiian Superman."

From his steel grip and imposing physique, you could tell that Alika Kealoha surfed big waves. His shoulders were wide and his arms massive, and his torso was shaped in a powerful *V.* He was a brawny iron-hard Atlas of a man.

If anybody knew Waimea, it was my Hawaiian cousin. Off the top of his head he could recite the various swells and their directions, the correct lineups for each, the dangerous riptides, and the sometimes risky shore breaks; he could also tell you who rode the biggest wave ever, who took the nastiest wipeout, who got hurt, who disappeared and was lost or found, and who died outright. With only a little prompting Alika remembered Corky McDahl's wipeout.

"Da *haole* surfah dat wipe out on Christmas Eve?" Alika asked me. "Da one dey nevah fin'?"

"Dat's him. You evah see him surf? Candy cane board, blon' hair, *attitude* . . ."

"Maybe at Chun's Reef. If dat him, brah, he OK for one mainland surfah. But bettah he wen' sit on da beach and watch us guyz, yeah? Big Waimea not fo' beginnahs."

"You surfing Waimea when he wipe out? Or your frien's?"

"Not me, brah, but maybe Bolo or Māpuna or Puka," Alika said, referring to his surfing buddies.

"Can ask 'em today?"

"Shoots," the Hawaiian Superman replied.

Out in the gravel lot we climbed into Alika's rusted-out Toyota truck, knobby tires crusted with red dirt. In the bed lay two big guns—sunshine yellow and lime green—similar in size and stiletto shape to Corky's missing board.

As my Hawaiian cousin wound through the gears and the tires began to sing on the blacktop, I recalled today's surf report for Waimea: *occasional twenty-five foot sets, or higher.*

This was a rare occurrence. Only a large winter swell, generated in the North Pacific and headed in just the right direction, causes waves to break like that inside the bay.

On these special days, liquid mountains loom on the horizon, sweep around the point, and explode with the percussion of a volcano. The booms can be heard halfway to Hale'iwa. The mile-wide bay transforms into a colossal outdoor amphitheater peopled by surfers and photographers and spectators from around the world. The road surrounding the bay chokes with double-parked cars. The lot at the beach park jams. Waimea takes on the elevated mood and bustle of a world-class amusement park. A Disneyland of waves.

But for big-wave riders this is serious business. The potential thrill of a lifetime can become, in unfortunate cases, the *end* of a lifetime. Mark Foo, drowned in 1994 at Mavericks, said it best: "If you want to experience the ultimate thrill, you have to be willing to pay the ultimate price."

When Corky wiped out, there was undoubtedly no shortage of photographers on hand with powerful telephoto lenses that can pick out a tattoo a quarter mile away. But since the wipeout occurred after sundown, the light would not have been best. The news clippings said a few bystanders had watched him get pounded by the first of several twenty-footers. No one reported seeing him after that.

As we approached Waimea, I noticed the bell tower of the Mission of Saints Peter and Paul soaring over the bay, familiar to surfers around the world. Less well known is the ancient cliff-top Mahuka *heiau,* or temple, for human sacrifice just beyond. Both the bell tower and the *heiau* have always suggested to me the sacredness of the bay. For surfers, coming here represents a pilgrimage, a confrontation with the ultimate power, and maybe even a meeting with destiny.

This morning the bell tower cast its long shadow across Waimea's wide beach, where countless caution signs pierced the sand like errant spears: High Surf . . . Hazardous Conditions . . . No Swimming . . . Beach Closed.

Despite these warnings, two surfers were paddling out to join many others in the distant lineup, where one of those liquid mountains was just now steaming in. As it jacked up, a dozen surfers flailed their arms and tried to climb over the massive cresting wave. Some few tempted their fate, turning and plunging down the almost vertical cliff.

Booooom! The mountain detonated in the bay.

"Chance 'um, Kai?" Alika's brown eyes taunted me as he pulled his truck into the jammed lot and parked illegally on a grassy strip.

Dry mouth again.

We stepped out and Alika nudged me. "Grab one board." He pointed to the two guns in the truck's bed.

Booooom! Another mammoth crashed, shaking the ground beneath us. A shiver of fear ran through me.

"Bettah do da interviews first." I wasn't deliberately stalling, but I wasn't in any hurry to paddle into those giants either.

"Da surfahs you need fo' interview stay in da waves, brah," my cousin replied, "not on da beach."

five

If I was going to go tight in the chest, to start breathing fast and feeling weak-kneed, or get butterflies in my stomach—if I was going to panic, the full-blown signs would appear now.

Had the unlucky Corky McDahl shown these telltale signs? I didn't know and right now I didn't care. My only job was to keep them away from me.

"*No Fear . . . No Fear . . .*" I said a little mantra to focus myself and stay loose.

I stripped off my aloha shirt and khakis, revealing the board shorts I was wearing underneath and the shark bite on my chest that Alika always referred to as my "tattoo."

Alika handed me a chunk of wax and I began reluctantly rubbing it onto the deck of his lime green gun. Out in the distant lineup riders and their surfboards looked like ants clinging to toothpicks. Little more than specks. Each breaker jacked up three or four times higher than the boards cutting white trails down it. The swell was still rising.

"*Ho,* brah!" Alika pointed toward the roaring bay. "Let's paddle out." I took a deep breath and tried to exhale.

We jogged down the beach to the water. The cool February sea and hiss of the distant foam gave me a few more shivers. The glassy surface near the beach lay deceptively calm, but suddenly an overhead shorebreak wave slammed the beach like a guillotine. We waited for a lull again, then mounted our guns and paddled quickly through the danger zone.

I am not an experienced big wave rider. The few surfers who are form an elite cadre whose door Corky McDahl was knocking on when he got knocked off by those twenty footers. I've often heard the names of big-wave pioneers of the '50s and '60s uttered by young surfers like Corky with reverence—if not a tinge of envy.

Greg Noll earned the nickname "Da Bull" for aggressively charging the biggest waves anybody of his day had ever ridden; Buzzy Trent, the consummate, muscle-packed athlete, resembled a Greek god; Jose Angel, all-around waterman, tragically died diving for black coral; Fred Van Dyke, the "Iron Man" of big wave riding, survived unimaginable wipeouts; Ricky Grigg, surfer and oceanographer, charted some of Hawai'i's famous reef breaks; Eddie "Would Go" Aikau vanished in the Moloka'i Channel while paddling to save a stranded boat crew; and Mākaha legend George Downing, to this day, directs the big wave competition at Waimea in Eddie's name. The roll call of legends also includes familiar names like Brewer, Brown, Cabell, Cole, Curren, Froiseth, Hemmings, Hoffman, Hollinger, Muñoz, Quigg, Strange, and such modern-day heroes as Ken Bradshaw, Laird Hamilton, Brian Keaulana, and the unfortunate Mark Foo. Striving to become one of them, had Corky—like Foo—paid the ultimate price?

Alika and I paddled for what seemed like a half mile deep into the bay. My arms felt tight, no matter how many "No Fear" mantras I said. In the lull between sets we paddled into the lineup, then over to three surfers on the edge of the pack. One looked like a brown bear. The second, in a red rash guard, was tiny by comparison. The third's scalp was shaved clean—*bolohead*. A bear, a shrimp, and a skinhead.

"Howzit, Bolo?" Alika asked the shaved head. "Howzit, Māpuna, Puka?" He turned to the bear and his tiny friend in red. "Dis my cousin, Kai."

"Howzit, Kai . . . ? Howzit . . .? Howzit?" All three responded in turn, checking me out on Alika's lime green gun.

"Kai one private eye," Alika told his three friends. "One Surfing Detective—Magnum P.I. kine."

"You really one P.I.?" asked the big brown bear whose name, Māpuna, meant "bubbling spring." He was the biggest spring I'd ever seen.

"Yeah, maybe you try help with my case?"

"Us guyz?" The three looked at one another, then broke into laughter.

"Yeah, you guyz." I said. "You know dat California surfah dat wipe out Christmas Eve? His name Corky McDahl."

"Nah," said the small one called Puka, a nickname meaning "hole." "Don' know no Corky."

"Maybe you wen' see him in da lineup—Waimea—day befo' Christmas?"

"What his board look like?" asked Bolo.

"Like one candy cane."

"I seen dat board, brah," little Puka said.

"Here at Waimea?"

"Nah—where wuz it?" Puka thought for a minute. "Ehukai . . . ? Sunset . . . ?"

"You remembah da guy—blon', green eyes . . . ?"

"Nah, but da board—yeah. Sunset, da guy wuz surfing Sunset."

Alika turned to the other two. "You know da guy?"

"Nah," they both said.

"But," bear-like Māpuna adjusted his giant frame on his slim board, "my frien' Ham tol' me he surf Waimea when da *haole* guy ate it."

"Your frien' Ham saw da wipeout?" I asked.

"Dat's what he say. Ham say da *haole* guy bin bury undah da soup, brah. Nevah come up, you know? *Nevah.*"

"Your frien' Ham here today?"

"Nah," Māpuna said.

"Ham working . . . Paradise Sandwich Bar," Puka added, "In Hale'iwa."

"Tanks, eh?" I said. "Alika, we goin' talk with Ham, sooner da bettah?" I tried not to sound too hopeful.

"You got your detective scoops." Alika flashed a dangerous grin. "Now les' *chance 'um.*"

I swallowed hard.

The bay lay eerily calm. A big set hadn't rolled through for several minutes. We sat on our boards and waited, which only made me more edgy. I started thinking about Summer. Why did I feel responsible for making things right? Her footloose husband had brought on her misfortune, not me.

"*Outside!*" Bolo yelled and paddled furiously toward the open sea. Little Puka and mammoth Māpuna followed. Alika and I paddled too. And behind us, the whole pack.

Out on the horizon where the sapphire sky met the sea, an ominous jade mass was building. It was dark and impenetrable, so thick the sun couldn't shine through. And it was rising.

"Outside! someone else yelled.

"Ho!"

"Big, big, *beeeg!*"

The jade mountain was coming. And there would be more behind it.

"Paddle, brah, paddle!" Alika barked at me.

After the nearly half mile stroke from the beach to the lineup, this sudden surge burned my arms. But I kept paddling until I caught up with the first jade cliff, just as it was about to let loose. The face looked to be twenty-five feet, easy. Maybe higher. Up, up, up I clawed, and over the top as it passed. *Phew!*

Craning my neck back, I watched the enormous white lip forming that would soon pound the bay. I was far enough off on the wave's broad shoulder to observe the monster crest and to see Cousin Alika turn, stroke just twice, then drop down the massive face. Alika crouched near the back of his yellow gun and spread his arms wide, like one of those ants I had imagined earlier clinging to a toothpick. His almost vertical drop looked impossible. *Impossible!* The Hawaiian Superman went anyway. I shook my head. No fear.

Boooom! The lip cracked like a thunderbolt. Alika and the jade mountain swept past, leaving only the gauzy lace of blown-back foam.

But there was no time to gaze. The second mountain was coming fast. I felt it rising underneath me. I paddled hard. But not hard enough. I couldn't scratch over the top.

Suddenly I found myself gazing down—straight down—a sheer cliff with only one way to go.

I swung my board around into a takeoff position. Thoughts raced through my mind: *feet wide . . . stance low . . . arms spread . . . stay back on the board . . . Holy . . . !*

six

"Kai, brah." Alika paddled back from his ride wearing a million-dollar smile. "Why you let da bes' one go by?"

I shrugged. "I took da nex' one."

Alika glared at me in apparent disbelief.

"It da truth, brah. Da board drop so fas'—*Ho!*—almos' pitch me off."

It *was* the truth. The lime green gun had dropped down that steep face like the bottom fell out, me barely hanging on. In only seconds I had cranked my turn and, just like that, the ride was over.

"Hana hou!" my cousin brightened. "Again, brah, again!"

"Nah, let's go to Hale'iwa and find your frien', Ham. Ask 'em 'bout da Christmas Eve wipeout."

Alika frowned.

"I goin' buy lunch," I offered hopefully.

"Laytahs."

Alika stroked out again into those jade cliffs and soon he took another impossible drop. And then another. And another.

It was afternoon before I finally coaxed my Hawaiian cousin out of the water. Luckily when we arrived at Paradise Sandwich Bar in Hale'iwa, Māpuna's friend Ham was still there.

"Da *haole* guy? He take off too late. Wen' over da falls." Ham spoke to us through the order window as he stacked a deli-style pastrami for Alika, and a *mahi* sandwich for me. Polynesian tattoos covered Ham's dark brown arms, and his chiseled face was crowned by sun-bleached dreadlocks. Alika told me Ham had battled drugs and lost, then wound up at "Oh-Triple-C," the O'ahu Community Correctional Center in Kalihi, and then in rehab. Struggling to stay clean, he now built sandwiches, surfed, and reported weekly to his parole officer.

"Da red stripe board shot in da air, *way high,*" Ham explained as his fingers danced over the Kaiser roll that was Alika's lunch. "Maybe twenty, t'irty feet—twirling, spinning, brah."

Behind Ham I could see a chrome carousel whirling a half dozen sandwich orders, slips waving like flags in the breeze. Ham watched over my *mahi* sizzling on the grill, then stuck his hand in a plastic container of pickles.

"You like pickles, Alika?" Ham raised his eyes to my cousin.

"Everyt'ing, brah. Da works!"

"So da California surfer's leash snap, or what?" I asked Ham as he flipped my fish fillet and piled pickles and onions and lettuce on Alika's sandwich.

"Fo' sure. Was not hooked to da board anymo'. No way could fly dat high."

"You spot him aftah da wipeout?"

"Nah, *da buggah* gone. Undah da water. Nobody in da lineup see him. Was late, brah, aftah sunset." Ham shrugged his shoulders, tattoos rippling over his brown biceps.

After downing our sandwiches, Alika and I cruised every surf shop in Hale'iwa, trying to track down Corky's missing board and the Sunset Beach woman who had found it. Tropical Rush, Strong Current, Surf n' Sea, again, and all the rest. I questioned everyone I could, but nobody knew much about Corky, other than his well-publicized wipeout. One person did recall seeing the California surfer showboating through Hale'iwa in a BMW convertible. Another mentioned a girlfriend.

"Girlfriend?" I was curious. "Was she blonde and pregnant?" Summer had told me she didn't accompany her husband to Hawai'i, but maybe that wasn't the full story.

"No, this lady had red hair," I was told. "And she didn't look pregnant."

Was Corky pulling the wool over Summer's eyes, stepping out with a redhead in a BMW? Or was it really Corky they had seen?

I left my card at each and every surf shop in Hale'iwa and asked to be called if any board resembling Corky's turned up. Though I had not yet discovered much, Summer was definitely getting her money's worth of my time.

Guiding my Impala back to Honolulu, the allegation that Corky had a redhead girlfriend started bothering me. I decided I wouldn't mention it yet to Summer. In her condition, she needed to think the best of her husband.

It was late afternoon by the time I returned to Maunakea Street. Beyond Mrs. Fujiyama's display cases I caught a glimpse of Leimomi in the back room, stringing a rosebud lei.

Leimomi. We had a date tonight. If I missed it this time, I'd be hard-pressed for an explanation.

Inside my office the red message light was flashing again. I first dialed Leimomi's Punchbowl duplex and I left a message that I would pick her up at seven. My conscience salved, I reached over to my answering machine and pressed Play.

"Hello, Mr. Cooke. This is Summer McDahl. Any chance I could see you? Same place? Tomorrow morning at nine?"

Why not at my office? When I returned Summer's call there was no answer, then a recorded announcement came on—a gravelly male voice with a thick foreign accent said: "Leave message at tone, if you please. Cannot talk right now."

The accent was different than any I had heard before. Middle Eastern? Asian? European? As I left my message I wondered if that voice might belong to the owner of a black Mercedes. I hung up and stared at the phone.

Before leaving my office that afternoon I tried to track down the convertible Corky was allegedly seen driving. There was only a handful of high-line dealerships in Honolulu that traded in pre-owned luxury vehicles like BMWs. I dialed up each number. Aside from trying to sell me one of their fine automobiles, none of the salesmen was much help. I moved on to Honolulu's sole BMW dealership. The salesman who answered was smoother, but just as persistent as the last.

"The Ultimate Driving Machine . . ." he announced, sounding like a TV commercial. "Can I put you behind the wheel?"

"Swell, I'd love to." I gave him hope. "How about tomorrow morning?"

Little did he know I could no more afford a new BMW than a Porsche or Ferrari. I made a mental note to park my old Chevy down the block.

That night I showered and dressed, then drove to Leimomi's duplex. She shared a dingy shack with three other women on the shadowy backside of Punchbowl. A narrow, pot-holed driveway led past two other duplexes to her place, which sat amidst a red tangle of bougainvillea. Aside from this splash of color, her only view was of laundry hanging on the neighboring *lānai*.

A full-time student with a part-time job, Leimomi was constantly strapped. My own threadbare life probably looked bright and glistening by comparison. At least I surfed and, through my work, traveled to the neighbor islands and sometimes to the mainland. Maybe that was part of my attractiveness to her?

Swinging into her dusky lane, I felt the same surge of excitement that I always did approaching her place. And an equally strong twinge of guilt. While the dank duplex gave off a certain moldy, rotting odor, it also smelled like . . . *love*.

This was the place Leimomi and I had discovered each other for the first time, her rusty bedsprings singing a high-pitched siren song that drowned out even her scratchy clock radio. The room got as steamy as a sauna. We stayed in bed through that first night and the whole next day—snoozing, whispering, making love. Leimomi cried. I comforted her. We made love again. Neither of us wanted to leave. By four in the afternoon we got so hungry we ordered two Domino's pizzas and ate them both.

With Leimomi's euphoric first taste of love came, for me, an unspoken responsibility. After our breathless twenty-four hours together in bed, she glommed onto me like a faithful pet. Every time I turned around, she was there. I hadn't counted on that. Sometimes, I had to admit, I longed for a way to slip away without hurting her.

Leimomi was unusually quiet on the ride to dinner at Cafe Diamond Head. She had chosen the Pacific-Rim establishment with its reputation for flamboyant fusion cuisine. Filet mignon *wasabe* with mango-macadamia chutney staked on Kahuku sweet potatoes. That sort of thing. Its high prices did something toward assuaging my guilt.

We sat at a table overlooking the soaring brow of the islands' most famous crater, barely visible in the fading twilight. I glanced at the pricy wine list and ordered a beer. Leimomi did too. We raised our glasses and I toasted Leimomi's beauty and good health. We were off to a good start. Her earlier upset seemed to be wearing off.

Sipping my beer, I noticed two men in black suits sitting across from us who appeared, from their overly formal attire, to be *malihini*. They were an odd pair in this chic Honolulu restaurant, where casual aloha attire was the norm. They kept gazing toward Leimomi, which kind of flattered me. They'd probably never seen a more beautiful island girl.

Just then I made the mistake of mentioning I had surfed that morning at Waimea Bay. The usually soft-spoken Leimomi reacted in a way that set my teeth on edge.

"I wish you wouldn't ride those huge waves," she said stridently. "Surfers get killed, you know."

"I know." I tried to put her mind at ease. "I'm working on a case involving that California surfer who died last Christmas Eve at Waimea. That's why I was there."

"What's to investigate?" she asked, still with a sharpness in her voice that surprised me.

"His insurance company won't pay because of some questions about his wipeout. Like, did he really die? Or was he faking it?"

"What did you find out?"

"Nothing for sure yet. But if he was trying to escape his pregnant wife and the responsibilities of fatherhood, I can think of a lot easier ways."

Leimomi gazed at me silently. Her cheeks colored. "Kai . . ." she began and then stopped.

"What, Lei?" She was starting to worry me.

"I'm thinking . . ." She paused again and tears welled in her eyes. "No, I can't burden you . . . until I'm sure . . ."

"Leimomi, you already have." I was getting agitated. She was dangling a carrot in front of me, though I wasn't sure I wanted to bite it.

"That surfer," she started again, "trying to escape the responsibilities of fatherhood . . ."

"What? Does he remind you of your father? How he skipped out on you and your mother?" I was grasping at something, anything, to steer the conversation away from me, and remembered that Leimomi's dad had been put away for dealing drugs.

"Well, I do wonder about Daddy and I miss him, but that's not what I was thinking about."

"What were you thinking?" I was starting to sweat.

"Kai, I'm pregnant." She studied my face for a response.

"Are you sure?" I asked, my expression frozen.

"I'm over a week late . . ." Leimomi blushed. "I'm always, I mean, I'm usually on time, like a clock."

"OK." My aloha shirt suddenly felt swampy. "Let's not overreact . . . I mean . . . it's perfectly natural. We'll figure something out. Let's stay calm."

"I'd love to have our baby, Kai," she went on, her tears flowing now, "but this isn't . . . the best time in my life . . . not until I finish my courses."

"Are you sure it isn't a false alarm, Lei?" Maybe she had calculated wrong. She sometimes did that, confusing dates or dollar amounts. God, I hoped she was wrong.

"I doubt it. I'm too long overdue."

I sat back in my chair and took another drink of beer, which now tasted pretty flat. I guess it was too late to slip away.

seven

I sat staring into my coffee at Denny's in Waikīkī the next morning. As much as I cared for Leimomi, I knew I didn't want to be the father of her child. *How did I let it go this far?* I tried to picture Leimomi in the same state as Summer, swollen with child, then shook the image out of my head.

Nine o'clock came and went. Summer still hadn't shown.

I tried to focus on the case. What about that gravelly thick accent at the Kāhala phone number Summer had given me? The voice didn't fit her profile. If she or Corky had friends in Hawai'i, they would more likely be people like themselves—transplanted Californians or *kama'āina haole* types, or maybe surfers who sounded local. But not wealthy foreigners who lived in O'ahu's poshest oceanside enclave.

Through the steam swirling skyward from my cup I watched the morning flow of beach-goers and surfers filing down Kapahulu Avenue. No rain today. The sun glowed over Diamond Head and glinted on the tiny shore break of Waikīkī Beach. I gazed down in front of Starbucks, figuring Summer would be hard to miss in the crowd. No sign of her.

At quarter after nine a bakery van painted with a big red heart with the word "Love's" inside it pulled to the curb by the ABC Store next to Starbucks. The driver began unloading donuts and sweet rolls and cinnamon buns destined for Denny's. I sipped my coffee. Then a black Mercedes pulled alongside the van. The van obstructed my view, so I couldn't see who got out. Two doors slammed, then the Mercedes pulled away. I kept my eyes on the van until I heard, behind me, Summer's whispering voice.

"Mr. Cooke?" She edged into the booth across from me. Today's maternity dress was baby blue. "Have you found any evidence yet?" She cut straight to the chase.

"I'm working on it," I said and sipped my coffee. "Yesterday I interviewed some surfers who saw Corky at different North Shore breaks. One named Ham Makanani was in the water Christmas Eve at Waimea and saw the whole thing. He doesn't doubt your husband drowned, but it's going to be tough to locate any tangible evidence."

"But isn't tangible evidence what we need to convince Mr. Gold?"

"More or less, and I will pursue every lead . . ." I thought for a moment about her husband's alleged redhead girlfriend.

"I hope you find something"—Summer glanced down at her enormous belly— "before the baby comes."

I followed her gaze and couldn't help but wonder aloud, "Should you have flown here, Summer, with your baby due so soon?"

"I had to make this trip." She peered at me with those intense violet eyes. "Without that insurance money the baby and I are lost."

"What about your family, or Corky's family? Can't they help?"

"Not really." Summer sighed. "Corky was estranged from his parents. He deeply loved his mother, but never got along with his stepfather. A few years ago they moved to Idaho. I don't even know where in Idaho. But Corky's folks never cared much for me. They didn't call or write when Corky died. I thought I'd at least hear from his mother."

"What about your family?"

"Just my mother is left. She lives on social security, from check to check. She usually needs help from me—not the reverse . . ." Summer paused. "If I didn't need that insurance money I wouldn't have come all this way."

The waitress refilled my coffee. I decided to take a different track. "The BMW convertible you mentioned. I'm going to visit the dealership later this morning, but I need more to go on. The model, the color, the year, the license— any specifics would help."

"Well, I'm not a car person." She uttered the phrase distastefully. "Cars, for me, are just a way to get from here to there. But Corky loved expensive, exotic cars, though he could never afford to own the ones he worked on."

"Were there any BMWs, even in California, that he may have detailed?"

"Mmmm . . . there was this one beautiful maroon car with cream-colored leather."

"Was it a convertible?"

"I think so . . ." She paused again. "Yes, the top was cream or beige, the same color as its seats."

"So the only BMW you can remember him working on was a maroon and cream convertible? Any idea what year it was?"

"Brand new. Or almost new."

"Do you remember the owner?"

"Only that it was a California customer." Summer looked puzzled. "But I doubt that car would be here in Hawai'i."

"You're probably right. But it's all we have to go on. I'll check it out with the dealer."

"Will you call me as soon as you find out anything?"

"Of course . . ." I hesitated. "You know, when I called you before, I wasn't sure I dialed the right number. There was a man's voice on the answering machine—an older man with a thick accent."

"I got your message." Summer looked away. She rose, her bulging figure setting her slightly off-balance. "Do you need any more money?"

"No." Evidently she wasn't going to explain the accented voice. "You've given me plenty of money for now."

Summer made her way toward Denny's exit, then down the stairs to street level. Where the Love's bakery van had been, Summer now waited by the curb. A man in a dark suit was talking on a cell phone next to her. Then I noticed he wasn't just standing next to her; he had his free arm hooked into one of hers, as if escorting her.

The black Mercedes pulled up again and Summer and the man climbed into the backseat. It whisked them off in the direction of Diamond Head, leaving me more than curious about Summer's mysterious friends.

Down by the Waikīkī Aquarium, where I had parked under a shady stand of ironwoods, I climbed into my Impala and headed for the BMW dealership. Chances were, if the car Corky was seen in had been purchased or serviced here, the dealer would know about it.

After a few minutes traveling ʻEwa on Kapiʻolani Boulevard, I pulled to the curb just beyond Ward Avenue, parking my old Chevy out of view from the showroom. I strolled down the street and then through the showroom doors, trying to look as confident as any potential new luxury car buyer.

The mirror-like marble floor reflected an impressive array of German automobiles. While waiting for the salesman I had time to admire them: sedans in midnight blue and metallic silver, a pastel yellow convertible, a flame red sports car. I eyed supple leather seats in one sleek driving machine after another. Had I forty or sixty or eighty grand to drop on a car, this would be a nice place to start.

I had paid only one grand for my thirty-year-old Impala and the grieving widow who sold it to me was very pleased to get that. The car would have gone for less, but somebody had told her it was a classic. A single alloy wheel on the gleaming sport sedan now in my gaze probably cost as much as my entire car. Does that mean the BMW would be more fun? I don't know. But as long as I can ride waves, any wheels that get me and my board to the beach will do fine.

"Can I put you behind the wheel of that sensational M5?" The grinning salesman approached me with his right arm extended. "You must be Mr. Cooke?"

"Yes," I said, shaking his hand, "But one problem—to buy it I'd have to sell my soul."

"Well"—the salesman's smile broadened—"how much is your soul worth?"

"Actually," I said, starting my spiel, "I'm trying to trace a certain BMW. I'm a private investigator."

His smile faded. "Oh, well . . . if I can help."

I handed him my card.

When he glanced at the longboard rider, he perked up again. "Do you know anything about the car?"

"Not much. The deceased's wife can remember only one BMW her husband detailed in his business in California."

"California?" The salesman looked dubious.

"I know. It's a long shot."

"Well, we do buy and sell a lot of cars—and some have out-of-state plates, occasionally."

"The car she remembers was a new or nearly new convertible—maroon with cream-colored leather and top."

The salesman seemed to be scanning his memory. "A few months ago we took in a maroon convertible, but with a black top and no California plates."

"It's worth following up."

"I didn't do the transaction. Another salesman did who's since moved on. Hold on a minute and I'll see what I can find out." He walked from the showroom and disappeared into an inner office.

Minutes later he returned with a handful of stapled forms. "Let's see, we took in the maroon convertible in December . . . December thirteenth . . . and I was wrong about the top. It *was* tan, not black." He studied some figures. "Boy, we got a deal on this." He flipped between pages. "It looks like the seller took way below wholesale bluebook for the vehicle—less than he had to if he would have done his homework. And I remember the car was in great shape."

"What was the owner's name?"

"DiCarlo." The salesman glanced at the colored forms. "Damon DiCarlo of Balboa, California."

"Damn."

"Not the guy you're looking for?"

"Afraid not."

"The car was registered in California," the salesman continued. "And had California plates."

Just then a woman in a silk dress and spiked heels— someone who looked like she could afford a new BMW— strolled in.

"Excuse me a moment." The salesman turned away from me and eagerly approached his new prospect. They talked briefly and then the woman must have uttered something to the effect of "just looking," and the salesman backed off.

"So what happened to this maroon convertible?" I asked as he walked toward me.

"We sold it to an attorney on Bishop Street. But since he's a current customer, technically, I can't give you his name." The salesman held a pink form carelessly within my view, his thumb next to the words "William J. Grossvendt."

"I understand," I said. "Confidentiality and all that."

The salesman winked. Then he seemed to have a flash of inspiration. "Now I remember—not one hour after the new buyer signed for the car, a foreign gentleman came in and wanted it—wanted it badly. He offered to pay more, to fork over a new retail price if I would sell it to him. But I couldn't, of course, because the car was already sold."

"Why do you think he wanted it so much?"

"Well, the strange thing was, we had another maroon convertible—a brand new one—out at the dock ready for pick up. That one must have had the black top I was remembering. Anyway, if the buyer could have waited one day—just one day—it would have been his."

"Did he wait?"

"No, we never saw the man again." The salesman arched his brows.

I thanked him and found my way out. By then he was trying his charm again on the woman in heels.

Down the street, parked alongside the curb, my old Impala looked ancient compared to those shiny BMWs. *It's a classic,* I told myself. *A timeless piece of Americana.* Besides, my longboard fits right in.

eight

I hurried back to Maunakea Street and cracked my Oʻahu phone directory. William J. Grossvendt was listed—both a home phone with an ocean-side Portlock address in Hawaiʻi Kai, and an office number on Bishop Street: Grossvendt, Weller, and Chang, Attorneys at Law. Bishop Street is where the swankiest attorneys in Honolulu hang their shingles, in the high-altitude offices of mirrored skyscrapers. Grossvendt certainly earned enough as a lawyer to purchase a new BMW, so why did he cheap out and buy a used one?

Since it was a Wednesday morning I tried his office first. The phone rang twice and then an upbeat receptionist said, "Good Morning! Grossvendt, Weller, and Chang—specializing in trusts and wills."

"I'd like to speak with Mr. Grossvendt, please."

"One moment, sir." The receptionist connected me, not to Mr. Grossvendt himself, but to a woman I assumed was his assistant or paralegal. She told me that the attorney was unavailable, but asked if I would like to leave a message. When I said I was a PI inquiring about Mr. Grossvendt's

BMW convertible, the woman abruptly stopped me in mid-sentence. "Hold, please."

Within seconds attorney William J. Grossvendt himself came on the line.

"Mr. Cooke," said a high, quavering voice, "you have information about my car?"

"Actually, I was going to ask you for some information."

"Have you found it?" the attorney asked excitedly. "Have you found it?" He sounded like a boy who had lost his favorite toy.

"Found what?"

"My BMW convertible!" he said impatiently.

"Is it missing?" I asked naively, hoping for more information.

"Why, it was stolen from my parking garage in early January, not two days after I bought it. It's been missing nearly a month. My assistant said you are a P.I.?" He sounded hopeful.

"Yes. Does HPD have any leads?"

"None," the attorney said. "And it was a professional job. That car had all the high tech anti-theft devices money can buy."

"Sounds like this theft was more about that particular car than about you."

"I wouldn't be so sure." His voice cracked. "I've had cars vandalized before—*keyed,* you know—and have received my share of threats, even death threats. Sometimes heirs cut from Grandma's will blame me, the attorney. They think I've taken their money. When my BMW was stolen, I had in mind a few people who might be responsible."

"I suppose there's a chance of that."

"So what's in this for you, Mr. Cooke?" the attorney asked in his anxious voice.

"I'm pursuing an entirely different case, but I think your car may somehow be related to it. The death of a California surfer at Waimea Bay last Christmas Eve."

"I heard about that. He died on a huge wave, right?"

"Right. And he was driving a BMW around on the North Shore before his wipeout. The car has been missing since his death—maybe the same car you bought."

"I really loved that car. And I'd love to have it back."

"Why don't you take the insurance money and buy another? I bet the dealership could get one just like it."

"I'm sentimental about that very car. My girlfriend helped me pick it out." He hit a somber note. "And she's since left the islands."

"I'll let you know what I turn up."

"Much appreciated."

"By the way," I said, "do you know my attorney friend, Tommy Woo?"

"Tommy? Yeah, I know him. But he's a sore subject around here."

"Why?" I asked.

The attorney cleared his throat. "One evening my former wife and I were at a party at Oʻahu Country Club—a very elegant white-tie affair—and Tommy was playing piano. On his break Tommy comes over to where we're sipping Dom Pérignon with a CEO friend, of a Big Five company, you know, and Tommy says, "Hey, Bill, did you hear the one about the Siamese twins hookers who offered a 'double-your-pleasure' guarantee . . . ?"

"Siamese twins hookers?" I recalled one of Tommy's crudest jokes.

"Yeah, the punch line made the CEO turn blue, I tell you. And my former wife, well, she looked as if she'd been bitten by a snake. That Tommy Woo, he's a prize all right."

I had to laugh. "I'll let you know if I find your car."

When the trust attorney hung up I wondered what Tommy Woo would say about stuffy Grossvendt, his blue-blood ex-wife, and the Big Five CEO. I pictured Tommy adjusting his tortoiseshell glasses with a flourish, puffing cherry blend in his meerschaum pipe, and uttering profoundly: "If they can't take a joke, f– 'em."

This mysterious car business wasn't making much sense. The convertible was registered in California, turned up in Hawai'i, and was purchased below wholesale by a Honolulu dealership, then sold to a Bishop Street attorney, *then* stolen from him two days later. Could it be linked to Corky McDahl?

I phoned information for Balboa, California, and got the number for Damon DiCarlo, the registered owner. DiCarlo's address was on East Ocean Front. From what I remembered about real estate in this pricy area of Orange County, Ocean Front was an exclusive seaside lane on the Newport peninsula. It adjoined the Balboa Channel and the famous body board spot called "The Wedge," a powerful, treacherous shore break that can hammer the unwary. Wicked huge swells pump up against a rock jetty, then slam the steep beach, spraying sand and foam every which way. It is one easy spot to break your neck.

I placed the call to DiCarlo. After four rings a melodic, Brando-like voice said: "Damon here. You know the routine. Leave a message and I'll call . . ."

I left my name and number, mentioning the BMW he sold. I wondered if this Damon would bother to phone back a complete stranger in Hawai'i.

I returned to the phone book and called all the surf shops Alika and I had visited in Hale'iwa. Still no sign of Corky's board. The candy cane had seemingly vanished. I wondered if the Sunset Beach woman who first found the board had kept it, and if so, why? By all accounts, it had been badly damaged. Were she and Corky's alleged red-haired girlfriend one and the same? I wasn't even sure if this elusive redhead existed.

Gradually I began to picture Summer's marriage to the California surfer as less than ideal. The young couple certainly remained apart for long stretches. But could they really be scamming the insurance company? I had a deep sense that Summer was not type to do such a thing. She was nervous, yes, and anxious. And she was evasive about certain details. Yet an underlying naive sincerity in her character seemed at odds with the idea of fraud. But I had to factor in the dark-suited men who "escorted" her in that hearse of a Mercedes. And that brought up questions. They weren't simple questions like "Did Corky really die?" or "Did Corky skip out on his wife and new baby?" These were more complex questions buried beneath the one she and the insurance agent were asking. Trouble was, I wasn't sure what they were.

It was time to fit in a quick session in Waikīkī. I hopped into my Impala and headed for Classic Surfboards on Kapahulu Avenue to get some wax.

Classic Surfboards is a groovy, sixties-style surf shop lined with more used boards than new, and hardly any glitzy logo apparel. The shop's motto warms my heart:

"No Gimmicks, No Bullshit, Just Surfing." A short walk from Waikīkī Beach, Classic Surfboards attracts local surfers and tourists alike. Since it can be cheaper to buy a board there than to rent one day after day at the beach, some boards for sale are dinged old tankers; but you can also find some nice ones at good prices. Surf'n Jenny, the sandy-haired proprietor and mother of two, always tells sellers: "Ask the very lowest price you will accept and your board will sell fast." I sold a ten foot T & C here in one day.

Inside the shoebox-sized shop I made a beeline for the glass counter piled high with cylinders of pastel-colored surfboard wax. My favorite is coconut-scented "Sex Wax." Expressly for warm water, this milky-white wax has an ambrosial island fragrance that never fails to raise the hairs on the back of my neck. I selected one disk of wax the size of a hockey puck and set it on the counter.

"Hi, Kai!" Jenny greeted me with a big grin. "Heading up to the North Shore?"

"Nah, I was just there yesterday at Waimea. Nearly killed myself on a thirty-footer." I exaggerated. "Today I'm heading out to Pops."

"Kai, for Waimea you need a gun." She looked concerned. "That nine-six nose rider of yours isn't built for big waves."

"I know, I borrowed a gun from my cousin Alika. It was OK. Didn't suit me exactly, but close enough."

"I took in a big gun nearly a month ago. It's got an amateur patch job, but it would have sold instantly if she hadn't put such a high price on it," Jenny explained. "She wants $350."

"A woman is selling a big gun? Not many women surf Waimea."

"She said she's selling it for a friend who left the island," Jenny replied. "I'm surprised she didn't put it in a shop in Hale'iwa, 'cuz the address she gave is on the North Shore. The board, though, was made in California."

"Wait a minute. Can I see this board?"

"It's over there between those two tankers." Jenny pointed to a wall lined with boards standing in file on their tails. There it was—red and white stripes like a candy cane, its narrow pointed nose rising nearly a foot above the longboards next to it.

Jenny gingerly plucked it out like a stick of gum from a pack. California surfboard label. No leash. And those telltale stripes.

"I want to buy this board." I tried to mask my rush of emotion. "How much does she want for it again?"

Jenny drew a card from a small file box behind the counter and glanced at it. "Too much, Kai. You're a good customer. How about I cut my commission and drop the price to three hundred."

"Did it come in with a leash?"

"You don't want that leash. It was sliced right in two—I only got the part still hooked to the board."

"Sliced or snapped? I think a surfer wiped out on this board at Waimea—the leash could have snapped or been shredded by coral."

"No, this one looks sliced like bologna."

"Do you still have it?"

"I threw it in the scrap bin in back. But that was weeks ago—and I'm not the only one who goes back there."

"I'll pay cash if you can find me that leash and give me the woman's name and address."

"Sorry, Kai, I can't give out her personal information. I promise all my customers confidentiality."

"I understand," I replied. Knowing Jenny's integrity, I didn't want to offend her or push my luck. To avoid trading in stolen boards, she was a stickler for gathering and protecting detailed information on her clients.

She set the card on the counter and covered it with the wax I had put there. Then she stepped into the back room.

I glanced at the card. The seller's address and other vital information were concealed under the wax. Out of respect for Jenny, I wasn't about to move it. On the edges of the card not covered by the wax, I could just make out a first name, "Maya," and the last four digits of a phone number. That was enough. I knew already the North Shore prefix. So I had myself a complete number. *Bingo!*

Jenny returned with a four-foot section of leash. I carefully studied the severed end. When a surfboard leash snaps in the heat of a wipeout, the broken surface looks irregular and jagged—with tiny peaks and valleys and burrs. But this leash appeared to have been sliced clean, as if with a knife. A few fine, curved parallel lines over the otherwise flat surface suggested the sawing movement of a sharp blade.

"Thanks for the cord," I said. "It may come in handy."

"A broken leash? Handy?"

I peeled off three of Summer's rumpled Ben Franklins.

Jenny eyed the bills. "I love cash."

"That makes two of us."

With sliced leash and badly-patched candy cane in hand, I stepped from the surf shop beaming.

nine

Nearly eleven feet of surfboard proved too much even for my spacious Chevy. Luckily, I always carry along a pair of soft roof racks. Within minutes I had positioned the racks on the wide teal roof, tightened the nylon straps inside the cabin, and lashed the candy-striped red board securely in place.

Back on Maunakea Street I maneuvered the lengthy gun between the cashier's counter and refrigerated display cases at Fujiyama's, and up the orange shag stairs. I got a few looks from Mrs. Fujiyama and her *lei* girls. Leimomi actually frowned. Did she think this telltale board proved her boyfriend had taken up big wave riding? Considering Leimomi's condition, that probably made me as irresponsible to her as Corky McDahl had been. The parallel made me wince.

Inside my office I set Corky's board on a rail along my longest wall and checked out the repair job. Amateur, as Surf'n Jenny had said. The patched board looked dappled like a roan pony, its dings unpainted, wavy, and irregular. I couldn't believe the seller had put such a high price on a wreck like this.

Before examining it further, I noticed the familiar blinking light of my answering machine and checked my messages.

"Mr. Cooke," said a singsong female voice, "this is Mr. DiCarlo's secretary returning your call from his office in Costa Mesa, California. Mr. DiCarlo is out of town, but he would appreciate any information you could provide him about his stolen car . . ."

Mr. DiCarlo's stolen car? Was this a twice-stolen car— heisted from both DiCarlo and Grossvendt? And if the former hadn't turned it in to the BMW dealership, who had?

Quickly I returned the secretary's call.

"DiCarlo Inc.," answered the same voice that had left the message.

I told her who I was and she became helpful.

"You've found Mr. DiCarlo's car?"

"Not exactly. I've found that it has been stolen—again. Not from Mr. DiCarlo, but from the car's new owner here in Hawai'i."

"In Hawai'i?" The singsong voice hit a high note.

"That's right. Did Mr. DiCarlo ship his car to Honolulu?"

"Not that I know of."

"Where is he now?"

"Well, this is a bit of a coincidence—Mr. DiCarlo is vacationing in Hawai'i."

"That *is* a coincidence. Are you in touch with him?"

"I can be."

"Would you give me his number or ask him to call me?"

"I'll ask him to call you."

"Fine," I said, feeling like we were finally getting somewhere. "One last question. Does the name Corky McDahl sound at all familiar?"

"Corky?" She paused. "Isn't he the fellow who washes Mr. DiCarlo's car?"

Bingo. "He apparently had an auto detailing business in Newport Beach."

"Then that's him, yes. Corky cleaned Mr. DiCarlo's car."

"The BMW convertible—maroon with cream leather?"

"Yes."

"Could Corky have taken that convertible to Hawai'i?"

"Why would he do that? Why would Mr. DiCarlo allow him to?"

"I don't know. It doesn't make sense. Are you sure you can't give me Mr. DiCarlo's phone number in Hawai'i?"

"I'd like to, Mr. Cooke. You sound very honest and sincere, but I can't. I'm sorry. I will call him with your number right away."

"What kind of business is he in?"

"Import-export."

"What sort of products?"

"The products change depending on what's available."

"Did his business take him to Hawai'i?"

"Mr. DiCarlo travels extensively on business," she said, "mostly to Mexico and South America. He speaks fluent Spanish."

"That so? I'd really appreciate hearing from Mr. DiCarlo."

"You will, I'm sure."

I then phoned the number Summer had given me and got that heavy accent again. "Leave message at tone, if you please . . ."

I asked Summer to call me, mentioning vaguely that I had made some progress.

Next I placed a call to the North Shore number of "Maya." A young woman answered.

"Maya?" I asked.

"No," she corrected me.   "Maya doesn't live here anymore."

"Where's here?"

"Who's calling, please?" She sounded agitated.

"Kai. I was a surfing buddy of Corky McDahl."

"You have the wrong number."

"Where might I find Maya now?"

Click.

No worries. I pulled out my handy directory that lists the addresses of all people on O'ahu by phone number, turned to the prefix "638," then scanned down until I found the last four digits of the number I'd just called. It belonged to an address off Kamehameha Highway called Kē Nui Road that fronts the ocean.

Kē Nui is a road of big wave riders. It looks out on the famous breaks of the North Shore—Sunset, Pipeline, and nearby Pūpūkea. Down the road a hop, skip, and jump is Waimea Bay. Kē Nui is near the center, in other words, of the surfing universe. Legends have called this street home— along with some young hopefuls. It didn't surprise me that Corky, by way of this woman named Maya, was associated with Kē Nui Road.

In less than an hour, with Corky's board lashed on top, my Impala rolled into the sandy lot overlooking blown-out Sunset Beach. The wind-whipped sea was the color of marbled jade—dark green riddled with stark white. Signs posted on the beach warned: High Surf . . . Dangerous

Currents . . . No Swimming . . . Beach Closed. Above these signs, Day-Glo orange flags stood stiff in the wind.

Nobody—swimmer, boogie boarder, or surfer—was out today. Not just because of the signs, but because even the regular crew at Sunset knows when to battle and when to retreat. The roar of the tumultuous waves resembled the H-1 Freeway at rush hour—amplified tenfold. It was a din that filled the air completely.

From Sunset Beach, I drove a short quarter mile to oceanfront Kē Nui Road, where the surf continued to roar. Maya's address was attached to a cottage with shake roof whose beach side stood on stilts in the sand at the high tide mark. You couldn't get much closer to the water than this without swimming.

I knocked and soon a wet-haired surfer girl stood before me in a string bikini top and skin-tight jeans. Her baby-white skin and pale blue eyes had mainland written all over them. She appeared to be about Leimomi's age.

"Is Maya here?" I whiffed the fresh scent of lavender on her.

"No," she said in a voice lower pitched than the young woman I had spoken with on the phone, but no less defiant.

"I'm a friend of Corky McDahl. I wondered if Maya could tell me anything about his wipeout—just to soothe my mind. I still have his photo." I showed her the snapshot Summer had given me.

The surfer girl didn't respond.

"Does Maya still live here?" I tried again.

"No."

"Do you know where I can reach her?"

"No."

"Did she leave a forwarding address?   Or a phone number?"

"No."

"Was Corky Maya's boyfriend?"

"You'd have to ask one of my roommates."

"May I?"

"They're not here," she said matter-of-factly.

"Would you please have them call me at this number?" I handed her my card, hoping the surfer image on it would reinforce my pose as Corky's wave-riding buddy.

"I can't guarantee they will." She shoved the card deep into a pocket of her jeans.

If she wasn't hiding something, someone was. Why else would she be so rude?

I knew the North Shore wasn't all good vibes and big waves. There were drug-related crimes and violence, like everywhere else. Recently at a birthday party at Laniākea two men were stabbed to death and several others beaten senseless. The culprits slipped away into a dark underworld the tourist bureau doesn't advertise. That makes the North Shore not a place to go poking around into other people's business, especially the wrong people. You might end up dead.

Up the road from Sunset Beach I stopped in at the Foodland, a chain supermarket and larger than you'd expect in the country setting of Pūpūkea. I wandered around until I found the crack seed display. I pulled a small package from the hanging rack and headed for the checkout line. A local guy, who from the width of his shoulders looked like he surfed, rang me up. I pulled out my wallet containing the photo of Corky. Handing a couple bills to the clerk, I flashed the picture.

"Evah see dis guy?"

"Dat's da guy wen' wipe out at Waimea . . ."

"Corky, yeah. Evah see his girlfriend? Redhead."

"Maya? Ho, nice!" He smiled suggestively.

"Yeah, Maya. Know where I can find her?"

"She live on da beach at Sunset . . ."

"Yeah, but her roommate say she gone."

"Gone?"

"Any idea where?"

"Maybe upcountry Maui?" the clerk said. "I t'ink she from Makawao."

"You sure?"

"Dunno fo' sure, brah." He shrugged.

"T'anks, eh?"

He was still leering at the thought of Maya as he handed me my bag.

ten

The bell tower at the Mission of Saints Peter and Paul loomed ominously over Waimea Bay as I glided by, heading for Hale'iwa town.

About halfway there, a black Mercedes with dark windows flashed by in the opposite direction. I couldn't have sworn it was Summer's escorts, but the men in the front seat looked hauntingly familiar. Were they going where I had been? Kē Nui Road? Pūpūkea Foodland?

At Surf 'n Sea in Hale'iwa I searched for a shaper from Oregon named Skipper who surfed occasionally with Cousin Alika. Although not born in Hawai'i, Skipper knew North Shore breaks and boards as well as many local surfers.

Surfboards in various degrees of ding patching leaned against the walls of the shop. The air was thick with the chemical odor of uncured resin. The floor felt sticky under my feet and was plastered with castoff strips of cotton-soft and resin-hardened fiberglass cloth. Skipper wore a surgical mask beneath his grey eyes and close-clipped hair of peroxide orange. A diamond stud in his left ear lobe glittered.

While I watched, Skipper squeegeed resin onto the deck and one rail of a surfboard—a gun with a slot-like hole in the deck where another surfer's fin had apparently dug in. In other words, the board had been "skegged."

When he was finished I showed Skipper Corky's poorly patched board and severed leash.

"Any idea who might have repaired this candy cane?"

"Ugly." Skipper shook his head. "No shop in Hale'iwa did this. I'd bet it was patched in somebody's garage. Maybe that guy out in Mokule'ia? I've never met him. He's military— from Schofield Barracks." Skipper eyed the board. "How much did you give for it?"

"Three hundred."

Skipper rolled his eyes.

"I needed the board for a case I'm working on," I explained, "the death of that California surfer who wiped out at Waimea on Christmas Eve."

"I remember that guy," said the shaper. "Too bad."

"You knew him?"

"Not really. Just to say hello. He brought in his lady once." Skipper raised his dusty brows. *"Nice."*

"What was her name?"

"I don't know, but I heard they were getting married and all. Then he wipes out at Waimea." He shrugged. "Foxy lady too—leggy, long red locks. She was older, but nice."

"Older? How much older?"

"Older than him. In her thirties, maybe."

"Any idea where I can find her?"

"Sunset Beach, I think."

"She's not there anymore," I said.

"Then I don't have a clue." Skipper shook his head.

As I left Hale'iwa town I turned west toward Mokule'ia, beyond which the paved road ends and the Waianae range drops down to a remote stretch of craggy coastline. Luckily, I didn't have to go that far. On oceanfront Crozier Drive in Mokule'ia, I searched for a novice *ding-meister* working out of his garage.

On the *mauka* side of the street in a carport, a crew-cut *haole* kid in a surgical mask was sanding a surfboard. He looked barely eighteen, skinny, and red-faced above the mask from too much tropic sun on fair skin. I pulled in front of the carport and removed Corky's board from my roof racks.

"You patch surfboards?"

He put down his sandpaper and flipped off the mask. A ring of white resin dust circled his mouth and nose like the outline of a goatee. "You bet. You need a ding repaired?"

I flipped over Corky's gun to display its mottled bottom. "This board has already been patched. I'd just like to know who repaired it."

"It's not the best repair job." He observed its wavy contours. "Hold on . . ." The novice *ding-meister* rubbed the freckles on his nose. "I remember that board."

"You patched it like this?"

"She was in a big hurry," he explained defensively. "She didn't want it done fancy. She wanted it done *fast*. She said she would pay extra if I could finish in two days, instead of my usual week."

"Who was she?"

"A good-look'n babe." He flashed a salacious smile.

"Did you ask her what happened to the board?"

"Didn't need to. She told me she hit a reef at Rocky Point."

"That so?" I replied straight-faced, trying not to betray my disbelief. Rocky Point is a popular winter break between Sunset and Pipeline. Everybody and his dog is out there on a good day. The reefs at Rocky Point could certainly damage a board, but not this one.

"Hey," said the teenager, "where did *you* get the board?"

"I bought it in town at a surf shop on Kapahulu."

"Oh." He rubbed the resin dust around his chin. "I figured she was going to sell it before she went to Maui."

"Maui?" I said, recalling that the Foodland clerk had said the same. "Did she say where on Maui?"

"Nah." He wrinkled his freckled nose. "Does it matter? Why are you asking all these questions?"

"Just curious."

"Ooohh," he uttered, as if we shared some kind of secret. "Yeah, she makes me curious too."

Back in my office, there was a message waiting for me.

"Kai, I'm worried." It was Leimomi, with that edge in her voice. "I'm really late now. And I feel funny—kind of sick to my stomach. Maybe I'm just worried sick, but I don't feel like eating. And when I do eat, nothing tastes right. All I can keep down are saltine crackers—the only food mother could stand when she was pregnant! *Call me.*"

Auwe. I decided to wait until I got home to call her back, then wondered if I should swing by to see her instead on my way.

I figured I should also check in with Summer, since my next move might be a long-shot trip to Maui and I'd be consuming more of her retainer. I dialed her Kāhala number and got that foreign voice on the machine again. "Leave message at tone . . ."

"Summer, I've made some progress but may need to fly to Maui to follow up on a lead. It's Wednesday afternoon at four. Please let me hear from you by tonight, either at my office or at home."

That evening I arrived at Ah Fook in Chinatown before Tommy Woo did. Inside the dinky chop sui house there was no place to wait for a cramped table except behind the swinging glass door, and I didn't want to stand there. So I joined the line of a half dozen customers outside on infamous River Street, where colorful thieves, con artists, drug runners, and occasional murderers once plied their dark trades.

Ah Fook's best-kept secret was a fancy menu for such a funky place: Shark Fin Soup, Stuffed Clams with Crab Meat, Peking Duck Dim Sum. Regular customers like Tommy and me never praised Ah Fook, for fear it would be overrun. Instead we embellished its deplorable reputation (which had some slim basis in fact): cockroaches roaming the walls, ants crawling on the tables, dog meat in the pork fried rice, payoffs to the health department and liquor commission.

Tommy was coming from a rehearsal for one of his jazz gigs and warned me he might be late. How he managed to wrap up a late-night session at 2:00 a.m., then cruise into his legal offices—eyes wide open—by eight the next morning is anybody's guess.

I checked my watch—ten after seven—just as a familiar dark profile emerged from the night and joined me at the front of the lengthening line.

"Hey, Kai, what do you call a guy who hangs out with musicians?"

Tommy Woo always wore black and always had a joke on the tip of his tongue. Over my shoulder I scanned the waiting customers lining River Street for ears that might be too tender or young for one of Tommy's doozies.

"Cooke, party of two." Fortunately, the hostess stepped out and led us inside. Our cramped corner table was so close to our fellow diners that I could smell their perfume and aftershave, but it was thankfully too loud inside the tiny restaurant to distinguish their words. A dozen animated conversations bouncing off the walls drowned out one another, making Ah Fook an unexpectedly intimate place.

I watched my friend's loose-jointed and lanky form squeeze behind the tiny round table. Divorced, pushing fifty, with a shock of grey hair and tortoise shell glasses, Tommy resembled a cross between a parish priest and Yo-Yo Ma. An only child, his father had been Chinese, his mother Jewish, he attended Catholic schools, and was exposed from infancy to the jazz and blues of Duke Ellington, Charlie Parker, and B.B. King. Tommy Woo had the wisdom of Confucius, the funny bone of a rabbi, the pomp and circumstance of the Pope, and the musical soul of an African. He could spin ethnic and off-color yarns until your face turned blue, then thrill and inspire you at the piano with "Take the 'A' Train" and "Body and Soul."

"*A drummer,*" Tommy uttered while taking his seat. "That's what they call a guy who hangs out with musicians."

"Oh." I scratched my head at the tamest tale Tommy had ever told. "You must not think much of drummers, I guess."

"Actually, I do." Tommy cracked a wry smile. "Good ones."

After two more of Tommy's salty and unrepeatable humdingers, we ordered the usual—the $8.95 dinner special: Egg Drop Soup, Sweet-Sour Spareribs, Shrimp Fried Rice, Lemon Chicken, Fortune Cookie (a rarity in Honolulu), and hot tea. The tea arrived almost instantly.

"So what's new with your practice, Tommy?"

"Jus' laugh'n 'n scratch'n," he joked. "Actually, I'm defending a mainland guy who sold some ice to an undercover cop. The narcs were laying a trap for the Sun organization, and my client—who has no connection to Frank O. Sun— got busted. He comes from a good family, has a good job here, and has never been arrested. Just thought he'd try a little meth on a lark. Then he got engaged to a nice local girl who reviles drug users and he tried to recoup his investment by selling the stuff to some other sucker."

"He should have flushed it down the toilet." I shook my head as the Egg Drop Soup arrived. "Do you expect a judge to believe him?"

Tommy sipped the hot soup and shrugged. "No, the narcs want to make an example of him."

"Frank O. Sun. What's his story? I've heard the name."

"Sun?" Tommy brushed back his shock of grey hair. "He comes from nowhere and everywhere. He's ubiquitous, my lad, *ubiquitous.* He wears his trademark Panama hat and sunglasses—always—day and night. Some say he's Korean, others that he's German or Bolivian. I doubt his real name is Sun. It may be *Sonne*—German, you know. But no one of my acquaintance has actually seen him in the flesh."

"Ubiquitous, huh?" I tried on Tommy's big word.

"Sun has a fairly complex organization of suppliers, distributors, dealers, money launderers, strong arms—the whole tamale. His group reaches from the islands to the Orient, California, and into Mexico and South America. Sun Imports, his front business, is a warehouse off Ward Avenue. The place has atmosphere—straw on the floor and steamer trunks full of pottery and exotic foreign goods. It's a popular store."

"I've seen it, just never dropped in."

"You're not the pottery type, Kai." Tommy grinned. "Neither am I."

The waitress brought our ribs and fried rice. Tommy went first for the meat. "And what these days occupies the Surfing Detective?"

We switched serving plates. "Another crazy case." I said. "This California blonde—very pregnant—who'll only meet at Denny's in Waikīkī. No explanation why. She's gorgeous, though. Never mind she looks as if she could give birth to a baby whale at any moment."

"So what does this pregnant woman want with you?"

"She wants me to prove her husband is dead."

"She doesn't know if her own husband is dead?"

"It's a life insurance claim for two hundred grand."

"Ah." Tommy nodded knowingly. "That ought to make her comfortable for a while."

I gave him the brief version of Corky's wipeout and the red flags that the insurance company was balking at.

"Any question in your mind that this surfer is dead?"

"If Corky was planning to skip, he couldn't have done a better job of preparing his nest egg: empty bank accounts, maxed-out credit cards, a missing BMW. But, except for a sliced surfboard leash, there's no real evidence. And I doubt he and the wife are in this together. I'd say she's a victim of her husband's irresponsibility."

The Lemon Chicken arrived, followed by more hot tea.

"By the way," Tommy asked idly, "what motive would your surfer have to skip?"

"To escape fatherhood, to keep on surfing free. That's the best I can come up with. But no way could he ever become the sponsored, big name surfer he dreamed of—not without his wife and the insurance company finding out. So what's the point in skipping?"

When our fortune cookies finally appeared, neither made sense to us, but they rarely do. My "An exotic companion awaits you" was at least more intriguing than solo Tommy's: "Family always comes first."

Later that night, back at the Waikīkī Edgewater, there were no messages waiting for me—not from Summer or Leimomi. Then I remembered, too late, that I had promised to call Lei. Once again, that unflattering parallel between Corky and me came to mind.

eleven

I didn't sleep well that night and awoke Thursday morning with a groggy head, fuzzy mouth, and a feeling of dread. The case was on my mind. So was Leimomi.

I flipped through the wad of green hundreds. A flight to Maui and a rental car for the day would cost less than a few bills. Hardly a dent.

Two people had told me that Maya was from Maui. And one of them had a hazy recollection that she'd resided upcountry in Makawao. If these tips turned out to be true, it shouldn't be hard to find her in the small mountain town. A few sloping blocks of wood frame buildings comprised the main drag of this commercial and cultural hub of upcountry Maui. Makawao could be canvassed easily in a few hours. I would have liked to discuss the trip with Summer first. But since she wasn't returning my calls, I might as well just *holoholo*.

The Aloha 737 quickly left O'ahu behind on this cloudless winter morning, crossed the wind-whipped channel to

Moloka'i, then skirted the sloping red plateau of its west end. Across from Moloka'i lay the tiny island of Lāna'i, the rural and remote Pineapple Isle, which is dominated by a three-thousand-foot volcano, Lāna'ihale.

The jet glided over cane fields on the isthmus between Maui's twin volcanic cones and touched down at Kahului Airport at ten, leaving me the better part of the day to poke around. The sub-compact I had reserved from Dollar was sold out, so at no extra charge they gave me a silver-blue Mercury Grand Marquis, whose overstuffed leather seats could have accommodated Summer's whole crew of dark escorts.

I pulled away from the airport and cruised toward Upcountry Maui, turning onto Baldwin Avenue at the former bustling sugar town of Pā'ia. Dubbed "noisy" in plantation times, today this rustic country town hosted quieter tourism. As the Grand Marquis climbed Baldwin past a rusting sugar mill and, by contrast, spotlessly white churches, the shoulderless road twisted higher into wide-open acres, ranches, and secluded luxury homes. The Mercury leaned precariously around each hairpin turn, as the mountain air grew cooler and more fragrant. It smelled pine fresh up here. High-country fresh.

Along with Kamuela on the Big Island, Makawao was one of the islands' last genuine cowboy towns and it looked the part: Old West wood-frame buildings with hitching posts recalled John Wayne movies. Settled near the end of the 19th century by Portuguese immigrants who raised cattle on upcountry slopes, this former rough and tumble mountain hamlet today boasts an eclectic blend of western, *paniolo*, Yuppie, New Age, and alternative. You can buy a saddle, have your palm read, attend a rodeo, order a veggie burger, and watch a glass blower. All in the same little town.

What did Makawao's character say about Maya? Was this North Shore surfer girl also a cowgirl or a hippie? An artsy type? A vegetarian? I aimed to find out.

Near the corner of Makawao and Baldwin Avenues, I stepped into a New Age bookshop called Om, where the musty smell of incense hit me like a wall. Besides herbal essences, bath oils, and scented candles, there were also a few books and tapes and CDs, most of the occult, astrological, and inspirational variety. Airy space music—from a group called Cosmic Tofu, said the display—wafted through the haze. *Tommy Woo would cringe.*

A wispy brunette, gold ring dangling from her nose, greeted me with penetrating cobalt-blue eyes that made me feel naked.

"How are *you* today?" she asked, sounding like she actually wanted to hear my answer.

"I have a favor to ask."

Her blue eyes didn't blink.

"I'm looking for someone named Maya—tall, red hair, maybe from around here. I don't have her picture, but I do have her boyfriend's." I showed her Corky's youthful face.

"Too bad he's taken." She studied the photo intently. "And you say his partner's name is Maya?"

"Right."

"You don't have a last name?

I shrugged. "I know it's a long shot . . ."

She shook her head. "I really wish I could help." She sounded sincerely sorry.

"Where else would somebody who lives around here shop?"

"Paniolo Trading Company.   And the natural foods stores—there are two—one on Makawao, one on Baldwin."

"She would need groceries, that's for sure. Thanks." I turned and left her behind in the incense haze.

Whole Earth Foods was just next door. But no one there had heard of Maya or recognized Corky. At Ambrosia, the second health food store on Baldwin Avenue, I did no better. Next I tried an antique shop and an adjacent real estate office. Same drill. Same response.

Trying not to lose hope, I stepped across Baldwin Avenue onto the plank boardwalk fronting the Paniolo Trading Company, whose rippled tin awning offered welcome shade as the scorching sun pierced thin mountain air. The old-fashioned general store smelled of roasting turkey and saddle leather and motor oil. This place had everything someone in a small cowboy town might need, from Band-Aids to videos to fresh *ahi*. Even an ATM machine. And, of course, Jim Beam. But no one I talked to knew of Maya or had seen a mug like Corky's—except in the Honolulu papers.

Bummahs. By now it was well after noon and everybody in Makawao was eating lunch except me. I found a yuppie deli tucked between some artsy shops in a courtyard shaded by a *hau* tree. I ordered a seared *ahi* croissant (the closest they had to a sandwich) and a Coke, hoping the caffeine and sugar might stimulate some new thought on the case.

Sitting under the hau's spreading boughs, I scanned the surrounding shops and wondered if Maya might patronize any of them: a seascape gallery, a second-hand boutique selling granny dresses and *da kine*, a jeweler specializing in sterling silver, and a glass blower.

I doubted if Maya had ongoing use for a glass blower, but it looked like the most interesting of the shops. I finished my *ahi* and wandered inside. The blower was hard at work. A molten orange blob at the end of his long tube glowed like fiery lava. As he turned it round and round, the orange glow became a perfect crystal sphere—evidently a paperweight, as the nearby shelves displayed. Brilliant orbs, they glinted with vibrant colors—turquoise, pumpkin, scarlet, saffron, peach.

I lifted up one in apple green, the size of a baseball. Sticker shock! It cost as much as the tab for this whole trip.

"That's one of our most popular crystals," said a woman with frosted hair who had crept up behind me. "Lovely, isn't it?"

"I might have to hock my car to buy it," I joked.

"We have a layaway plan," she said with a straight face. "The smaller weights are less."

In spite of myself, I checked one in ocean blue the size of an Easter egg. Inside the crystal were delicate turquoise-tinted swirls like undulating waves. It was beautiful. And only half the price of the larger green one. I wondered if Leimomi would like it.

"You can almost see the ocean inside, can't you?" the woman purred.

You could. On an extravagant whim, I replied: "I'll take this one for my girlfriend."

"She'll love it."

Then I pulled out Corky's photo. "I'm looking for an old friend named Maya who may be with this man. I can give you his name if that would help."

"I don't need his name," she said proudly. "He looks different without his beard, of course, but I would recognize that boyish face and those green eyes anywhere. That's Charles, Maya's husband."

"Yes." I tried not to betray myself.

"They were in last week. Maya bought a crystal vase for their cottage. I think they're renting. Just moved in about a month ago."

"Is it near town?"

"You can't miss it—the yellow one about a mile down the road."

I thanked her, paid for the crystal orb, and headed to my waiting Mercury.

She was right. The yellow cottage wasn't hard to find. Beyond the weathered tombstones of St. Joseph's Catholic Church, it sat just outside of town among velvet green horse pastures. I pulled into a gravel drive and walked up to the tin-roofed cottage. The place looked deserted.

"Hello, anybody home?" I said through a screen door.

No one answered.

"Hello?"

No response.

I peeked in the mailbox and I found a phone bill addressed to "Maya Livengood," and a letter forwarded from Kē Nui Road—also in her name. There was a third forwarded letter addressed to "Charles McDahl" that was postmarked January third—over a month ago—in Lewiston, Idaho, but just forwarded a few days past. The handwriting looked feminine and shaky. And the sender's last name was the same as Corky's. Maybe his mother?

Tampering with U.S. Mail was a federal offense, punishable by serious jail time. A PI could lose his license. I stuffed the letter in my pocket. Climbing into the Grand Marquis, I aimed down the gravel drive and headed back to Kahului Airport.

twelve

Until my Honolulu-bound jetliner was wheels up and climbing, I resisted opening the envelope. The letter was written in the same feminine shaky hand.

Dear Charles,

Son, thank God you are alive! The story of your surfing accident at Waimea Bay was carried on all the TV networks and CNN, on the radio, and even the Lewiston paper. They all believed you were dead. But I prayed to God that you survived. My prayers have been answered.

It's a shame you have to hide from those bad men and can't even let your wife know you are alive. I fully understand and will keep your secret.

Please send me your new address.

Love,
Mom

Corky was more of a fool than I had imagined. If you are planning to disappear, the last person on earth you want to tell is your own mother. Any halfway decent insurance investigator would start with her. If Mr. Gold had not, he wasn't doing his job. But, then, if he had, maybe this mother who wasn't bright enough leave her fleeing son's name off envelopes *was* bright enough to fool an insurance investigator.

I returned to Maunakea Street late that afternoon, letter in hand—my only piece of hard evidence that Corky McDahl was apparently very much alive.

Mr. Gold had good reason to be suspicious. But I wasn't working for Mr. Gold. I was working for Summer, who was now more mysterious to me than ever. Was she totally in the dark, as the letter suggested? Or was she working with Corky? And perhaps Maya? And who were these "bad men"—the same men with Summer in the black Mercedes? Or were the "bad men" just some excuse Corky had given his mother to justify his running out on his pregnant wife and taking up with another woman?

The red light on my answering machine reminded me that Summer had never returned my call. I pressed Play and heard Tommy Woo's voice.

"Hey, Kai, did you hear the one about the Chinese, Filipino, and Hawaiian astronauts . . ." After a punch line that would get Tommy himself punched in some circles, he added "My client got hung out to dry by the Sun organization. He took the rap for that ice he sold. Thought you'd like to know."

Why did Tommy think I would like to know? Because the same thing had happened to Leimomi's father, who was still cooling his heels in prison? Her dad could have plea-bargained for a lighter sentence, and been out by now on parole, had he testified against the kingpin. But that meant harassment, bodily harm, or death.

As I erased Tommy's message, there was a gentle *tap . . . tap . . . tap* at my door. I reached for the knob and found Leimomi standing there, still wearing her *lei* stringing clothes—white Bermudas and a pink T-shirt that said "Fujiyama's Flower Lei's" and carried the ambrosial scent of ginger and *pīkake*. I glanced involuntarily at her tummy, wondering if it had already started to bulge like Summer's.

"I'm worried, Kai."

I took her warm hand and walked her to my client's chair. "Sit down and tell me what's happening."

"Nothing's changed," she said looking distracted. "Nothing at all has changed."

"Tomorrow's Friday." I tried to cheer her up. "Let's go out to dinner and have a relaxing evening together. It might do you good. Pick you up at seven?"

"A nice dinner won't change anything. It will be the same problem tomorrow."

"Wait and see. Here . . ." I pulled a twenty from my wallet. "Why don't you buy one of those test kits and then you'll know for sure."

"What if I don't want to know?"

"Leimomi . . ." The next hour was spent talking in circles, with Leimomi crying, me consoling, and nothing getting resolved. After she left, I realized I had completely forgotten about the ocean blue crystal egg I had bought for her. *Auwe!*

I tried calling Summer later and was surprised when she actually answered.

"What evidence have you found?" she asked matter-of-factly. There was a coolness and distance I hadn't heard before.

"I've found evidence, but not that Corky died."

"What do you mean?" She sounded curious, but not ecstatic.

"If you are not sitting down, Summer, I suggest you do."

"I'm already sitting. What is it?"

"Corky may be alive."

Silence.

"I've just come from upcountry Maui where he is most likely staying with a friend."

"What friend? He doesn't have any friends there."

"I'm not sure," I lied. She didn't need to be told just yet that not only had her husband faked his own death and skipped out on her, but also was living with another woman. Or maybe it was Summer who should be telling *me* these things.

"I want to see you," she said suddenly. "I want to see this evidence."

"OK. But let's meet in my office. The evidence is confidential and I don't want to carry it out of here."

"Alright." She agreed. "When?"

It was nearly four. "Can you get over here by 4:30?"

There was a long pause, as if she were consulting someone. "Yes. How do I get there?"

I gave her directions, then hung up the phone. I tilted back in my swivel chair, feet up on the desk, and puzzled over my client and her husband and his redhead girlfriend. Love triangle? Co-conspirators? At this point, the jury was still out.

Suddenly I got chicken skin—goose bumps—as if surfing in wintry conditions without a wetsuit. I took my feet off the desk and opened its wide center drawer.

Way in back under a tablet of yellow legal paper lay my Smith & Wesson. The blue-black .357 Magnum felt cold and heavy in my hands. It was loaded with six rounds. I put it on one corner of my desktop, artfully covered with a loose arrangement of bills and receipts I had neglected to file.

I put the letter from Corky's mother under the plastic liner in my wastebasket. If Summer decided to bring company, I didn't want anybody to walk off with it.

The longer I thought about my client's visit, the more uneasy I felt. On impulse I called Tommy.

thirteen

"Hey, Kai," Tommy answered on the second ring, "Did you hear the one about the curvy local girl who went door-to-door as a handy-man?"

"Can the jokes, Tommy," I cut him off. "I've got a quick favor to ask."

"Shoot."

"Somebody's coming to my office at four thirty and I'm a little concerned—not about her—but about who she might bring along."

"The pregnant blonde? The wife of the dead California surfer?"

"He's not dead. He's living in upcountry Maui with his new girlfriend."

"So he skipped out after all." Tommy didn't sound surprised.

"Looks like it, but there may be another angle. I'm wondering if the wife is caught up in something much larger."

"Yeah? Well, what can I do for you, Kai?"

"She's coming at four thirty . . . Would you call me at quarter to five? Just to see if I'm still breathing?"

"Sure."

"Thanks." I checked my desk clock. "She'll be here any minute. Talk with you later."

I hung up and waited. If Summer stayed true to form, she would show up at least ten minutes late. I should have told Tommy to call at five.

At 4:25 a faint knock sounded at my door. Before I could reach the knob, the solid mahogany swung open to reveal two men in black suits. No Summer.

One of the men had dark hair and complexion, maybe Middle Eastern or Mediterranean. I recognized him as Summer's escort. The other had bleached white hair and the washed-out skin of an albino. The whites of his eyes were a mouse-like pink. This odd pair of men stood in my doorway, silently—me looking at them, them looking at me.

"Mr. Cooke?" The dark man broke the silence. He didn't look angry or belligerent. He actually cracked a smile—which worried me.

"Yes, I'm Kai Cooke."

He reached into his pocket. I edged toward the Smith & Wesson. If he was pulling out his piece, I wanted mine too.

"'Gratulation!" blurted the white-haired one. Then his partner handed me a wad of green bills—Ben Franklins—rolled cylindrically like *sushi,* with money where the rice and Spam would go, and bound by a rubber band.

"Mr. Sun say investigation over," announced the white one.

"Mr. Sun? But Summer . . ."

"No, sir," said the dark one in the accent of an English gentleman. "You are under the employ of Mr. Frank O. Sun.

And when Mr. Sun says your investigation is over, Mr. Sun means your investigation is over. *Understood, sir?"*

"Sure, I understand." It appeared there was only one right answer.

"Thank you, then," the dark one replied. "We bid you good day, sir." They headed out the door.

"Wait"—I tried to stop them—"Summer . . ." The door was shut on my words.

The roll of hundreds in my hand began to feel heavy. I set it on my desk and slumped into my padded chair. I was gazing at the ceiling when my phone rang.

"You OK, Kai?" It was Tommy.

"Yeah, I'm OK. Tell me about Frank O. Sun."

"Is that who she brought?"

"Summer didn't show. Just two extremely well-dressed gentlemen—*malahinis*—who dropped several grand into my hands and told me to stop my investigation. They said *Mr. Sun* wanted me to stop."

"Drugs," Tommy said, "or drug money. Those are the only things that move Frank O. Sun."

"But how does Summer fit into this?" I wondered aloud. "She might be in danger."

"Or she might be pulling the wool over your eyes," Tommy smirked. "I've always thought you're too much of a choir boy to be a private dick."

"Help me think here, Tommy. Could Corky be connected to Sun? What would a surfer do for a drug lord?"

"Who knows? Sun has a big organization . . ." Tommy was silent for a rare moment. "You said your surfer made lots of trips between California and Hawai'i. Did he ever surf in

Mexico? Maybe he's a small-time supplier, or a dealer, or a mule."

"Then what about Summer?"

"Maybe Sun couldn't find him and had her hire you to do it for him, which means Sun wants this Corky *badly*. He probably skipped out with cash or drugs."

"And a BMW convertible."

"That too. I would guess if they get to him before you do, he's toast."

"Not good."

"Why should you care about him?"

"I don't. I'm just worried about his pregnant wife if Sun has her. Once he deals with Corky, what value is she?"

"You really think she's not involved?"

"I think she's innocent."

"You might be surprised, my friend."

Tommy's words rang in my ears after he hung up.

fourteen

Removing the rubber band from the green roll on my desk, I peeled off one bill after another. These were not crisp new notes, but well worn, high-mileage currency that had wandered the streets.

I counted to fifteen and still had more than half the roll left. Then I wrapped the loose bills back into the wad, and slipped it into my desk's top drawer, by the Smith & Wesson.

I decided to leave a message for Summer. I made it brief: "Summer, please call me if you need further assistance."

I didn't really expect to hear from her. She was spinning in Sun's powerful orbit; who was I to pull her out? Tommy was very likely right. I had been merely an errand boy—and now Mr. Sun was through with me. I wasn't going to give up, but I did take his message seriously. A shadowy drug lord was often a businessman of many enterprises.

My job now was to find Summer's wayward husband before Sun did, if it meant saving her. I wondered if Sun's men would stop tailing me just because my investigation had been declared over.

I locked the two dead bolts of my door on my way out, then navigated the incense haze wafting from Madame Zenobia's shop. Descending the stairs I spotted Leimomi in the back room stringing blue-dyed carnations and perfumy tuberose. *Tourist lei.* She sat by herself, looking glum, so I rushed on before she could catch my eye. But I didn't evade Mrs. Fujiyama.

"Mr. Cooke." Her courteous smile straightened.

"Hello, Mrs. Fujiyama. How are you today?"

"Very good," said the silver-haired matriarch. "But not so good my *lei* girl."

"Anything wrong?" I acted puzzled, but a sinking feeling told me what my landlady was about to say.

"Leimomi." Mrs. Fujiyama's smile now turned down at the corners.

"What's wrong?" I asked the obvious.

"Maybe *you* know?" She peered at me over her half glasses. "You her friend, yes?"

"Yes, I'm her friend . . ." What else could I say? *She thinks she's pregnant and I'm the father?* That wouldn't do. So I settled for, "We're having dinner tonight. I could ask her then if anything's wrong."

"Leimomi very young." Mrs. Fujiyama's eyes darkened.

"Yes, Leimomi is young," I conceded.

"Time for Mr. Cooke to marry?" She held me in her gaze. "Maybe you like have family—wife and *keiki*. Single life not so good, you know."

"Plenty of time," I said uncomfortably. "I'm only thirty-four."

"Thirty-four," she echoed. "Old man already. You be surprise'. Time fly. Before you know it—too old for family. Wife want young man. Not dry old man."

I was about to say something I'd probably regret, so I let her remark pass and made for the door.

Later that afternoon I headed for a quick session at Paradise. There was still one hour of light. I intended to use it.

Off shore of the Halekūlani Hotel, Paradise is one of the most remote and least crowded spots in Waikīkī, producing a narrow, peaky break that pumps up into crystal-blue curls. Takeoffs are steep and lightning fast. Rides are brief and intense. Though compared to the liquid mountains I had scaled at Waimea Bay, these small swells were tiny anthills.

But today I had them nearly to myself—one pristine swell after another—since most dedicated surfers were still haunting the North Shore. At the first glimmers of sunset, the sweet strains of an *'ukulele* and the twang of a slack key guitar from the Halekūlani echoed across the water. The spendthrift setting sun painted the sky with more gold than all the kings and queens of the world ever owned.

Out here I felt immeasurably rich. Out here I felt at peace. But back on shore trouble was brewing.

Friday morning I flew to Maui for the second time in less than twenty-four hours. On the plane in first class sat a pale, white-haired man in dark glasses looking eerily similar to Sun's albino. I watched him disembark at Kahului Airport, then waited until he had claimed his luggage and hailed a taxi before I picked up my rental car.

Find Corky first. That's what ran through my mind as the grey Nissan climbed twisting Baldwin Avenue into the cool upcountry. I glanced again and again in the rear view mirrors. Nothing but winding road.

Soon the eclectic town of Makawao came into view. Today I bypassed the general store and the New Age book shop, and drove straight to the yellow cottage. It hadn't changed since yesterday. The overgrown cane field—stray stalks bending forlornly—still climbed the sloping hillside beyond it. I knocked on the screen door.

"Anyone home?"

No answer, though the inner door was open and what I saw inside didn't look right.

"Hello?" I knocked again and waited.

No reply.

The screen door made a chilling squeal when I pulled it open. The cottage was in shambles. Either Corky and his lady friend lived like pigs, or they had been visited by pigs. Papers and magazines were scattered on the floor. A wastebasket was overturned. Unwashed dishes filled the sink. On the dining table, breakfast sat uneaten: two bowls of cereal soggy in milk, a glass of orange juice in which floated a drowned fly, and a full cup of coffee. One of the chairs had been turned over on its side; another, pushed back far from the table, tilted rakishly against the sink counter. From the look of this barely touched breakfast, someone had evidently split in a hurry.

I walked to the one and only bedroom, where a similar disorder prevailed. A double bed with sheets and blankets ripped off revealed a naked mattress stained in suggestive places. Dresser drawers lay open and emptied onto the floor. Bikini panties and jockey shorts were strewn and draped about.

I peered out a back window. After the mayhem in the cottage, the tidy rows of young salad greens in a vegetable garden struck me as odd.

"Anybody home?" I said a little louder than before.

Still no answer.

I wandered out into the yard and toward the overgrown cane field. And there, at the edge of the property where a split-rail fence separated a shaggy lawn from the field, stood a tall redhead whose hair glowed like copper wire in the morning sun. Her long slender arms were spread wide on the top rail resembling wings. She was gazing straight down at her feet. Her stance almost cut the figure of a crucifix: forlorn, solemn.

"Hello?" I edged toward her.

Her head slowly rose and turned in my direction. She had the face of a boy—a handsome, animated, sad boy. Grey-green eyes contrasted her copper hair. Rainbow-colored love beads hung around her neck. She wore faded denim bellbottoms and a scarlet tie-dyed T-shirt that revealed the silhouette of bare breasts.

"I'm looking for a Charles McDahl." I moved in for closer inspection. "Have you seen him?"

Her sad face, up close, was lightly freckled and a little less boyish. Fine, delicate lines around her eyes recalled Skipper's observation that Corky's "lady friend" was several years his senior. Maybe she actually *was* a child of the sixties.

"You're looking for Corky?" she replied in the high, husky tones of an adolescent whose voice is changing. "He's out there."

She pointed to the fallow field. There was a faraway look in her eyes. "They just left. They took him into that field. Except the older man. He stayed in the car."

"Frank O. Sun?"

"I don't know." She glanced away. "They kept me in the cottage. I heard a pop. Then they drove off."

She turned her distant eyes on me. "I'm Maya, Corky's wife." She offered me her fine-boned hand.

"Kai Cooke. I'm a private investigator." As my own hand closed over hers, I tried not to look too astonished at her declaration. Corky now had two widows?

When she began climbing over the split-rail fence, I followed her. She didn't try to stop me. I noticed she was in fact wearing a band on her ring finger, though dull like brass rather than gleaming like gold. We stepped warily through the uncultivated fields, searching the sod for what seemed inevitable.

"What did the men want from Corky?" I asked as gently as I could.

She didn't answer, just scanned the barren ground. Then she stopped and turned to me. She had begun to cry.

"They just kept shouting at him," she said through her tears. "'Where is it? Where is it?' . . . Everybody shouting . . ."

She started to walk away again, her steps now a stagger.

"Can you remember what the men looked like?" I tried another question, but too late.

Maya had frozen in place, suddenly silent and pale. I followed her gaze to the shallow ravine ahead of her.

fifteen

The red earth was stained black with blood. The biggest stain formed a ragged circle the size of a car wheel. Smaller spots dotted a meandering path. It looked as if someone had been shot and then dragged away. *He bled profusely,* I said only to myself. *They must have shot him point-blank.*

Maya mechanically followed the trail of blood, heading in the direction of the yellow cottage. Part way there, she bent down to pick up a black rubber *zori*. It was large and a local brand—"Surfah."

"His slipper," Maya said without emotion. "That's Corky's slipper."

She then picked up a pair of mirrored sunglasses that even I recognized. In the photo that Summer had given me, hanging around Corky's neck by thick cords was this same pair—the expensive kind some surfers wear. Surfers with money.

I figured the body of Corky McDahl was probably riding in the trunk of a car at this very moment, or his remains had already been dumped in an upcountry field or into the ocean.

I turned to Maya. "It looks like they took him away," I said in the most innocuous way I could. "It looks like they removed him from the scene."

She didn't respond but kept walking toward the cottage. I wondered why Sun had left Maya behind alive. She knew of Corky's dealings with Sun, I would bet, and now she could identify the men who'd taken him, if not Sun himself.

"Can you think of what they might have wanted from Corky?" I asked her again as I opened the screen door. Maya walked ahead of me, then stopped at the sight of the half-eaten breakfast. She ran her spider-like fingers through her hair and then looked up and studied my face for a long time. She appeared to be weighing my trustworthiness.

"It would help with the investigation," I coaxed her gently. "I wouldn't want you to be next."

Maya righted the tilted chair and slumped down into it. "Corky worked for a man in California named Damon," she began hesitantly, "Damon DiCarlo. At first Corky just took care of his BMW, but then DiCarlo said he would give Corky the car if he helped ship it to Honolulu. All Corky had to do was pick it up at the boat dock in Honolulu—and it was his."

"After Sun removed the drugs?" I helped her story along.

"Ice." Maya nodded. "Forty pounds hidden in the car."

"That's what, a million in street value?"

"I guess. But Sun never got it. Corky picked up the car at Sand Island and drove off."

"Was he *crazy?*"

"Corky had it in for DiCarlo, not Sun. He never intended to deliver his car, or the ice, once he found out DiCarlo was sleeping with his wife."

"His wife?" I stared. "But you said . . ."

"Yeah, Corky and I really are married. And he's still married to her too." Maya said this with a weird kind of distance. "But her baby's not Corky's. It's DiCarlo's."

"What? Is that what Corky told you?"

"When Summer got pregnant she wanted Corky to bring home more money, so he agreed to ship DiCarlo's car."

"And DiCarlo is a supplier for Frank O. Sun."

"Yeah, he brings drugs from Mexico into California and then ships them to Hawai'i. Corky hid the ice, sold the car, and faked his wipeout at Waimea Bay," Maya said matter-of-factly. "We hid out on the North Shore for a while, then on Lāna'i, now here."

"Where is the ice?"

"On O'ahu. Corky didn't tell me where exactly—to protect me."

"Or it was to protect him?" I said. "I'm sure you've thought of this, but what makes you think he wasn't going to skip out on you too?"

Maya seemed unfazed. "Then why would he tell me about the map he drew to the very spot?"

"There's a map?" Her story was getting loonier by the minute.

"On Lāna'i."

I figured she was either setting me up for a really wild goose chase, or this was the key to the whole thing. "Then I guess we better get ourselves over to Lāna'i and find that map before Sun does."

"Go to Lāna'i? Now?" Maya's freckled brow furrowed. "Give me a minute." She disappeared into her bedroom.

I considered phoning the Maui police, but decided against it. We couldn't afford the time for police reports and the interrogations that always follow a murder. Maya herself, as Corky's girlfriend—or "wife"—would be a crucial witness to his death, if not a suspect. And without her, even the tiny island of Lānaʻi would seem like a huge place to hunt for one solitary map.

A few minutes later Maya emerged with a small duffle slung over her shoulder. Her sad face now showed an eerily vacant smile. Her hippie look had been replaced by Hawaiian chic: a hibiscus print sundress in blood red that echoed her fiery hair. The neckline was cut tantalizingly low, and she hadn't bothered to wear a bra. It was easy to see how Corky might have been drawn in by Maya's seemingly unconscious sexuality. She had a gypsy, footloose quality about her that seemed to lure one on an exotic journey.

But even though she lived up to everybody's intoxicating description, her empty smile so soon after the murder did make me leery of her. *What is this woman made of?* Was Maya simply trying to make the best of a traumatic event? Or was she traumatized herself— her face a plaster mask reflecting the numbness that covers pain?

Maya slipped into the front seat of my rental car and we pulled away. With her sitting so close to me in that splashy red dress, it was a chore keeping the Nissan on Maui's twisting roads. But I did. All the way back to Kahului Airport.

sixteen

By mid-morning we were airborne to Lānaʻi. Cotton candy clouds floated lazily above the pitched roof of Lānaʻihale. Maya held onto her seat and her vacant smile as the Twin Otter shuddered through the clouds, then swept over Lānaʻi's towering sea cliffs to a tiny asphalt strip.

Dwarf *kiawe* dotted the plains beneath us where pineapple once grew, the *kiawe's* ashen, salt-bitten stalks rolling endlessly up to the horizon. Atop a distant slope, Norfolk pines marked off Lānaʻi City and the grand sprawling Lodge at Koele.

The Twin Otter bounced twice on the slender strip before settling into an even roll. At the cozy little airport on the Pineapple Isle you can't hire a rental car; you must catch a shuttle bus upslope to Lānaʻi City. We hopped off the Otter and onto the bus. The shuttle climbed the slanting plateau toward those statuesque Norfolk pines, providing sweeping views of the small island.

Given my hurry to find that map, I was glad of these visual reminders that the teardrop-shaped island of Lānaʻi stretches only about eighteen miles by a dozen. The austere, bone-grey landscape brought to mind Hawaiian legend portraying this as a forlorn, desolate place haunted by the spirits of buried *ali'i* and, therefore, uninhabitable by mortal beings. Although since the 1990s two elegant resorts—the Mānele Bay and the Lodge at Koele—have combined to employ more workers than did the nation's largest pineapple plantation here.

The shuttle climbed slowly toward Lāna'i City—too slowly for me. We didn't have endless time. Sun would soon enough figure out, if he hadn't already, that I had with me the only person other than Corky McDahl who could lead him to his stash. Maya wasn't saying much about the missing ice, or her departed lover, though she spoke freely enough about herself through that eerie smile that hadn't left her face since we left Maui.

Maya was forty-six. She told me this with pride, since she apparently knew she looked ten years younger. A military kid, born "Mary Leavis" to an artillery captain and a nightclub dancer in Texas, she grew up in the sixties bouncing from base to base. She later married and divorced twice, then changed her name to "Maya Livengood" when she became a free spirit in Hawai'i, drifting from island to island. Since then she had occupied herself swimming and diving and haunting the beaches of Hawai'i's famous breaks—and hooking up with guys like Corky who surfed them. To hear her tell it, she relished her mellow footloose lifestyle.

"I'm into astrology," Maya announced, with an artful flutter of her long eyelashes. "That's how I knew Corky and I were right for each other. We were both water signs. He was a Pisces—a fish. And I'm a Cancer—a crab. His wife was all wrong for him. She's an earth sign—Virgo the virgin—too distant and proper for a fluid, free-wheeling Pisces." She looked at me intently. "What's your sign, Kai?"

"No signs for me, thanks. Whatever my horoscope says, I'm sure I don't want to know."

"You're bull-headed." Maya shook her long hair. "What are you, a Taurus?"

"You missed my point, entirely."

She got quiet again. But that ghost of a smile didn't leave her face.

The shuttle bus crested the rise into Lāna'i City—sixteen hundred feet above sea level—where the pines pointed into the sky like giant green arrows. The stately evergreens lent the plantation town an air of mountain serenity and coolness. Surrounded by these soaring Norfolks, grassy Dole Park lay at center of the village. A bank, a general store, a few diners, and other small businesses sat on the park's perimeter with rustic sun-faded facades suggesting an earlier era. The village's nearly deserted streets reinforced the sense of desolation that had set in at the airport.

We stepped off the shuttle by the kelly green Lāna'i Plantation Store, whose red tin roof covered gas pumps, a small convenience store, and the island's only car rental agency.

"It's time you told me," I said, opening the store's door. "Where's the map hidden?"

Maya didn't hesitate. "On Shipwreck Beach."

"Shipwreck Beach? That's eight miles of sand and junk."

"Corky told me the map is inside a sunscreen bottle."

"Eight miles, and we're looking for one sunscreen bottle?" I couldn't help but sound exasperated.

"There's more . . ." Maya paused. "Corky told me to walk the beach to that stranded Navy ship—the huge one that ran aground offshore."

"That narrows it down some," I said, a trace of exasperation still in my voice.

By noon Maya and I were twisting down the sun-bleached highway to Shipwreck Beach in a Jeep Wrangler—rear-view mirrors, for the moment, empty. A conventional car would have done us little good on this rugged island, whose roads other than this narrow paved highway were mostly sand and dirt and mud. Soon we would need all four wheels pulling.

The road wove down six miles to the blustery windward coast of Lāna'i. This remote wind-swept slope would be a great place to get lost. And never found. There were few signs of civilization here, not even such beginnings as lines for electricity, telephone, and cable TV. The sloping terrain, like the bleached highway, looked scorched. Stunted *kiawe* and red rock—that was it. Over the craggy landscape the wind howled.

Before long Maui and Moloka'i lay in the distance on the blue sea. Then the rusty hulk of the grounded ship came into view, listing and battered into a bare skeleton. Many years ago the Navy tried to sink the mammoth World War II liberty ship in the channel between Lāna'i and Maui. But the vessel had a mind of her own. She ran aground and all attempts to remove her failed. Today she still haunts the beach like a rotting corpse yet unburied by the sea.

Unreal. As unreal as the likelihood of our finding a sunscreen bottle on eight miles of beach presided over by this hoary wreck.

As the highway bent down to the shore and the pavement turned to sand, we found ourselves driving along the beach on a powdery path bordered by *kiawe* thickets. The wind swirled a sand contrail behind us as the Jeep got squirrelly. I shifted into four-wheel-drive.

Another mile brought a huddle of fishing shacks, erected of timbers washed ashore from capsized vessels, and the first human faces we'd seen on this desolate coast, two local fishermen mending a net. Beyond the shacks where the path ended, I did a U-turn and stopped, pointing the Jeep back toward the highway in case we needed to leave in a hurry.

"The ship is about a mile down the beach." I broke the news to Maya. "We'll have to hike."

As we stepped from the Jeep, grains of wind-blown sand bit into our bare limbs like a swarm of mosquitoes. *Gusty trades.* The tide was high and getting higher, leaving a narrow strip of beach bordered by thorny *kiawe* and littered with fishnets, ropes, Pepsi and Bud cans, driftwood, crab skeletons, rocks, and plastic containers of every color and shape. The sand literally blasted our every step as we fought our way down the inhospitable beach.

Suddenly, out of nowhere, two more Jeeps, kicking up a cloud, came flying down the sandy road.

"We've got company."

Maya glanced back, saying nothing.

The Jeeps stopped well short of ours and as I watched the sand cloud settle, two men in dark suits piled out of one and began striding slowly toward us. Another one or two remained behind in the other Jeep. *Frank O. Sun?* A good hundred yards stood between them and our own Jeep, which was beginning to look dangerously far away.

"Let's turn around."

"Turn around?" Maya arched her brows. "What about the map?"

"If we find it, Sun is going to want it too. We better head back to Lāna'i City, where there's safety in numbers."

Maya nodded and we jogged to our Jeep, hopping in before the suits came close enough to do us harm. I cranked the motor and mashed the pedal down. Sand swirled behind us, spraying tiny shrapnel on the two men as we whizzed by. I sucked in a deep breath and held it, hoping they weren't going to start waving guns. I recognized the white hair of the man who had visited my office; the other man I could only see was dark.

We flew past the Jeeps. One had a suit-and-tie now standing beside it; inside sat a man in dark glasses and hat.

When the sand settled behind us, the odd couple had shrunk to tiny stick figures in the distance running for their vehicles. Before long the two Jeeps were filling our rear-view mirrors, where they stayed all the way back to Lāna'i City.

seventeen

When I swung into the pine-lined drive to the Lodge at Koele, one of Sun's Jeeps swerved in behind us and almost spun. At remote Shipwreck Beach Maya and I were easy targets. But here at the Lodge, it would be harder to avoid witnesses.

The Lodge at Koele rambled over acres of highland woods and tropical gardens and expansive lawns. Though its patina copper roof, cozy dormer windows, and wide shaded *lānai* echoed the plantation-style architecture of the humble village below, this palace was definitely not humble. The portico over the grand entrance displayed a larger-than-life hand-painted golden pineapple, the Hawaiian symbol of hospitality.

With Sun at our backs, I was pinning my hopes on that legendary hospitality right now. Since there was no way to get back to Shipwreck Beach before nightfall without being followed, we'd best get a room.

At the reception desk a bow-tied local woman greeted us cordially, with a well-trained *"Aloha."* It was Friday in prime season—when the American heartland was buried in snow—and we had no reservation.

Predictably all standard rooms were booked.   She straightened her tie, apologized, and then explained that the Lodge was happy to offer us, instead, some of its more luxurious accommodations.   We could score a spacious "plantation" room with king-size poster bed for nearly four bills, or a two-bedroom suite for a grand. *Ho!*

"We'll take the plantation room," I said, without even glancing at Maya. I handed the receptionist my credit card and signed in: "Mr. and Mrs. Cooke." Never mind that I had no wedding ring; my companion did.

"A porter will assist you with your luggage."

"Thanks, we can manage." I pointed to Maya's small bag and then mumbled some line about preferring to travel light.

We passed through the Lodge's Southwest-inspired Great Room, an open-beamed expanse whose sunny skylights glowed on countless wingback chairs and sofas and oriental rugs, then across a wicker-chaired verandah. Out of the corner of my eye I saw two Jeeps pull under the Norfolks at the Lodge's entrance, then one man jumped from each Jeep, both as overdressed and out of place on Lāna'i as they had been on O'ahu.

"Company again." I turned to Maya, who I began to notice was rather accomplished at being unfazed.

The two men stepped into the Lodge, leaving one man inside each Jeep. Even at this distance, inside the trailing Jeep I could see the Panama hat.

"Sun seems to think we know something he doesn't," I said. "Did Corky tell him about the map?"

"No, that's why Corky was killed."

Maya said "killed" nearly as dispassionately as if she were referring to a cockroach. Now I've seen more than my share of grieving widows and lovers. And, hands down, Maya was the coolest of all. When it registered that this was the first she'd referred to Corky's death since leaving Maui, I wondered again what else this forty-six-year-old redhead wasn't talking about.

Our airy, pale blue room had enough soft angles and plush furnishings to put one in the mood for relaxation. The king-size bed, a four-poster of knotty pine, reigned over the spacious room, but left plenty of extra territory for overstuffed chairs and lounges and billowy blue curtains framing bucolic views. We had everything anybody might need: a wet bar, a safe, color TV and video player, two phones, a koa ceiling fan, and our own personal *lānai* overlooking our own personal banyan tree.

I stepped onto the teak-furnished *lānai* and watched Sun's two Jeeps, drivers only, pull into the Lodge's parking lot. Maya reclined on the four-poster bed, each post topped with a carved miniature pineapple resembling a hand grenade.

"*Lovely.*" Maya ran her fingers over the powder-blue comforter. "Try the bed, Kai."

As she oozed admiration over our temporary lavish surroundings, I couldn't help observe, "You don't seem too broken up over your boyfriend."

"*Husband,*" she corrected me. "Anyway, I had my cry." Fluffing a downy blue pillow, Maya turned her eyes to me. "What do we do now?"

"Wait."

"For what?" She stretched her lanky limbs on the bed like a cat.

"Darkness," I said. "In the mean time, you can make yourself comfortable."

"I will." Maya continued her feline stretching. Her copper hair glowed against the blue pillows. She made that poster bed look awfully inviting. So I made myself turn away and walk over to the desk.

Paging through the Lāna'i phone directory, I searched for the number of a surfing buddy whom I had first met years ago in the lineup at Cunahs in Waikīkī. I hadn't seen Conrad Figueira recently, and I didn't even know if Rad or his family still resided on Lāna'i. But having just one friend on this island might be a lifesaver.

I tried dialing "Angel Figueira," the first of two "Figueira" entries in the tiny book. The phone rang and rang. On the sixth ring an out of breath young woman gasped "Hello." I explained my old relationship with Conrad.

"Rad?" she said excitedly. "You're a friend of my big brother?"

Catalina told me she lived in the family home in Lāna'i City with her two children, Felipe and Maria, and their grandfather, Angel, who worked the early morning shift in the kitchen at Mānele Bay Hotel.

"Come visit us," Catalina said with warm and sincere Filipino hospitality. "Felipe and Maria would love to meet you. And Papa too. He's napping now. He goes to work every morning at five."

She gave me directions to their house on 'Ilima Avenue, and we hung up. If Maya and I ran into trouble, Catalina might just become our new best friend.

I then phoned Leimomi and left a message that I was working a case on Lāna'i and was *very* sorry to miss our date tonight. I left neither a phone number nor said at what hotel I was staying—I didn't even want to think about what kind of explaining I'd have to do if Leimomi called and Maya answered.

Maya and I stayed in the room most of the afternoon, her watching infomercials about age-defying miracle beauty cures, me sitting on the *lānai* keeping an eye on Sun's Jeeps in the parking lot. Around four, I took a walk to the sundry store and bought two penlights.

As I was leaving, I saw my albino friend in the cavernous Great Room sunk into an overstuffed leather sofa with a newspaper in front of his nose. He acted as if he didn't see me, but as I passed he peered at me over his *New York Times* and then pulled a cell phone from his shirt pocket.

When I returned to our room, Maya's impression remained in the blue comforter, but she was gone. *I knew I shouldn't have left her alone.*

Ten minutes passed. I imagined as many scenarios in which she played victim to Sun's goons as those in which she played their accomplice, compliant with their plots to an extent that did not threaten her "widow's" inheritance.

When she finally let herself in, I asked where she had been.

"Reliving beautiful memories," she explained, reclaiming her comfy spot on the poster bed.

"You and Corky stayed here?"

She nodded, her smile becoming annoyingly serene.

I walked over to the phone, definitely feeling more relaxed at the thought of Maya not being one of Sun's pawns.

"I hope you liked the food then, because I'm about to make reservations for dinner. Seven?"

She nodded.

I phoned in the dinner reservation, then pulled a frosty Heineken from the wet bar and offered it to Maya.

"I don't drink," she said, recovering her voice.

I popped the cap and began to down the Heineken myself. As I was nearing the bottom, the phone rang. I let it go.

Maya looked at me as the phone rang and rang. "Aren't you going to answer it?"

"No."

I sat silently and watched Maya. She didn't move. Finally the phone stopped ringing. A message light began blinking.

I picked up the handset and played the message.

"Kai . . . ?"

Leimomi had tracked me down. And she sounded desperate.

"I did what you asked. I bought a pregnancy test kit. We need to talk. I can't bear this alone."

Pilikia. I shook my head. Trouble.

"And, Kai, why did the hotel operator say she was connecting me to the room of 'Mr. and *Mrs.* Cooke'? Who's Mrs. Cooke?"

"What's the message?" Maya was asking in my other ear.

"Wrong number." I hung up the phone.

Maya rose abruptly from the poster bed. "I'm going to take a bath in that blue tub. Do you mind?"

"Why should I mind?"

Maya said nothing more as she ambled toward the gleaming tub, leaving the door partway open behind her.

I could see her reflection in the bathroom mirror. Behind her, powder blue was the dominant hue, with soft, indirect lighting and fixtures of polished brass. Gauzy shower curtains, draped from a brass rod the size of a canon, fell into sweeping festoons with plenty of pomp and circumstance. Cream-colored throw rugs and fluffy terry towels made the scene that much more luxurious.

Maya began to undress, revealing the shapely breasts I'd been glimpsing at all day. The freckles on her face, I discovered, had cousins elsewhere. And they were sexy— each and every one. She definitely didn't look her forty-plus years. Her slender limbs were smooth and gracefully sculpted. Only around her neck could I detect the first faint lines that someday would show her age, but not yet. When she shed her panties, the triangular puff of copper hair between her legs sent shock waves through my brain.

"Join me in the bath?" Maya's voice snapped me out of my reverie. *Say what?*

Maya bent, gorgeously naked, toward the brass tub faucets and cranked on the hot. A steamy flood poured out as a war went on inside me. There was something more than a little unsavory about climbing into that steaming tub with the redhead whose "husband" had just died violently only hours before. Then there was Leimomi, whose looming pregnancy had my future hanging in the wind.

I watched as Maya sprinkled in a packet of bathing crystals. A rich, dewy, seductive scent instantly perfumed the room. *Jasmine.* I could see the hot water rising, bubbling and shimmering.

Maya swung one long bare leg over the baby blue tub rail, then the other. She slipped down into the fragrant bath.

Soon only her slender neck and fiery hair showed above the rising water.

"*Ahhhh . . .*" was all she said.

I don't know how it happened exactly. It wasn't a decision I consciously made. When I slid in behind her, she remained silent. She turned and glimpsed the shark marks on my chest. But even they didn't move her to speak. The water was almost too hot—on the edge of scalding. But before long I got used to it. I breathed in deeply and the jasmine sent filled my lungs. I cupped my hands around her breasts as she eased up onto me. Instantly she was moving and communicating, not with words, but with sighs.

We climbed higher and higher, taking each other up to an invisible summit. When we finally tumbled over it together, Maya screamed and grabbed my thighs so tightly that her nails left deep red impressions. I felt the sting, but didn't care. By then I was floating on a blue cloud.

Making love with someone I'd just met was kind of crazy. There was a sense of knowing her intimately—the warmth of her touch, the taste of her skin and hair and private places, and the exquisite feel of her love—yet I hardly knew *her* at all. Who she was, how she lived, or what she lived for.

Before the floral euphoria of the blue bath faded, there was a knock at the door. "Room Service," said a male voice.

"Did you order Room Service?" I whispered into drowsy Maya's ear.

"No, sweetie, I didn't order anything," she cooed back.

I stepped dripping from the tub, wrapped a fluffy towel around me, and headed for the door.

"Who are you looking for?" I asked through the thick wood.

No reply.

I heard a tray settle to the carpet and some china and silver clinking. Then I heard footsteps—not one pair but two or three—quick footsteps making tracks down the hallway from the door.

I dialed Room Service. "Did you send a tray to our room?"

"One moment, sir . . . No, sir, Mr. Cooke. Nothing was sent to your room. Would like to order from the room service menu?"

"No, thank you. A waiter apparently left a tray by mistake at our door. You might want to send someone for it."

"Yes, sir. Immediately."

As I slipped back into Maya's warm blue world, I got to thinking. *What was on that tray?*

eighteen

Inside the dimly lighted Lodge dining room the ambiance was Old World, island-style: crystal chandeliers glinting against dark paneling of *koa* and mango; landscapes of Provence hanging beside Hawaiian quilts and a lava rock fireplace. When the *maître d'* seated us, the pearly twilight was fading to grey and I was just hashing out my plan. It wasn't an elegant plan—not so elegant as this high-toned eatery. No matter. So long as the plan worked.

Smelling fresh from her jasmine bath, Maya hardly glanced at the menu and announced, "I'm a vegetarian," then ordered portobello mushrooms with Waimānalo greens. *Whatevahs.* The four-star Pacific Rim establishment boasted fresh Island ingredients with Continental flair—Moloka'i venison carpaccio, Lāna'i mixed pheasant and quail sausage with Pinot Noir sauce, *onaga* and Kahuku mashed potatoes, and fancy wines staring at seventy clams. I went with the catch-of-the-day—fresh *'ō pakapaka*—grilled solo with no sauces, chutneys, salsas, or other fussy stuff. Just the way I like it.

If Sun were watching us dine, he kept himself hidden through the entire meal.

When the check came, it took my breath away. *Oh, well, Sun's money.* I put the meal on our hotel tab and we strolled arm-in-arm back toward our room, past illuminated orchids and lily pads and cascading bougainvillea. Beyond the lighted pathway were bubbling blue spas, and beyond the spas were darkened golf links and hills and woods. Suddenly sensing someone behind us, I stopped under a torrent of bougainvillea and drew Maya to me. I whispered, "Let's put on a show."

Maya kissed me as her roving grey-green eyes glanced over my shoulder and found one of the bubbling spas. "Want to make love in the spa?"

"Later."

Her slender fingers ran down the buttons of my aloha shirt, past swaying palms and *hula* dancers.

"Later," I said again, though she was getting good at distracting me. "Listen, if Sun's man drops back, we can slip into the darkness and then run to the golf clubhouse. Up there on the rise." I pointed. "Follow the cart path and stay behind the trees so no one can see you."

"You're no fun." Maya pinched my behind.

"Have you forgotten why we're here?" I reached into my khakis and pulled out one of the two penlights. "Take this. But don't turn it on, if you can avoid it."

Behind us, our tail lit a cigarette and slowly edged away. Since we'd been at the Lodge, Sun's men had appeared to be working in solo shifts, perhaps hoping not to arouse suspicion about their un-resort-like attire and conduct.

"Let's move," I whispered. We split off and jogged through the maze of gardens and up the cart path toward the first fairway.

Behind the clubhouse we finally met up, both of us puffing. When the blood stopped pounding in my ears, I listened to reassure myself we hadn't been followed and then, clasping her warm hand, led Maya quietly into the dark woods.

Snapping on our penlights, we huffed up a foothill trail through a grove of ironwoods and pines. In less than half mile of meandering, the trail intersected the road to Shipwreck Beach.

Six miles stood between the Lodge at Koele and Shipwreck Beach. *Six miles.* Sun would be watching our Jeep, so that was out. But it was a nice evening for a hike. The air was cool, even a bit chilly at this elevation, and luckily the blustery trades had died down.

We stepped along the sloping highway, alone under the stars. Any approaching vehicle would give us plenty of warning to conceal ourselves, for headlights and a motor's hum would carry a long way in this silent night. The terrain looked less desolate by night than by day, a dark country road winding down an endless grade. We could have been in any rural spot, except for the lights of Lahaina flickering across the channel.

The moon soon rose above the sea, painting Maui's distant twin mounds pale amber. The highway took on an eerie glow. I hoped Maya would complain of sore feet—so I could too. But she kept on, her hips swaying rhythmically in front of me.

I glanced behind us, looking for two pairs of Jeep headlights. I glanced behind us again and again. No sign of Mr. Sun.

It was past midnight when we finally reached Shipwreck Beach. A low tide offered more sand for our throbbing feet to tread on than the narrow strip of the morning. Bleached remnants of sea creatures scattered about glowed like ghouls in the moonlight.

Our every stride brought more cans, containers, and debris to sift through—Miller Genuine Draft, Kikkoman soy sauce, a lonely flipper, Tide detergent, a rusty fire extinguisher, frayed rope—in search of our sunscreen bottle.

"What kind of sunscreen are we looking for?"

"Coppertone," Maya said. "Bronze bottle. Number 8." She paused. "Oh, yeah, Corky said to look by a rusty freight container washed ashore near the stranded ship."

She tells me this now? Could she really be that much of an airhead? I stepped gingerly among the debris. *Or was this a wild goose chase after all, with Maya in the lead?*

As we hiked the beach toward the wrecked ship, behind us I spotted two flashlights, about a quarter mile back, combing the sand like search beacons. They could have belonged to fishermen, but I doubted it.

"Guess who?" I pointed to the roving lights.

Maya didn't even hear me. Her mouth had dropped open.

Before us loomed the moonlit ship, its rotting, ghostlike corpse still unburied by the sea. Heavy swells were battering it and exploding like skyrockets in the moon's glow. I got chicken-skin.

Opposite the distant ship sat the freight container on the beach, sprayed by the shore break. The rust-orange container had apparently plunged from a freighter, spilled its cargo, and washed ashore. One of its two doors had been ripped off and lay twenty yards away in the sand.

I glanced down the dark beach. The roving beams kept coming. Now human figures crossed in front of the beams, picking their way through the debris as they walked. "Where's the map?" I asked again.

Maya shone her penlight inside the rusty freight container. Crabs with big menacing claws scuttled every which way through the dark and shallow sloshing seawater. Their powerful pincers and beady eyes seemed to threaten intruders: "Don't even think about it setting foot in here!" Only those twin searchlights closing in on us could possibly prompt me into that container.

No need. Maya evidently knew right where to look. Under the lip of the doorsill—high above the crabs and sheltered from wind and sea, there it was: a bronze bottle. Coppertone 8.

nineteen

"Unscrew the cap."

Maya's eyes met mine, and something in them glinted like a devious child's. She twisted off the cap.

I shone my penlight on a rolled piece of paper inside the neck of the bottle. It looked dry and clean. A pencil or car key or small finger could, with patience, fish it out.

"That's Corky's map." Maya peered at the rolled paper and smiled strangely.

"Screw on the cap and let's go."

"Go? Don't you want to see it?"

I pointed down the beach at the wandering beams. "Let's move."

"Where?"

"Hiking trails head *mauka* every mile or so along the beach. They're full of *kiawe* thickets and out of our way, but they may be our *only* way."

Maya nodded and we took off down the beach, away from the lights.

About a mile beyond the wrecked ship, we came to a sandy trail twisting up several miles toward Lāna'i City. It didn't make sense to go back to the room now, where Sun's men would be waiting for us. It'd be better to push ahead and try to get off this island. It was now two a.m. We had miles to go before dawn. And the twin beams kept coming.

We took the *mauka* trail.

Hours later, in the distance, we saw a faint flickering. Lāna'i City. The moon in the west was setting over the tranquil sea, while the eastern sky behind us was turning the color of a blushing peach.

No more roving beams. No head lamps. Had we shaken them?

The twinkling village stretched out before us in a luminous grid. Cottage windows of early risers glowed pale yellow against the brighter checkerboard of streetlights. We headed for one of those cottages, the home of Angel Figuiera.

Tin-roofed plantation dwellings with postage stamp-sized lawns lined 'Ilima Avenue in colors that, even under glaring street lights, looked wild: lemon yellow, cinnamon red, cornflower blue. Evidence of family life abounded: boogie boards, bicycles with training wheels, barbecues, toy Jeeps, Igloo coolers. A puppy whined. A lone rooster crowed. Hard to believe that among this reassuring domesticity a drug lord might be lurking.

Most cottages didn't have legible numbers, but from the few that did, we seemed to be moving in the right direction. There it was—537 affixed to a lavender cottage with a rust-freckled GMC truck occupying the lawn.

Five in the morning is a strange time to knock at someone's door. We had little choice.

A short, wiry old man appeared in a white chef's apron that contrasted his wrinkled, raisin brown skin. He must have lived seventy years, maybe more, under the tropic sun. Despite his weathered appearance, Angel Figuiera's lively eyes sparkled like an excited boy's.

"Mr. Figuiera? I'm a friend of Rad's from Oʻahu—Kai Cooke."

"Eh, Kai, Catalina bin tol' me you call." Out came his sunny smile and his pidgin.

"Sorry we come so early." I shifted to pidgin myself. "Dis my frien' Maya. We get some kine *pilikia*. Can help us out, or what?"

"Shoots . . ." The old man smiled.

"We need catch da firs' boat to Lahaina from Mānele Bay dis morning, so dat"—I hesitated—"so dat nobody see us."

"No need explain. You n' Maya come wit' me to Mānele Bay Hotel. I work dere."

"You go to work soon?"

"Yeah, right now in da truck." He waved toward the GMC. "Climb in da back, in da shell. Nobody see you in dere."

I was grateful for local-style hospitality. No need to explain motive, however bizarre, even shady. After our nightlong hike, I had little energy to spin a yarn about what we'd been through, or what we might face ahead. Sometimes mysteries are best left that way.

Angel's pickup rattled through the few blocks of Lānaʻi City, then turned down Highway 44, the two lane blacktop also known as Mānele Road that ran about five unswerving miles, then began to weave as it approached the cliffs of Mānele Bay.

"Da boat to Maui no leave 'til eight in da morning," Angel said through the sliding window between the cab and the shell.

"Dat's OK," I said.

"Da harbor jus' one short walk from Mānele Bay," Angel explained. "You like come to da hotel?"

"You sure no problem?" I asked.

"Nah, I take you t'rough da kitchen. I'm one *preparation chef*." Angel said in formal English, pronouncing each syllable of his title carefully. "I prepare da pineapples and papaya and mango fo' da guests' breakfas'—lunch too. I experience' wit' pineapple," Angel laughed. "T'irty years in da pineapple fields—I pick 'em. Now in da resort, I slice 'em. I da 'pineapple man.'"

As Angel approached the cliffs, Maya gazed longingly at Mānele Bay, dead ahead in the gauzy twilight.

"Over dere, dat's da resort where I work now," Angel said. "Job mo' easier, mo' bettah pay. Go figgah."

The Manele Bay Hotel spread its meandering Mediterranean-tiled wings around the sheltered bay where dolphins are known to play and *malahinis* bake in the tropic sun. Unlike the cool Lodge at Koele, this oceanfront resort embraced the typically sun-splashed beach.

But there wasn't much sun at quarter past five, just a pink glow heightening in the east. Nearly three hours to cool our heels. The more time we gave Sun to find us, the more chance he would. But what was the likelihood of Frank O. Sun thinking to look for us in a resort kitchen? Zilch, I hoped.

Angel punched in at 5:28 a.m., then we followed him through a maze of hallways to the huge kitchen, where he donned a chef's cap embroidered with the resort's name in royal blue. At stainless preparation tables *sous chefs* were already at work slicing tangy tropic fruits for the breakfast buffet: kiwi, mango, pineapple, papaya—while mingled whiffs of cinnamon, coconut, and buttery oats suggested that the pastry chefs had started work even earlier.

My stomach growled. I saw Maya eyeing a tray of fragrant muffins. Since we had just hiked through the night without food, I suspected she was as ravenous as I. Angel must have seen the look of hunger in our eyes.

"Dis way," he smiled warmly. "Da employees' dining room."

Angel led us a short distance from the kitchen to a room where resort workers were eating a very early breakfast. A smaller sampling of the hotel's guest fare was laid out in a buffet line.

"OK wit' da boss if we eat?" I wondered out loud.

"He don' min'," Angel winked. "He don' know and he don' min'. Or he put 'em on my tab, no worry."

Maya and I filed through the buffet line heaping on fruits of every variety, elegant pastries, and, for me, scrambled eggs and breakfast meats. We filled our plates, then dug in, as if only hours earlier I hadn't forked over two bills for dinner at the Lodge's swanky restaurant.

After breakfast Maya found an unnoticed corner of the employees' lounge to snooze in, and I kept watch on a secluded terrace overlooking the bright blue bay. To ensure we didn't miss our ferry, I set my alarm watch for seven thirty. Even if

I had dared to, I was too wired to sleep. I kept turning over our options for escape once we reached Maui. None of them perfect.

When I stepped back into the employees' lounge to wake Maya, she was gone. As my watch ticked toward eight I wondered if she and the sunscreen bottle had flown. I tried not to worry. Her disappearances were becoming routine.

A few minutes later she casually strolled into the lounge.

"Where have you been?" I asked the obvious with all the enthusiasm of a soldier after a twelve-mile forced march.

"Reliving beautiful memories of Mānele Bay," she replied. "Corky and I—"

"Do you still have the map?"

"Why wouldn't I?" She opened her purse and fished out the bronze sunscreen bottle.

"OK, let's go." I led her to the employees' dressing rooms where—with the blessing of Angel, if not his boss— we changed into a couple of unattended wait-staff uniforms: royal blue aloha shirts, slacks, and embossed baseball caps. Maya slipped the sunscreen bottle into the pocket of her aloha shirt, where the staff customarily kept their order pads and pens, then twined up her long hair under the blue cap. I practiced slouching in my new outfit, so I might be taken for a tired waiter on whom onlookers would spare no more than a casual glance. With my sore feet, working up a shuffling gait was no problem.

We tracked down Angel again, thanked him for the food and clothes, and asked about getting a ride to the ferry.

"No worry," he said, smiling his *aloha* smile. He led us up a spiral staircase to the resort's marble-columned entrance.

From there a van whisked us to Mānele Harbor like two hotel workers heading for a weekend getaway on Maui.

The Lahaina-Lāna'i ferry idled into the harbor as we arrived. About the size of a city bus, the boldly red-white-and-blue-striped vessel floated high in the water and had two decks spacious enough to accommodate more than the few passengers waiting with us to board. The lower deck was enclosed by dark glass; the upper, behind the wheelhouse, was open to the morning sun. At the stern, four gaping pipes rumbled with the throaty authority of twin diesels.

This appeared to be no "chug-chug" ferry, but one that could get up and move. The twenty-five mile trip between Lāna'i and Lahaina was scheduled to take only forty minutes. The fast clip would suit me just fine. The sooner we got away from the Pineapple Isle, the better.

The ferry docked and the engines shut down. I scanned the other passengers who boarded with us. None of them looked the type to run drugs. Maya and I took comfy velour seats on the lower deck. Soft fusion jazz—Kenny G's mellow sax—wafted through the air-conditioned cabin. I thought of Tommy. The pseudo-soothing ambiance inside the ferry was at odds with the increasing tension I felt every minute we remained docked. I looked up into the wheelhouse, where the captain's digital clock said 7:58. I took a deep breath.

One minute later the twin diesels started up with a roar, then settled into syncopated hum. The steward removed the boarding plank. Maya put her head on my shoulder. "It's almost like being on vacation," she said.

"Almost," I replied. She sure was taking this mad dash for our lives in stride.

I scanned tiny harbor, a lava rock breakwater sheltering a half dozen sailboats and small fishing vessels, but saw no evidence of Frank O. Sun or his well-dressed lieutenants. Not on the breakwater. Not on any nearby boat.

Then up on the distant rise, I caught sight of a Jeep weaving down toward us in a hurry. No, two Jeeps. Moving fast.

Maya looked up then and clutched the sunscreen bottle in the pocket of her aloha shirt. As the ferry chugged toward the harbor's mouth, the two Jeeps stormed into the parking lot. A man in dark glasses and suit jumped from one of the Jeeps and waved his arms. He shouted something at the boat. I couldn't hear his words over the throbbing motors.

"Captain," the steward shouted up to the wheelhouse, "More passengers?"

I looked at Maya. She looked at me. Neither of us said a word.

twenty

The steward shouted again. "Take the passengers aboard?"

The cabin clock read 8:01. The captain cranked the wheel toward the open sea and revved the twin diesels. In a cloud of salt spray and billowing exhaust, the ferry roared from Mānele Harbor.

As we began climbing swells outside the breakwater, the two Jeeps became mere specks behind us. Soon the ferry swung around the rocky southern tip of Lāna'i and into the channel to West Maui. Lahaina was not yet visible, only the green cane fields scaling the mountain behind it. The drone of the diesels, the bow rising and falling over the swells, and my lack of sleep would normally have made me doze off. But not today. My mind was racing.

Before we hit Maui we needed a plan. *How to get back to O'ahu?*

We could try to evade Sun by boarding a flight from Kahului to Kaua'i or Moloka'i or the Big Island, then connecting to O'ahu. Wandering Kahului Airport, however, could be risky. Or we could drive to remote, tiny Hāna Airport in East Maui where Sun surely wouldn't go. But the trip would set us back half a day. Our best bet was to try the commuter airport at Kapalua—just up the road from Lahaina. Island Hopper flew Twin Otters from Kapalua almost hourly. Even if Sun pursued us there, we would most likely take off before he arrived.

As the ferry cruised across the channel, we were surrounded by islands: Lāna'i fading behind us, brooding Kaho'olawe on our right, cliffy Moloka'i on our left, and cloud-wreathed Maui dead ahead.

Maya was missing this awesome array of islands. The twin diesels' rhythmic hum had put her to slack-mouthed sleep. I heard a clack on the floor under her seat, then spotted an object near her feet the size of a cigarette pack. I plucked it off the deck. *A cell phone.* There was a call-back number on the screen, but no messages. I watched Maya's even breathing as I tried to memorize the number before returning the phone to the floor. Then I peeked into the pocket of her aloha shirt. The bronze sunscreen bottle was still there.

The crossing from Lāna'i to Maui took every one of the scheduled forty minutes. But before long the engines quieted down again to a syncopated idle. Ahead, Lahaina Harbor's antique lighthouse pointed skyward like an ivory needle. Coconut palms and spreading banyans stood sentinel over the old whaling port, with its vintage square-rigged ships and legendary Pioneer Inn. I'd never been so glad to see the red roof of that storied old inn—a place where whalers once imbibed their grog, and whale watchers still do today.

At nine on Saturday morning in prime whale-watching season, Lahaina Harbor was jumping. Sunburned *malahini* lined the decks of dozens of vessels, powered and sail, that ply the sea in search of those leviathans. Near the harbor's entrance, surfers rode lazy little rollers. I envied those board riders, *surfing free.*

As the ferry docked I scanned countless cabs and vans and passenger cars flanking the Pioneer Inn, and on bordering Wharf and Hotel Streets. I focused momentarily on each vehicle, looking for telltale signs of Frank O. Sun. Though I saw none, I wasn't fully reassured.

Maya and I disembarked and lost ourselves in the after-breakfast crowd on Front Street. Lahaina town was as lively as its harbor. The main drag bustled with tourists eyeing I Got Lei'd on Maui T-shirts, Cheeseburger in Paradise, time-share condo deals, you name it. On Front Street we boarded the Lahaina Trolley, which runs north to the resorts of Kā'anapali, and blended in with the rest of the aloha shirts and bikinis on their way to work or play.

The trolley, a mock cable car, breezed through town, then along the coast a few miles to Whaler's Village at Kā'anapali. From there we caught a shuttle up slope to tiny Kapalua Airport. On the tarmac stood a Twin-Otter, my old friend: eighteen seats, two propellers, the boxy shape of a mini-van. Small, but enough airplane to fly us back to O'ahu.

Minutes later, the Twin-Otter lifted off over the golden sands and pale jade reefs of Kā'anapali's famous beach, then the deep blue channel between Maui and the shadowy cliffs of Moloka'i.

"Open the sunscreen bottle," I shouted into Maya's ear above the engine roar.

"Here . . . on the airplane?" she yelled back.

We were seated at the rear of the Twin-Otter—the last row by the door—enduring a ear-shattering din. The turboprops screamed, the cabin vibrated, the whole airplane audibly throbbed.

"Nobody's looking," I yelled. I had already reassured myself that no one aboard appeared to be employed by Sun, and no one was manifesting much interest in how two resort workers were spending their Saturday off.

Maya scanned the passengers, then she unscrewed the cap. She stuck her little finger in the tiny bottle neck and coaxed out the rolled paper.

"It's not a map," she said, even before unrolling the small sheet. "It's directions."

I suspected she had already peeked.

The document was handwritten in blue-black ink on buff stationary imprinted "The Lodge at Koele," where Maya and Corky had apparently spent a lost weekend. At the end was a little crude drawing of what looked like a church steeple. Corky had damn lousy penmanship. Or he must have scribbled this thing in a big hurry. It read:

Hey, Babe,
    Drive to Waimea Bay. Look for the bell tower at the mission on the n— side of the bay. The stuff is in the tower. Go there when the church is open for mass on Sunday so you can climb the tower. At the top is a bench under the windows where you can s— the whole bay. Look under the bench seat.
    If you read this, it means I'm gone. Sorry I didn't make it with you, Babe. But this map is your insurance policy.
                    Luv ya,
                    Corky

"Is it what you expected?" I yelled into Maya's ear over the roar.

"Yes and no," she said. "Corky took me to Mass once at that church. It was strange because he wasn't religious. He was *spiritual*—but not conventionally religious. It all makes sense now."

"Sunday may be our best bet to climb the bell tower. But we'll go have a look today anyway. Most Catholic churches hold a mass or two on Saturday evening."

After the Twin Otter touched down in Honolulu, we headed for the car rental agencies—no way could we stroll up to my Impala in the lot without being spotted. As I waited at the Hertz counter, craning my neck to spot any dark suits lurking, I called my office for messages. Off O'ahu now for nearly twenty-four hours, I wondered if Summer had checked in.

The first message was from Leimomi—she needed me. I had forgotten to return her last call. I felt terrible, but it would have to wait longer still.

There were three other messages.

"Mr. Kai Cooke? Your Jeep is overdue." The Lāna'i Plantation Store. I wondered how much not returning that Jeep was going to cost me. Or Sun.

The next message was from attorney Grossvendt. "Any news about my BMW convertible . . . ?"

I had news: He would never see his beloved BMW again, unless Sun got busted and all his assets were seized. If so, the car would probably come back in pieces.

The last message was in a low and heavily accented voice: "Mr. Cooke, I think you make some fatal mistake. I say 'Investigation over.' And I mean *over.*"

Frank O. Sun. I envisioned his dark glasses and Panama hat.

"You are paid handsomely. Is this not true? I give you one last chance . . . like a gentleman, yes? A word to the wise: consider most carefully."

I heard a click. No message from Summer.

Maya and I piled into a Hertz Ford and drove to Waimea Bay. We didn't talk much. Just as well. I was thinking about Summer and wondering whether my beating Sun to the ice would help her, or hurt her. I hoped the former. But it was now out of my control.

As we pulled onto the H-1 ramp, I checked the rear view mirrors. If Sun knew we had the only map to his missing treasure, he wouldn't let us out of his sight for long. He had to be back there somewhere.

When we got to the bay, Kamehameha Highway surrounding it was choked with traffic. I braked and we were stopped momentarily on the ridge. The air was pregnant with mist. Spectators, two and three and four deep, lined the road gawking at the drama below.

Waimea was breaking!

The whole crew was out. Big wave legends and newcomers and wannabes. A dozen surfers on stiletto-like big guns stroked for each massive swell. The sets looked good. Probably eighteen to twenty feet.

Nearly every surfer on earth knows the view from this ridge. The classic scene is portrayed often in the surf media—the horseshoe-shaped bay, the mountainous waves, and their daring riders. And in the background, always, rises the mission's bell tower, higher than the highest winter waves.

That surfer Corky McDahl had chosen this tower in which to hide his treasure, his deliverance, his salvation, made perfect sense. As it loomed into view, the huge monolith took on new meaning for me: the end of the line for this twisted and deadly treasure hunt.

We crawled in the traffic, a solid line of cars and vans and trucks wrapping around the bay. Finally passing the beach park entrance, where police were turning vehicles away, we crossed Waimea stream and curved around the bay's north side.

The gravel lot in front of the mission looked deserted. *No Saturday Mass?* I got out and stepped to the church. It was locked up tight. The front doors were bolted, as were the side entrances. And the bell tower.

I walked around the building until I found a sign: Mass Every Sunday—7:30 and 9:30 a.m.

Corky had been right. Our treasure hunt would have to wait until tomorrow.

twenty-one

We followed Kamehameha Highway north past ʻEhukai and Sunset. Both breaks, like Waimea, were cranking and the highway and beaches packed.

At Kahuku Point, the highway bent east and then south to Lāʻie, where a narrow side road marked by a single sign led *makai* to the Mālaekahana Bay campgrounds. We turned in. Mālaekahana's tranquil beachside campsites in February lay mostly empty, unlike in spring and summer when tents sprout like wild mushrooms. Technically, a state permit is required to camp at Mālaekahana, which means driving downtown to Punchbowl Street. We had no time for that.

"Do you like sleeping on the sand?" I asked Maya.

She knit her brows. Surprisingly, the footloose redhead didn't appear to relish the idea. She didn't even suggest sex on the beach.

"It's not exactly the Lodge at Koele," I said, "but at least there are cold showers and Sun shouldn't look for us here."

Strong trades bent the ironwoods along the shore as we stepped from the car onto a bed of their pine-like needles, within a stone's throw of the rumbling surf. It was wild out there. Wet and wild.

I borrowed Maya's cell and called Tommy Woo. But before punching in his number, I left her at the campsite and hiked to the restrooms. I didn't want her to hear the details of my dealings with Sun.

After Tommy told his obligatory first joke, I gave him Sun's telephone number and asked Tommy to call him. I wanted to contact Sun personally, but not reveal our location or that I was calling from Maya's phone.

"Block your caller ID," I added.

"It's always blocked," Tommy said. "Let's keep it simple. You talk and I'll record your voice and play it back for Sun."

"OK." I took a breath. "Here goes . . . ."

"Recording," Tommy said.

"Frank O. Sun, listen up: Harm Summer McDahl and you will never see your ice again. I'm not talking more until you let Summer go . . ."

I thanked Tommy, then left a voice mail for Detective Brian Tong at Narco-Vice, telling him succinctly what I had learned about Sun and his organization. If I didn't make it through the day tomorrow, at least the authorities would profit from my investigation. I then hiked back to the campsite where Maya was gazing out to sea, as if searching for a lost and lonely speck in the boiling surf.

For the rest of the night we lay low. Night comes quickly to the tropics in winter. After sunset, twilight briefly appears, then vanishes. Suddenly we were in the dark.

I set my watch alarm for 6:00 a.m. and we slept under the stars, not on the beach, but on ironwood needles. The needles might as well have been cast from iron, for all the sleep I got.

Maya made no overtures that night. She even stopped asking for my birth sign. Her game was over, I guessed. Or maybe last night's hike had just taken the starch out of both of us.

When my alarm rang Sunday morning, a razor-thin orange line glowed above the turbulent sea. By six-thirty we were heading north on Kamehameha Highway.

The surf was still up. Following a pickup truck with a half dozen boards piled in back, we stopped just short of Waimea Bay and pulled into the mission. The car behind us also turned in. Then another. Early arrivers to seven-thirty Mass.

The mission's doors, unlike yesterday, were wide open. We followed in a young couple and their ponytailed *keiki* who walked down the center aisle, stopped by a pew, genuflected, stepped in, and turned down the kneeling bench to pray. The mission was as small as the typical side-chapel of a larger church, and was overshadowed by the massive bell tower behind it. The pews were polished dark mahogany with kneeling benches upholstered in red vinyl. Overhead, ceiling fans whirred. It was cool and quiet inside, except for the shuffling of parishioners' feet and the crack of the wooden benches being turned down against the floor.

"Find us a seat," I said to Maya as I stepped toward the rear foyer. "I'm going to look around."

When I glanced up from the foyer's skylight at that huge tower looming overhead like a medieval fortress, I couldn't help thinking: *The view of the bay from up there must be awesome.*

One thing was clear: to climb to the top I would first have to break in through a solid wood door with an old fashioned keyhole lock, the kind you find these days only in antique chests and steamer trunks. A lock like that can usually be picked, but it would have to be picked quietly.

I rejoined Maya in the chapel just as the priest rose in a long white robe, spread his arms wide like a cliff diver, and uttered in a deep, resonant voice:

"In the name of the Father, and the Son, and the Holy Spirit . . ."

"Amen," the rising parishioners responded in unison. I said "Amen" too, hoping for divine intervention to guide me up that tower.

I looked around us. The mostly local crowd filled the little church to the brim: babies in mothers' arms, toddlers, teens, *tūtū,* uncles, cousins. It was a family affair and the feeling was good. Behind the priest a vaulted arch was inscribed God Is Love. And through open windows framing the bright blue bay I could hear the thunder of surf. *Big* surf.

"The grace of our Lord Jesus Christ . . . be with you all," intoned the priest.

"And also with you," the parishioners responded.

On each pillar between the church's open windows hung a bas-relief depicting one of the fourteen stations of the cross—Via Dolorosa, the way of suffering—seven stations on either side of the chapel. White marble statues of Mary and Joseph stood behind us, each adorned with a green *haku lei.* Not the kind of scene for Sun in his Panama and shades.

"The grace and peace of God our Father . . . be with you," the priest continued.

"And also with you . . ." the parishioners replied.

Then the tuneful choir, a dozen strong, began singing their hearts out. I mumbled along. The Hawaiian *wahine* leading the choir broke into a solo, while strumming a guitar and directing three *keiki* playing 'ukulele. Soon everybody was singing merrily. Me, I kept mumbling and watching and waiting.

Maya and I did our best to rise and kneel and pray with the faithful. Though we were always off a beat. Personally, I could have used some soul cleansing right then, but I had work to do.

When the priest took up the sacred host, the chalice and the wafers for Holy Communion, I prepared to make my move. The priest raised the chalice and solemnly crossed himself, then the choir sang like earth-bound angels, *"Al-le-lu-ia! Al-le-lu-ia!"* Parishioners rose one pew at a time and filed forward to take Communion. I tapped Maya on the shoulder. "Wait for me at the car after Mass."

Maya stepped toward the altar with the others. I slipped to the back of the church, then into the foyer adjoining the bell tower.

Danger—No Admittance said a sign on the dark lacquered door leading to the tower. With only my keys and a tiny keychain jackknife so small it passes airport security, I worked the lock, while the Communion hymns covered the clinks and clanks of my lock picking. First I tried my keys: Apartment key. Office key. I wiggled each key inside the keyhole. I even tried the rental car key. No luck. Suddenly the choir's sweet *"Al-le-lu-ia!"* ceased and the priest said: "The Lord be with you . . ."

I didn't have much time. Then I tried my Impala's key— old-style, long and skinny. I heard a promising *click* . . . but then that was all. The tiny jackknife was my last hope. I opened the longer blade, slowly inserted it, and moved inside the lock. Another promising *click* . . . followed by a louder *click . . . click. Yes!* Finally, the lock sprung.

The bell tower door opened to mustiness and semi-darkness. Rusty folding chairs and card tables layered with dust leaned against two walls. In the center, a spiral of wooden stairs. I mounted the creaky wood that serpentined up into the shadows. Through the viewing ports above came a brilliant light. With each creaking step, I rose toward it.

The choir cranked up again, guitars and 'ukulele and off-key voices:

> *Kindness and truth shall meet;*
> *Justice and peace shall kiss . . .*

The choir's voices grew fainter as I climbed, their fading hymn soon blending with another. The hymn of booming surf.

When I finally reached the tower's summit, I saw a bench lining each wall of the empty belfry, just as Corky had said. The benches doubled as storage bins; each could be lifted to reveal an enclosed compartment. In one of these compartments would be the prize. One million worth of methamphetamine ice.

As I moved toward one wall, I couldn't help but gaze out the viewing port. The bay was cranking! Swell after swell steaming in. And plenty surfers taking the big drop.

I tore my eyes away and considered the bench compartments. There were four—four chances.

I tried the bench opposite Waimea first, facing down the coast toward Pipeline and Sunset. Prying the seat up with my fingers produced cobwebs and a coil of rope. That was it.

Next I tried the bench facing *mauka* toward the sacrificial *heiau* and Waimea Stream. Empty.

I tried the one facing out to the open sea, where those huge rollers swept around the point into the Bay. More junk: a stack of yellowed copies of the *Daily Missal,* a mousetrap with a decapitated mouse, a cheap screw cap bottle of wine, a used condom.

That left the last bench facing Waimea Bay, where Corky had started this whole mess. I should have guessed. It made perfect sense.

Slowly I pried up the bench seat. My eyes scoured the empty space.

twenty-two

Nothing.

Or was there something? I noticed some sparkling dust and reached down and with my fingertips, extracting a gleaming speck. It was almost crystal-clear, like rock candy.

The ice had been here and now it was gone. *How could Sun have found it before we did?* We had the only map, according to Maya. Had Corky, before he died, revealed the location to the drug lord? If so, why was Sun still following us?

"It's gone," I told Maya in the mission's gravel lot.

Her face went blank. "It can't be," she said.

"This is all that's left." I held in my palm the little crystal of ice. "Somebody got here first."

"They lied to me." The words spilled out as if Maya were alone. Her eyes darkened to the impenetrable jade of a Waimea wave.

"Who lied?"

"The men who took Corky."

"*Took* Corky? You said they *killed* Corky. Remember his slipper and sunglasses, his spilled blood?"

"They told me to say that"—she looked away from me—"to tell you, so you'd think I was the only one left who knew where the ice was." She ran her fingers through her hair. "And they did kill a man, right in front of me. But not Corky."

I didn't know whether to believe anything this woman said anymore. I started up the car.

"It was the guy who hired Corky—Damon DiCarlo." She sounded pleading now. "They told me if I didn't lead them to the ice, the same thing would happen to Corky."

"Then why didn't they take both of you?" I turned off the engine and looked hard at her. "Why leave you behind?"

"Corky wouldn't tell them where the ice was. And he convinced them I knew nothing. But they thought *you* did and told me to go with you. Once we found the ice, they said they'd release Corky and pay me ten thousand dollars."

"And you believed that?"

She shrugged. "I had to."

"So all along you've been cooperating with Sun?" Her seduction routine suddenly made sense—it wasn't my irresistible attraction, but my usefulness in retrieving her boyfriend.

"What else could I do?"

"Think, Maya. You're not getting anything from Sun, probably not even your boyfriend."

"I'll see Corky again," she said defiantly.

"Did you call Sun and tell him where the ice was hidden?"

"*No!*"

"Can the lies, Maya."

"Mr. Sun gave me a phone number, but I didn't call. *Honest.*"

"You mean, you didn't call since Lāna'i. That's why you kept disappearing, isn't it?"

"Yes, but it was before we found the map. I haven't talked with Mr. Sun since. I swear. That's why he kept following us."

"If you didn't tell Sun, he obviously got it out of Corky. And if Corky was alive, he's not anymore. Your boyfriend double-crossed the organization—look what Sun did to DiCarlo."

"I want to go back to Maui," Maya said abruptly. "Corky will meet me there."

"Let me see your cell phone and then I'll drive you to the airport."

She looked befuddled, but reached into her pants pocket and handed me her tiny Motorola. I checked her call log for Sun's number and dialed.

On the first ring a heavy voice said "Sun."

"Mr. Frank O. Sun?"

"Yes. Who is speaking?"

"Kai Cooke."

"Ah, Mr. Cooke. You follow still errant ways? You forget investigation over, do you?"

"Mr. Sun, you've got your ice—thanks to me. If I hadn't found Corky, you'd be nowhere—like you were before I took this case."

"Beware of pride, Mr. Cooke. An emotion most unwholesome."

"My message is simple . . ." I paused for effect. "Let my client go. Narco-Vice would love to hear all I know about your organization. If you hurt Summer, I'm on the phone. Think about it." Sun didn't need to know I had already called Narco-Vice.

"You forget the husband, Mr. Cooke."

"I didn't forget. I just don't believe Corky McDahl is alive." I watched Maya flinch. "Good-bye, Mr. Sun."

I hung up.

Maya bristled. "You didn't have to say that about Corky."

"Not to be cruel, Maya, but if your boyfriend is still walking this earth, I'd be very surprised. You can call Sun and speak to him yourself, if you like." I handed back her cell phone.

She was quiet for a moment. Then she said, "I want to go home to Maui."

Minutes later we were cruising by Haleʻiwa, then pineapple fields, coffee groves and Schofield Barracks. Finally we caught the freeway to the airport.

I dropped Maya at the inter-island terminal. I wasn't worried about her. She knew how to take care of herself.

"Sorry to have to ask you this, Kai," she said stepping from the rental car. "I need airfare."

"You need what?" I couldn't believe my ears.

"Airfare to Maui." She shook her copper hair, which in the full sun seemed to burst into flame.

More than anything I wanted to be rid of this woman. I reached into my wallet. From the wad of hundreds Summer had given me that fateful morning at Denny's, one was left. One green Ben Franklin—the *only* bill in my wallet. I gave it to her.

"Bon voyage."

She grinned and then kissed me passionately. I admit I didn't stop her. With her arms tight around me, her breasts pressed against me, I recalled that jasmine-scented blue bathtub at the Lodge at Koele. When she broke off the kiss, she announced: "You're warm-hearted and generous. You must be a Leo." Maya nodded. "Yes, I bet you're a Leo."

Still smiling, Maya glided into the terminal. She had lied to me for most of the forty-eight hour blur we were together. And I felt guilty that I had given into her seductions. I also felt oddly sad upon seeing her go. I watched as she stepped gracefully into the terminal, then broke into a run. Was she running to or running from?

Whatevahs. Maya was gone.

When I returned the rental car at the airport, it seemed as if we'd had it for days. I put the charge on a credit card, then walked to the parking garage to retrieve my Impala. I had no idea what Sun might have done with my classic Chevy. But the teal Impala was still there, looking a little dusty but unharmed. I peeked under the car for explosive devices. *Nah, they wouldn't waste the powder on me.*

It started up on the first try; I swung in line to pay for parking and suddenly realized my wallet was empty. The bill for parking nearly three days would be at least thirty dollars.

When my turn at the window came I pulled in front of the attendant, a woman in a flowered mu'umu'u the size of a tent. "I was just dropping off a friend at the terminal," I said. "I got in the wrong lane."

"Ticket?" she asked.

"Don't have one. I must have left it at the lot entrance."

A cloud crossed the attendant's face. She scanned the thin layer of dust on my Impala's hood. Obviously the car had sat several days in the garage. "Got to talk to one supahvisah."

"I'm really in a hurry," I pleaded. "It wasn't my fault. I mean it was, but I won't do it again."

"*Auwe!*" She let out an exasperated breath. Horns blew. The line of cars behind me was growing.

"I return da favah someday, yeah?" I hauled out my pidgin, winked, and hoped for the best.

She gave me serious stink eye, then suddenly the gate went up.

"Tanks, eh?" I drove away.

Maunakea Street never looked better. I was glad to be home. I walked through the flower shop, saying hello to Mrs. Fujiyama, who peered at me sourly over her glasses. I glanced to the rear of the shop where were Chastity was working, and Joon and Blossom. No Leimomi.

"Upstairs . . ." Mrs. Fujiyama said without apparent reference to anything. Did she mean Leimomi?

I climbed the orange shag and marched past Madame Zenobia's. The psychic shop was shut tight. Ahead I could see the full-color surfer on my door and, yes, someone was waiting, sitting on the floor, hunched over as if in pain.

"Leimomi?"

The woman turned, then slowly dragged herself up. She peered at me with violet eyes.

"Corky's alive," Summer said. "I want you to find him."

"Are you OK?" I scanned her body for evidence of abuse. She appeared fine, though from her now even lower-slung burden, it looked like the baby might come any minute.

"Corky didn't die at Waimea." Summer ignored my question. "He's alive. And I need him now." Her voice was still a whisper, but a determined one. She glanced down at her enormous tummy.

I wondered if now was the time to quiz her about her association with Sun. Maybe it didn't matter anymore. She was unharmed and, by the looks of it, at this moment very in need. Besides, she was still my client and I had yet to produce her husband—dead or alive.

"How do you know he's alive?" I asked.

"It's an intuition—a strong intuition."

"OK, for argument sake, let's say that Frank O. Sun did the unthinkable and let Corky live—where do we start looking?"

"Is the surf up?"

I should have thought of that, but I hadn't had a full night's sleep in three days.

"Give me a minute." I opened the door to my office. The familiar mustiness of the place felt reassuring. "What about the baby?" I scanned again her bulging middle.

She grimaced. "I've felt a few small cramps."

"Contractions? Do you need a hospital?"

"Find Corky first. Then I'll go to a hospital."

"Let's talk." I gestured to my client chair. She sat down as I walked behind my desk.

"Somebody has to tell you this, Summer, even at this inopportune time." I paused to gather my thoughts, but there was no gentle way to deliver them. "Corky may not want to see you as much as you want to see him. He thinks your baby isn't his. He thinks it's Damon DiCarlo's."

"This baby is Corky's." Summer stared into my eyes without blinking. "Damon and I never made love. He asked but I refused. I've been faithful to Corky, despite what he thinks. There was never anyone else."

"I believe you." I meant it.

"I think we should go to Waimea Bay." Summer looked at me anxiously. "I want to find Corky before the baby comes."

"You're sure?"

She nodded.

"OK," I sighed. "Back to Waimea."

twenty-three

On the ridge overlooking Waimea Bay I parked my Impala—leaving Summer sprawled in the passenger seat—and began searching for Corky McDahl, again.

Stepping from the car I felt a tug of the Smith & Wesson I had tucked into the right front pocket of my khakis. It felt heavy and cold, and made a bulge in my pants that Summer could have easily noticed, had she been in any condition to look.

I hoped I wouldn't need it. Frank O. Sun had his ice, Summer was free, and Corky was God knows where—on earth or in heaven. Or maybe hell.

So why did I need the revolver? I don't know. I just didn't feel comfortable showing up at Waimea without it.

With my field glasses I scoped out countless surfers in Waimea's lineup. The swell had gone down since this morning. The waves were big enough—twelve to fifteen feet—to attract a crowd, but not too big to frighten anybody off. A half dozen surfers dropped down each precipitous face.

In the unlikely event that Corky actually *was* out there, whose board would he be riding? His own patched candy cane sat safely in my office. I scanned the crowd and managed to pick out Cousin Alika on his sunshine yellow gun and a few of his friends. I also spotted a blond mop head here and there. But nobody who looked like Corky. After searching for several minutes, I gave up and walked back to the car.

"I don't see him," I told Summer.

Hunched over inside the Impala, she glared at me with an intensity that was almost scary.

"Here, let me find him!" She lumbered from the car, reached for the binoculars, and took up a shaky position on the ridge overlooking the bay. I steadied her and suggested she sit down. But she wouldn't.

She swung the field glasses to one side of the lineup, then to the other—coming back again and again to the same spot in the thick of the farthest break.

"Oooohh!" she groaned.

"Are you alright? You should really sit down."

"No." She kept standing, focusing the binoculars. *"That's him,"* she said. "That's Corky. He's on an orange board and he's grown a beard."

"Let me see."

She handed me the glasses and I focused on a bearded blond guy on an orange gun. "Could be," I admitted.

"It *is* him. *Aaahh-Aaahh!*" Summer winced. Her paper white face bore an expression of pure pain.

"Are you—"

"A huge contraction . . ." She grimaced and then buckled over.

"We're finding a hospital." I reached for her hand.

Summer no longer resisted. Inside the car I stretched her out in the front seat, her head on my lap. She was beginning to writhe. *"Aaaaaaahh!-Aaaaaaahh!"*

Neither of us paid anymore attention to the surf or the scenery on the way to Kahuku Community Hospital, about five miles up Kamehameha Highway. By the time we pulled up to the emergency entrance, Summer was breathing fast and hard. I felt totally helpless.

The green-smocked medics wheeled her off in a flash, so I waited. I thought about Leimomi, her pleading voice was echoing in my head. I picked up a *People* magazine and flipped through it without seeing a thing.

Summer delivered a healthy eight-pound, two-ounce baby girl.

"You're the father?" one of the ER nurses said to me in the waiting room.

"Y—" I started to say, then realized where I was. "No, the father is surfing at Waimea Bay."

"Oh . . ." she said.

"Is she OK?" I interrupted any further questioning.

"The mother and daughter are doing fine," the nurse reassured me. "Both are fine."

"Can you tell her I'll be right back?" I stood up. "She'll understand."

"I . . . yes, I can." The nurse looked at me curiously as I turned and made for the door.

I fetched my Impala in the hospital's lot and roared back to Waimea, even faster than the trip over. There was no place to park legally in the bay's lot, so I double parked and walked across the beach, hoping the officer directing traffic was too busy to notice.

Of the dozens of surfers we had seen earlier in the water, a few were now coming in, while others were just paddling out. I looked around hoping to see someone I knew. Cousin Alika on his yellow board was still in the water. I scanned the faces on the beach.

"Ham!" I said, seeing Alika's surfing buddy. "Get off work fo' check out da surf?"

"Kai, bruddah," Ham said and shook my hand local-style, the Polynesian tattoo on his bicep dancing. "Yeah, I wen' make sandwiches fo' da lunch crowd, den I dig out."

"Ham, you do me one favor?"

"Shoots," he said, tossing his sun-bleached dreadlocks.

"One *haole* guy in da lineup on da orange board—see um?" I pointed.

"Yeah, brah," Ham squinted. "Jus' one orange speck way out dere."

"Dat's him, da California surfah named Corky, you know, da guy dat wipe out Christmas Eve. Tell him come in. If he no come, you round up Alika and da boyz and encourage him, OK?"

"He alive? Da surfah dat wipe out stay alive?"

"Yeah, his wife *hāpai* and jus' deliver one *keiki* at Kahuku Hospital. I goin' drive him down dere."

"Dis guy goin' come in." Ham's serious face looked determined.

"Tanks, 'eh?"

"No mention." Ham mounted his board and paddled into the boiling surf.

I sat on the beach and waited. For the first time since this whole twisted case began, I actually felt peaceful. Summer was alive and well, and so was her baby girl. And

Summer's estranged husband, by some miracle I might never understand, was also still alive. I wondered how he might react. Would he believe the child was his? Would he care?

A half hour went by before I saw the orange gun coming in. The closer he got, the more he looked like the photo Summer had brought to Denny's in Waikīkī that rainy Monday morning. Straw yellow hair. Boyish face, and now that blond beard. Not until he walked up the beach could I see his green eyes clearly and understand how both Summer and Maya might have fallen for him. Something about his churlish expression said, "I'm cool."

He scanned the beach with the board under his arm.

"Corky McDahl?" I approached him. He had a totally pissed off look on his face. "Your wife has just given birth to your new daughter."

"Says who?" he blustered with boyhood bravado.

"Kai Cooke." I replied. "I'm the private detective she hired to find you."

"The kid ain't mine." Corky was all attitude. "You got no right to pull me out of the water on such a good day." He turned back toward the waves.

I reached for his arm, but he was already trotting down the beach, heading for the shore break. I ran after him and grabbed a rail of his surfboard.

"Chill!" He yanked away the orange gun. As his toes touched the water, from my khakis I pulled my own gun—the Smith & Wesson.

"Hold on." I pointed it at his head.

"Piss off." He kept walking into the water.

I aimed at his board and fired, ripping a hole through it the size of a silver dollar.

He peered back at me. "You're f—k'n *crazy,* man!"

"Let's go." I pointed the smoldering Smith & Wesson toward my Impala in the parking lot. "I won't hurt you enough to get charged with anything serious, but if I were to drop my gun, say, and it accidentally discharged into your foot, you could miss a lot more than one day of good surf."

Corky scratched his blond mop with the hand that wasn't cradling his damaged board. Then he started walking with me toward my car. A small crowd had gathered around us and followed behind. I figured someone had already dialed 911 by now, so we needed to move fast.

I gestured to the racks on my Impala's teal roof: "Strap your board up there and be quick."

Without snarly comment or surly retort, Corky lifted his surfboard onto my racks. I could see blue sky through that silver dollar-sized hole.

"You drive," I said, as much as I hated turning over the wheel to anybody, especially this guy. "I'll make sure we get there." I held the gun level. Corky climbed into the driver's seat. I shut the door behind me and glanced over my shoulder. No police escorts yet.

Corky didn't say a word during our brief ride. So I decided to break the ice.

"DiCarlo isn't the father, according to your wife. The baby is yours."

Corky didn't respond, his green eyes fixed on the road.

"Look. You and your wife can sort it out. But right now she needs you."

"Like I really care." He kept looking straight ahead.

A few miles from Kahuku Hospital Corky suddenly glanced at me.

"So where's Maya?" he asked.

When I told him she'd flown back to Maui, Corky just shrugged. I had a feeling he was going to leave it that way.

"You're fortunate to be alive," I said, truly curious about his dumb luck. "Why did Sun let you go?"

"I told him where the stuff was hidden," Corky explained.

"I was just at the mission and the ice was gone."

Corky seemed to smile slightly. "I moved it to a locker at the Y before Maya and I split Oʻahu."

"So why go to all the trouble to bury a bogus map on Shipwreck Beach?"

"To throw him off. Sun finally realized he could never find the ice without me. So I took him to the Y. He left with the bundle. I left with my life. Not because Sun is generous, but because I convinced him Maya would squeal if anything happened to me."

"Did you know Sun was also holding Summer?"

"I didn't know she was even here." He took a deep breath and a hint of concern spread across his face. Maybe he did actually care. "I'd heard she hired someone to look for me and Maya, but I had no idea she came to Hawaiʻi herself."

"I think DiCarlo may have brought her against her will. And now he's dead."

"His blood splattered all over me," Corky said, expressionless.

"You know it wasn't an accident. Sun made an example of him. DiCarlo was killed entirely for your benefit."

Corky didn't respond. When we pulled up to the emergency room, I let my Smith & Wesson rest in my lap.

"Just go in. They're expecting you."

Corky eyed the gun, then released his grip on the wheel and looked out the window. Finally he opened the door and let himself out.

I watched the reluctant Californian unlash his orange board, cradle it under his arm, then step slowly into the emergency room. He looked back at me only once.

twenty-four

Back on Maunakea Street I peeked in on the *lei* girls. No Leimomi. *Where was she?*

Upstairs in my office the red light on my answering machine was blinking. I pressed Play.

"Mr. Cooke, this is Meyer Gold, investigator for Acme Life, calling about Charles Corky McDahl, the surfer who died at Waimea Bay last December. Acme has concluded its investigation and is prepared to settle the policy for Mrs. McDahl, who we understand has retained your services. But I'd like to compare notes with you before authorizing the check."

Ho! Mr. Gold was in for a surprise.

I knew who the next message was from even before I heard it.

"Kai? Are you there? Please pick up the phone. Kai . . . ?"

I lifted the receiver before her message ended and dialed Leimomi's number.

"Kai? Is that you?" She answered on the first ring. *"Finally.* Where have you been? I've called your office five times."

Leimomi's tone wasn't angry or depressed or even scolding. She just sounded happy to hear from me.

"Sorry, Leimomi—really sorry—it was a case, the California surfer who wiped out at Waimea. The case is over now. I'll be here for you—"

"Kai, the most amazing thing has happened." It was her turn to cut me off.

"What?" I held my breath.

"Daddy is getting out on parole. He's coming home to Kaua'i and I'm going to go there to meet him."

"Well . . . that's great, Leimomi." I was expecting news of her *condition.* "Did your father get out early?"

"Yeah, he's agreed to testify against the drug supplier who got him in trouble."

"I thought your father feared for his life?"

"He did, until the supplier got indicted. It just happened and now Daddy's getting out."

"Wait a minute . . . what's the drug lord's name?"

"Moon or Star or something like that."

"Sun? Frank O. Sun?"

"That's him."

I suddenly recalled my phone message yesterday to Narco-Vice. Could Detective Tong have worked that fast?

"Kai? Are you still there?"

"Uh-huh."

"Anyway, Daddy and Mamma are getting back together. And that leads up to what's so important I wanted to tell you. Kai, I'm sorry, but . . . but I'm not just going to Kaua'i to visit, I'm going back for good. I'm moving home. I miss Daddy and Mamma, and I miss Kaua'i. Honolulu is too big and busy for me—too many people, too much traffic, too much everything."

"Well . . . what about the baby? I mean, what do you want to do?"

"Didn't I tell you?" she said.

"Tell me what?"

"I must have miscounted, or I was just late, or something."

"You said you took the pregnancy test and couldn't bear it alone?"

"No, you didn't listen. I couldn't bear to take the *test* alone. I was afraid of the results. I wanted you with me when I took it . . ."

I was speechless.

"We can still see each other, Kai." Leimomi sounded sympathetic. "You can visit me on Kaua'i. And I could visit sometimes on O'ahu."

"That would be . . . great," I said, still stunned.

"I'm sorry to do this to you. I feel so guilty, leaving you like this. It's not that I don't love you. I do. It's just that I have so much to catch up on with Daddy. I want to be at home for a while."

"Don't feel guilty." If she only knew how much I meant that. "I understand. Can I help you? Give you a ride to the airport? Maybe we could go out to dinner before you leave?"

"I'd like that," she said.

We hung up and I rocked back in my office chair. All that built up emotion. All that reservoir of guilt. All for nothing.

I thought of the ocean blue crystal egg I had bought Leimomi in Makawao. It was the day I discovered Corky was alive, the turning point in the case. I figured the egg would mean more to me than to Leimomi at this point. I dug through my drawers and finally found it, placing it gingerly on my desktop. The turquoise-tinted waves glowed in the sunlight streaming through my office window. A beautiful sight.

I gazed over at Corky's candy cane-striped surfboard lying on a rail against my office wall. After getting my butt kicked the other day at Waimea, I doubted I would ever be riding it. Maybe I could give it to Summer and Corky as a present. Though Corky might not be riding too many more big waves himself. He had become a daddy. And who knows how the drug trial would shake down—whether he would be indicted and, if so, what kind of a plea bargain he might be able to swing.

I spent the rest of the day in a daze, still reeling from Leimomi's surprise announcement and feeling slightly abandoned, both by her and, as much as I hated to admit it, by Maya. I knew it was just my ego, since I didn't really envision a future with either of them. But just the same—those ego beatings can kind of hurt.

Later I wondered if my phone message to Detective Tong, telling all I knew about the Sun organization, could have had any bearing on Sun's indictment or on the early release of Leimomi's father. I doubted it. The wheels of justice turn slowly.

No matter, it was provocative to imagine myself helping to turn those huge wheels.

twenty-five

Monday I took off from work. I counted Sun's sushi-roll of hundreds, glad I had stored it safely in my desk. After expenses—airfare, the lodge, rental cars, and meals—I had cleared nearly three grand.

It took some talking to settle my accounts on Lāna'i. The Jeep Wrangler I rented had to be retrieved from the lodge's parking lot. Late fee, plus an extra day's charge. On the other hand, even though I'd failed to check out at the lodge, the nice folks there were so full of *aloha* that they credited my account for the second night.

When I called the surf line later that day, Waimea had gone down a few feet, but was still pumping. So were Sunset and Pipeline. But the crowds would be out. And I'd been up to the North Shore twice in the last twenty-four hours. Here in town, Waikīkī was breaking two-to-three feet.

I grabbed my longboard and headed for Pops.

Paddling out through Waikīkī's shore break, my arms still felt tight from the other day at Waimea. But after the first few strokes, the stiffness wore away and I felt fine. Truly fine.

I waited in the lineup for a good set. The little swells lifted me up and gently set me down again. They resembled ripples on a pond compared to the thundering mountains up on the North Shore. But I'd had enough of big wave riding for one winter.

MURDER
AT VOLCANO
HOUSE

A Surfing Detective Mystery

CHIP HUGHES

SLATE RIDGE PRESS

Acknowledgements

Many thanks once again to my wife, collaborator, and inspiration, Charlene, and to brilliant and extraordinarily generous Honolulu private detective Stu Hilt. *Mahalo* to Sher Glass, President, Volcano Community Association; to Doug Crispin, National Park Service ranger and long-ago CSU-Chico housemate; to John Broward, Emergency Operations Coordinator and Eruption Crew Supervisor, Hawai'i Volcanoes National Park; to Christine Matthews, consummate mystery editor and Secretary, Private Eye Writers of America; and to Doug Corleone, whose fast-moving narratives I've tried to emulate. For editorial suggestions and proofreading, I'm grateful to Nathan Avallone, Les Peetz, Laurie Tomchak, and Lorna Hershinow. Finally, special thanks to Alan Cressler for the cover photo of Halema'uma'u Crater.

In the time-honored tradition of fiction writing, the author has taken artistic liberties in the depiction of certain sights, facilities, and geographic features. The hotel of the book's title is not intended to be the Volcano House of today. The hotel was shuttered when the story was written and on-site research was conducted a decade earlier when flames of the old hotel's famous fireplace still flickered. And, of course, characters that populate the story are products of imagination rather than actual persons.

Holmes: "There is a realm in which the most acute and most experienced of detectives is helpless."

Watson: "You mean that the thing is supernatural?"

—*The Hound of the Baskervilles,* Arthur Conan Doyle

one

It's Friday afternoon in late March—one of those mild and calm days in Honolulu when coconut palms outside my office above Fujiyama's Flower Leis barely whisper in the slack trade winds. I'm about to close up shop and paddle out to Pops in Waikīkī.

My phone rings. *Maile?*

No such luck. Caller ID says: TOMMY WOO. Attorney-at-law, jazz pianist, jokester, and friend.

"Howzit, Tommy?" I answer.

"Hey, Kai," he says, "how do you get a lawyer out of a banyan tree?"

"If I knew, Tommy, you'd tell me anyway." There's no stopping him.

Tommy is quiet for a moment. Then he says: "Cut the rope."

"That's it?" I ask.

What a mistake. A barrage of blue ones follow.

When the jokes finally end I say, "What can I do for you, Tommy?"

"I've got a customer for you."

"A paying customer?"

"Absolutely," he says. "And she needs your services now."

"Now? As in immediately? I'm on my way out the door."

"You don't need to start until Monday. But she wants to see you today—to make arrangements."

"Arrangements for what?"

"She'll explain. She's here in my office. Well, she just stepped out when I called you. She wants me to come with her."

There goes surfing!

"How soon can you get here?" I glance at the clock on my desk. It's already four. I want to be in the water in twenty minutes.

"Give us fifteen," Tommy says.

"It's got to be a short meeting, Tommy. I have to be somewhere at four thirty."

"I'll bet you do," he says. He knows my ways.

"Who is the woman?" I ignore his sarcasm. "She a client of yours?"

"Never met her before. She lives on Kāua'i. But I recognized her and you will too. I did some work for her husband a long time ago—before she married him. Anyway, that's how she found me. Being married to him, she's got money. And the case will take you to a neighbor island. 'SURFING DETECTIVE: CONFIDENTIAL INVESTIGATIONS—ALL ISLANDS,' like your card says. Eh, Kai?"

"A case on Kāua'i?"

"No, on the Big Island."

Now I'm really confused, so I simply say, "I'm already working a case—that Pali Highway crash."

"Tragic," Tommy says, revealing his softer side. "I feel for those girls' parents."

"Me too. Actually, I'm waiting on some things and can spare a day or two. But that's all."

"Perfect," Tommy says. "A few days are all you'll need. I'll bring her over."

two

While I wait for Tommy and the mystery woman whose name he assures me I'll recognize, I dial Maile's home number. Maile probably won't pick up, so I work out a message for her in my head. I've given up calling her cell phone. I guess trust is one of those things that's easy to lose and hard to recover.

Her home phone rings and then her machine kicks in. "Hi, this is Maile Barnes, tracer of missing pets. How can I help?"

"Maile, it's Kai." I start to spew out my rehearsed message: "I wondered if you wanted me to take Kula surfing again. It's been a while and I haven't heard from you—I mean, Kula hasn't been in the water—unless . . ." I'm wandering, so I try to get back on course. "Well, I can take him Sunday . . . Uh, just let me know. Call me, text me, email me. Whatevahs."

I had a crush on Maile in high school. When I was off to college, she married someone else, became a K9 cop, and then, suddenly, a young widow. She quit the force and started a pet detective agency.

Recently Maile helped me on a case. We hit it off like a house on fire. She warned me never to cheat on her, since she'd been burned before. I didn't, exactly. But my explanations have fallen on deaf ears. Now she won't speak to me—except about Kula. Kula is the golden retriever she helped me rescue for one of my former clients. She's fostering the dog, since my client is unavoidably detained. He's spending the rest of his life in jail.

I gaze out my office window onto Maunakea Street's *lei* shops, dim sum parlors, fish markets, vegetable stalls, and art galleries, whiff the sweet odors and reeks wafting up, and wonder why I'm so stuck on Maile. Is it because the spunky ex-cop and I are so much alike—that old-fashioned romantic notion of soul mates? Or because I'm still haunted by her soft curves and jasmine-scented sheets?

I don't come up with an answer before there's a knock at the door. Tommy steps in, adjusts his tortoiseshell glasses, sweeps back a lock of silver hair, and gestures to the woman next to him. "Kai Cooke, meet Donnie Ransom."

I draw a blank on her name. But I do vaguely recognize her face. When Tommy announces—"Miss Hawai'i finalist"—I know why.

"My name was Lam then," she says. "Not Ransom. That was twenty years ago."

It's coming back to me now. Donnie Lam was not just a finalist, but first runner-up. Though she missed the crown by a sliver back then, she strides into my office with the grace and elegance of a reigning beauty queen. Her hair is long, lustrous and black; her eyes sparkle like agates in the sun. She wears more mascara and brighter red lipstick than I'd say is necessary for a daytime meeting with an attorney, but they make her eyes and smile all the more vivid.

Tommy says: "She has a job for you."

I expect to hear what sort of job, but she seems more interested in the locale.

"On the Big Island," Mrs. Ransom says, "at Hawai'i Volcanoes National Park." Leaving Tommy standing, she takes the one extra chair in my office. "We'll put you up at the Volcano House, all expenses paid."

"The Volcano House?" I say. "There's nothing like sleeping on the edge of an active crater."

Tommy smiles and so does Mrs. Ransom. I look at her more closely. She has that harmonious blend of Hawaiian, Asian and *haole*, or Caucasian, we call local girl. There are only a few visible hints of the two decades that have passed since she almost became Miss Hawai'i: faint lines around her eyes and mouth, and a little fullness in her neck and figure.

"Like I told Tommy, Mrs. Ransom, I'm working another case at the moment and can spare only a few days."

"Please call me Donnie," she says. "And don't worry, we'll have you back on O'ahu by Tuesday evening. Wednesday morning, at the very latest."

"That might work," I say.

"I'm so glad." Her youthful complexion glows against her black silk dress. Tommy, also in black, as usual, looks rumpled by comparison.

"Now just what is it exactly you'd like me to do?" I ask.

She perks up. "I want you to come with my husband and me to the Volcano House. To—sort of—chaperone him."

"That's it?" *Did I miss something?*

"Let me explain. My husband is Rex Ransom. You may have heard his name. Rex was founder and CEO of Ransom Geothermal, a drilling operation on the Big Island in the Wao Kele O Puna rainforest. Rex pulled out of there years ago and sold the company."

"I remember him," I say. But I don't like what I remember. I've got nothing against geothermal energy—and other alternatives to burning foreign oil—but what this man did was something else.

"Rex and I are going to the Big Island for the funeral of his former corporate attorney, Stan Nagahara. Stan died recently in the national park and his service will take place at the military camp chapel there. He's the second from Rex's company to die there in as many years. Stan's death was no accident. Neither was Karl Krofton's two years ago. They were both killed by Pele."

"Excuse me," I say. "Do you mean Madame Pele, the goddess of fire and volcanoes?"

"Exactly. Pele's going to take revenge on Rex, just like she did on the other two."

I try to keep a straight face, but it's tough, because behind Mrs. Ransom, Tommy is cracking a smile. So I say: "Why do you think Pele took revenge on those two, and plans to do the same to your husband?"

"Pele's followers believe that by drilling in the rainforest Rex and his company violated and desecrated her. They believe what Ransom Geothermal did amounted to rape. I'm afraid they're right. And if Rex puts himself in Pele's domain, she will strike him down."

"What makes you think those other two were killed by Pele?"

"There's no doubt. Look at these." Mrs. Ransom hauls out two newspaper clippings, one slightly faded, the other newer, whiter. She hands me the faded one first—from two years ago in the Hilo newspaper.

I read it aloud, in case Tommy also needs bringing up to speed.

Clues Sought in Volcano Accident

Hawai'i Volcanoes National Park: Park Service rangers are asking residents and visitors in the Volcano area to provide information about an accident that left former Ransom Geothermal executive Karl Kroften dead. Kroften's crushed BMW was found Thursday morning by a park visitor. The car had apparently careened off Crater Rim Drive near the Halema'uma'u Crater, flipped, and landed on its roof in a hardened lava bed. Speed may have been a factor. Kroften had no prior accidents, traffic citations, or arrests. He was known to friends and former co-workers as a quiet man who lived alone, enjoyed motor sports, and did not drink.

Earlier that evening a park visitor reported seeing a grey-haired woman smoking a cigarette climb into a silver BMW sedan like Kroften's with a white dog. When the wrecked car was recovered, no trace of the old woman or her dog was found. Volcano residents familiar with the legend of Pele say that what the park visitor saw was the fire goddess in one of her many *kinolau* or guises.

"You see," Mrs. Ransom says, "Karl Kroften's death was the work of Pele. It couldn't be clearer. Pele has the *mana*—the power—to take many forms. That's what *kinolau* means. *Kino* is Hawaiian for body and *lau* for many."

Tommy raises his brows.

I say something vaguely neutral like, "Uh-huh." And then, "Or maybe he was driving too fast?"

"Rex says Karl was an excellent driver," she goes on. "Rex rode with him many times to job sites. No, it was Pele."

Then she hands me a week-old clipping from the Honolulu daily.

Volcano Attorney Found Dead in East Rift Zone

Hilo: Big Island attorney Stanley Nagahara, who once represented Ransom Geothermal Enterprises, was found dead yesterday in an inactive lava tube in the East Rift Zone in Hawai'i Volcanoes National Park. A search and rescue effort began late Tuesday evening when Nagahara, who had been hiking alone, failed to return home. His body was discovered early Wednesday morning in a crevasse of nearly one hundred feet into which he had apparently tumbled. Family members and friends were at a loss to explain the accident. Nagahara was an avid and experienced hiker who often explored

> lava tubes and caves in the area. He is the second former Ransom Geothermal executive to die accidentally in Hawai'i Volcanoes National Park in as many years. Two years ago drilling engineer Karl Kroften died in a single car accident near the Halema'uma'u Crater . . .

"It's a pattern," she says. "Rex would be the third. Bad things come in threes. He's Pele's next victim."

"A car accident . . . a fallen hiker . . . two years apart," I reply. "How is that a pattern?"

"Pele makes the pattern. She's behind it all. Both deaths happened in her domain—on her 'aina. Both involved high-ranking people in Rex's company. This is her revenge. But the one she wants most is Rex. He was the head of the whole operation."

"Two high-ranking officials from your husband's company have died, out of how many?" I try to be the voice of reason. "Isn't it just a coincidence?"

"I'm not willing to take that chance," she replies. "I wish Rex wouldn't attend the funeral, but Stan was his friend as well as his corporate attorney. They endured a lot together. Rex says he must go and pay his respects."

"I have to admit," I say, "I was sympathetic back then to Hawaiians who opposed drilling in their rainforest." Images surface in my memory from the news coverage of Ransom's crews and their machinery ripping and scarring the fragile forest. The ongoing protests could do nothing to stop the devastation.

"I was sympathetic too," she says.

"In good conscience," I hear myself say, "I don't see how I can go with you."

Tommy frowns.

I'm hoping the conversation will end here.

three

The conversation doesn't end.

Donnie Ransom's beauty queen smile tightens. She pushes on, sounding desperate now.

"I promise you—Rex is a changed man. He's beginning to feel his own mortality. He had a heart attack back in September. And two days of tests last month at Wilcox Hospital confirmed he could have another. It's been so hard."

"It must be difficult for you." I try to be sympathetic.

"I went to Lānaʻi while he was in the hospital. Caregivers have to take care of themselves, you know." Donnie keeps going. "Rex has developed a fear of Pele. He has nightmares about her in her various guises—beautiful young woman in red, old lady in white, and so on. He wakes up screaming. Believe me, he's not the hard-charging conservative from Montana he was thirty years ago. He's even renting our guest quarters to an openly gay man."

"Why don't you have your renter escort you and your husband?" I say, still looking for a way out.

"Jeffrey? Oh, I don't think Jeffrey could protect anyone. He's a lovely, sensitive man, but . . ." She hesitates. "He's boarding the *Pride of Aloha* this Saturday with his friend, Byron, for a week-long inter-island cruise."

"Why don't you hire a Big Island PI?" I try again. "You won't have to pay travel expenses."

"Money is no object," she says. "Besides I don't know anybody on the Big Island. And Mr. Woo says I can trust you."

Tommy winks. I know what that means. The Ransoms could bring him more business, if I do well. Plus I owe him. Tommy helped me recover Kula, the golden retriever Maile is now fostering. I glance at my attorney friend again and see the writing on the wall.

"I'll pay your room, airfare, car, everything, plus your daily fees," she says. "All you have to do is follow my husband at a safe distance and make sure nothing happens to him. He's proud and wouldn't hear of being protected, so you'll have to do it incognito."

"Incognito?" I'm surprised she knows the word. But what she apparently doesn't know is that following someone unnoticed is not easy, especially in the wide-open spaces of a national park. If you're far enough away not to be seen, you may be too far to protect the client from sudden violence. The job is nearly impossible.

"That's right," she says. "I'll keep in touch with you when I can by cell phone and let you know our movements."

Tommy gives me a look.

It's only a few days, I rationalize. *And I won't have to be seen with the man.*

"Okay," I hear myself say.

When Tommy and the woman finally leave my office and clear the building I rush out right behind them. I can almost smell the waves.

I don't get far. At the bottom of the stairs I see Blossom, one of Mrs. Fujiyama's *lei* girls, crying. She's a slim, sweet local girl, barely out of high school. Mrs. Fujiyama is looking distressed, but doing nothing. Chastity and Joon, her other *lei* girls, are sitting stock-still.

I see what the problem is. Blossom's boyfriend—or her ex-boyfriend—Junior has tracked her down at work. He's got his big mitt on her and he isn't letting go. Blossom tries to pull away. That makes Junior clutch on harder. He's about twice her size. And he must outweigh me.

"You're hurting me," she cries. She's broken up with him before, but he just won't go away.

Mrs. Fujiyama tells Junior if he doesn't leave she's going to call the police.

I'm standing on the stairs, looking down on this. *What can I do?* Punks like Junior are bad news—they punch first and talk later. I can handle him, if it comes to that. But I don't want to antagonize him, unless I have to. He starts flinging Blossom around like a ragdoll and Mrs. Fujiyama screams she's going to call.

That's it. I can't watch any more. I step down and say, "No need. I'll call." I pull out my cellphone, look directly at Junior, and dial 911.

The line rings and rings. Finally an operator answers.

"Police," I say. "Emergency." I keep looking at Junior, wondering if he's coming for me.

There's a bit of a wait before a dispatcher gets on the line. I hold the phone to my ear, never taking my eyes off the punk. He's not pulling Blossom now. In fact, he's let go of her. I suspect there's a warrant out on him, or he's on parole, because he's starting to look uneasy.

Finally, I get a dispatcher.

"Assault in progress," I say. "Corner of Maunakea and Beretania. Fujiyama's Flower Leis."

The dispatcher asks me what's happening. But before I can answer, Junior is hustling out the door. He turns back and flips me the bird. "I get you, fuckah!"

After things calm down in the *lei* shop, I give HPD my version of events in a witness statement. Then I head for the beach.

Junior, it turns out, does have outstanding warrants. But they've never been served. There's a backlog of warrants in the City and County of Honolulu and not enough personnel to serve them. So guys like Junior sometimes go on their merry way.

Me, I've got enough on my plate already without dealing with him. There's the Pali case, not to mention that Big Island errand I'd rather not think about. But as I cruise down Maunakea Street with the nose of my board riding on my Impala's dash, the brown haze hanging in the dying afternoon sky won't let me forget.

It's vog—volcanic smog—drifting up from the Big Island and signaling another eruption in the East Rift Zone. Volcanoes down there have been going off sporadically for months. Red-hot molten lava flowing to the sea brings out the crowds. The Volcano House will be busy.

It's sunset when I finally paddle out to Pops. Usually I can leave my cases on shore, if I choose, but the vog keeps me in mind of Rex Ransom. No way I'd work for the man—ever—except to repay a favor. I'm hoping the waves will let me forget. At least, temporarily.

As I'm paddling to the lineup I glance back at the Sheraton Waikīkī, soaring directly opposite the break. In old times, many Hawaiians lived on the oceanfront land the hotel now occupies. They named the surf spot offshore of their home Populars, because it was a favorite break in the area. There's a reason, beyond proximity, why it was popular with Hawaiians back then, and remains popular with surfers today. Though we call it simply Pops.

On a good day, Pops serves up long, hollow, right-breaking curls that you can ride almost forever. As the wave peels and swings toward shore, it often bowls in sections. A couple hundred yards offshore, and far from the more accessible Waikīkī breaks, Pops is a long paddle from anywhere. And that keeps the crowds small and mellow, except during a big south swell.

Then look out. The waves are packed, the riders more aggressive, and the vibe more edgy. On one of those big days a hotshot once ran right over the top of my board—slicing my deck with his skeg. Then he had the gall to ask if he could see the damage he'd done. I covered the scar with my prone body and told him he didn't hit me after all. He paddled away looking disappointed.

As the sun sinks in the west, the brown haze on the horizon turns glittering gold. A few riders are paddling in, and a few dozen remain. Friday afternoon. *Pau hana*—quitting time. I should've known. I don't like crowds, even small crowds, so I paddle next door in the *Ewa* direction to the peaky breaks of Paradise. There I'm one of only three surfers. The waves are fewer and farther between, but when they jack up there's plenty for everybody.

In between rides, thoughts of Rex Ransom return. Sherlock Holmes had his pipe—I have my surfboard.

Floating on the glassy sea, scanning the horizon for my next wave, sometimes I can solve problems that elude me on shore. Out of the blue I recall memories from the distant past. Ransom's controversial drilling operation at Wao Kele O Puna and the disputed land swap that enabled it made him a very unpopular man, especially among Hawaiians and members of the SPC—Save Pele Coalition. They believed Ransom had despoiled the rainforest—essential to their cultural practices and gathering rights—and defiled, if not raped, their goddess. I can't say I fully understand the depth of their belief in Pele and other Hawaiian deities. But it's hard to miss her power among her followers.

Donnie Ransom knows the score. But she's worried only about Pele—not about the protesters who had tried to defend her. Their revenge seems more likely than hers. My prospective job is looking hairier by the minute. It's tough enough to fend off a goddess—not to mention a raft of mortal foes. Better find out more about Ransom's human enemies before catching my flight to Hilo on Monday.

I glance out to sea. Here comes another Paradise roller. The wave builds and peaks like a liquid pyramid. I swing my board around, paddle, and rise. The drop is steep and fast. I make my turn. *Stoked!* Before I know it, the ride is over.

I pivot my board around and paddle back to the lineup, smiling ear to ear. I try to remember what I was thinking about. *Rex who?*

four

Saturday morning, on my way to the Pali Highway, I pass by the Aloha Tower. The big white cruise ship *Pride of Aloha* is moored just to the right of the tower. Above its flower-festooned bow and soaring stack the brown haze of vog from the Big Island still hangs in the air. I remember Donnie Ransom saying that their renter will board the ship tonight for the weeklong inter-island cruise. I'd like to trade places with Jeffrey. Let me take the cruise and him shadow his landlord. All my years in the islands—born and raised—I've never been on one of those ships.

"You're not the cruise type, Kai." I hear Tommy Woo's sardonic voice in my ear. Tommy may be right. But I imagine myself gazing from a porthole onto the sunlit sea. *Nah.*

I shrug it off and aim my old Chevy up the Pali Highway toward the windward side of O'ahu. My Impala's big V-8 growls up the highway, called Route 61 on the map, climbing through lush Nu'uanu Valley to the tunnels at the *pali,* or cliff. Beyond the tunnels, the *pali* drops more than one thousand feet.

The sheer plunge has caused many deaths, some long before the three I'm investigating today. The first road was built back in 1845 over an ancient Hawaiian footpath that carefully navigated the cliff. When the second was blazed in 1898, hundreds of skulls were found, believed to be the remains of warriors who jumped or were forced from the cliff when Kamehameha I conquered the island of O'ahu. The present highway replaced the old road in 1959 and introduced the tunnels where the accident I'm working on occurred.

Even as I pursue the Pali case, thoughts of Pele keep intruding. *Da goddess stay* pa'a *in my mind!* Just before I reach the ramp to the scenic Pali Lookout—with its sweeping views of the Windward coast—I remember the story about Pele preventing cars from passing through these tunnels. Motorists reported their vehicles mysteriously stopping and not starting again—until they removed pork they were packing. *Lolo?* Not in Hawaiian legend. The goddess once intercepted a half human, half hog god named Kamapua'a and did not allow him, or any form of pork thereafter, to pass. Since I've got no bacon on board, my Chevy glides through the tunnels without incident.

Not so for those unfortunates involved in the case I'm working. On the Windward side of the tunnels, about a week ago, a Honda Civic plunged from the cliff and landed upside down, killing everyone aboard—the driver, Freddie "Fireball" Furman, and his two passengers, twin sisters Heather and Lindsay Lindquist. The twins had been celebrating their twenty-first birthday at several clubs in Honolulu when Fireball offered them a ride home to Kailua. All three were intoxicated—well over the legal limit. Fireball was double over.

I pull off at the next scenic lookout—a lesser version of the dramatic Pali Lookout above—after the big bend in the road about a quarter mile below the tunnels. I walk toward a trailhead that will lead me down to the scene of the crash. I'm hiking this steep trail because the twins' father is suing the clubs that served his daughters and the driver. I'm working for Mr. Lindquist's attorney, a partner in a Bishop Street law firm. Tommy recommended me—another reason I owe him. What the job amounts to—in addition to searching the crash site and the vehicle—is investigating each club the doomed threesome went to that night and then interviewing the employees and tracking down other patrons who were there.

This sad job—I know because I've done it before—is complicated by two things: First, club owners don't want their employees to go on record with anyone except their own attorney, who would be defending the clubs in court. Second, ferreting out club goers after the fact can consume more client dollars than the resulting information is worth. Sometimes you get lucky. One witness may clinch the case. Question is: which one?

Despite these challenges, I took this case, and others before it, because too often drunken and/or stoned racer-boys like Fireball—hell bent on killing themselves—take innocents like the Lindquists with them. It makes me angry. And heartsick. These cases, for me, tend to become more like missions. I can't bring back the dead. But I can try to give their grieving families and friends the satisfaction, if not the consolation, of knowing exactly what happened and why.

I'm just starting to look into this particular accident. And the Bishop Street attorney who hired me is in a hurry.

The only reason, besides a favor to Tommy, I will go to the Volcano House tomorrow is that I'm waiting on a few things. My HPD friend Creighton Lee says he can get me access to the impound lot to examine the wrecked Honda. But that won't happen until later in the week. And another contact, through Tommy, says he can provide liquor commission reports on the clubs where Fireball and the twins did their drinking. The reports could help determine the history of over-serving in those clubs and whether or not any claims have been made or any litigation filed. But I have to wait for the reports.

From the trailhead I hike steeply downhill toward where Fireball's Honda landed after its dive from the highway above. The terrain is rugged and the underbrush thick. It's slow going. The picture emerging of the accident is pretty much what I expected from the facts of the case.

A dozen or so friends had been drinking at the clubs. Neither girl knew Fireball. He was a friend of a friend whom they met at the last club. They hitched a ride home with him when their pal Ashley, who had driven them to the celebration, left earlier than they did to catch a redeye to Denver. Ashley hasn't returned my calls. But that's another story.

Leaving the last club, the Lollipop Lounge, the three climbed into Fireball's Honda and headed up the Pali Highway. His Honda was tricked out with lowered suspension, aftermarket turbo, nitrous oxide kit, and one of those angry-bee mufflers. *Fast & Furious*. Fireball had accumulated a raft of citations, arrests, and DUIs. His license had been revoked recently for driving 110 mph. On the Kailua-bound ascent, which was slick from a passing shower, Fireball no doubt mashed the gas pedal to the floor. The twins must have been terrified—if they weren't already knocked out from all the alcohol they'd consumed.

When his car screamed into the first tunnel, Fireball was already in trouble. He wasn't as good a driver as he thought. Especially drunk. The Honda's four tires, those essential points of contact with Mother Earth, lost traction on the slick pavement. The car started to slide. Impact marks entering the first tunnel suggest that the Honda's driver's side fender, doors, and rear quarter hit hard as the car began to swerve. It probably entered the second tunnel half-sideways, passenger side of the vehicle leading the way, and failed to negotiate the acute right curve immediately following that tunnel. The Honda collided with the low concrete barrier that separates the two elevated sections of the highway, flipped, and disappeared. An astonished motorist in the town-bound lanes saw the car vanish.

I hug the *pali* and carefully measure my steps. The trail continues steep and slow. But I finally reach the accident site. The impact of the falling car has crushed dwarf *kiawe* and caused a minor landslide. Debris from the wreckage is scattered. There's not much left, just bits and pieces. I scour the scene. I'm looking for physical evidence—receipts, bottles, personal items, and vehicle parts—anything that might corroborate that the three accident victims were sold drinks while intoxicated.

I find several jagged pieces from the car and broken glass on the dark-stained earth. No receipts or bottles. But there is something.

Off in the brush to the side of the debris a small object gleams gold. I step toward the gleam, reach in, and extract a Hawaiian bracelet. It's bent, but not mangled. And it's engraved. *A woman's name?* Apparently not Heather or Lindsay. Odd. Why would the twins, or Fireball, carry another woman's bracelet in the car?

The letters on the bracelet are ornate and difficult to read. Turning it to the light, I think I have the name. The twins' friend who drove them to the party and then flew to Denver. The same friend who hasn't returned my calls. *Ashley.*

five

Sunday morning I'm snoozing when my phone rings. I check my watch. It's not even seven. *Maile?*

I look at the phone. No such luck. Why do I keep hoping? Caller ID says: RANSOM.

I pick up.

"Hello, Kai?" says the now familiar feminine voice. "It's Donnie. I hope it's not too early."

"No worries," I say. "I had to wake up anyway."

"Oh." She seems ever so slightly taken aback.

"What can I do for you?" I ask.

"I just wanted to fill you in about the arrangements for Monday morning," she says. "You have an e-ticket on Hawaiian Airlines from Honolulu to Hilo, departing at nine-forty. Rex and I will be on the same flight—in first class. Your seat is in the back of the coach cabin. That way, Rex won't suspect you're following us."

"Makes sense," I say.

"At the Hilo Airport Rex and I will be picked up by a chauffeured limo. I've reserved a rental car for you. You can follow us to Volcano House at a discreet distance."

"Your limo will have a head start," I say. "It'll take me a while to pick up the rental car."

"That's okay," she says. "I'm not concerned about Rex's safety on the drive to the hotel. Just once we're there. We'll be staying in a crater-view room on the first floor in the main building. You'll be in a second-floor crater view room in the adjacent building, not far away, but far enough that we won't run into you every time we go out in the hall. I'll stay in touch with you when I can by cell phone."

"Got it." I'm still wondering why she called me at this hour on a Sunday morning.

"Now let's go over the instructions," she says. "You're going to follow Rex, but he's not to know. You'll stay with us—at a distance—everywhere we go. You'll eat in the hotel dining room when we eat, but not at our table. You'll act like any other hotel guest. You and I won't talk when Rex is around. Understood?"

"Yes," I say, not much liking her tone.

"I'll be in touch when I can to let you know my husband's comings and goings."

"Okay," I manage.

"You don't sound too concerned," she says. "This is really important. My husband's life is at stake."

"I am concerned. But it's early and—"

"This was the only time I could call when he wouldn't overhear me," she interrupts. "He's in the shower now. When he's out we'll be together all day."

"Don't worry," I say. "I'll stick with your husband. I won't let him out of my sight."

"Aloha." She hangs up.

No chance of sleep now. I grab a bowl of cereal and flip open my laptop. As I'm spooning in my breakfast I begin a quick and dirty investigation of Rex Ransom. Google provides lots of hits.

What I'm looking for are potential threats to the man I've been hired to protect. Donnie Ransom has already briefed me thoroughly about Pele. Whatevahs. Realistically, I'm concerned more about mortal enemies. Some of what I see brings back memories from two decades ago. Some is new to me.

There's a lot about the protests against the former CEO of Ransom Geothermal, a Montana-based corporation that spearheaded a controversial drilling in the Wao Kele O Puna rainforest. The Save Pele Coalition—the native Hawaiian group that protested the project from the get-go—claimed it violated a state land trust that set aside the pristine rainforest for preservation and for their use and gathering rights. They alleged that this last existing lowland rainforest had been illegally swapped for comparatively barren and worthless land many miles away. And that drilling in their goddess Pele's domain was, to them, tantamount to rape. These were highly charged issues involving the Hawaiians' land, cultural practices, and religion. Before the age of the internet, the protests splashed the headlines and made the radio and TV news.

Ransom received threats. The one act of violence against him came at the hands of SPC radical Ikaika "Sonny Boy" Chang who dragged the CEO from his car into the red mud road Ransom's crew had cut into the forest. Sonny Boy was arrested and denounced by the SPC, since it advocated nonviolence. He did time for the attack, was released, and then arrested again for violating parole. Over the last two decades he'd been in and out jail. Currently it appears he's out. That could be trouble.

Ransom's geothermal operation ultimately failed to produce enough electricity to be commercially viable. He bailed out and the disputed land was ultimately returned to a trust for the benefit of Hawaiians, after years of continued protests and legal wrangling. When the CEO walked away, his former partner Mick London went bankrupt, sued Ransom, but did not prevail in court. London apparently lost everything, including his home. After the court battle, it appears the two men never reconciled. If London still lives on the Big Island, which seems to be the case, he might attend the funeral of a former Ransom company officer. That could also be trouble.

At the same time Ransom pulled out of Puna and was being sued by his former partner, the CEO was going through an ugly divorce from his first wife, Kathryn Bates Ransom—while former beauty queen Donnie Lam waited in the wings. During their bitter divorce, Kathryn, who apparently still resides in the family home in Kona, was questioned by Big Island police about a knife wound to her husband's hand that was treated at Hilo Medical Center. Ransom claimed the wound came from a cooking accident. Those who knew the couple thought otherwise. Kathryn had finally snapped, one neighbor said, and given her cheating husband what he deserved.

It wouldn't surprise me if Rex's ex showed up at the funeral too. Kathryn no doubt knew the family of the deceased and might want to pay her respects. More trouble?

I close my laptop. Three potential threats to my charge over breakfast are three too many. And they only confirm my suspicion that Pele should be the least of Donnie Ransom's worries.

six

Monday morning I show up at the interisland terminal more than the required hour before the nine-forty flight to Hilo. When I check in, there's no sign of Donnie Ransom and her husband. I'm a seasoned island hopper, so I know enough not to check a bag. Especially if I have to pay for the privilege.

I get my carry-on and myself through security, go to the gate, and take an inconspicuous seat in the waiting area. It's early. Only half a dozen passengers have beat me here. I glance at my boarding pass. Seat 26E, at the back of the Boeing 717, as far from first class as you can go. Donnie wasn't kidding. She's put a lot of seats between her husband and me. The Ransoms are probably in row one. I know her type. First class isn't enough. She must be in the first row of first class.

Minutes pass and the boarding area fills. Still no Ransoms. Then I hear the preliminary boarding announcement. The usual stuff. First, families with small children and those who need assistance. Then, first class and elite high-mileage fliers board. And finally the likes of me and everyone else. *Steerage class.*

Where are Donnie and Rex Ransom? Their cabin is about to board.

Then comes another announcement: *Ladies and Gentlemen, at this time we welcome aboard our first class passengers.*

Still no sign of the Ransoms. Then it dawns on me. They're probably in the elite fliers' lounge with other well-heeled passengers. They should emerge now that their cabin has been called.

Sure enough. First Donnie appears. Then, behind her, an old man. He bears faint resemblance to the robust Rex Ransom in the media two decades earlier. The contrast between those images and his present self couldn't be more pronounced. Or the contrast between his bent profile and the erect form of his younger wife.

Rex Ransom in his heyday—ice-blue eyes, raven hair, prominent jaw, barrel chest, massive arms, and aggressive, in-your-face posture—is all but gone. In his place is a pale-eyed, silver haired, bent and frail septuagenarian who walks with a cane and looks not ahead, but down at his unsure footsteps. A lifelong smoker who recently suffered a heart attack, has he finally kicked the habit? Whatevahs. The damage has obviously been done.

Time has ravaged the once powerful CEO more than his foes ever did. I can see no reason why anyone, even his worst enemy, even Pele herself, would want to punish him further. The years have taken their toll. The transformation would sadden me more if I hadn't just been refreshing my memory about what he did at Wao Kele O Puna.

I watch Donnie Ransom take her husband's arm, the one not holding the cane, and lead him down the jetway. The age difference between them glares. To the casual onlooker

Donnie must appear to be a faithful daughter assisting her aged father. The fact that Donnie looks local and Rex is obviously a mainlander doesn't alter the impression. I wonder about their relationship as husband and wife. Twenty years ago when they met, he was a CEO in his mid-fifties accustomed to calling the shots. She was barely thirty and a beauty. He had money; she had youth. Now he's so clearly dependent on her that their roles have obviously changed.

They disappear down the jetway. Minutes later, after most passengers have boarded, my turn finally comes. I lug my carry-on down the jetway and onto the airplane.

I was right. The Ransoms are sitting in row one in plush royal purple lounge chairs. I try not to make eye contact with them, but I'm stopped by traffic in the first class cabin. Rex Ransom turns toward me and before I can avert my glance we make eye contact. He smiles. His smile is warm and disarming. I'm surprised. I find myself being drawn to him and smile back.

Then I walk on slowly down the aisle, kicking myself for this slip. I'm off to a bad start being incognito. Donnie, who's buried in an airline magazine, has fortunately missed the encounter.

I pass between the purple curtains that separate the first class and coach cabins and work my way to the back of the airplane. 26E is not only in the very last row, but also in the middle of three seats. I wedge in.

The airplane finally gets pushed back from the gate, taxies to the runway, and takes off over Keʻehi Lagoon. The engines howl. I look straight ahead at the purple seatback in front of me. It says: "Life vest under your seat." That's probably more reassuring to passengers who are in the ocean less than I am.

The Boeing soars by the skyline of Waikīkī and I glance out the window. Vog. The brown haze is still drifting up to Oʻahu from the ongoing eruption. Hilo Airport and the roads to and within Hawaiʻi Volcanoes National Park will be choked with onlookers. I wonder how the potential crowds may affect my keeping tabs on Ransom.

Time slips by. Molokaʻi, Lānaʻi, and Maui pass under our wings. No sooner do I down the passion-guava nectar a flight attendant offers me than the Big Island comes into view.

Snow-capped Mauna Kea towers above the clouds. This tallest mountain in Hawaiʻi—tallest in the world measured from the sea floor—evokes memories for me no doubt different from those of most who fly by this looming giant.

My parents died here. I was eight. After their plane crash I was *hanaied* by my auntie's *ohana* on Oʻahu's North Shore and then sent to an uncle in California to attend prep school. Later I toted my surfboard to college at Point Loma. How I ended up in the army after my freshman year and eventually made it back to the islands is a story longer than this Honolulu to Hilo flight. Laydahs.

The airplane descends along the emerald-green Hamakua coast and lapping waves that shimmer in the morning sun. The liner banks steeply and then touches down in Hilo—delivering me to my strange gig.

The cabin door opens and I see the Ransoms stepping off the airplane. Five minutes later I finally wrench myself from my seat and navigate the narrow aisle. I'm almost the last passenger off. No Ransoms in sight.

I catch up with them as they're leaving Baggage Claim, follow them from the terminal to the curb, and watch them climb into a black Lincoln. He gets in first. Before she follows him, she turns, sees me, and nods—discreetly, of course. Then the door closes and they're gone.

The air is thick with vog—formerly rare in Hilo—and the airport thick with people. Word has gotten out about the eruption. I walk to the car rental agencies located in the tin-roofed longhouse across from Baggage Claim. Directly behind is the lot that's usually full of cars. Not today.

I step to the agency whose contract I hold and take my place in a line of a half dozen customers. I wait a minute or two. Nobody's moving and nobody's driving away in a car.

Finally the first customer in line waves his contract angrily and stalks away muttering. The next screams that he and his wife have flown from Canada for a Hawai'i vacation planned for years. But where's their rental car? More customers walk away, instead of driving away.

By the time I reach the desk I know the score. There's been a run on rental cars because of the eruption. A contract means nothing.

"I'm not just going *holoholo*." I tell the agent, which means something like to go on holiday. "I've got a job to do. I need some wheels."

"See those three cars over there?" She points across the lot to a red Ferrari, a black Maserati, and a bright yellow Porsche Boxster. "Those are our exotics—the only cars available."

My contract is for a subcompact, not an exotic. So I ask: "How much?"

She explains that I can rent the Ferrari for five bills a day, the Maserati for four and a quarter, or the Boxster for three and a half. I have no idea if Donnie will pay, but I hear myself saying, "I'll take the Porsche."

I sign the papers, grab the key, and slip into the yellow roadster. Twenty-three miles on the clock. Brand new. I put down the top and head for Volcano. This is hardly the kind of car to tail someone. *I hope she pays.*

I take the airport service road from the rental lot and turn left onto the Māmalahoa Highway, more familiarly known as Hawai'i Belt Road. Then I cruise the outskirts of Hilo town, savoring the whine of the flat six motor behind me. *How the other half lives. Or is it the 1%?* There's little chance I can catch the Ransoms' limo, but I can have fun trying. Too bad the Porsche is an automatic. Sports cars are for shifting.

Not too long ago this part of Hilo was sparsely populated, but now I find myself passing Toyota and Honda dealers, Walgreens, Macy's, Pizza Hut, and Jack in the Box. The national chains are sprouting like poisonous mushrooms in the lush soil of this island. Inspired by the lure of tropical paradise, tourists come from thousands of miles to eat fast food and shop in big-box stores, just like at home. Go figgah.

The road begins to climb. The scent of ginger fills the air.

I leave Hilo and its strip malls behind. The Hawai'i Belt Road circles the entire island, but I'm only taking the thirty-mile portion that rises four thousand feet to Volcano. My quibble about the Boxster's automatic transmission disappears when I feel how quickly and seamlessly it shifts. The Porsche purrs into the greener and cooler stretch of highway.

By the village of Kea'au I pass the turnoff for Kalapana, once famous for its black sand beach. That beach, a victim of flows from the East Rift Zone, is now buried under tons of lava. *Pele at work.*

Moving into the goddess's domain, where the evidence of seemingly supernatural power shows all around in the very earth, sea, and sky, sparks a weird thought: What if Donnie's right—I still can't wrap my head around it—and Pele actually *is* out to get her husband? I remind myself that I agreed to this madness for one reason—and one reason only. I owe Tommy.

I concentrate on the road ahead and try to catch the Ransoms. It's a short road. And things could be worse. I could be driving a subcompact instead of this rocket.

So I push the pedal and the Porsche instantly responds. The roadside becomes a blur of farms and forests and macadamia orchards. Ginger and lavender grow wild on the shoulder. The hamlets of Kurtistown, Mountain View, and Glenwood barely interrupt the countryside. Altitude markers count the climb: 2,500 feet . . . 3,000 feet . . . 3,500 feet. The air streaming through the roadster grows cooler.

When the scenery changes from lush green to the grey-bitten of higher altitude, I catch the black Lincoln and hang back. We pass the village of Volcano. And just beyond it comes the entrance to Hawai'i Volcanoes National Park.

The limo turns left and stops at the ranger station. I pull off to the side of the highway and put up the top. I don't want to sit directly behind the Lincoln while the driver pays admission. When the limo moves on, I pull up, pay, and swing into the Volcano House, barely a stone's throw away. The Lincoln parks under the portico and the Ransoms climb out.

I keep my distance.

Beside the limo sits a white Ford Expedition with emergency lights on top and PARK RANGER emblazoned on the side. Did Ransom have an official escort? The Ranger himself is nowhere in sight.

After the old man crawls from the limo he steadies himself with his cane and his wife takes his free arm. Once they disappear inside the hotel and the limo drives away, I park at the far end of the nearly full lot, as much out of sight as I can get the yellow Porsche.

When I climb from the car, the odor of sulfur hanging in the cool air hits me like a wall. Fumes from the volcanoes can be hazardous, especially for the elderly.

Bad idea to bring him. But his own, according to his wife.

seven

If you've never been here, the barn-red clapboard façade of the Volcano House resembles, well, a barn. Don't let the hotel's plain and unadorned exterior fool you into thinking that inside, by contrast, is a luxury resort. What you see is pretty much what you get. But you don't come here for luxury. You come for the view. This is the only hotel I know of, at least in this part of the world, that's perched on the rim of an active volcano.

I step into the Volcano House and recall from previous visits that a hotel by this name dates back to an 1846 grass hut and a later wooden structure containing the famous fireplace whose enduring flames are immortalized in *Ripley's Believe it or Not*. The hotel expanded in 1891 and remained in operation well into the twentieth century, until it burned to the ground in 1940. Legend has it that the fireplace's celebrated flame kept going even after the hotel burned. Embers were rescued from the ruin and returned to the hearth when the hotel reopened. That's why the management says, "Volcano House, where the fire and aloha spirit never go out!"

I navigate a huddle of guests in the lobby admiring those perpetual flames, and head to the registration desk. A Park Service sign there confirms my fears about the poisonous air around the volcanoes.

> **CAUTION**
> VOLCANIC FUMES ARE
> HAZARDOUS TO YOUR HEALTH
> AND CAN ALSO BE LIFE-THREATENING.
> VISITORS WITH BREATHING AND
> HEART PROBLEMS, PREGNANT WOMEN
> AND YOUNG CHILDREN
> SHOULD AVOID THIS AREA.

The Kīlauea Caldera is bulging. The Halemaʻumaʻu Crater, Pele's traditional home, is a lake of fire. Steam vents along the Crater Rim Trail are spewing noxious gas. And, of course, the East Rift Zone continues to erupt. But nobody seems concerned. Because that's why they're here. To experience it all.

There's a line at the registration desk. I take my place at the end and look around. Things haven't changed much here since my last visit. Behind the veneer desk are cubbyholes for room keys and guests' mail, an ancient phone with three dozen buttons for the various rooms, an adding machine with a paper roll, and a yellowed keyboard and monitor that look like they've been around since the dawn of the personal computer. Plaques on a nearby wall, dating back a few years, attest to the hotel restaurant's culinary excellence.

The guest at the front of the line rings the bell—one of those old-fashioned chrome thingies with a clapper on top. A *mu'umu'u*-clad woman appears and begins to assist. She's the essence of Hawaiian hospitality. Warm smile. Soft voice. Genuine *aloha*. How a people whose land, government, and culture were stolen from them can be so pleasant to the heirs of the thieves is a miracle to me. I guess that tourist cliché about warm-hearted, generous Hawaiians has a nugget of truth.

The receptionist's job isn't easy. Apparently some in line don't have reservations. She has the unenviable task of informing them that the hotel is full. I'm glad my room has been booked in advance by my client. That's what she tells me, anyway. And I hope the hotel doesn't give away my room like the rental agency gave away my car. The desk clerk calmly and courteously explains the situation to those without reservations. One by one they step away, crestfallen.

"So sorry," she says. "*Mahalo* for understanding." Her gentle voice sounds vaguely familiar.

When my turn comes she looks me up and down, smiles warmly, and says, "Kai, long time no see!"

"Shoots," I respond, recalling her face now. But not her name.

"You remembah me, yeah? Pualani." She shifts to Pidgin. "I wuz working hea when you come 'bout your parents."

"I remembah," I say. More than a decade ago I came to the Big Island to investigate their airplane crash. I was a *keiki* when it happened. So by the time I returned in my late twenties the trail was cold. But it was something I had to do. I didn't find much, but afterwards I spent a few nights at the Volcano House to unwind. That's when I met

Pualani. She was sympathetic to the tale of my orphaning, which her warm friendliness coaxed from me. One evening after her shift we strolled the Crater Rim Trail under the stars. We talked-story. I liked her but never saw her again. Until now.

"Same job still," she says. "But I get one teenager. Imagine dat!"

"Nah," I say. "You stay so young." She's filled out a little since then and her still pretty face shows the passage of time.

"You get *keiki*, Kai?" she asks. "You marry?"

"Nah." I shake my head. "Working too much."

"So why you hea? Anoddah investigation?"

"Holoholo," I say. I can't tell her why I'm really at the Volcano House. "Can fin' my reservation?"

"Shoots." She types on her ancient keypad and peers at the yellowed monitor. "Mr. Kai Cooke—fo' two nights. Lucky you get one reservation. We bin sold out. Turn lots of customahs away. Dey all come to see da eruption. Pele at work again!"

"She da boss ovah hea," I joke. "Don't mess wit' Pele."

"Fo' sure," she says. "I afraid fo' one hotel guest—afraid Pele gonna get 'em. He check in awready. He old man now, bent n' walk wit' one cane. But I rec'onize 'em. He da guy dat drill in Pele's rainforest. She gonna get 'em."

"You really t'ink so?" I didn't expect that time-ravaged Rex Ransom would be so easily recognized.

She nods. "He come for da funeral," Pualani says. "But he bettah watch out or his own funeral gonna come bumbye— jus' like da oddah two."

"So you t'ink Pele *make* da oddahs?" I wonder if she's pulling my leg. "And she gonna *make* dis old guy too?"

Pualani gives me a room key, a map of the hotel, and a wink—a wink that seems as mysterious as the goddess herself.

"T'anks, eh?"

I step away from the desk and glance at the map. About half of the rooms in the hotel have crater views, some in the main building, some in an adjacent addition. I did my homework, so I know that Donnie and her husband are staying in the main building on the first floor in room one, the largest crater-view room. My room also overlooks the crater but, as Donnie explained on the phone, is in the addition on the second floor at the other end of the hotel. Close enough to watch over Ransom, but far enough to keep out of his sight.

I walk from the registration desk through the main building to the addition. On the way I pass the Ransoms' room. The door is slightly ajar. I hear voices. I stand against the opposite wall out of view and listen. Donnie is talking to her husband.

"What about me?" Her voice rises in irritation. "I'm your wife!"

"You have nothing to worry about," Rex Ransom replies.

"That's easy for you to say!" she shouts.

The door bursts open. Donnie stalks out. I start walking again toward my room.

"*Kai?*"

I hear my name called in a stage whisper and turn around.

Donnie closes the door and steps gracefully toward me, her lustrous black hair shimmering even in the dim hallway. "Did you check in?" Her tone sweetens. She smiles.

"Yes, just now," I say. "Howzit going?"

"Fine," she says, her red lipstick punctuating her smile. "We're having a wonderful time—never mind my worries about Rex."

I let that one pass. "Did Mr. Ransom see me on the airplane?" I know the answer, but at this awkward moment I can think of nothing else to say.

"I doubt it," Donnie says. "Even if he did, to my husband you'd be just another coach passenger hiking to the back of the airplane."

"That's good, I guess," I say. "I better go—in case he comes looking for you."

"Oh, I don't think we have to worry about that." Her mascaraed eyes sparkle.

"Aloha—for now." I start walking.

"I'll be in touch, Kai," she says and moments later the door to the Ransoms' room snaps shut.

I walk the passageway to the addition, hike the stairs to the second floor, and step to the end of the hall. The door to room thirty-three opens with my key to a flowered carpet, Hawaiian quilt on a double bed, small bath, and a *koa* desk and rocker. That's about it. No TV. No WĪFi. No minibar. But there's something better: serenity.

The room has good vibes—and two windows overlooking the crater. I open them. Cool air wafts in—expected at four thousand feet—and that omnipresent smell of sulfur. I gaze down on Kīlauea Caldera, the collapsed but still active volcano nearly three miles long. Fifteen Aloha Stadiums, they say, could fit inside. Smoke twirls up from vents in the charred and cracked floor. The mottled surface resembles the scorched remains of a wildfire.

Far in the distance at the southern end of the caldera gapes the half-mile wide Halemaʻumaʻu Crater. The view from the hotel of the fire goddess's home is obscured by spiraling smoke. Yet the crater looks majestic, haunting, and huge. *Pele.*

The air suddenly feels cooler and I get chicken skin.

I leave my bag in the room, shut the windows, and head downstairs to the hotel's famous fireplace. I walk past the Ransoms' room again. Their door is closed now, but I can still hear voices. Can't make out words, but I can hear tone. It's the tone of a couple disagreeing. Though there's no screaming, I find myself wondering about the picture of devotion I saw earlier at Honolulu Airport.

A brusque word now and then, a crisp exchange, might not be all that unusual in a marriage—especially if one spouse persists in doing something the other believes is dangerous. Donnie Ransom fears for her husband's life at the Volcano House. He insists on coming anyway. Wouldn't she be upset? Wouldn't she feel ignored, hurt, and angry? Wouldn't she naturally speak out? Not to mention that she's a bit haughty anyway.

I walk on. What do I know? I'm just a guy who has a lot to learn about women. Otherwise, Maile would return my calls.

I head for the fire. The Ransoms obviously don't need my services at this moment. Especially as a marriage counselor.

eight

At the registration desk I see the olive trousers, khaki shirt, and smoky-the-bear hat of a park ranger. I remember the white Expedition in the hotel's lot and wonder again if he's here because of Rex Ransom. The ranger turns from the desk and walks toward me. His brass nametag says DOUGLAS CRISP.

"Aloha, Ranger Crisp," I say, hoping to test my theory. "What brings you to the Volcano House?"

"Escaped mental patient," the ranger says. "She may be hiding in the park. I just left a BOLO at the front desk."

"Be on the lookout?"

"Right," he says. "We're warning hotel guests. She's a grey-haired old woman who wanders around half naked. She appears harmless, but she's unstable and should be considered dangerous. Her name is Serena Barrymore."

"Serena Barrymore?" I repeat. "Sounds made-up."

"It may be," Ranger Crisp says. "Another name she uses is Goddess Hiʻiaka. Hiʻiaka, in Hawaiian myth, is Pele's youngest and favorite sister—keeper and protector of the rainforest and flowering ʻōhiʻa tree. Barrymore took that identification to the extreme and actually killed a man for chopping down one of those trees."

"You're kidding."

"I wish I was," the ranger says. "Barrymore shoved him into the path of a Hilo bus. When she was apprehended she claimed to be above human law. Her victim was in a coma for months until his family decided to remove life support. Barrymore was indicted for second-degree murder. She never stood trial, though. She was evaluated and deemed unfit."

"Sad case," I say.

"Back when they were drilling Wao Kele O Puna she threatened people involved in the project. We've increased our presence in the park because Stan Nagahara's funeral tomorrow will bring back some of those same people. She might target them."

"I'll keep my eyes open." I head for the fireplace.

I'm right. The ranger is concerned about Rex Ransom. I add another potential threat to my list—this one embodying the all-too-real impact of the legendary goddess—as I walk to the Volcano House's famous fireplace.

The *koa*-paneled room where the celebrated embers glow looks like the lobby of an Old West inn. Two saddle-leather sofas and a log table between them sit on a wine-colored carpet. The room is dim except for those eternal flames and sconce lights on the paneled walls. Two *koa* rockers flank the hearth. One is already occupied by an aloha-shirted local man rocking slowly like he's in no hurry. I take the other and say, "Howzit?"

"'Kay, brah." He smiles.

I smile back and gaze at the fire. Those hundred-year-old flames lick up the chimney and radiate warmth into the room, taking the chill out of my bones. I move closer to the fire. Above the mantel a likeness of Pele herself, carved in bronze-hued lava rock, peers down on me imperiously. No soft, gauzy, delicate angel, this woman. She's a broad-featured, large-breasted, tough-love goddess whose huge hands reach out to either side of the mantel, embracing and dominating the flames. Here's another reminder of her power.

"Das Pele," says my fellow rocker who sees me gazing at her. "She da queen, brah."

"She da real t'ing," I reply.

"You like study her, or somet'ing? Serious kine?"

"Nah, jus' looking."

"Sure, brah," my companion says. "Me, I jus' waiting. Limo drivah, you know. Deliver my passengers awready. Jus' waiting fo' drive 'em aroun.'"

"Who dey?" I ask.

"Not suppose to say, brah."

I suddenly realize why he's not saying. "Black limo? You drive from da Hilo airport one hour ago? One couple in da car?"

"Yeah. How'd you know, brah?"

"I recognize 'em. Dey famous, eh?"

"Not famous anymo'. I know 'em back when. Da wahine wuz one beauty queen, brah. And she still look pretty good! And da guy, he wuz da geothermal king."

"You mean da guy dat drill on Pele's lan'?" I want to keep him talking.

"Yeah, brah," he says. "Lots of people dey talk stink 'bout him, but he always treat me good. Da protestahs dat fight geothermal bin all *pakalolo* growers. Dey no like him drilling in dere *pakalolo* patch. Das all."

"Really, brah?"

"Is true," he says. "One protestah get jail time fo' *pakalolo* and firearms."

"Whatevahs," I say.

"You no hear 'bout dat?" he continues. "Da geothermal king jus' follow da example of King David Kalākaua. Da King talk wit' da guy Thomas Edison, dat invent electricity, 'bout making power from da Kīlauea Volcano. Dat was mo' den one hundred years ago, brah! "

"Fo' sure? Kalākaua and Thomas Edison?" It sounds improbable.

"Is one fact of history," he says. "Happen in 1881." He keeps talking. "Geothermal not all bad. Get da power outta da groun', brah, so we nevah depend on foreign oil. Plus da geothermal king make jobs for da people."

"You know 'em long time?"

"Yeah, brah. Maybe twenty years. Use to drive 'em when he da boss. Know his firs' wife too. But dey divorce now. Ho! She *hūhū*. Really hate 'em, brah. Try stab 'em once."

"Da firs' wife? She stab 'em?" I recall Googling the same information. Small world.

He nods. "Mr. Ransom nevah press charges. No like his wife fo' go to jail—even though they getting one divorce."

"Da ex-wife here for da funeral?"

"Dunno, brah," he says. "I no drive her anymo'."

"I'm Kai." I offer my hand. "Maybe buy you one drink sometime?"

"Shoots," he says and we shake local-style. "Cannot drink on da job."

"Maybe latah?"

He nods. "I'm Kawika."

"Aloha, Kawika." I rise from my rocker and leave behind the everlasting flames. And the everlasting gaze of Pele.

nine

I pass the Ransoms' room again and this time nothing's shakin'. Door closed. No voices. I cross to the addition, climb the stairs to my room, and check the phone. No messages. My cell isn't ringing either. All I can do is wait.

I'm not what you'd call a patient person. Since there's no TV in the room, I crack a glossy book on the desk about Hawai'i Volcanoes National Park and flop on the bed. I fluff the pillow behind my head and gaze at the full-color plates of craters, caverns, fissures and vents. It feels good to get horizontal after the flight to Hilo, the drive to Volcano, and the busywork of checking in and getting settled. The park, the book says, was established in 1916 and includes more than five hundred square miles of land and two active volcanoes, Mauna Loa, the world's most massive, and Kīlauea, one of the world's most active. Little wonder Pele has such a lively following, since her volcano just keeps on keeping on.

My cell phone rings. RANSOM.

"Kai," Donnie says in a whisper when I answer, "we're going to walk the Crater Rim Trail to The Steaming Bluff."

"Steaming Bluff?" I say. "Did you see the warning at the hotel desk?" A picture of the almost mystical steam vents comes to mind: wisps of vapor floating up from dozens of openings in the lava rock and hovering over the trail. Eerily beautiful. But the super-heated underground water that rises in misty beauty can carry potentially lethal fumes, such as the Park Service sign warned about. Fumes that may make breathing difficult for even the most robust tourist.

"There's no stopping Rex," she says. "If there were, we wouldn't be here. And you wouldn't either."

"Okay, I'll follow you."

I hop off the bed, head downstairs, and step outside onto the Crater Rim Trail, where it passes in front of the Volcano House. I move around the corner of the hotel and wait for the Ransoms to show.

Five minutes pass, and finally they come hand-in-hand, working their way across the lawn to the trail. She's steadying him as they step onto the path. Rex Ransom looks no more healthy than he did on the airplane. He's bent and his eyes point down. He hobbles along, a cane in the hand that isn't held by his wife. Stroll is too elegant a word for how they walk. It's more like a crawl. But the picture of the two together looks like devotion, despite the harsh tones coming from their room earlier.

The Ransoms head in the westerly direction, toward the steam vents and Halemaʻumaʻu Crater. The trail by the hotel is more like a sidewalk, asphalt and a yard wide. A lava rock retaining wall, about waist high, stands between the cliff and the Kīlauea Caldera, hundreds of feet below. It's late afternoon and the smell of sulfur hangs in the cool air. Aside from the sulfur, I can spot no immediate threat to the former geothermal king. I give the Ransoms a minute to clear the hotel before I come out of hiding.

Just as I emerge, a middle-aged man also steps from the hotel and onto the trail. He's got a touch of grey in his sideburns and is talking on his cell phone. He shuts the phone and heads in the same direction as the Ransoms.

This is good. If the man stays on the trail between them and me, he will provide concealment. But the more I consider this, the less likely it seems. The man looks fit and should easily overtake the toddling couple. I follow him, not expecting to see him for long.

Ahead of both of us, the Ransoms are barely moving.

To my surprise the man with a touch of grey travels as slowly as they do. And it's not because he's stopping at every turn to gawk at the caldera below. He's just ambling along, eyes ahead, keeping pace with the Ransoms. I maintain the same pace, at a distance. The trail loses the asphalt and the lava rock wall upon leaving the Volcano House and turns to gravel, bordered by tree ferns. The caldera side of the trail sprouts guardrails. The tree ferns called *hapu'u* climb high overhead like giant green umbrellas. They look primitive and Jurassic. I might expect a dinosaur as much as a human assailant to jump out around the next bend.

The air warms as we approach the steam vents and smells increasingly like rotten eggs. The sun tries to burn through the sulfur-infused vapor, but manages only a pale wafer in the sky.

Ahead on the misty trail I can barely make out the red blooms of the native flowering *'ōhi'a,* the tree that mad woman Serena Barrymore, a.k.a. Goddess Hi'iaka killed for. As I get closer I see a bird hovering above the *'ōhi'a,* whose breast and head are also red——the Hawaiian honeycreeper called ʻApapane. The man with a touch of grey isn't noticing the tree or the bird. He's watching the Ransoms. I'm thinking this is no coincidence. I know what to look for. And this guy is a professional. Or an amateur masquerading as a professional. Is this another foe to add to my list?

The man keeps pace with the Ransoms. He walks by the pale-yellow and red berries of the ʻōhelo plant——a traditional favorite of Pele——growing about waist high on the side of the trail. He doesn't seem to notice the berries. It's a little early in March to harvest the ʻōhelo, but already the plants have clusters about the size of blueberries. Donnie Ransom could pick the berries and offer them to the goddess, if my client truly believes Pele plans revenge on her husband. A ritual offering thrown into the fire pit might just do the trick. Or at least make Donnie feel better.

But the Ransoms walk by the ʻōhelo. And so does the man following them.

The trail keeps meandering, and I keep losing the Ransoms and then picking them up again. At one turn when they stop, the man stops too, and glances back at me. I see him make what appears to be a mental note. Does he think I'm following him? Does he think I'm following the Ransoms? He pulls his cell phone again and makes another call. He's done within twenty seconds. *Strange.*

We all start moving again——the Ransoms, the man between us, and me. The trail twists and turns, emerges from the overgrown jungle, and then weaves along the cliff to The Steaming Bluff.

The Ransoms stop at the first vent along the trail, a gaping hole in the earth the size of a compact car. Steam wafts up thicker than chimney smoke. The fumes can't be good for Ransom, who looks every bit the candidate for another heart attack. The only thing between the former CEO and the smoldering abyss are two slim guardrails on the edge of the trail. But a man of his size could easily slip through them. He leans over the top rail to get a better look. Mrs. Ransom is a half step away from becoming a widow. She scolds him.

Seeing him precariously balanced like that recalls the story of the young park volunteer who tumbled into one of these same vents. She was overcome by scalding vapor and didn't make it out. This happened a few decades ago when Ransom was drilling nearby, and quickly turned into a cautionary tale at this park. So he must have heard about it. I hope he remembers. An elderly man in his condition is no match for a steam vent.

As Rex Ransom gazes into the gaping hole, I stop. The man between us also stops. Then things change quickly.

The vague outline of someone emerges from the mist at the opposite end of the trail. He seems to be wearing a black mask and running towards the Ransoms. He reaches into a pouch at his waistline, pulls a metallic object, and points it in the couple's direction. The thick vapor makes it hard to tell what's happening. He keeps coming.

Alarm bells go off in my head. A Touch of Grey snaps to attention and starts running toward the Ransoms. I break into a run too, staying right behind him. I don't like this guy being between my clients and me.

The masked man keeps coming.

Damn! Already I feel like I've failed. I didn't really believe the old man was in danger here from anything more than old age. Guess I was wrong.

I close in on the Ransoms and so does A Touch of Grey. We're both flying at top speed, evenly spaced. But the masked man beats us to point blank range.

The vapor distorts everything. But this much I can see. Before he reaches the couple and the masked man, A Touch of Grey veers off the trail to the right, away from the scene, and disappears. *Where's he going?* Rex Ransom, still gazing into the vent, doesn't appear to notice him. Or the masked man.

Now I'm almost upon the couple and the approaching man. I halt. The man passes the Ransoms and keeps going— metallic object still in his hand. Now he's heading for me. I'm about to duck off the trail myself, since I'm unarmed. As he approaches me he raises his hand not holding the object. *What's he doing?*

The mist clears enough that I get a better look at him and the object. It has a cord leading to his ears. It's not a gun. It's a digital media player.

The runner passes and I see that his mask is actually a kerchief over his mouth and nose, probably to filter the toxic air. And from his graceful gait and curvaceous figure I'm convinced this man is actually a woman. She moves her hand again. Now I understand. She's waving to me. I wave back.

Maybe the goddess is playing tricks on me?

ten

After following the Ransoms through the hotel's breakfast buffet the next morning—with no sign of A Touch of Grey—I'm in the driver's seat of the yellow Boxster at quarter to nine, ready for the funeral. Ready for anything.

The black Lincoln pulls up to the portico and the waiting couple climbs in. He's in a dark suit and she's in a flowered but also dark *muʻumuʻu*. When the limo passes me and swings onto Crater Rim Drive, I wait about thirty seconds and then fire up the Boxster. The flat six motor roars. Aiming the ragtop in the direction of the limo, I keep my distance so this bright yellow machine isn't a dead giveaway. But I know where we're going. And it's not far.

The Kīlauea Military Camp chapel is less than a mile away, just beyond the Steaming Bluff. Stanley Nagahara, the deceased, was a veteran and a longstanding resident of Volcano, the village just outside the park's entrance. His memorial service will draw neighbors and fellow veterans, as evidenced by the mix of aloha attire and uniforms now climbing from cars and trucks around the chapel. But others, including myself, my client, and her husband, have trekked here because Nagahara had been a corporate attorney who, during the company's heyday, represented Ransom Geothermal to Hawai'i county and state governments, after having worked for the state himself for many years.

I park in an unobtrusive spot in the camp and wait. Across the picturesque rolling lawns are a few dozen cottages that flank a small headquarters and reception building. Behind these, more cottages straddle the meandering tree-lined roads. The camp looks more like a resort than an active base because its main purpose in recent years has been to provide a vacation spot for current and retired military personnel. The chapel resembles a barracks, though, except for a raised section of roof above the entrance resembling a bell tower.

The Lincoln pulls in front of the chapel and the Ransoms climb the steps to its open doors. They file in and other funeral-goers follow. I lock the Boxster and join them.

I stride in wearing my one black aloha shirt—reserved for funerals, weddings, and other somber occasions. I don't know a soul except my client, and I know her only slightly. So I opt not to leave a sympathy card—typically filled with cash to help defray funeral expenses—as the Ransoms do, or walk through the receiving line. But I do go through the motions of signing the guest book, at least, and then try to disappear as the sort of casual acquaintance who shows up at funerals but avoids open caskets and grieving widows. I grab a seat in the back, power off my cell phone, and watch the Ransoms as they approach the casket.

The chapel has a dozen mahogany pews on either side of a carpet runner. Up front there's a portable pulpit and a communion table and, behind those, a royal blue curtain. Grey-green walls reinforce the barracks feel.

I'm ready to get this funeral over. The start time is nine, but the service won't likely begin until family and friends finish paying their respects. And the line is long.

Up front someone speaks his name and Mr. Ransom waves. Even at this distance, I notice a nasty scar in the webbing between his thumb and first finger. I'm contemplating the scar when someone slides into the pew next to me.

"Howzit?" he says. "Remembah me? Kawika, da limo drivah."

"Eh, Kawika," I say. "Howzit?"

"I no expect to see you hea, brah," he replies. "Know da guy?"

"Nah, jus' one frien' of a frien'," I say, hoping he'll let my vagueness slide.

We talk story quietly and time passes. I pump him for information about the Ransoms without seeming to pump. As we're talking A Touch of Grey enters the church and sits across the aisle from us. I don't really like this guy, whoever he is, hanging around my clients. But there's not much I can do about it inside the chapel.

Kawika doesn't notice the man, but turns to watch a tall middle-aged woman in black stride elegantly in and join the line. She stands out. It's not just her black dress. There are plenty inside the chapel. But the way she wears it. And her coiffured hair. She's in a class by herself.

By now Donnie and Rex Ransom have made their way through the receiving line with handshakes and hugs and even a bow, and are finding seats near the front of the chapel. As they pass the statuesque woman, Donnie winces and the old man nods but does not smile. The stately figure that provoked these reactions doesn't move.

"Das da ex." Kawika points to the tall woman. "Das her."

I recall the story about Ransom's ex cutting him with a kitchen knife. And that is some scar on Ransom's hand. Kathryn Ransom doesn't look the type to have carved it there. But I keep watching her. After she works her way through the line, she strides to the back of the church. She stares straight ahead blankly, without turning in her ex-husband's direction, then takes a seat next to A Touch of Grey. They exchange glances. Do they know each other?

A younger version of Ransom's ex, mid-twenties I'd guess, hurries into the chapel. If she's not huffing, she's certainly breathing fast. She slides into the pew that holds the former Mrs. Ransom and sits next to her, on the other side of the mystery man.

The two women in black look like a matched set. Same posture. Same elegant gestures. Same coiffured hair. I ask Kawika and he confirms: Ransom's daughter. And he sounds impressed when he tells me she attended Vassar College.

On the other side of the chapel a bearded, dreadlocked local guy in camouflage wanders in looking lost.

Kawika sees me studying him and says, "Das Sonny Boy." The unlikely figure passes. "Must be outta jail on parole. He da *pakalolo* king."

"Who Sonny Boy?" I ask, surveying his gaunt, tortured face, but I recall even before Kawika speaks. I let him talk.

"Da protestah, brah. Da one dat attack Mr. Ransom. Get nine mont's in prison fo' dat. Sonny Boy wen hate da drillers. Surprise he hea."

"T'ink he jus' come to pay respects?"

"Dunno, brah. Sonny Boy no like da geothermal drilling. He no like Mr. Ransom. Or da oddah guy. Maybe he jus' glad Mr. Nagahara dead. Maybe he wish Mr. Ransom dead too."

When the service finally starts, it's full of platitudes about the deceased: good father, loving husband, loyal servant of the state, respected attorney, etc. But I don't sense much compassion in the church for the man, despite the occasional wet eye in the crowd. A few friends and family members file up to the pulpit to offer a few words about the departed. Nobody says boo about Nagahara's role in the geothermal project in the rainforest, which suggests that most in attendance would rather forget that episode in his life.

Ransom himself sits in the front of the chapel motionless. But once when he turns, I see his face. It shows no grief. It shows nothing. The former CEO appears to have come out of a sense of obligation rather than a feeling of friendship.

As the speakers drone on I find myself feeling blue. A man has died and few who knew him seem deeply moved. When my time comes I'd rather just vanish in a giant wave, without fanfare, than be remembered with such little affection.

A commotion at the back of the chapel makes me turn around. So does Kawika. A man who resembles Father Time, long white beard and all, stumbles down the aisle. He looks for a seat, but no one is making room. As he passes I get a whiff of him. It's barely mid-morning and he smells like he's been knocking 'em back since dawn.

The current purveyor of platitudes at the pulpit tries to ignore the bearded figure, but he's already stolen the show.

Finally he finds a seat. Those sitting by him slide this way and that—giving him a wide berth. Ransom turns around, sees the old drunk, and the color drains from the CEO's face. He knows this man. And he's not overjoyed to see him.

"Das Mick," Kawika says. "Mr. Ransom's old partner. Mick—he go broke when Ransom Geothermal pull out. Belly up. Fo' sure."

"Mick London?" I recall his name from my web browsing.

"Das him, brah."

That makes three enemies of the man I've been hired to protect under this one roof—his ex-partner, his ex-wife, and the ex-protester who did jail time for attacking him. Not to mention the operative who seems to follow the CEO everywhere. And possibly knows his former wife.

Will the next one to stumble into the church be Pele's favorite sister Hiʻiaka? Or maybe the fire goddess herself?

eleven

I'm making my way out of the chapel after the funeral, just turning my phone back on, when it rings.

"Kai?" It's Donnie. "He's in the restroom," she says. "Just to warn you, he wants to drive to Wao Kele O Puna."

"Why?" I ask.

"I don't know," she says. "Memories, I guess. All the rigging and equipment and buildings are gone. There's nothing to see. It's just an empty hole in the rainforest at the end of a lava road."

"The Puna forest is isolated," I say. "It'll be tough to follow you and not be seen. I'll have to lay way back."

"Good idea, Kai. Rex joked on the way over here: 'That guy in the yellow Porsche seems to follow us everywhere.' I guess he must have seen you coming up from Hilo."

I gulp. Ransom's eyes appear not to be aging as fast as the rest of his body. "The Porsche wasn't my idea. The agency was out of all but exotic cars. It was either this or walk."

"Here he comes," she says nervously. "I've got to hang—"

I hurry to the Boxster. Kawika has already pulled up to the chapel door and the Ransoms are climbing into the black limo. They pull away. I follow at what I hope is enough distance to evade Ransom's view.

In the parking lot we pass an old beat-up truck that has faded letters on the door: LONDON DRILLING EQUIPMENT. Ransom's ex-partner. Smashed Father Time with his flowing beard is inside trying to start the old beast—and not having much luck. Should he be driving in his condition?

I aim the yellow Porsche back onto Crater Rim Drive, well behind the Lincoln. It passes the park entry station and heads down toward Hilo. I let two vehicles come between us, and then follow.

The rainforest. Ransom's going back.

When reaching the town of Kea'au, the limo turns right onto Kea'au-Pāhoa Road. Wao Kele O Puna, the upland rainforest of Puna, is another ten miles almost due south. But first we pass through the quaint town of Pāhoa that looks like a snapshot from the Old West—plank sidewalks under wood-railed balconies and false-front clapboard buildings. The balconies are festooned with bunting and flags and flowers, giving the little town a cheerful, festive feel. But we quickly leave that cheerfulness behind.

I lay back further because now there are no cars between the limo and me. Soon the Lincoln makes a sharp right off Kea'au-Pāhoa Road and heads into the forest. The road eventually turns from asphalt to crushed lava. The Ransoms' car is alone. I try to get lost in its dust contrail.

I slow down and glance from one side of the road to the other, taking in the amazing diversity of the forest that Ransom had so casually disregarded in his effort to exploit the supposed energy sources in its depths: the scarlet flowers of the mossy-trunked 'ōhi'a tree; the pendulous fronds of the *palapalai* clump fern; the soaring umbrella-like *hapuʻu* tree fern; the silver-leafed and orange blossomed *paʻiniu* lily; and the smooth, shiny twining leaves of the fragrant *maile* vine. These trees, ferns, flowers, and vines in the rainforest, protesters argued, were vital to native Hawaiian gathering rights and cultural practices—from securing natural remedies to making *lei* and adornments for sacred *hula*. The SPC sought to reclaim what they believed was rightfully theirs.

Into this culturally rich and fragile ecosystem Ransom brought his drilling operation, apparently ignoring the traditional admonition to tread lightly and treasure this wonder of nature.

> *E nihi ka hele i ka uka o Puna,*
> *mai ʻako i ka pua*
> *o lilo i ke alao ka hewahewa*

> Approach cautiously the forests of Puna,
> do not pluck flowers lest
> you be lost in the pathways of error.

After a mile or two of thick forest, a clearing comes into view. The limo drives straight in. I pull off into a break in the road. I park the Boxster between two *ʻōhiʻa* trees, hoping Ransom on his way out won't spot the yellow roadster among the bright red *lehua* blooms canopying the trees.

Stepping back onto the road, I gaze into the hole in the forest and recall news coverage of the drilling and the protests. The clear-cut, geometrical scar of nearly eight acres looks hauntingly familiar—like a science fiction movie in which a giant flying saucer has landed and scorched the earth.

The rigid straight lines and totally denuded land-scape in the midst of lush greenery bring to mind the opposing camps that spurred the protests. Those who would preserve and protect the land vs. those who would exploit and develop it. There wasn't much middle ground between these champions of untamed nature and champions of untamed industry.

On one corner of these barren acres sits an eerily square reservoir of milky zinc green. I don't know what chemicals the reservoir contains or what purpose it served, but its murky surface looks as unnatural as the stripped land.

I hear something that makes me turn around. Another car raising dust pulls up about twenty yards behind me. The driver climbs out. A Touch of Grey. *He's everywhere.* He just stands by his car, looking past me to the Ransoms. He must wonder about me like I wonder about him.

I turn back to the clearing in the forest and watch the old man step from the limo, hobble with his cane a few paces toward the green pond, then stop in his tracks and scan the entire clearing. I can't see the expression on his face. He's too far away. But I can see him shrug as if to say, "What was all this about?" I imagine him reflecting on his drilling on the disputed land, the anger and resentment it aroused, and then the ultimate failure of his operation to produce enough steam and energy to be profitable.

Why he wanted to return here is anybody's guess. Could it be that his ill health and the death of two of his former executives have heightened his feelings of mortality? Or is he merely lamenting that fate defeated his reign as the geothermal king?

He shakes his head. He bows. He moves closer to that milky pond, almost stumbles, and his wife dashes from the limo to right him. She turns him around, guiding him back to the car. They both climb in. I hide among the ʻōhiʻa trees when the limo passes, raising a dust cloud. A Touch of Grey briefly disappears among the trees, then jumps into his car and raises a dust cloud of his own. I fire up the Boxster and follow both dust clouds back to the Volcano House.

* * *

Tuesday evening the Ransoms leave me alone. Donnie calls once to say they are dining in their room. I'm relieved and re-pack my bag. Their flight to Kāuaʻi via Honolulu departs at noon. Except for following the Ransoms back to Hilo tomorrow morning, I'm done. Well, I'll continue to keep an eye out for A Touch of Grey—*whoever he is.*

I phone Ashley in Denver again. And leave another message. I want to ask her about the Hawaiian bracelet with her name on it I found at the scene of the Pali crash, and about the party she attended celebrating the Lindquist twins' twenty-first birthday. Frustrating as it is not to hear from Ashley, I'm glad to have a case waiting for me when I return to Maunakea Street. And also glad to put this glorified chaperone gig behind me.

I eat alone that night. On my way back from the hotel restaurant I walk by the Ransoms' room. I hear tapping and stop. The tapping seems to be coming from the room next door. Is it the toe tap of a hotel guest listening to music? Or maybe some kind of secret code?

Or just my overactive imagination?

twelve

Wednesday morning, I'm awakened by a call. I was wrong. Donnie does need my services. She says her husband insists on walking the Crater Rim Trail again before breakfast. For his health, she tells me. And he's going alone. She doesn't say why. No worries, I reply. I'll be waiting for him by the trail.

Same drill as before. I hide behind the corner of the hotel when Ransom appears. The old man hobbles out the side door, makes his way awkwardly across the lawn with his cane, and sets out even more slowly than before—with no one now to support his feeble progress. I let him get ahead of me, far enough so he won't think he's being followed, but not so far that I lose sight of him.

The air is chilly and thick with mist. The sky is ghostly white. Visibility is even worse than yesterday. We're walking in a cloud. Double exposures, odd outlines, and shrouded images distort even the most familiar objects. I stick close to Ransom. He shouldn't be left alone in this murk.

I look behind me. No Touch of Grey in the parade. To track Ransom today he'd have to be close. He's not. Why go to so much trouble to follow a man and then just quit?

Not me. I'm still on the case. I follow Ransom, just the two of us, alone on the trail. Not even any other tourists at this hour. We leave the Volcano House behind and head into the tree ferns. The old man is under those green umbrellas when he puts his cell phone to his ear. He talks briefly, and then hangs up.

He hobbles on. Finally he reaches The Steaming Bluff, the goal of his solo hike. He stops at the first gaping vent and leans against the top guardrail. The steam, billowing thick with sulfur, still appears to be the most visible threat to his wellbeing.

A young woman approaches him from the opposite direction. Even through the steam I can tell she's oddly dressed for the trail: flowing crimson gown, shimmering black hair, flame-red lipstick, and eyes vivid with dark shadow and liner. She's attired more for a prom than a hike. Ransom sees her and they appear to lock eyes briefly.

Who is this woman? She looks hauntingly like a well-known *kinolau* of Pele. Donnie mentioned this guise of the goddess in my office—the seductive young woman in red. My client didn't describe her in detail. She didn't need to. Like most people who grow up in the islands, I know. That *kinolau* and this woman on the trail appear to be one and the same.

Can't be. I scratch my head. Is she why the old man insisted on walking alone? Was the call from her? Or has she merely bumped into him by chance?

Now my own phone rings. It's Donnie. *"Kai!"* She sounds hysterical. *"I'm so afraid!"*

"What's wrong?" I say. "Where are you?"

"I'm running toward you on the trail." She's breathless. "Now I can just barely see you through the mist."

I turn around and see the vague outline of a person, motioning rapidly toward herself.

"I'm so afraid!" Her voice is lower now, but still on the verge of hysteria.

"Wait there." I run to her. I don't like leaving Ransom behind, but he's not so far away that I can't return to him quickly. I keep glancing back as I move further from him and the woman.

When I reach Donnie she's clutching a piece a paper in her trembling hands. She grabs my arm and pulls me a few steps off the trail into the tree ferns, out of sight of her husband.

"What's wrong?"

"This." She hands the paper to me. The words on it are cut and pasted from a newspaper.

---

as you value your health and your life
keep away from Pele
Deadly

"Where did you get this?"

"It was slipped under my door just after Rex left," Donnie says, still trembling. "What does it mean?"

"You tell me. You know your husband and his enemies better than I do." I step back onto the trail to catch another glimpse of Ransom. The air is thick and I can barely see the shadowy outlines of two people.

"Maybe it's Rex's ex-wife?" She shrugs.

"What motive would his ex have to produce a note like this? Just to make him, or you, uncomfortable?"

"I don't know." Donnie shakes her head. "I'm so scared, I can't think straight."

I believe her.

Donnie tries again. "Maybe the insane woman who escaped from the mental hospital?"

"No matter who delivered the note," I say, "we can't do anything about it now. I better get back to your husband." I fold and put the note in the pocket of my aloha shirt and start with a quick stride toward Ransom. Donnie's next words stop me.

"I warned Rex already," she says.

"That was you who called him?" *There goes my theory about the woman.*

"He told me I was worrying about nothing. Then he hung up."

From the direction of The Steaming Bluff I hear what sounds like a thud and a groan. Donnie seems too out of it to notice.

"Why don't you go back to your room now and let me handle this?" I say. But I'm not waiting for an answer. I'm already moving through the mist.

I start running. I race through the fern grove. I can hardly see my own feet. But I keep going.

I hear my shoes pounding the trail. Soon I reach The Steaming Bluff. But I don't see him or the woman in red. The vapor is so thick now I can't even make out the caldera below. I approach the vent where I left Ransom. The closer

I get, the hotter and more rotten-smelling the steam rising from the cavernous hole. Pele's at it again.

"Mr. Ransom?" I call his name, abandoning my cover.

I doubt the old man could have made it much beyond the vent in the short time I've been gone. But he's nowhere in sight.

I lean against the guardrail, like he did, and peer in. The smell of sulfur suddenly combines with a more noxious odor. The stench of burning flesh.

My eyes follow my nose down into the abyss, blinking to avoid the reeking steam. About a dozen feet down, lodged on an outcropping, lies a man. His skin is lobster pink. His lips are puffy. His eyeballs bulge like poached eggs.

He isn't climbing out on his own. He's been boiled alive.

thirteen

It's him. The man I was hired to protect.

No doubt about it. His cane, already discolored by the searing steam, is wedged in a crack just a few feet below his body.

The woman in red—a dead ringer for Pele—has vanished.

Unreal. My brain rebels. But I have to admit what I saw. And it seems I saw Pele, in the flesh.

Maybe she had nothing to do with it? I rationalize. *Maybe Ransom just got too close, succumbed to the fumes, and stumbled into the vent?*

I shake my head. I walk in slow circles, trying to figure out what to do. Then I get a grip on myself.

Survey the scene.

I'm the first one here and presumably nothing has been touched. It's not often a PI gets first crack like this. It may sound cold, since the old man is lying in the vent, but there's nothing I can do about that. What I can do is try to find out why he died. And what, if anything, the woman in red had to do with it.

I scan the trail near the vent. The hard-packed dirt, trodden by countless park visitors, reveals no discrete shoe- or footprints. Neither Ransom's nor the young woman's. Just off the trail I notice a broken 'ōhelo branch and small depressions in the vegetation that suggest someone scrambled through the brush toward Crater Rim Drive, about fifty yards away. The woman? Unlikely, given her attire.

My first look gets me nowhere.

When I'm satisfied I've combed the scene the best I can in short order, I dial 911. I'll wait to inform Donnie until the Park Service arrives.

Within minutes a smoky-the-bear hat shows up. It's Ranger Crisp. He peers into the vent. He asks me the expected questions. He's calm and deliberate. I give him my card and explain that I've been following Mr. Ransom incognito and why. Then the ranger calls in emergency services.

Seconds later, A Touch of Grey shows up. He sees the former CEO at the bottom of the vent, looks at the ranger and me, and asks, "What happened?"

"We're not sure yet," Ranger Crisp says. "Do you know this man?"

"I know who he is," he replies. "I'm with Puna Security." He also hands the ranger a card. "I've been shadowing Mr. Ransom."

"On whose orders?" the ranger asks.

"A former exec of Mr. Ransom's company—an old friend of his—hired me to follow him because of what happened to Mr. Nagahara and Mr. Kroften."

"With the victim's blessing?"

"He didn't know."

"So that makes two of you tailing him?" The ranger says. "And neither of you saw what happened?"

"I almost did. The old man was approached by a woman." I describe her and her resemblance to Pele. "Then Mrs. Ransom, my client, called me away for a moment." I save the warning note until I can discuss it privately with the ranger. "When I returned, the woman was gone and he was in the vent."

The Puna Security man chimes in just as my cell phone rings. It's Donnie.

"Kai," she says, "Where's Rex? He should be back from his walk by now."

"Stay where you are," I say. "I'll be right there."

I hang up and tell the two men I'm going to inform the deceased's wife. That's normally the job of the official investigating agency, but since the ranger isn't about to leave the body, he does not object. I hike back to the Volcano House. On the way to her room I stop at the front desk and ask Pualani to photocopy the note.

Pualani glances at it and is comfortable enough with our friendship to read it silently. I watch her lips move as she reaches last word and whispers *Pele*. She gives me a look as mysterious as her earlier wink, places the note on her machine, and then hands back the original and copy.

I say, *"Mahalo,"* and put both in my shirt pocket.

I knock on Donnie's door and she lets me in. From the look of concern on her face I can tell she already knows something is wrong. No sense beating around the bush.

"I'm sorry to inform you," I say, "that your husband is dead."

She buries her face in her hands and starts to sob. "I knew we shouldn't come here! I knew Pele would get him!"

I put my hand on her shoulder. "I'm very sorry."

She keeps her face buried in her hands. She seems resigned rather than shocked. She doesn't ask how it happened or where. She just sobs.

"Your husband wasn't well," I say. "He might have had another heart attack, even if he didn't come to the Volcano House." I don't mention the woman in red. Donnie doesn't need to hear about her now.

"I want to go to him," she says. "I want to be with Rex."

"It's not a pretty sight. I'll take you if you want, but it's not a pretty sight."

"I don't care." She goes into the bathroom and rinses her face.

Then we walk the Crater Rim Trail to where Ranger Crisp and the Puna Security man have now been joined by a dozen onlookers, a state sheriff, and an emergency staff in rescue garb resembling space suits. They've got ropes and pulleys and other equipment. Ransom is still down in the vent. He's not going anywhere.

"Are you sure you want to see this, Donnie?"

"I don't want to," she says. "I have to. Rex is my husband."

"Okay." I take her to the edge of the trail. She peers over the railing and into the vent. "I knew it would happen!" she cries. "I knew it!"

"We better go," I say.

"I need to talk to her," the ranger says to me. "The sooner the better."

"She'll be in her room. This is no place for her now."

The ranger nods and looks at me. "I need to talk more to you too."

"Whenever you're ready," I say and lead the widow of Rex Ransom back to the Volcano House.

fourteen

"You should show this to the ranger when he interviews you." I hand Donnie the original note when we return to her room, keeping the copy in my pocket. She scans it once again.

"Once the ranger is through with us, would you like me to accompany you back to Kāua'i?" I ask. "Sorry to say, your husband's body may have to stay here with the medical examiner for now."

"That's very kind of you," she says. "I'll manage, but can you wait while I make a call?"

"No problem," I say, assuming she's going to inform family members of her husband's death.

When she takes her cell phone from her purse, I excuse myself. "I'll be out in the hall."

"Stay here," she says. "I'm just calling our renter, Jeffrey Bywater. I don't want him to be shocked when he watches tonight's news on the cruise ship." She punches in a number she seems to know by heart.

"Hello, Jeffrey? This is Donnie."

She pauses. I hear a male voice on the other end of the line, but I can't make out his words. She whispers to me, "He's aboard the *Pride of Aloha*."

"Are you and Byron enjoying the cruise?"

He responds in more words I can't decipher.

"I'm glad," she says. "Jeffrey, I'm afraid I have some bad news. Rex apparently had another heart attack while he was walking a trail by the Volcano House. He was found in a steam vent." She pauses. "Jeffrey, he's dead."

I overhear Jeffrey telling someone what Donnie just said. The other person, I assume, is Byron, Jeffrey's friend.

Donnie starts to sob again. "I'll be okay," she says into the phone. "I just wanted you to know." Another pause. "That's not necessary. I'll be fine. I'm with the private detective."

She puts her hand on mine. I wonder what's going on.

"Okay, do what you like, but it's not necessary. Goodbye, Jeffrey."

She puts down her phone.

"Jeffrey and Byron have decided to cut their cruise short," she explains. "They're going to leave the ship when it docks at Nāwiliwili Harbor on Kāuaʻi tomorrow morning, pick me up at Lihue Airport, and drive me back to Hanalei. I told them it wasn't necessary. But they're such caring guys."

"Sounds like you'll be in good hands," I say, but am frankly relieved she no longer needs my services.

"I'll be fine to fly back to Kāuaʻi by myself tomorrow morning," she explains, "since both of them will meet me there."

She barely gets out her words when there's a knock at her door. I open it to Ranger Crisp. He wants to interview Donnie first. Alone. So I step into the hall. The ranger tells me, "Don't go far."

"I'll be in the lobby," I say.

Soon I'm warming my bones by the perpetual flames of the famous fireplace. Time passes. I'm not thinking about Rex Ransom. Maybe his death is too gruesome. The crackle and piney scent of the fire makes my mind wander—back to the Pali case and those unreturned calls, back to Blossom and her abusive ex-boyfriend, back to Maile and Kula. I drift off into a reverie that's suddenly interrupted.

"I'm ready for you," the ranger says.

We walk into the hotel dining room, empty at this time of day, take a table, and the interview begins.

Ranger Crisp proceeds to ask me more expected questions, this time to corroborate what he's been told by Donnie. How long I'd been working for her. What my duties entailed. Who I was protecting Mr. Ransom from. And how I went about it. The ranger also asks about the last time I saw Ransom. He seems to assume I'm the last person to see the victim alive. But I know I'm not.

I mention again the young woman in red. "It may sound crazy, but this woman looked amazingly like Pele in one of her guises. It's probably just a coincidence."

"Stanger things have happened," the ranger says. "Some people will say Pele has claimed another victim, because of Mr. Ransom's role in the geothermal operation at Wao

Kele O Puna. His death makes three. And three looks like a pattern."

"And then there's the note," I say. "I assume Mrs. Ransom showed it to you."

"She did," the ranger says. "We'll follow up on it."

"Pele wasn't Mr. Ransom's only enemy—real or imagined," I say. "He had mortal enemies too, but you probably know that."

"We know about some others. Who did you have in mind?"

I tell him.

He nods in agreement, as if we have the same list. Then he says, "Park Service personnel just removed the body."

"I bet his wallet was found on him," I say, "with no evidence of theft."

The ranger nods. "We're going on the assumption, suggested by Mrs. Ransom, that her husband had a heart attack. The autopsy will determine the exact cause."

"I would have been there," I say, "but she was hysterical about that note."

"It's a sad coincidence, isn't it?"

"How's that?"

"Well, she hires you to protect him. You follow him everywhere and nothing happens. And then you leave him alone for barely a minute—to comfort her—and he turns up dead."

Before long the interview is over. I walk back to Donnie's room to express my sympathy again and say goodbye. She's not there. Just as well.

Minutes later my overnight bag rides beside me in the yellow Boxster, heading down the Volcano Highway to Hilo Airport.

fifteen

Thursday I get in early to my office with a copy of the morning paper. The front page poses a provocative question: "Pele's Third Victim?" Below is a photo of a younger Rex Ransom in his geothermal days. And below that, instructions to turn to the local section for the full story. I do.

Pele's Third Victim?

Another Former Ransom Geothermal Executive Dies

Hilo: Big Island geothermal developer Rex Ransom was found dead yesterday morning in an active steam vent at Hawai'i Volcanoes National Park. The former CEO of Ransom Geothermal Enterprises apparently fell into the vent after being overcome by fumes. He was walking by himself on the Crater Rim Trail near the Volcano House when he fell.

Ransom and his wife were staying in the park while attending a funeral for attorney Stanley Nagahara, who once represented Ransom Geothermal. Nagahara's body was discovered recently in a crevasse in the East Rift Zone after a solo hiking accident. Nagahara was the second former Ransom Geothermal executive to die in the park. Drilling engineer Karl Kroften died nearly two years ago in a single car accident near the Halema'uma'u Crater.

Ransom's death yesterday brings the number to three. The men's connection with the controversial geothermal project in the Wao Kele O Puna rainforest has not been lost on devotees of Pele, legendary goddess of fire and volcanoes.

"Pele get her revenge," said one lifelong Puna resident who asked not to be identified.

But a Park Service spokesman explained that steam vent deaths are not unexampled. "This has happened before," said Ranger Benjamin Cabato, referring to a park volunteer who died from a fall into a steam vent in 1992.

The young woman in red. She's not mentioned. Just as Pele devotees saw the goddess in the grey-haired old woman with her white dog climbing into Karl Kroften's BMW before it crashed, so too would they see the goddess in the young woman who appeared before Rex Ransom fell.

But I have no time to dwell on the newspaper. I have to put Ransom's death out of my mind. The Pali case needs attention.

I take the orange shag stairs down into the flower shop. Blossom is not there. But Mrs. Fujiyama is, tidying a refrigerated display case filled with fragrant *pīkake*, plumeria, and white ginger *lei*.

"Morning, Mrs. Fujiyama." I whiff the perfumed air. *Lucky you live Hawai'i.* Where else can a PI hang his shingle above a *lei* shop?

"Good morning, Mr. Cooke." She glances at me over her half glasses, always politely formal, and smiles. If she's still worried about Junior, she's not showing it.

I hustle to my parking garage. Maunakea Street is in peak form as I step onto the early morning sidewalk. The floral scents of the *lei* shop are soon replaced by other aromas of Chinatown: the reek of the open dumpster against Mrs. Fujiyama's building, the tropical tang of mangos on a fruit vendor's cart, the earthy scent of *bok choy* and other Chinese cabbages at a vegetable stall, the sweet-sour smell of *char siu* hanging in a lunch counter window, the pungent waft of the morning's catch in the fish market; and the cheap perfume of a lady of the evening strolling home from her night's work on Hotel Street.

Before long I'm leaving Chinatown behind, driving down Maunakea to Nimitz Highway. I turn right and glance back at the Aloha Tower—no *Pride of Aloha* today. Donnie Ransom's tenant, Jeffrey, and his friend Byron no doubt by now have disembarked at Na-wiliwili Harbor and retrieved their landlady at Lihue Airport. I'm off the hook because of those two guys. And glad the whole Ransom mess is behind me.

I turn off Nimitz Highway on Ma-punapuna Street, drive a few blocks *mauka*, and pull in front of HPD's contract vehicle impound lot, operated by Stonehenge Recoveries. On any given day on the island of Oʻahu more vehicles are towed than can be accommodated on police property. So one lucky towing company wins the lucrative contract to perform this function. I got a green light from my friend in blue, Creighton Lee, to visit Stonehenge Recoveries.

Stonehenge. Curious name for a Honolulu wrecking yard. Does the name allude to that prehistoric circle of mammoth stones outside London town, in the direction of Dartmoor? *Never been, but would like to go.* Maybe the tow company wants patrons to think solid and reputable and enduring?

The yard itself is not much to write home about. A doublewide trailer, with a couple of wrecked cars in front of it, serves as an office. The office has two windows where you can pay your fine and liberate your car. By the windows are instructions in big red letters telling you what forms to fill out and how to pay.

Speaking of luck, as I step from my car some unlucky guy is standing at one of the windows, arguing with the unlovely woman on the other side. She *looks* okay. What's unlovely about her is her tongue. The poor guy whose automobile she holds hostage is getting an earful. She's grown thick skin, I guess. Dealing with irate motorists day after day can do that. She's telling him he owes not only a fine, but also a towing and a storage charge. She's telling him he must pay it all in full and in cash before he sees his car again.

He objects. She has an answer for everything: You think the charges are unfair? Fill out a complaint form. You want a copy of your completed form? Sorry, no copies. You've heard complaint forms mysteriously disappear? Can't be. We carefully file every form and act on it promptly. Any other questions?

Now he's fuming. Soon the unlucky guy at the window and the woman on the other side are really going at it. She doesn't even see me as I slip by the doublewide trailer and walk behind it into the impound lot. Despite my friend in blue's assistance, technically I'm not supposed to be here. But I don't let that stop me. I'm poor at following rules and regulations.

It's a clear March morning and the metallic paint on dozens of impounded cars sparkles in the sun. The car I'm looking for won't have much sparkle left. It won't have much of anything left. Vehicles involved in serious accidents are typically winched onto a flatbed truck, sometimes in pieces. That's what happened in the Pali crash, after the Honda Civic plunged from the cliff. I've seen photos of the wreck, but not the actual vehicle. Until now.

I'm not a curious onlooker or morbid spectator hovering over a wreck that killed three people. My mission is different. I'm looking for material evidence for a civil trial, much the same sort of evidence I looked for at the scene of the crash: cash register and credit card receipts, bottles (intact or broken), clothing or pieces of clothing, shoes, slippers, fluid and other stains—anything that might pertain to the accident. Like that Hawaiian bracelet belonging to Ashley.

She still hasn't returned my calls. So I still have no explanation why her bracelet rode in the doomed car when she didn't.

The deeper into the yard I walk, the more desperate the shape of the cars. There must be a hundred here, easy. At the very back are the worst cases—whose makes and models are almost impossible to determine. This is where I find the remains of the metallic red Honda, looking less like a car than a coffin.

Why am I always on the trail of death?

Fireball really did a job. The only way to tell that this mangled mess is a Honda is a bent badge on what remains of the hood. The car's sides are sheared almost flat from slamming the walls of the Pali tunnels. Its roof is crushed nearly to the windowsills. Its windshield pillars flattened to the dashboard. All the glass is gone.

Inside is a world of hurt. Two deflated airbags sag to the floor, dotted with dried blood. Bloodstains on the passenger seats must belong to the birthday twins; stains on the driver seat to Fireball.

I reach into the car, wishing I was wearing latex. Gingerly I run my fingers across the discolored seats, looking for anything. Then I stretch into the foot-wells, trying to follow my fingers with my eyes. I come up empty. No receipts. No bottles. No clothing or swatches of cloth.

I turn to the glove box—covered now by one of the deployed airbags. I fold the stained bag up onto the dash and try the glove box's door. It won't budge. No surprise. The Honda has been twisted and torqued by its catastrophic collision. Bare hands won't do. I scan the surrounding wrecks for something to pry open the box. Under an old Pontiac, a classic almost as old as my Impala, I see a piece of broken trim—metal, not plastic—about a foot long. I grab it, wedge it in the uneven seam surrounding the glove box, and pry the door open.

I find what you might expect—an owner's manual, service records, a pen, a little bong pipe. I pull everything out. Nothing is left in the empty box. Except for one thing. A slip of paper. A cash register receipt

Bingo! But there's not enough readable print on the receipt to tell much. However, there is a phone number on the back. It's written in a woman's hand. No name. Just the number. And it's not a Hawai'i number. Area code 303.

I have no idea where 303 is. But I'm going to find out.

sixteen

Back in my office I get a call from Tommy Woo. I'm sure the first topic of conversation is going to be the death of Rex Ransom at Volcano House.

I'm wrong. Tommy starts off: "Hey Kai, did you hear the one about the sushi bar on Bishop Street that caters exclusively to lawyers?"

"No, Tommy." *Another lawyer joke?*

"It's called Sosumi," he says. "You get it? *So sue me.*"

After Tommy reels off a few more I finally bring up the Ransoms. "I wonder how Donnie will make out."

"Just fine," Tommy says. "Ransom had lots of money and Donnie has lots of time to spend it."

"They seemed devoted," I say. "Well, she and the old man did have their moments."

"You're a choir boy, Kai. How do you make it as a private dick? Ten bucks says she's got a young stud on the side. Watch *The Garden Island* for a wedding announcement."

"What do I know about women?" I admit. "Or weddings?"

"Speaking of weddings," Tommy says, "I'm going to ask Zahra to marry me. What do you think?"

Zahra is Tommy's new girlfriend—a ravishing exchange student from Kenya about half his age whose visa is about to expire. That's probably the reason for the sudden wedding plans.

"I dunno, Tommy," I say. He's been married twice and both marriages were disasters. "You've known her, what, about a month?"

"I knew all I needed to know from day one." Tommy sounds defensive. "Women from Africa have souls a mile deep."

I just listen. I don't want to dig myself deeper. Plus I'm sure Tommy is savvy enough not to get taken in by an immigration scam.

"Sorry I brought it up." Now Tommy sounds hurt.

I try to recover. "You have my blessing—I wish you two every happiness."

"*Shibai,*" he says and hangs up.

And I'm thinking: *What crazy things people do for love.*

After Tommy's call I try the number I found in the glove box of Fireball's crushed Honda. But first I look up the area code—303. It's Denver.

Ashley. She flew to Denver on the night of the accident.

It's not her cell number—I check—which has a Hawai'i area code—808.

When I dial the 303 number I'm thinking I may get lucky and Ashley will be on the other end. I really need to talk to her.

The number rings and rings. Finally voicemail kicks in. "Hi, this is Ethan," says a twenty-something male voice. "Please leave me a message."

"Hi Ethan," I say. *Who the heck is Ethan?* "My name is Kai Cooke. I'm a private detective in Honolulu. I'm trying to locate a girl named Ashley who may be able to help me with a case I'm working on—an auto accident on Oʻahu that killed Heather and Lindsay Lindquist. Do you know Ashley or the twins? Yes or no, either way, would you please give me a call?"

I leave my phone number and hang up—hoping I'm getting closer to the elusive Ashley.

On my way out of the office later that day I stop in the *lei* shop and ask Blossom how things are going. She's a good kid and I fear for her.

"Junior scares me." She trains her luminous eyes on me. "Sometimes he hurts me."

I gaze upon her reed-like figure and long brown hair thinking, *No woman—young or old—deserves that punk.*

Mrs. Fujiyama overhears our conversation and steps to the *lei* table.

"Junior—bad man," she says. "He keep coming back. What I can do?"

I try to reassure her. "A TRO may help."

"TRO—what that?" she asks.

"Temporary Restraining Order," I explain. "It's a legal document that will forbid Junior to come near Blossom or your shop."

"Piece of papah," she says. "What good dat? How one papah stop angry man?"

I see her point. "I'll keep an eye out for him," I say.

No sooner do I say that than a dusty black pickup truck with big knobby tires screeches to a stop in front of the shop. Junior storms in. A floral funeral wreath on a tripod awaiting a bereaved family comes crashing down. Mrs. Fujiyama watches in horror as perfectly arranged flowers break loose and roll across the floor. A silken banner—OUR BELOVED MOTHER—twirls in the air on its way down.

Blossom's ex has a scowl on his face and he's coming fast. Blossom grips me. *Does he think I'm her new guy?*

Blossom screams. Mrs. Fujiyama runs for the shop phone. Then I realize Junior's not coming for Blossom. He's coming for me.

He takes a jab at me with his right fist. Since my arms are shielding Blossom, all I can do is turn away. He catches me on the side of my face, just above my left eye. It's a glancing blow but breaks the skin. The results are instantaneous. My blood drips onto Blossom's hair.

I release Blossom, rise from the table, and start for him. Mrs. Fujiyama comes back with the phone in her hand. "Police," she says in a surprisingly calm voice.

When Junior sees Mrs. Fujiyama talking on the phone, he runs for the door. Then he turns back and glares at me. "Nex' time I *kill* you."

He jumps into his black truck and tears away, smoking the tires down Maunakea Street.

Blossom collapses on the *lei* table. Mrs. Fujiyama comforts her. I'm not seeing so well, as blood fills my left eye. I grab for my handkerchief and daub the wound. The broken skin only stings. But the volume of red is amazing. It must look worse than it feels because Mrs. Fujiyama calls my name repeatedly: "Mr. Cooke! Mr. Cooke!"

"I'm okay," I tell her.

I barely get these words out when I hear sirens and then two HPD officers charge into the shop. They look at me and one says to the other, "Call EMS." I try to talk them out of this, but the other officer takes my arm and sits me down in one of the *lei* girl's chairs.

"Take it easy, sir," he says. "Help is on the way."

I don't bother to dissuade him. I just sit and wait. Somehow one of the officers produces a small towel and I bury my bloody face in it.

"What happened here?" the first officer asks Mrs. Fujiyama and her girls.

They start to explain. I try to talk, but the officer who handed me the towel puts his hand on my shoulder and says, "You can give a statement later."

So I just listen. Mrs. Fujiyama explains and fills out a witness statement. Junior is in trouble. He's looking at assault and battery, terroristic threatening, and property damage. In addition to outstanding warrants, he's also violated the terms of his parole, which stems from arrest and incarceration for domestic abuse of his girlfriend before Blossom. When HPD catches him, he's going back to jail. No question. But while he's still on the outside he's going to be all the more desperate and dangerous.

Another siren. Soon through my clouded vision I see flashing lights in front Mrs. Fujiyama's shop. Two medical techs rush in, see my bloody hand towel, and kneel down in front of me.

"We better get that looked at by a doc," one says.

"I'll be fine," I say. "It's just a scratch."

"We can't take you against your will, sir," says the other, "but you really should have it looked at."

I nod.

They put me on a gurney, wheel me to the ambulance, with Mrs. Fujiyama and her *lei* girls looking on. I should feel like a hero.

Before long we're at Queens Medical Center emergency room. The good thing about coming to the hospital in an ambulance is that you get to see someone immediately. I'm quickly processed and put on an examination table behind drawn curtains. A nurse has me remove my bloody shirt and then a doc looks me over. The nurse cleans the wound. Whatever she uses makes it sting again. Then the doc shines a floodlight on it and looks closely.

"Well, you're in luck," he says. "An adhesive strip should do the trick. No stitches today. Unless you want some?" He cracks a smile.

What's with the humor of ER doctors? I almost say

"Stay out of the ocean for a few days," he says. "You're a surfer, right?"

"Yeah, how'd you know?"

"Those teeth marks on your chest," he says. "Dead giveaway."

My shark bite. I don't like his choice of words. But I repeat: "Stay out of the ocean."

After a cab ride I'm back at the office with more adhesive strips and ointment and a list of instructions. When I check myself out in the mirror in the closet-sized bathroom used by Mrs. Fujiyama's five office tenants, I'm surprised that the strip the nurse put on my forehead camouflages the entire wound.

I get off easy. But I keep hearing Junior's menacing voice inside my head: "Nex' time I *kill* you!"

seventeen

By Friday Ashley still hasn't returned my call. Neither has the guy named Ethan. *Does nobody in Denver return calls?* I'm wondering even harder now why Ashley's Hawaiian bracelet was at the scene of the accident when she wasn't riding in the doomed car, and why Ethan's phone number was in the glove box. I could leave each another message, but in my experience too many messages can make witnesses less willing to talk. In-person interviews are always best, but difficult when the persons are in Denver and I'm in Honolulu.

So I face a stack of papers on my desk begging to be filed, and prepare a bill for Donnie Ransom. I have feelings about billing her so soon after her husband's death—a death I was hired to prevent—but I get over them. The charge on my credit card for the three-day rental for the Boxster alone is over a grand.

Before Friday is over, the bill is in the mail to Kāua'i and I'm glad to put the Volcano House case behind me.

On Saturday, against my own advice, I leave two more voicemails for Denver. I don't expect to hear soon from Ashley and Ethan, given recent history. But I've got to make something happen. Even if I have to resort to something unorthodox—like hiring an undercover operative.

A young guy I know named Nicholas, an apprentice carpenter, really likes his beer. Nicholas is a big guy and looks older than his years. He's just shy of twenty-one, the legal drinking age in Hawai'i. Since it's Saturday, he'll be knocking back a few. I give him a call and make him an offer he can't refuse. Today Nicholas is working for me.

I pick up Nicholas at the house off Kapahulu Avenue in Kaimuki he shares with another guy and a girl. I beep and he ambles out with an open beer in his hand. He's got a big smile on his face, like he's the happiest twenty-year-old on earth. Twenty year olds have a lot to be happy about.

"Hey, Nick," I say, as he steps into the car. "Leave the beer here."

"Shoots, Kai." He sets the open bottle in the street. "Geev' me five, *braaahh!*" The way he's talking makes me wonder if he's up to the task. But there's no use doubting or turning back now. He's my best shot.

I give him a high-five and ask: "You ready?"

"*Right on!*" he says. And then: "Thanks again, man, for findin' my tools. I hope that guy that took 'em gets twenty freakin' years."

Nicholas is referring to the favor I did him. Somebody took a bunch of tools from his pickup truck. I tracked down the thief, tipped off HPD on where to find him, and recovered most of the tools. I doubt he'll get much more than probation, but at least I nabbed him.

Once Nicholas is buckled in, I aim my old Impala toward downtown Honolulu to a club called the Lollipop Lounge. En route I give Nick instructions.

"Now here's what you do," I say. "You walk into the Lollipop, take a seat, and order a beer. Give the server your credit card when she brings the beer, and make sure you don't leave without your signed receipt. Get the server's name, if you can. I'll come in after you, take another table, order a beer myself, and watch what happens. If you get carded, the game is up. We'll try another club."

"Got it," he says. "My kind of work!"

When we get to the Lollipop Lounge, on a seedy block of Kona Street not far from Ala Moana Shopping Center, Nicholas follows my instructions to a tee. We're in luck. Business is slow, late on a Saturday afternoon, and he doesn't get carded. Nor does the server, a woman twice Nick's age, notice that he's already had enough to drink.

We're here for a reason. I'm tying to establish that this club serves minors and intoxicated patrons. The Lollipop is the last club that served Heather and Lindsay Lindquist the night they died. The Lollipop also served the driver of the car.

Luck stays with us. I observe Nick, who is underage, being served when he is already clearly buzzed. I observe him using his credit card and getting a receipt. The receipt will have the time and date stamped on it and, of course, Nick's own signature. For good measure, I also buy a beer and pay with my credit card, getting the name of the server from a tag that says STORMY, in the event Nick doesn't.

If the case goes to trial, and the Lollipop is a defendant, I may be deposed to present this evidence against their claims of not serving either the Lindquist twins or Fireball when they were intoxicated. If we're really lucky the same server who served Nicholas was working the night the twins died.

I let Nicholas stay for a second beer, while I nurse the one I ordered. At the bottom of his second, I gesture to him to meet me outside. He does and I drive him home. The beer he left in the street in front of his Kaimuki house is still standing there.

"Take this inside," I say to Nick. "T'anks, brah."

He picks up the bottle, nods, and wobbles into his house. I'd feel bad about contributing to the delinquency of a minor if it wasn't in the interest of stopping the kind of illegal practices that get other minors killed.

On the way back to my apartment on Ala Wai Boulevard my cell phone rings. It's against the law in the City and County of Honolulu to talk on a hand-held cell phone while operating a motor vehicle. But when I think a call may be crucial sometimes I bend that law. If this one is from Denver I really need to take it. I look in my rearview mirror. An HPD cruiser, a white Crown Victoria, is right behind me. *Damn!* I don't even look at caller ID. I let the phone ring.

I can only hope if this call is from Ashley or Ethan that she or he leaves a message. One or both may have information that could help me wrap up the Pali case. But there's nothing I can do now. That HPD cruiser is still riding my bumper.

About a minute later my cell phone beeps. *Phew.* I have a new voicemail. Once I pull into my parking spot at the Edgewater I dial my voicemail and hear a young woman's voice. *Ashley at last?*

"Hello, Kai," she says. A promising start. "May I see you on Monday?"

Better than I expected. But the message doesn't sound right. Why would Ashley ask to see me in my office? All I requested was a return phone call. Plus, the pleasant female voice sounds sophisticated, with none of the rising pitch at sentence endings—*Like everything is a question, you know?*—of Heather and Lindsay Lindquist's other friends I've interviewed.

Then comes the answer.

"My name is Caitlin Ransom. I'm Rex Ransom's daughter."

Rex Ransom's daughter wants to see me?

"I understand you were with my father at Hawai'i Volcanoes National Park. I would like to talk with you about . . ." she pauses, "his death." Then an even longer pause. "Sorry, this is hard for me."

I try to remember if I have a box of tissues in my office. This could be a tearful meeting.

Caitlin Ransom leaves her number in that lovely voice and says she hopes to hear from me soon. I call her back immediately. The phone rings and then her voicemail kicks in.

"Aloha, Caitlin," I say. "Kai Cooke. I'd be happy to see you on Monday. Around nine? If that's okay, no need to call back. I'm very sorry about your father."

I hang up. *And wonder.*

eighteen

On Sunday morning we still have vog and I still haven't heard from Denver. But I'm still stoked about scoring big with Nicholas at the Lollipop Lounge.

I'm hanging out this morning at the Waikīkī Edgewater with the Sunday newspaper. When I was a *keiki,* Sunday was family day. My mom and dad and I would take a picnic to the beach, go for a hike or a drive, or visit my auntie's *ohana* in Punalu'u. It didn't really matter what we did—as long as we did it together.

I scan the front page. I don't have a problem with being alone on Sunday. I can always go surfing. Never mind the scratch over my eye. Never mind doctor's orders.

I flip pages to the local news and see this:

Geothermal CEO Overcome by Fumes

Hilo: A Big Island medical examiner retained by the National Park Service has determined that former geothermal pioneer Rex Ransom, who died last Wednesday at Hawai'i Volcanoes

---

National Park, was overcome by toxic fumes before he apparently slipped into an active steam vent. Ransom, 70, was discovered in the vent last Wednesday. Volcanic fumes, said the examiner, Elton K. Tamura, MD, can be especially hazardous to the elderly, and to those with heart and lung conditions.

The former CEO of Ransom Geothermal Enterprises, a previous heart attack victim, was by himself on the Crater Rim Trail near the Volcano House when the accident occurred. The day before, he and his wife attended the funeral of former Ransom Geothermal attorney Stanley Nagahara, who also died recently in the park. Another member of the firm, Karl Kroften, died two years ago near the Halemaʻumaʻu Crater.

The deaths of three people closely associated with the controversial geothermal project two decades ago in the Wao Kele O Puna rainforest continues to cause speculation among devotees of Pele that the legendary goddess of volcanoes had a hand in the deaths. The medical examiner's report on the cause of Ransom's death has not put this speculation to rest.

Overcome by fumes? You'd think that would quiet talk of Pele's revenge. Or would it? Was I right to think Ransom's worst threat was the noxious air near the craters?

Still no mention of the young woman in red who approached Ransom on the trail before he died. Or the warning note. Should I bring these up at my Monday meeting with Ransom's daughter?

The Volcano House case just won't go away. Sitting around on Sunday morning doesn't help. I slip on my board shorts and grab my wax. Hard to believe I haven't been in the water since going to the Big Island. *Sorry, Doc.*

Then I get a better idea. Why not take the golden boy? *If Maile will return my call.* I grab my cell, punch in her number, and take a breath. She won't answer. But I'm used to that.

Her phone rings and then I hear her warm familiar voice: "Hi, you've reached Maile Barnes, tracer of missing pets. How can I help?" *If she only knew.*

"Hi, Maile. It's me again. Okay if I take Kula surfing? Been a while since the boy's been in the water. Would you please give me a call? It's now"—I check my watch—"almost nine on Sunday morning. I can pick him up in thirty minutes."

I could say a few other things about missing her and hoping she forgives me, but I don't. She's heard it all. I just say goodbye.

Now the waiting game. I'm stuck until I hear from Maile.

So I reflect on how I messed up. I finally reconnect with the woman of my dreams. And then the relationship goes up in smoke. I could blame it all on Madison Highcamp. She told Maile in a drunken phone call that she—Madison and I—were engaged. It was a lie, but the message stung. Maile had been burned before. She said *never again.* I tried explaining, but no dice. My mistake was not breaking up with Madison sooner. No, my mistake was dating the rich, idle, tycoon's wife in the first place.

My phone beeps. It's a text message from Maile: "OK. Kula in yard."

That's it.

The ex-K9 cop is conveniently not around when I arrive at her Mānoa cottage. *No surprise.* Maile's feelings run deep. She doesn't get over things quickly. And I have to admit—I hurt her. Kula is like a child of divorce, and I have visitation rights.

I walk around to the back yard and there he is—mane and feathering luminous in the sun. He glides toward me with the grace of a stallion. His blond lashes set off dark brown eyes. *Golden boy.* I open the gate and he sidles up to me.

"Hey, Kula." I stroke his sunny fur. "Let's hit the waves."

He barks. His tail sweeps like a golden plume. *He's stoked already.*

From Maile's carport I fetch the tandem board on perpetual loan from my cousin Alika and strap it on my roof racks. Then Kula and I head for the surf. The retriever sticks his head out the window—fleecy ears flapping in the breeze. He's got a big goofy smile on his face.

Dogs aren't allowed in Waikīkī. That's why we pull into Kakaʻako Waterfront Park, to the uncrowded break called Flies. When Kula hears the waves crashing beyond the dune and smells the salt spray he goes ballistic. A boy after my own heart.

I grab the board and Kula prances over the dune to Flies, at the *Ewa* end of the park. I set the big board in the water and Kula steps onto the nose. He knows his spot. I hop on behind him and paddle toward the break.

The one and only surfer in the lineup this early on Sunday is gazing out to sea. In the distance he sees a set coming. He paddles for it. When the first shoulder-high roller reaches him, he's on it.

I paddle into the spot he leaves behind. Another wave rolls in. I swing the tandem board around and point the nose toward shore. The retriever hunches on the nose. I paddle until I feel the rush of water under the board. The nose drops and the board takes on the steep pitch of the wave. I pop up, turn right, and try to stay in front of the curling lip. Kula balances as I trim the board, keeping his paws spread. He barks and barks. *What a rush!*

When the wave fizzles and the board glides to a stop, I swing the nose around to paddle back into the lineup. Kula suddenly pitches into the water. *Oops.* He swims back like nothing happened, and I help him on. He stands on the deck on all fours and shakes. The salty spray flies all over me.

"Good boy, Kula." I pat his wet fur.

He barks again. And doesn't stop until I paddle back into the waves.

Kula's a lucky dog. He almost died after his rescue. The guy who shot him, a pet thief named Spyder Silva, wasn't so lucky. It's a long story, but the short version is that the retriever was trying to protect Maile—held at gunpoint by Silva. When I saw Kula go down I pulled my Smith & Wesson on Silva. I had to answer to homicide detective Frank Fernandez. Ultimately Fernandez grudgingly agreed

I'd acted in self-defense. I was in the clear. But Kula barely hung on. It took months for him to recover. Kula and Maile bonded around that experience. I should be glad she lets me take him surfing. But I'd be gladder if she'd talk to me.

While we wait for another wave I wonder again what I can possibly tell Ransom's daughter, other than I'm sorry for her loss. I wonder even more why she wants to see me.

After Kula and I catch our fill of waves at Flies, I bathe, dry, and return him to Maile's yard. Carrying cousin Alika's tandem board back to her carport, I notice she's home this time. I get bold and pop into her cottage to say thanks.

Maile's three cats curled up on rattan chairs—Coconut, Peppah, and Lolo—barely crane their necks. They know me. Lolo, the shy calico, doesn't even bolt. Scattered about the living room are Kula's toys—rawhide chews, yellow tennis balls, braided tug ropes—and food and water dishes inscribed with his name. He lives like a prince here. *Wish I did, too.*

Maile steps from her bedroom in her Nikes, running shorts, and sports bra. Seeing her tanned limbs and lovely curves again kind of smarts. I remember them too well.

Her face used to light up when she saw me. Not today. She doesn't offer me a chair. I ask how she's doing. We exchange a few terse sentences.

I can see we're getting nowhere fast. I just say goodbye and head for the door. Then she surprises me.

"Too bad about your client at Volcano House," she says with some real feeling.

I turn back. I'd like her to keep talking. "How'd you know he was my client?" I don't remember telling her about Ransom. And my name wasn't in the news reports.

"Tommy," she says. "We were talking about something else and it came up. I was interested because a guy I used to know dated Ransom's wife, Donnie Lam, when he was at Stanford."

"Donnie went to Stanford?" That doesn't sound right.

"No, I don't think so. She was living in the bay area and they met in a bar. He fell hard for her and was broken up when she married some old rich guy."

"You mean Rex Ransom?"

"No. Apparently she was married before. When that husband died she returned to Hawai'i and married Ransom. Or so I heard."

"Really?" Then as an afterthought: "Did Tommy tell you he's getting married again?"

"Yeah." Maile shrugs. "I wished him luck. He'll need it."

"My sentiments exactly." At least we agree on something. So I get even bolder and ask: "How about dinner this week?"

"We'll see," she says noncommittally.

"I'll call you."

I almost float to my car, so pumped up I nearly forget Maile's curious story about Donnie being married before. Almost, but not quite.

She's been widowed by two rich old men?

nineteen

Monday morning that amber haze still hangs over Maunakea Street. I'm waiting for Rex Ransom's daughter. I don't have to wait long.

She's ten minutes early.

When she strides in I recall seeing her at the Kīlauea Camp chapel—she and her dark, statuesque mother looking like a matched set.

"Caitlin Ransom," she says—pleasantly, but business-like. She offers me her hand. I take it and she shakes mine vigorously. *Shades of her late father?*

She's got to be in her thirties, given her parents' age, but she looks barely twenty-five. Grey eyes. Brown hair trimmed smartly to the shoulders. Little black dress flowing gracefully over her lean frame.

"Kai Cooke," I say. "Won't you have a seat?" I gesture to my client chair.

She sits and adjusts her dress. Her stylish attire and fine features give her that cultivated look young women get in pricey private schools.

"I'm sorry about your father." I say the line I rehearsed in the surf.

"I miss him," she says. "Every day." The mist in her eyes tells me she means it.

"Did you stay in Volcano after Stan Nagahara's funeral?" Since Caitlin vaguely resembles the young woman in red I saw on the trail, I try to make a connection.

"Mother did," she says, "but I had to get back to school in Honolulu. I'm doing graduate work in anthropology."

"So you didn't see or talk to your father the next day—the day he died?"

"Unfortunately not."

"I wish I could have prevented what happened," I start to explain. "You see, Donnie—"

"I'm sure it wasn't your fault." She saves me from rehearsing the lamentable event. "And I'm grateful you agreed to see me."

"So how can I help you?" I ask the question I've been wondering about since her unexpected call.

"My father's death was no accident," Caitlin announces.

"You don't accept the medical examiner's report that he was overcome by fumes?"

She slowly shakes her head. "Dad knew he had a heart condition and he knew the fumes around the volcanoes could be dangerous."

"A woman approached him on the trail moments before he died. I hesitate to say this, but she looked amazingly like one of Pele's well-known guises."

"I know Donnie believes Pele took my father's life," she says. "But I don't."

"Okay, let's say for argument sake you're right. If it wasn't an accident and it wasn't Pele, how did your father end up in the steam vent?"

She trains her grey eyes on me. "That's what I want you to find out."

I don't know why I suddenly feel uncomfortable. I grab for any words I can find—and hope they won't sound flip: "Do you have someone in mind?"

"Maybe Sonny Boy Chang? He assaulted my father two decades ago and has been in and out of prison ever since. He's out now."

"I saw Sonny Boy at the funeral." I recall the bearded, dreadlocked man in camouflage. "If we strike out with him, then who?"

"Lots of people on the Big Island fought geothermal development and disliked my dad." She rattles off a list of essentially the same names that were on my own list. Then she says: "My father sent me a generous check before he died. I'm willing to spend every penny to find out who did this."

"I've got another case going, but I can look into your father's death around it." Then I say, "When the deceased is divorced, like your dad was, it's customary to interview the former spouse. That would be your mother."

"My mother could have nothing to do with this," Caitlin insists.

I remember the nasty scar on her father's right hand, but keep it to myself. "I just want your okay to talk with her."

"You have it." Caitlin gives me her mother's phone number in Kona.

"I should also talk again with your father's second wife," I say. "Did you know she was married once before she met him?"

"I heard her first husband died," Caitlin replies. "Donnie's not my favorite person, as you can imagine, but she doted on my father."

"That was my first impression," I say. Caitlin doesn't need to know my second.

Caitlin Ransom gives me a retainer before she strides from my office. She's hardly out the door when I go on line and book a flight to Hilo for the next morning. I get Pualani at the Volcano House on the phone, we talk story, and I explain why I'm returning so soon. Then I phone Caitlin's mother, Kathryn Ransom, at her Kailua-Kona home and she agrees to see me. Finally I try Ransom's ex-partner Mick London in Kamuela, with a cell number Caitlin provided. He sounds drunk again—*or still?*—but he too agrees. I'm batting one thousand. Except there's no phone number for Pele.

Before I leave the office Monday afternoon, I call Denver again. Neither Ashley nor Ethan answers. I leave more messages—against my own better judgment. I can await their return calls just as well on the Big Island.

Then I phone Tommy Woo. He tells me some jokes too salty to repeat. I ask about his contact with the liquor commission and explain that I need a history of over-serving of customers at the Lollipop Lounge. All Tommy can talk about is Zahra and their wedding plans. I try to change the subject. I ask him about a TRO for Blossom's abusive ex, Junior.

"Worthless," Tommy says. "A TRO may only piss him off more. A piece of paper won't stop a desperate man."

"Mrs. Fujiyama said the same," I say. "Well, sort of."

"She's right." Tommy says. "Best thing your *lei* girl can do is disappear for a while."

Before I lock up for the day I make one final call—to Maile. I get her voicemail. "Hi Maile. It's me. I have to go back to the Big Island for a few days on the Ransom case. When I return I'll give you a call about dinner."

I glide down the shag stairs, feeling almost giddy. But the air comes out of my sails as soon as I see Blossom. I don't have to ask how she's doing. I can tell by the look in her eyes.

"Junior keeps hanging around my apartment," she says. "He keeps driving by the *lei* shop. I don't feel safe anywhere."

I recall Tommy's advice. "I'm going off island for a few days," I say, as the other *lei* girls, Chastity and Joon, look on. "Why don't you stay at my place while I'm gone?" As soon as I say this I realize it's a terrible idea—Tommy's advice, or not.

Blossom perks up. "You sure?"

"I'm sure," I say. But the old saying—*No good deed goes unpunished*—comes to mind. "You can stay tomorrow night. And probably a few nights after that." I explain where I live and how to get into the building. Then I climb back up the stairs and fetch her my extra apartment key.

When I return, Junior's black pickup truck is pulling up in front of the shop. He sees me giving Blossom the key. I make eye contact with him and he flips me the bird. *Again.* Then he lays rubber down Maunakea Street.

"I'm scared." Blossom trembles.

"Come tonight," I hear myself say. "I can walk you through the place so you know what's what." Then it dawns on me that I have a studio apartment with only one bed. "There should be space enough for two," I say, trying to convince myself. *Ah, I'll sleep on the* lānai.

"Oh, *mahalo,* Kai!" She hugs me. *"Mahalo."*

Mrs. Fujiyama—always the protective mother hen—frowns when she sees me lead her *lei* girl out the door. Doesn't she remember I learned the hard way already not to date her girls? Plus this one is nearly half my age.

I glance back at my landlady and shake my head.

twenty

The tiny *lānai* of my studio apartment looks thirty-five stories down into Waikīkī. The only thing between the *lānai* and a very long drop is a thin plate of glass. All night long I listen to traffic below on Ala Wai Boulevard, the chirping tires of racer-boys like Fireball, and sirens of HPD cruisers chasing them. Scrunched into a patio chair, hanging in the air above the noisy streets, I dream of Maile's hillside cottage.

My dream is interrupted by Blossom bouncing off my sofa bed, turning on lights, pacing the apartment, and talking on her cell phone. To whom, I don't know. She's in a new place. And maybe she's anxious. I don't blame her, but I also don't get much sleep.

By morning, I'm a wreck. *No good deed goes unpunished.*

After an impromptu breakfast, Blossom and I walk the carpeted hallway to the elevator. One of my neighbors lifts an eyebrow at me when he sees my pretty companion. I drop Blossom at the *lei* shop on my way to the airport. Fortunately, we don't get the same look from Mrs. Fujiyama. I guess by now she's figured it out.

* * *

My plane lands in Hilo at a little before eleven, I pick up a rental car—no wait and no hassles this time, *but sadly no Porsche*—and climb once again to the Volcano House. I pull through the portico of the barn-red hotel, park the car, try not to breathe the sulfur-laden air too deeply, and pass the fireplace on my way to the registration desk. The Park Service sign cautioning about the fumes is still posted.

I don't have to ring the bell.

Pualani greets me with her warm Hawaiian hospitality. She knows why I'm here, but she says playfully, "Kai, why you nevah come back sooner?"

"Was here only las' week," I say. "Remembah?"

She turns to her yellowed keyboard and peers at the monitor that's been around since the dawn of the personal computer. She types on the ancient keys. "Geev you one deluxe crater-view room dis time," she says. *"Kama'aina* rate."

"T'anks, eh?" On my own dime, or should I say on my client's dime, I had reserved the cheapest room in the hotel facing the parking lot rather than the crater.

"Room numbah one," she says. "Da same room da geo-thermal guy stay in dat wen' *huli* inside da steam vent. Spooky, yeah?"

"Das okay," I say, secretly stoked. I ask Pualani if I can see the guest register for the night before Ransom died. I don't expect to find anything obvious. But maybe a name will pop out. Or maybe a name that means nothing to me now will mean something later.

"I remembah da date," she says. "How I can fo'get?" Her fingers dance on that yellowed keyboard again. When she finds the appropriate record she wrestles the monitor in my direction.

The names on the screen include my own, those of Rex and Donnie Ransom, and the man from Puna Security. The other names don't mean a thing to me.

So I ask Pualani: "Anyt'ing strange happen on dat day?"

"Nah." Then she thinks for a moment. "Wait!" she says. "One guest wen insist fo' crater view room numbah t'ree. He make like big fuss. Said he mus' be on da groun' floor. Afraid of heights. Da hotel full, yeah? But I move da guests suppose to be in numbah t'ree to anoddah room upstairs. He says he come to see da eruption. Den what he do? He check out early da nex' morning—no time to see da eruption."

I glance at the hotel map. Crater view room three sits right next to room one—the Ransoms' room and now my own.

"When he leave da nex' morning?" I ask

"I dunno . . . maybe eight," she replies, which would be before Ransom died.

"What his name?"

She points to it on the screen. Lars Stapleton.

The name doesn't ring a bell. "What dis' guy look like?"

"Small kine *haole* guy," she says.

"Hair color? Eyes?" I try to jog her memory.

"So many people, dey come to da desk," she says. "How I can remembah dem all?"

"Where he from?"

She goes to another screen and scrolls down. "New Jersey."

"Nah." The more I hear about this Stapleton, the more I'm losing interest. His name could be an alias, but his profile doesn't fit any pieces of this puzzle.

"Don' fo'get Pele." Does Pualani want to help—or to pull my leg some more? Here in the park, so close to Pele's home and the mist that surrounds it, how could I forget the legendary goddess or deny her power? Pualani insists: "Pele knows. She da one you need talk to."

"But how I goin' investigate Pele?" I ask like it's a serious question. "How I goin' track down one goddess?"

"I tell you bumbye," she says, by which she means soon enough. Then she winks again.

I walk just a few steps from the registration desk to crater-view room one. This is the biggest view room in the hotel and usually costs double what I'm paying. Not a bad place to cool my heels before the long drive tomorrow to Kona and Waimea, on the other side of the island. Pualani must still like me. Or she's just full of *aloha*.

Though the best room in the house, it's spare like the rest. No TV, no radio, no cable or WīFi. Just a *koa* desk and chair, a small bath with shower, and a closet with a sliding door. There's a beautiful Hawaiian quilt on the double bed. But best of all is the sweeping view of Pele's domain.

I open the windows overlooking the crater, whiff sulfur in the air, and scan smoldering Kīlauea below. Across the desolate expanse, smoke plumes waft lazily into the sky. Despite their slow twirling, beneath them lies a massive unstoppable force—molten magma miles below the surface. And Pele stands for the power behind all this. No wonder so many believe she's a force to be reckoned with.

Turning my gaze away from the windows to the wall against the bed, I see a small door that appears to connect to the next room—crater view room three where guest Lars

Stapleton stayed. I unlock the door, not even stopping to think about any guests in the adjoining room who might not welcome my intrusion. The door opens to another identical door. That door is locked. To enter one room from the other, both doors must be unlocked. Obviously, guests in both rooms must desire and welcome such intimacy.

What this has to do with the death of Rex Ransom, if anything, I don't know. Ransom didn't die in his room. And when I was here with Donnie the door to room three was not open. Lars Stapleton from New Jersey remains off my list of suspects, for now.

At one I walk to the hotel dining room overlooking Kīlauea. It's been less than a week since I watched Rex and Donnie Ransom enjoy their last supper together at a candlelit table. The dining room looks different by daylight. Red oilcloths on the tables glint in the sun. The caldera appears to run for miles. It must be an optical illusion, but it looks like forever. At the far end, nearly out of sight, the smaller but more active Halema‘uma‘u Crater smolders.

I have my pick of tables, so grab one by a window. Just me and a bottle of Tabasco on the red oilcloth. While I wait for the waitress the image comes to mind of Donnie Ransom walking into the dining room leading her husband by the hand. A picture of devotion. But my cynical side chimes in: *He's loaded and she's half his age.* Then my more charitable side: *If she wanted him dead, why would she hire me to protect him?* But now I wonder again about the secrecy she insisted on. Was it to protect his pride, or to hide that she was having him watched?

I order a Volcano Burger and the waitress leaves me with the view and with my thoughts. When my burger arrives, I pass on the Tabasco and dig in. What Maile said about Donnie pops into my mind. Rex Ransom was not the first rich old man Donnie married. Now she's twice widowed. I look across the caldera and count the steam plumes twirling into the air. I get to twenty-two and stop. I'm procrastinating.

I pay for my burger and step outside onto the Crater Rim Trail. I hike through the tree ferns to The Steaming Bluff. The rotten-egg odor intensifies as I approach the vents. I stop at the exact spot where I found Ransom, lean over the railing, and peer into the gaping hole. It's warmer today and less misty, but the memory of what happened is seared into my mind.

I'm following him, the young woman in red approaches, Donnie calls me and frantically shows me the note, and then I return to find the woman gone and the old man in the vent. Before I dial 911, I survey the scene. I find nothing. No footprints, not even Ransom's. The trail reveals zero.

Since it's clearer today and the sun has broken through, I try my search again. I'm sure the guardrails by the vent have been dusted. But the fact that no suspects were pursued suggests that no usable prints were found. I go off the trail and explore in a circular, falcon-like pattern, making wider and wider sweeps as I walk in the tall brush. A couple strolls by arm-in-arm, giving me a look. I smile. I'm almost done and still find nothing.

Then I see a glint in the tall brown grass and reach for it. It's lipstick. I remove the cap and crank up the stick. Red.

Fiery red.

twenty-one

Wednesday morning I start early for Kailua-Kona. I take the Belt Road almost due south from Hawai'i Volcanoes National Park to the southern tip of the island—and the southern-most point in the United States. It's a craggy stretch with plenty to see—if you like rocks.

The Big Island, as its name implies, is the biggest island in the Hawaiian chain. It has more land area than all the other inhabited islands combined. The drive from Volcano House to the west side's most populous city will take me more than two hours. And the Kona district is not my only stop. From there I'm driving another hour north to Waimea, in the island's northern-most region of Kohala. Adding the return, I'll be on the road the better part of the day.

The long drive gives me time to think. I pull from my aloha shirt the lipstick I found near the steam vent where Ransom died.

Fiery red.

Any hope of usable prints has been dimmed by the lipstick's exposure to days of mist and sun and rain. Was this the same lipstick worn by the woman who approached Ransom?

Why would she take it along hiking? Maybe to freshen her appearance before meeting a man? An old man?

I slip the lipstick back into my shirt.

Finally come the outskirts of Kailua, the once sleepy fishing village and home of Hawaiian royalty. Kailua and the Kona District have experienced some of the same growing pains as other places in the islands. More building, more traffic, more tourist-oriented development.

I consult my map. Kathryn Ransom lives far from the congestion of Kailua's tourist trade. It wasn't always so busy here. I remember visiting family on the Big Island when I was a *keiki*. I'd fish from the lava rock seawall along Ali'i Drive, dangling my toes in the crystal-clear water and casting my line into blue Kailua Bay. Just a few hotels lined the shore back then, frequented by *kama'aina* and *akamai* travelers who knew about this quiet getaway—a world apart from the bustle of Waikīkī.

I turn off Hawai'i Belt Road just outside of town and weave my way into a gated retreat perched above the sea. Her home is hidden behind a grove of areca palms and a green-patina copper gate.

I call on an intercom and get buzzed through. The gate swings open and I edge down a gorgeous flagstone drive. More palms—stately Royals—line either side. At the end is an estate rambling over several prime oceanfront acres. I park under a granite-columned porte-cochere by a carriage house. I step out to the sound of pounding surf. *She did well in her divorce.*

I follow more flagstones to sea-blue stained glass doors and knock. Soon the statuesque woman I'd seen at the funeral appears. Kathryn Ransom smiles. Her shoulder-length brown hair is no less meticulously arranged than on the day of the funeral and, though silver-flecked, reminds me of Caitlin.

"Thank you for seeing me on such short notice, Mrs. Ransom," I say. "I'm very grateful."

"Please call me Kathryn," she says in a voice as lovely as her daughter's and leads me in. Up close, she's just as elegant as I remember. She's in cream today, rather than black, and it sets off her coloring nicely. I guess her age in the sixties—about twenty years older than Rex Ransom's second wife.

Kathryn Ransom's home looks way too big for one person; clearly it was the family residence before the divorce. As we walk there's a glimpse, on the right, into a spacious kitchen of oak and granite and stainless steel. A knife rack above one of the stone countertops glints with what looks like pricey German blades.

We pass into a magnificent living room overlooking the sea. The golden bamboo floor glows in the streaming sunlight. We sit on a white leather sofa, almost as immense as the white grand piano across from it. Lettering on the piano says STEINWAY & SONS.

Tommy would drool.

I start things off easy by gesturing to the piano. "That's a beautiful instrument."

"It's a concert grand," she says. "We bought it at the New York factory and had it shipped here." She pauses. "Do you like music?"

"I do. Would you play something for me?" I don't know why I say this. It just pops out.

Kathryn Ransom's face glows. "Yes, of course. What would you like to hear?"

"Maybe one of your favorites?"

"Okay." She rises and walks to the piano, sits, and lifts the fallboard covering the keys. Her profile at the white piano is silhouetted against the blue sea. She settles herself, takes a breath, and says, "This is a calm, contemplative little piece. It helped me through the divorce."

"What's it called?"

"'Gymnopédie' by Eric Satie." She pronounces it *zhim-no-PAY-dee*. And it might as well be Greek, because I have no idea what it means. Then she says, "Satie was French." So I know I'm way off.

She starts to play—slowly and softly. The tune is simple, serene, and haunting. Her fingers move gracefully over the keys. The piano sounds bell-like and brilliant. I can't believe I'm hearing concert hall music in a private home in Kailua-Kona. The melody calms me, yet makes me yearn. I know I've heard it before, but don't remember where or when.

As the serene tune continues I wonder what an equally serene world would be like—a world in perfect harmony. And while I know that's not possible, the piece puts me in a space where I can imagine it. Everything is ordered and beautiful. Everyone loves and cares. All work for peace and the common good. Nobody gets divorced. Nobody steals. Nobody cheats and lies. Nobody murders.

My reverie continues as long as the piece does—just a few precious minutes. When it's over, my hands feel damp.

She turns to me. "Did you like it?"

When she asks this I suddenly recall her ex-husband's limo driver saying, "She wen stab 'em, brah!" I can't picture it. *These graceful hands wielding a knife?* Then I remember her eyes turning blank at the funeral when she saw her ex with his second wife. *No love lost.*

A strained look now crosses Kathryn Ransom's face. Finally I choke out, "That was beautiful. You're very good."

"Thank you." She seems relieved. "Satie wrote two more variations. But I'll spare you for now."

With the musical prelude over, I start my questions. "Would you mind telling me about the time your husband checked into Hilo Hospital with a knife wound? I can't imagine you had anything to do with it. You just don't seem like the kind of person . . ."

Her eyes go blank—like at the funeral. I sit quietly and wait.

She doesn't speak. She turns back to the piano and starts to play again. The musical prelude is *not* over. The piece sounds like rippling water. It's beautiful. I'm entranced, by both the tune and her refusal to talk. I almost don't care. The melody carries me away.

When it ends she says, "That's Bach's 'Prelude in C'. So simple. So exquisite. Another little piece that helped me through the divorce."

I nod and wait.

She finally starts to talk. "Kai, I wasn't myself during the divorce. I was self-medicating to get through it—if you know what I mean."

I nod again. That's a euphemistic way of saying she was blasted.

"I just sort of snapped. I'd given him everything for thirty years. I gave him three children. I followed him everywhere—from one drilling site to another around the world.

I was devoted and loyal and loving. And—with him—that wasn't always easy."

"I understand." I let her keep going.

"But when he lied to me . . . when he deceived me . . . when he took up with that woman half his age behind my back." She pauses. "I'm not proud of what I did. At that moment, I wanted him dead."

"Do you mind if I ask you where you were on the morning your ex-husband did die?" I wonder if she's going to start playing again. She doesn't.

"I was driving from Volcano back to Kona. I stayed overnight with Stan Nagahara's wife. We've always been close and she wanted me with her after the service."

"Do you remember what time you drove?"

"Not exactly. I ate breakfast first with Kyoko. Maybe nine or nine-thirty?"

"Anyone ride with you?"

"Just me. Caitlin flew back to Honolulu. She had classes at the University."

"When did you learn of your ex-husband's death?"

"Oh, it wasn't until that night. Nobody official called me, of course. I'm not his wife anymore. I saw it on the TV news. Caitlin hadn't heard, nor her brothers on the mainland. I had to tell them."

"I'm sorry," I say.

"When the divorce was over, I just wanted to put him behind me. But my children still needed him. And he wasn't there. I'm sorry for them. Before he died they were just getting close to him again after a long estrangement. Why would I kill him? He was finally coming to his senses and considering his own family."

I shift gears. "Are you still in touch with Mr. Ransom's ex-partner, Mick London? I'm going to see him this afternoon. Anything you can tell me about him might help."

"Mick lost everything when Rex pulled out of Puna. I talked with him about six months ago. He's living in a tiny shack and drives an old beat up truck.

"I saw the truck," I say, "at the funeral."

"His belated entrance was hard to miss." Kathryn shakes her head. "From what I've heard, Mick ekes out a meager existence by scavenging scrap metal. Other than that, he just drinks and fishes. If he didn't fish, he wouldn't eat. This is a man who was once very successful. But when the company failed he discovered he was too old to start over. He blames Rex entirely."

"He's bitter about losing his business?"

"That's only half of it. Mick was dating Donnie Lam before she married Rex. She was some kind of PR person the company hired. She was already widowed, from what I heard. Then she latched onto my husband. I'm not much for women who do things like that."

I pull the lipstick I found on the Crater Rim Trail from my pocket and crank it open. "Does this look familiar?"

She studies its fiery red hue. "No. Should it?"

"Is it a color that you or, say, your daughter might wear? Or anybody you know?"

"I doubt it," she says. "Well, maybe Rex's second wife. That looks like her style. Where did you find it?"

I fudge. "Somebody dropped it and I picked it up."

We talk a while longer. What I finally take away from the interview is that Kathryn Ransom admits to stabbing her husband during their acrimonious divorce. She also admits to being in or around Volcano on the morning her husband died. She has no alibi as to her exact whereabouts. She says she was driving back to Kona alone. She had the opportunity to kill her husband. But to hear her talk now, not the motive. She claims she's over the divorce and over her late ex-husband. And I can't link her, at this point, to the young woman in red.

I find myself believing Kathryn Ransom. For now.

twenty-two

It's after one when the green copper gate at Kathryn Ransom's oceanfront estate closes behind me. I make tracks for Waimea.

The highway north of Kailua along the Kohala Coast looks like a bomb went off. From the mountains to the sea, the roadside is charred and empty. It wasn't a bomb that did this. It was a volcano. Hualālai, the island's third most active. The lack of rain in this arid region doesn't help recovery. The lava flow looks like it happened just yesterday, not two hundred years ago. The only things that seem to sprout in the blackness are the luxury oceanfront resorts at Waikoloa and the cryptic white coral graffiti along the highway: "Shade Dada," "Thelma + Louise," and "sadkids.com." And the not so cryptic: "Aloha, Mom," "Suck it up," and "Jess loves Bryan." Or is it "Jeff loves Byron"?

I pass the sprawling resorts along the shore and then climb northeast into the ranchlands of Waimea, officially called Kamuela. The air cools and the roadside greens. This is the high country of Parker Ranch—famous for its fine beef cattle—where verdant pasturelands roll gently from snow-capped Mauna Kea toward the sparkling blue sea.

Kathryn Ransom wasn't exaggerating when she said Mick London lives in a shack. An abandoned utility shed, really. Weathered grey boards. Rusty tin roof. One window and one door. Next to the shed is his beat-up truck. The bed is heaped with scrap metal. And one fishing pole. The faded letters on the door—LONDON DRILLING EQUIPMENT—make little sense now.

The shed's door doesn't have a knob. Only a hasp and padlock. The lock is open. The key in. I assume that means Mick is home. I knock on a grey board, my knuckles managing to avoid splinters.

"Jus' a min—" drawls a slurred voice from behind the boards.

I wait. Crashing sounds make me think I've come at a bad time. I check my watch. It's a little after two.

The door finally creaks open, revealing the white-bearded Father Time I saw at the funeral. Mick London is hunched over and smells like a barroom. His flushed face suggests too much whiskey and too much Hawaiian sun. And his murky eyes more of the same. The grime on his tattered shirt and holey jeans reminds me of the Chinatown winos who hang out by Mrs. Fujiyama's dumpster.

The shack smells like he does. A half empty whiskey bottle sits on the dirt floor by his unmade cot. He motions me to sit in the only chair in the place. He stumbles to his cot.

"Wan' some?" He reaches for the whiskey.

I shake my head. "I'm good."

"Doan mine if I do." He takes a swig.

I thank him for seeing me on short notice. Then I start off friendly and easy. I ask him where he fishes.

"Fissssh?" he looks surprised. "Near Mauna Kea Resor'," he manages to say. "On the rocks."

"What do you catch?"

"Ulua," he replies.

"Really?" *Ulua* is a large, white-meat game fish, prized by local fishermen.

"Yeahhh." He takes another drink. "Fur dinner." Fish seems to be, as Kathryn Ransom said, his only sustenance. Besides whisky.

I ask him how he teamed up with Rex Ransom.

"Tha' *sonofabitch!*" Mick reddens. "We go *waaay* back." Mick says he came with Ransom Geothermal from Montana to be Rex's plant manager in Puna. But then he started a side business with his boss's blessing and sold his wares exclusively to him. It was a great deal for Ransom, I gather, since Mick took the risks of acquiring and stocking the equipment. He admits he made good money while the arrangement lasted, but was not prepared—not even told—when Ransom abruptly pulled out of Puna. Mick eventually filed for bankruptcy.

"Did Ransom help you in any way?" I ask.

"Tha' *sonofabitch?*" Mick is about to boil. He explains he took Ransom to court, but the CEO's shifty lawyers prevailed.

"Too bad," I say, trying to keep him going.

"An' tha' *bitsch* he marry—" Mick spits out the words. "She wuz gonna marry meee!"

"Donnie?" It sounds unlikely.

"Yeahhh, tha' *shlutt!*" Mick goes on to say that when Donnie sniffed what was coming—his bankruptcy—she jumped ship.

"Make you angry to see them together at the funeral?" I ask.

Mick's face reddens. He gawks at me.

He's right. It was a stupid question.

"Dey deserff eash other!" He sneers. "Doze two!" Mick claims Donnie only married Ransom for his money. Which gives her a good reason to want him dead. "If Pele didn' keeel 'em," Mick says, "Donnie did!"

"How could Donnie kill Rex?" I ask. "I was with her when he died."

"Jus' kiddin'," Mick says. "Sour grapes."

I shrug. "Do you mind if I ask where you were when he died, the Wednesday after the funeral?"

"Doan remember," he says. And I believe him. He was smashed.

"Did you drive home after the service? Did you stay another night in Volcano?"

Mick looks puzzled. "Now I remember—I drove but I got shleepy. I pulled off an' shlept."

"Where?" He obviously couldn't see straight.

"I dunno."

"Did you get a room?"

"Nah. Wadda I wan' a room fur? Got my truck."

"Did you see or talk to anyone?"

He shakes his head. He's got no alibi. He seems to know that. But I've got no evidence against him. He seems to know that too.

We talk more. I ask more questions. Time passes.

"Thanks," I finally say. "Gotta long drive back to Volcano."

He nods and I stand. Mick rolls back on his cot and hoists his whiskey. "To yo' healff."

I let myself out and soon begin winding down the Hamakua Coast, mulling over the interview. *Opportunity.* Mick London has no alibi on the morning Ransom died. *Motive.* He's still bitter about his old boss taking away his livelihood and, Mick claims, his woman. *Means.* But how could he do it? Even if he showed up on the Crater Rim Trail that fateful morning, Mick was in no condition to kill a flea. And what possible connection could he have to the young woman in red?

* * *

Back at the Volcano House Wednesday evening I get a call from Tommy Woo. He tells his obligatory jokes and then asks, "Whatever happened to your little *lei* girl and her thug boyfriend?"

"Blossom may be little, Tommy. But she's not a girl. She's twenty. If you want to know, she's staying in my apartment while I'm on the Big Island."

"*Bad* idea," he says.

I know he's right, but I say, "You yourself advised she should disappear for a while."

Tommy shrugs it off. "What are you doing back on the Big Island?"

"Didn't I tell you? Ransom's daughter hired me to look into his death. She doesn't believe an accident put him in that steam vent."

"You're investigating *Pele?*" Tommy's tone suggests he's ribbing me.

"Yeah," I respond in kind. "I've got her on the ropes. I'll have a complete confession before I leave. Guaranteed." Then I go him one better. "And if the goddess refuses to confess, there's a few human suspects I like for the crime."

"Good man . . ." Tommy pauses. "But you better be careful about lending your apartment to the *lei* girl. When her ex-boyfriend finds out, he's gonna think you're her new guy."

"His name's Junior and he already thinks that. He's wrong."

There's a beep on my cell phone indicating an incoming call. I glance at caller ID. *Maile?* No. Area code 303. *Denver.* The Pali case. *I've got to take this call!* But just as I tell Tommy to hang on, the number disappears.

"*Sh—!*" I say.

"What's wrong?" Tommy asks.

"I got another call, from Denver—probably the Lindquist twins' friend who may be the key to the Pail case. I've been waiting on her for a week."

"She'll leave a message," Tommy says. "Anyway, you better watch your back for this Junior dude. I bet he's got a rap sheet as long as his arm."

"And outstanding warrants," I say. "He's gonna do some time, once HPD gets him off the street."

Then Tommy coyly asks, "Remember what I told you about Zahra?"

At first I draw a blank. "Oh, yeah. You're going to ask Zahra to marry you."

"Right," he explains. "Otherwise she has to go back to Kenya."

My phone beeps again—this time with the tone indicating a new voicemail. *From Denver?*

"Sounds like you've got it all figured out." I'm getting impatient because I've already reminded him about his two marriages. After the second he got his cats, Miles and Charlie, and swore off marriage forever. Truth is, Tommy isn't cracked up to be a husband. His late-night gigs after long days at his office mean he's seldom home. I'm surprised his cats haven't left him.

"I've got to pull the trigger soon," Tommy continues. "I've got to co-sign that fiancé visa, or she has to go back."

"Tommy, you already have my blessing. Whatever makes you happy, my friend."

"Well, I have a favor to ask you about the wedding." He pauses and I wonder what's coming. "Would you be my best man?"

"Do I have to wear a tux?" I'm looking for a way out. I'm not much for weddings, or any kind of formal events. Sunset on the beach with a few beers. That's my kind of celebration.

"Nah," Tommy replies. "Zahra and I are wearing African wedding robes. You can wear whatever you like."

"Swell," I say. "I'll be there."

"T'anks, eh?" Tommy hangs up.

I call my voicemail and retrieve my new message.

"Hi, this is Ashley," says the twenty-something female voice. "I'm totally sorry I haven't called you back. I like left my cell phone on the airplane, you know?"

Is she asking me or telling me?

"It took the airline a really long to find it! *Bogus.*"

Bogus?

"Whatever," Ashley continues. "I'm flying back tomorrow—okay?—and can meet you Friday, like at noon. I work at Safari in Ala Moana Shopping Center. For sure I'll bring my pics of Heather and Lindsay's twenty-first birthday party. *Way* sad."

Then she says as an afterthought. "Oh, Ethan got your messages. He's like just a guy I know in Denver. He wasn't at the twins' party."

Okay, Ethan wasn't at the twins' party. But why was his phone number riding with them in Fireball's car?

I save Ashley's message. Now I have another question to ask her on Friday.

twenty-three

Thursday morning I stop by the desk at the Volcano House and ask Pualani if she has any idea where I might find Ikaika "Sonny Boy" Chang. It's a big island—but not that big. Like most island communities, this one is tight.

Hearing Sonny Boy's name seems to startle her. She composes herself and then says that after the Save Pele Coalition disowned him for dragging Ransom from his car, Sonny Boy has been in and out of prison, but recently returned on parole to Volcano, where he lives only about a mile away. She claims he's a new man. *We'll see.*

"Sonny Boy stay only one mile from da Volcano House? You got one address fo' 'em?"

"No need address," she says. "Volcano one small kine village, yeah?" She tells me how to find his digs. "But he no *make* da geothermal guy. I know. Pele da one."

"How you know he no do 'em?"

"Jus' know." She gets a tortured look on her face. "Sonny Boy at home," she says.

I wonder how she knows. "You okay?" I ask.

She nods, but her eyes tell a different story. Leaving the desk I ponder what just happened and what Pualani has to do with Sonny Boy.

* * *

I drive Hilo-bound on Highway 11, from the main gate of Hawai'i Volcanoes National Park to Volcano Village. The journey downslope is barely one mile.

In less than a minute I turn off the highway into Volcano Village. The village's scattered homes and B&Bs spread over several miles of high rainforest at the cool elevation of nearly four thousand feet. Its post office and dozen or so small businesses—restaurants, hardware store, and two general stores—all straddle Old Volcano Road, once the main highway around the island. Frequent rains keep everything in Volcano green and mossy.

The old highway that connects the village's main streets is damp. It's not raining now, but the next shower is always coming. Only a few thousand people live here. The village gives off a hang-loose-aging-hippie vibe. It's a place where independent-minded artists, crafts- and trade-persons, retirees, wilted flower children, and corporate dropouts end up after long years of playing the game. Not the mention lifelong residents who are none of the above.

How Sonny Boy fits into this vibe, I don't know. He certainly wasn't hang-loose when he dragged Ransom from his car some two decades ago. I recall the CEO's limo driver, Kawika, saying Sonny Boy grew *pakalolo* back then on the land cleared for drilling. Maybe protecting his crop made his protest turn violent? When I asked why Chang had attended

Stan Nagahara's funeral, Kawika said the former protester was probably just glad to see Nagahara dead. And would also be glad to see Ransom dead.

No surprise Caitlin named Sonny Boy her suspect number one.

Off the old highway sits a plantation-style cottage on an overgrown jungle that's seen better days. I pull in. That's not where Sonny Boy lives. He lives down an equally overgrown path that weaves out of sight behind the cottage. I drive down the path, just wide enough for one car, into a clearing. Sitting on blocks is a rust-orange shipping container, the kind you see on Matson ships, with a window cut in at one end and a door at the other.

I knock on the rusty metal door. I expect it to open to the sweet-sour odor of *pakalolo*. No. The container smells like wild ginger. Has he kicked the habit?

He steps toward me. He's not a big man, but wiry and muscular.

"Ikaika?" I say. "I'm Kai. Pualani say maybe you like talk wit' me?"

"Shoots," he says, "Call me Sonny Boy." He shows me in.

The ginger scent intensifies as I follow him. Then I see why. In one corner a plastic bucket that says London Drilling Equipment—a relic of his protesting days?—brims with the yellow ginger that grows along the highway.

"You know Pualani long?" I ask and check him out more closely.

Mop of brown hair. Sun-bleached dreadlocks. Dark, intense eyes—with the martyr look in those biblical illustrations of Jesus. But Sonny Boy's eyes are fiercer.

"Pualani no tell you?" His fierce eyes warm.

"No tell me what?" I say.

"I'm Malia's daddy."

Whose daddy? Then it dawns on me. *Pualani's tortured look. Her teenage girl.*

"Shoots," I say. Sonny Boy and Pualani must have hung out together during the protests. Then on one of his return trips from prison, I guess, Pualani had his baby.

"You surprise?" he asks. "Das why I here in Volcano. To be wit' Malia."

I shrug and look around the rusty container. On the plank floor sits a small bookshelf with volumes on Hawaiian history and law. And a photo of a smiling teenager who looks like Pualani. No TV. No electricity, I guess. There's one short stool and a sagging single bed against one metal wall and a surfboard against the other. That's it.

I try to connect with him. "Where you surf, brah?"

"Pohoiki in Lower Puna." Sonny Boy gestures to the stool. I plant myself on it and he sits cross-legged on the floor. "Da bes', brah. But when I can go surfing? No wheels."

"Maybe we go togeddah sometime," I say. "I got one car hea, but no board."

He perks up. Regardless of what I've heard about him, I'm starting to like Sonny Boy. His daughter is his life. He surfs. Maybe he is a changed man?

"What you t'ink 'bout da guy Rex Ransom wen' *huli* in da steam vent?" I ask.

Sonny Boy's eyes turn fierce again. "Good riddance. He deserve 'em. He rip up da rainforest and he rape Pele."

"You like tell me, brah, you hea when he wen' *huli?*"

"Wuz hea in Volcano," Sonny Boy says. "Pele did 'em. Case close. When I pull da guy outta his car, I do 'em fo' Pele. She acting t'rough me."

"Maybe Pele act t'rough again?"

"Nah," Sonny Boy says. "Dis time she no need me, or anybody." He looks me in the eyes. "No mo' jail again fo' dat guy. *Nevah.* I stay wit' Malia."

Sonny Boy didn't get off lightly. Most men in Ransom's position, for PR sake, would have let an incident like this go. But he pressed charges, attended court hearings, and spoke out against Chang at every opportunity. Why wouldn't Sonny Boy carry a grudge? Not to mention that he seems to think his actions were divinely inspired.

"Why I *make* Ransom?" he continues. "No need. Pele do 'em. All t'ree dead now. Firs' da plant manager. Den da attorney. And now da beeg boss. It more den one coincidence. Don't you t'ink, brah?"

"Could be," I say. And I wonder: *Would he risk parole to take another hack at Ransom? Would he risk being with his daughter?*

"If you don't believe me," Sonny Boy says, "ask Pele's sistah, Hi'iaka. She see da whole t'ing."

"She see Pele kill Ransom? Da crazy woman? Da escape mental patient?"

"Sure t'ing, brah. Go ask her yourself."

"Where I fine' her?"

"Secret place," Sonny Boy says. "You got one car?"

I nod. "Told you awready, brah."

"I take you, den," he says.

twenty-four

Sonny Boy and I climb into my car. He's carrying a plastic shopping bag half filled with papayas and apple-bananas. We start to roll and he says, "You like take one *makana,* one gift, to Hi'iaka?"

"What *kine* gift?" I ask.

"One bottle of gin," Sonny Boy says. "An' one pack of Camels." He tells me Hi'iaka should be honored in the same way her sister Pele is honored.

"Fo' sure?" I'm thinking this is a scam. I'm thinking the gin and Camels will end up in Sonny Boy's hands.

He nods. He's not kidding.

Sonny Boy directs me to a little general store on the Old Volcano Highway. It's one of those tiny, all-purpose marts where villagers can get everything they need without having to drive to Hilo. The fifth of gin and pack of Camels sets me back nearly twenty-five bucks. I pocket the receipt, wondering how to justify this expense to my client.

We climb into the car again and head into the park. I take Crater Rim Drive past the Volcano House and start to circle the three-mile Kīlauea Caldera. Sonny Boy is not saying where we're going.

So I ask, "How you know da goddess?"

"Hiʻiaka?" he asks.

"Yeah, Hiʻiaka—Serena Barrymore."

"From da protess'," he says. "Not name Serena anymo'. Dat was befor' da protess'. We protess' togeddah da drilling in da rainforest."

"You know da guy she *make*, da guy she push in front da bus?"

"Nevah know da guy. Was in prison den."

I nod and keep driving. The caldera stays on our left as we continue along the counterclockwise circle. It's midmorning and The Steaming Bluff, where Ransom died, raises a thin mist into the sapphire sky. The odor of sulfur seeps into the car, despite closed windows.

I turn to Sonny Boy. "Where we going?"

He nods in a forward direction.

I keep my eyes on the road ahead. We pass the Kīlauea Military Camp, site of Stan Nagahara's funeral, and then the Jaggar Museum and the Southwest Rift Overlook.

Sonny Boy's face looks confident, even amused. He's got a secret. And he knows I want it. But at least he seems to be cooperating with me. Or is he leading me into some remote, quiet place where I could easily disappear?

Soon we approach Halemaʻumaʻu Crater, where Karl Kroften's crushed BMW was found.

I shrug. "Here? Where Pele live?"

Sonny Boy gazes ahead and grins, like the cat that ate the bird. He's enjoying himself. He likes to keep me wondering.

We swing around the bottom of the circle, where Crater Rim Drive carves into lava flows of the 1970s and 1980s. As long ago as that was, the roadside still looks charred. Only a few sprigs of green sprout from cracks in the black rock.

We pass Devastation Trail—a winding path into a scorched forest. Then Thurston Lava Tube, a tunnel as big around as an airliner that was formed by a river of molten lava. Sonny Boy raises his brows and says, "Almos'."

I drive by the Thurston Tube. About a half-mile later he says, "Pull ovah."

I do and we climb out. He grabs his shopping bag with papayas and bananas and I grab my gin and smokes. We walk back toward the lava tube.

"Where we goin', brah?" I ask.

"I show you." He keeps walking.

We walk in single file along the shoulder of the road. Soon Sonny Boy steps through a break in a fern hedge and we find ourselves on a trail that weaves through a forest. The air is moist and cool. An invisible stream gurgles. A chorus of crickets and birds serenades us.

"Dis where Hi'iaka live?" I ask. "On dis trail?"

"In one secret lava tube, brah," Sonny Boy says.

I consider what he's said. The Thurston Tube is the most famous, but there are hundreds in the park and in the East Rift Zone where lava flows to the sea. Some tubes have been charted and explored, by the likes of Stan Nagahara who died in one, but others remain mysteries.

Sonny Boy leads the way. The trail gets narrower and the forest thicker. This would be a perfect place to rub out a PI who's too *niele*—too nosey. If the ex-con has anything to do with Rex Ransom's death, or the deaths of his two officers under equally suspicious circumstances, he could disappear me here—if not forever, for a very long time. I size up Sonny Boy again and decide to take my chances.

"We there yet?" I'm already breaking into a sweat. The sun is blazing, we're hiking up and down and around, and there's not much air among the giant ferns.

"Almos'," he says again.

And, true to his word, not one minute later he slows down, stops, and scans the trail as if he's searching for something. He looks and looks and then says: "Hea." Meaning, this is the place.

He squeezes through some more tree ferns into one of those hidden, uncharted lava tubes. While the Thurston Tube is lighted for the convenience and safety of park visitors, this tube is dark.

We head in. We've got no flashlight. But Sonny Boy lights a match. We can see again. The tube starts off barely high enough to stand, then gets smaller. We duck our heads. The floor is rough and uneven. Sonny Boy lights another match.

I'm smelling sulfur again. The tube narrows. I see a dim light ahead. And then I smell fresh air.

"Almos' dere," Sonny Boy says.

Finally we step into full light. And a fairy tale.

A rainbow arches over a grove of *'ōhi'a* and a gently rolling stream. Brilliant red birds, *'I'iwi,* the Hawaiian honeycreeper, hover over the colorful *lehua* blooms. Everything is green and dewy and luminous in the sun. It looks like an enchanted rainforest. *Unreal.*

"Dis where da goddess stay," he says. He points in the direction of the rainbow.

Under the resplendent arch above that *'ōhi'a* grove a bare-breasted woman dances the *hula*.

"Das her?"

Sonny Boy nods.

twenty-five

She's wearing a red *haku lei* on her grey head and a ti-leaf skirt. Another red *lei* hangs around her neck, resting on her breasts. She's not ample like Hawaiian goddesses of legend. I can count her ribs as she dances the *hula*—her hips swaying, her arms undulating, her hands in gentle fluid motion. Her eyes are closed and she chants as she moves.

Sonny Boy puts a finger to his lips. *"Ssssshh,"* he says.

Quietly we come closer. Barrymore's red *lei* are *lehua* flowers from the *'ōhi'a* tree. The tree she killed for.

She stands on a mossy perch above us, her delicate *lei* contrasting with her leathery skin. Neither her complexion nor her features look Hawaiian. Nearly three decades ago she threatened Ransom and accused him of raping her sister and of desecrating her rainforest. Back then, Barrymore was considered crazy, but harmless. That was before she committed second-degree murder. If she could push a man into the path of a bus, she could push Ransom into a steam vent.

An escaped mental patient can't make it long on the outside without help. *Sonny Boy.* Why is he helping her? Did they conspire to kill Ransom?

Her eyes suddenly open and she peers down on us.

"I am Pele's favorite sister, Hi'iaka, patron of *hula* and protector of trees and ferns and rainforests." She speaks slowly and distantly, like she's in a trance. "I bring new life and heal the land after Pele's lava flows. I was conceived in Tahiti, daughter of Haumea and Kāne. My beloved sister carried me to Hawai'i cradled in her bosom."

"Hi'iaka, it's me," Sonny Boy says. "I bring you one *makana,* one gift."

She perks up when she hears the word *makana*. Sonny Boy hands her the papayas and apple-bananas. She takes them.

"Dis Kai." He gestures to me. "Kai bring one *makana* too."

I hand her the gin and cigarettes. She sets them on her mossy perch next to Sonny Boy's gift.

"Kai like talk wit' you," he says.

She smiles eerily, which I guess means, "Okay."

I start to ask a question, but get distracted by her breasts. I'm not used to seeing women unclothed in broad daylight. I try to keep my eyes on her face. Some words finally tumble out: "Beautiful *hula*—beautiful forest."

"This is my *'ōhi'a* grove," she says in perfect English. "The *'ōhi'a* is sacred to me. I am its protector."

"To cut them down is a sacrilege," I say. "Just like drilling in the Wao Kele O Puna rainforest. Do you remember the drilling?"

"Hi'iaka never forgets," she says.

"And the protests in the rainforest against the man you called 'the evil one'?"

"He deserved death at Pele's hands," she says.

"Not death at *your* hands?"

"Pele took her own revenge. I saw with my own eyes."

"You saw Pele pitch him into the steam vent?"

"Yes, I saw."

This conversation is getting loonier by the minute. But I'm beginning to wonder who's loonier: her for telling me this wacky stuff, or me for asking questions that prompt it.

"Okay, Goddess Hiʻiaka." I play along. "Tell me what you saw."

"Pele was in her most provocative *kinolau*—flowing red dress, shimmering long hair, vivid eyes, and lips as fiery as a lava flow."

Barrymore didn't have to see the woman on the trail to get these details. This guise is legendary. I'm not convinced.

I turn to Sonny Boy, who's taking it all in.

"It da truth," he says. "The goddess nevah lie."

She continues: "The old man—the evil one—saw Pele coming and tried to run. But he fell to the ground, gasping for air."

Was that the thud and groan I heard? I wonder. But I reply, "How did he get into the vent?"

"Pele," she says again. "Then she ran down the trail past me."

"You're sure you saw her?"

"I'm sure because she dropped something."

"What?" I ask, expecting more nonsense.

"The lipstick that makes her lips fiery red."

"Can't be." The words slip out.

"I held the lipstick in my own hands," Barrymore insists. "Then I left it along the trail, in case my sister came back for it. She didn't. She kept running."

From my pocket I pull the lipstick. "Did it look like this?"

"Yes," Barrymore says. "Just like that."

Sonny Boy turns to me. "Believe now?"

twenty-six

We make our return trip through the dark tunnel. My skeptical side is protesting. I almost believe the young woman I saw on the trail—the same woman Serena Barrymore says she saw—was a *kinolau* of Pele. Almost. I air my doubts.

"Madame Pele immortal, yeah?" I ask Sonny Boy.

"Das right," he replies.

"Den why she need one mortal lipstick? Why not she jus' make her lips any kine color she want?"

"Dunno, brah," answers Sonny Boy. "Pele do whatevah she want. If she want one mortal lipstick, she do 'em."

"Or maybe Goddess Hiʻiaka jus' dress up like Pele? Maybe Hiʻiaka herself pitch Ransom inside da vent?"

"Don't t'ink so, brah," he says. "Hiʻiaka too old. Maybe she can pitch 'em inside da vent, but she no can look like one young *wahine*."

Sonny Boy has a point. The woman I saw was definitely young. Serena Barrymore could not have resembled that woman, even in the mist. As we emerge from the tube into daylight and walk back to the car, I realize my investigation so far has turned up more evidence implicating Pele than any human suspect. That's fine—if you believe in goddesses.

For the sake of thoroughness, I have Sonny Boy write in my spiral notebook his recollection of Barrymore's story, signed and dated—the loony tale of a crazy woman verified by an ex-con on parole. *Solid evidence?* The best I've got.

* * *

Back at the Volcano House I grab a sandwich in the hotel dining room. After lunch I'm walking by the reception desk where Pualani has just been extending her *aloha* to a hotel guest.

"Eh, Kai," Pualani says, "So you meet da *lolo wahine* dat t'ink she one goddess?"

"How'd you know?" I ask, before I put two and two together and come up with the inevitable: Sonny Boy.

"Jus' know." Pualani says again. "She no mo' Goddess Hi'iaka den dis bell on da desk." *Ding!—Ding!* Pualani rings the little chrome bell for effect. "She *lolo*. Da *wahine* sick."

I agree with her. "She say she see Pele, in da *kinolau* of one beautiful young *wahine*, pitch da geothermal boss inside da vent. You evah see one woman like dat 'round hea?"

"I no see her," she says, "but was Pele. She *make* da oddah two. Why not da boss? Pele your suspect numbah one!"

"You t'ink so?"

"Fo' sure. You gotta go to Halema'uma'u Crater at sunset wit' *'ōhelo* berries. Make her one offering. She come to you. Guarantee."

I slowly nod.

But, Pualani warns me, it's not the best time to visit the crater. Its floor—the thin crust resting on a lake of boiling lava—is bulging. Park volcanologists worry another eruption is coming. She describes fiery fountains spewing ash and molten rock into the air. She cautions me to be careful.

"T'anks, eh?" I think of the cliché: *fool's errand.* Then I go it one better: *dangerous fool's errand.*

Back in my room I catch up on paperwork. I write out detailed notes about my four interviews on the Big Island with Kathryn Ransom, Mick London, Ikaika "Sonny Boy" Chang, and Serena Barrymore, a.k.a. Goddess Hi'iaka. I will refer to these notes when I report back to my client. I can't count out any of these four suspects just yet. But while all four had, to varying degrees, motive, opportunity, and means to kill Rex Ransom, the interviews lead me to believe none actually did kill him. Unless one of the four incriminates him- or herself, or unless another suspect surfaces, I'm left with only *Pele.*

Barrymore claims she saw the goddess heave Ransom into the vent. I can dismiss her description of Pele's widely-known *kinolau,* but not the lipstick I later recovered on the trail. Barrymore had to be there for that. And so I'm stuck with her story. Stuck at least with part of it. To believe it all, I'd have to believe that the goddess materialized bodily on this earth and caused the death of a mortal man.

That's a huge leap.

I lie back on the bed and decide that it might not be a bad idea to at least check in with Pele later at the Halema'uma'u Crater. Maybe it could help me get into a frame of mind to understand how so many people, some of them at least apparently sane, could conclude that it had to be the goddess who pushed the old man to his death.

I'm not a normally a napper, but the long drive yesterday and fitful sleep last night make me drift off.

Suddenly I'm on the edge of the crater at sunset gazing into the fiery pit. Standing over the hiss and roar, I wait for the goddess to appear. Finally she does. Pele rises out of the flames as the seductive young woman I saw on the trail. She says my name and promises to tell me everything. Before she does I awake.

It's late afternoon—little time to spare before sunset. I drag myself out to gather an offering for Pele. Yes, I actually do this.

I don't have to hike far on the Crater Rim Trail. Just to The Steaming Bluff. Sulfur fills the air. By the vent where I found the old man I spot the green-leafed stems of the *'ōhelo* plant reaching skyward and carrying pale yellow to bright red clusters of fruit, about the size of blueberries. There's plenty to choose from. The *nene,* or Hawaiian goose, loves these berries and disperses their seeds widely. The berries aren't fully ripe. I'm a bit early to pick, since peak season is June through October, but I doubt the goddess will mind. Or even notice.

One stem yields up two or three berries, another nearly a dozen. I end up with several stems—berries and leaves and all—and carry them back to my room.

Since sunset comes at quarter to seven in early April, I make reservations for dinner at eight. An hour should be more than enough time to interview a goddess.

But what do I know? I've never done it before.

* * *

Fifteen minutes before sunset—I hate being late—I pass the registration desk where Pualani is still working. I hold up my stems of *'ōhelo* berries and say, "On my way."

"Bettah go fas'," she says. "Da Park Service gonna close da Halema'uma'u overlook."

"Why dey close da overlook?"

"Cuz da crater floor bulging. Maybe dey t'ink one eruption coming."

"I going." I make tracks to my car.

I head south again on Crater Rim Drive toward Halema'uma'u. About half way there I pass the Jaggar Observatory and Museum where Park Service personnel are loading barricades into pickup trucks. I mash the gas pedal. Once the barricades go up, I've got no chance with Pele.

Even from a mile away I can see the smoke—a massive column spiraling into the sunset sky.

I pull in at the Halema'uma'u overlook, grab my sprigs of *'ōhelo* berries, and walk toward the hissing and rumbling. The sulfur smell thickens. It's hard to draw a breath.

The sun sinks to the crater's western rim. I consider turning back. But I keep walking.

twenty-seven

The first thing I see on the path to the crater's edge is this sign:

> **WARNING**
>
> STAY ON ESTABLISHED TRAILS.
>
> STAY OUT OF CAVES AND CRACKS.
>
> POTENTIALLY LIFE-THREATENING
>
> CONCENTRATIONS
>
> OF CARBON DIOXIDE.

I'm hiking just to the overlook—only a short distance on the three-mile Halemaʻumaʻu Trail—but I make a mental note and look around. The landscape is rock. There's nothing green. Smoke from the crater keeps billowing. The hissing and rumbling grow louder. I move on and pass another sign.

THE "FIREPIT" OF HALEMAʻUMAʻU

Halemaʻumaʻu Crater is the site of the most eruptions at the summit of Kīlauea Volcano. Between 1905 and 1924, a period of about 20 years, a dazzling lake of molten lava circulated within its walls. Then, in 1924, the lake drained away, allowing groundwater to penetrate deep inside the volcano. Enormous steam explosions resulted, showering the landscape with rocky debris, still visible around the rim today.

When the floor of the pit abruptly rises or falls, as is occurring now, things can happen fast. I plan to be outta here if they do.

Upon reaching the overlook, I peer down. The crater is about a half-mile across and a hundred yards deep. Molten lava gurgles through cracks in the bulging floor. The fiery pool is a fraction of the whole, but it's liquid and moving. Flames lick up the crater wall. And from the flames comes that twisting column of smoke.

My eyes smart. I blink away tears.

The last beams of the setting sun flicker over the crater's edge. The sky around the sun whitens like a halo, but elsewhere darkens. Lava below in the pit takes on a crimson glow. Flames flare like torches. The molten lake becomes luminous—in the same hot hue as the flames.

By the overlook there's a small platform surrounded by a picket fence and another sign that I can barely read in the diminishing light:

> 'Āina a ke akua e noho ai
>
> Land where the goddess dwells

Pele's home. The sign reminds me of the warning delivered to Ransom's wife moments before he died: "As you value your health and your life keep away from Pele . . . Deadly." Had he heeded that warning he might still be alive. And I would not be here.

Turns out I'm not the only one bringing her an offering tonight. Standing by the fence, a few feet in front of me, a ponytailed girl drapes a *lei* around the pickets. The fence is already festooned with half a dozen *lei*. Just beyond sits a plate of mangos and papayas and a bottle of liquor—I can't make out the label—wrapped in *ti* leaves. And on the barren earth around the plate are more *lei* and flowers, and sprigs of *'ōhelo* berries like I've brought.

Ponytail whispers several words I can't hear and one I can: "Pele." She's smiling through her tears. *Tears of joy— unlike mine?* I don't know. I'm a guy. But something has just happened here that's meaningful to her.

She's so into her feelings that she doesn't even notice me as she walks by, leaving me alone at the overlook. The sun's afterglow fades above the crater's rim. The fire pit's hue deepens. And it growls.

I feel like a fool. I'm standing here teary-eyed with these sprigs in my hand like they're flowers for a blind date. Will that seductive woman I saw in my dreams appear? *Right.* I have no idea what to say. But I don't have forever to say it. This crater could blow, or the barricades go up. Either way, I'll have to leave.

I'm about to screw up my courage when I hear another kind of rumbling in the lot. A motorcycle. A man dismounts his bike in the growing darkness and makes his way up the trail to the overlook.

Another guy? Another offering?

He struts up to where I'm standing like he really knows what he's doing. He's in black motorcycle leathers. His face is seriously sunburned. His salt and pepper beard is windswept. On his right hand, which is clutching a book, is tattooed an image of a Sunday school Jesus; on his left the words, GOD'S CHILD.

"Hello, brother," he says. "I just rode all the way from Kona." He may have ridden from Kona, but his words and appearance suggest he's from the mainland.

"Howzit," I say. I could use a little support, so I ask: "Are you here on a mission?"

"Right on, brother," he says, and holds up the book. It's a Bible. "I'm here to deny Pele exists. I'm going to say so right over this burning pit."

"It's been done." I relate to him how Princess Kapiolani defied the goddess over this same pit in 1823. Her followers warned her not to. But she did anyway and survived—a fact that put a big dent in the cult of Pele and furthered the efforts of the Christian missionaries in the islands.

"Never mind about the Hawaiian Princess. I need to do this for myself." He steps up to the picket fence. "It's a test of faith."

He opens his Bible to the first of about a dozen bookmarks. He announces: "Exodus, chapter twenty." Then he shouts: "'I am the Lord thy God, who have brought thee out of the land of Egypt, out of the house of bondage.

Thou shalt have no other gods before me.'" He lists various forbidden idols and graven images, adding Pele to the lot, and then shouts: "'Thou shalt not bow down thyself to them, nor serve them, for I, the Lord thy God, am a jealous God.'"

The fire pit grumbles. Lava shoots into the air.

He flips pages to his next bookmark and says: "Deuteronomy, chapter eight." He shouts: "'If thou forget the Lord thy God, and walk after other gods, and serve them, and worship them, I testify against you this day that ye shall surely perish.'"

More thunder. More fountains. He turns to another bookmark and says, "Leviticus, chapter twenty-six. Again he shouts: "'Ye shall make no idols . . .'"

The ground shakes like an earthquake.

I'm afraid the crater's ready to blow. And I haven't said a single word yet to Pele. Meanwhile this guy has maybe ten bookmarks to go. It's not my style to argue with complete strangers about religion, but I have only one shot at this offering to Pele, and he's making it impossible.

"Hey, brah. You have your god," I hear myself saying. "Why not let Hawaiians have theirs?"

But he turns back to the fiery pit and shouts: "Pele, you false god, you have no power over me. You have no power over anyone. I dare you to show yourself—"

A lava jet shoots into the darkness.

He slaps his Bible shut, turns, and starts back to his motorcycle. He's not four strides from me before I know we're in trouble. Another fountain goes off. The ground shakes again. Then more jets. Soon a shower is coming down on my head. A shower of ash.

I toss my ʻōhelo berries over the fence onto the edge of the pit. "For you, Pele." Then I hear myself saying: "If you're real, show me a sign."

I run for the lot, catching up to the bearded biker as he mounts his ride. Ash is falling thicker now. Pebbles the size of hail ping on the tank of his bike, making little dings in the metal. Then pebbles give way to rocks.

"So long, brother," he says. When he starts his motor-cycle, a rock the size of a baseball cracks his helmet and he tumbles to the asphalt lot.

"You okay?" I ask.

He struggles to his feet, looking dazed. "Pele is the whore of Babylon!" he seethes.

"I thought you said she didn't exist?"

He gives me a sour look, hops back on his bike, and rolls away. I run across the lot to my rental car, sure it's dinged beyond repair from the fallout. I don't take time to look. I just hop in and tear away.

As I motor to the Volcano House, out of harm's way, racing toward me are two Park Service trucks with flashing lights and those barricades stacked in back. They're closing the overlook. I may be the last person to make an offering to Pele for a long time to come.

Back at the Volcano House I carefully check the roof, trunk, and hood of my rental car. This could cost me.

Not a single ding. *Impossible.*

twenty-eight

Flying from Hilo Friday morning I notice vog still hanging over the Honolulu skyline. Pele has followed me home.

Back on Maunakea Street my message light is blinking. CAITLIN RANSOM. She's anxious to see me this morning. I return her call and she tells me she'll be here in thirty minutes. Then I sift through the stack of mail that arrived while I was away. There's a check from Donnie. She's paid me in full and included a generous tip. A sticky note attached to the check says, "Mahalo, Kai." That's it.

Before Caitlin arrives I pull out my interview notes to review them. My eyes wander to this morning's paper lying unread on my desk. The front page nearly knocks me off my chair.

A Fourth Death at Pele's Hands?

Kona: Another former officer of defunct Ransom Geothermal Enterprises was found dead yesterday in Waikoloa near the Mauna Kea Resort. The body of Michael "Mick"

London lay on a barren stretch of volcanic rock near this west-side resort. Investigators say London had been fishing on the craggy coastline when he apparently fell and struck his head. Alcohol may have been a factor.

Mick London formed his own drilling supply company in the late 1980s that sold exclusively to his former employer. When Ransom Geothermal ceased drilling operations on the Big Island, London's firm went into receivership. Litigation followed in which London claimed Ransom owed him thousands of dollars on leased and purchased equipment, but London failed to prevail in court.

Rex Ransom was found dead in a steam vent at Hawai'i Volcanoes National Park in March. Two other officers from his firm, Stan Nagahara and Karl Kroften, also died in or around the park in the past two years. London's death yesterday makes four.

Each man's connection to the controversial geothermal project in the Wao Kele O Puna rainforest has persuaded some devotees of Pele that the legendary goddess of volcanoes has taken revenge.

Caitlin Ransom is early again. She's in a floral print dress that does nice things for her grey eyes. No handshake this time—businesslike or otherwise. She just slides gracefully into my client chair.

I show her the headline. She's already seen it.

"It's so sad," she says. "Mick was really a nice guy. After he and my dad had their falling out, Mick's life has been so miserable."

"I talked with him three days ago," I say. "He was broke and bitter, but very much alive."

"Did he shed any light on my father's death?" She chokes a bit on the word "death."

I summarize my interview with Mick. And then with Sonny Boy. I mention seeing her mother, but I spare Caitlin the details. I also spare her my encounter at the Halemaʻumaʻu Crater. And I keep the found lipstick to myself, for now.

"And what are your conclusions?" Caitlin asks.

I tell the hard to believe, but equally hard to reject story that Serena Barrymore, a.k.a. Goddess Hiʻiaka, told me. "She claims she saw the same woman in red I did pursuing your father on the Crater Rim Trail. Barrymore says she also saw this woman push him into the steam vent."

"But isn't Barrymore an escaped mental patient?"

"True," I say. "Not the most reliable of witnesses."

"Who could the woman in red be?" Caitlin furrows her intelligent brow. "And why would she want to hurt my dad?"

"The woman can only be Pele, or someone made up to look like her. Trouble is, I interviewed every potential suspect, and none of them even remotely resembles her."

"Leaving only Pele?" Caitlin says.

"Afraid so. Or someone not on our list who's good at costume and make-up. Maybe someone involved in the protests who's willing to kill for Pele."

"Who? I can't think of anyone," Caitlin says "But it's some comfort that you're ready to admit my father's death wasn't an accident. At least now I'm not alone."

"There's three of us," I say. "You, me, and a woman who's certified insane. We need more to go on. Can you think of other people who might have wanted to harm your father?"

Caitlin draws a blank.

I try a different tack. "Maybe your father mentioned someone or something in your last conversations with him?"

She comes up with a few things that don't sound promising. Then she says: "He said more money was coming."

"More money?" I perk up. "What did he mean by that?"

"Remember I told you he sent me a generous check?"

I nod.

"Dad said he was sending more. Both to me and to my two brothers. He said it had to do with estate planning, or something like that."

"Did you receive another check?"

"No. My brothers didn't either."

"What about your father's will? Do you know what it says?"

"No. We never discussed that. I just assumed he left everything to Donnie, since my mother's estate eventually goes to my brothers and me."

"It might be worth checking into."

"I'll do that," she says.

After Caitlin strides from my office it's almost noon. Time to leave for my appointment with Ashley at a shop at Ala Moana Center called Safari. She's supposed to show me photos of the Lindquist twins celebrating their twenty-first birthday, before Fireball drove them off the Pali. I'm not hopeful her photos will be much use. Still, I head down the stairs.

Mrs. Fujiyama is sitting at the *lei* table with Chastity and Joon. No Blossom. Is she still in my apartment? This morning I came straight from the airport to my office, so I don't know.

I ask and Mrs. Fujiyama slowly shakes her head. "She go back to him."

"Back to Junior?" I shake my head too.

"He know she staying wit' you," Mrs. Fujiyama says. "He get furious mad. He say he gonna kill her. And you."

I'm alarmed that Blossom has gone back to Junior. Not for myself. But for her.

"You bettah watch out," my landlady says.

Before I can get out the door, his black pickup truck pulls up. The passenger door opens and Blossom slinks out. She's crying. He shouts at her before she closes the door. "I be hea at six. You be ready!"

Blossom runs from the black truck as if she's fleeing a coiled snake. He squeals away. Though it may make me late to my appointment with Ashley, I stop. Blossom looks up at me and I see a fresh bruise on her cheek. She looks down again, ashamed.

"I'm sorry, Blossom," I say. "Your staying at my place was a mistake—*my* mistake. Junior got the wrong idea."

"I tol' him you like one uncle to me," she explains. "But he no belief'."

"Uncle?" I say, surprised to hear myself referred to that way.

Then she surprises me even more. "'Nuff, awready!" she raises her voice. "Junior not going to hurt me anymo'."

Encouraged by the first inklings of a changed attitude—from victim to survivor—I don't know what to say. So I settle for, "I'll be back in an hour. Then let's talk."

She nods.

twenty-nine

Ala Moana Shopping Center at lunchtime is a zoo. Throngs of people patronize this place—the largest open-air shopping mall in the world. And they're all driving in circles right now with me, looking for a spot to park.

I hate to be late. It's already noon. Maybe Ashley won't mind—or notice.

At last I find a spot on the street level near Macy's at the Diamond Head end of the center, climb to the mall level, and head *Ewa* toward the luxury outfitter called Safari. I rush past some of the center's nearly ninety eateries and two hundred stores—mostly high-end icons like Louis Vuitton, Tiffany & Co., Chanel, Ralph Lauren, and Neiman Marcus—seeing more tourists inside than locals. I finally show up at Safari, across from Long's Drugs, huffing. It's ten minutes after noon. I hope Ashley hasn't already left for lunch.

I dash across the swanky hardwood floors and plush area rugs, and gaze at the elegant casual threads like you'd take on a big game hunt. Nice stuff. *And pricey.* Images of lions and giraffes and elephants grace the pastel walls, but

I would bet none of these duds are going on safari. Except at Disneyland.

Two young women are working the floor. One is a jaunty strawberry blonde in a pink polka dot dress. The other is in dark gothic mode—with powdered white face, red lips, and jet-black hair. I glance back and forth between the two, befuddled. Then I take the easy way out. I ask a guy behind the register, "Which one is Ashley?"

He points to the blonde. Makes sense. She appears to be about the same age—twenty-one—and from the same crowd as the late Lindquist twins.

"Sorry I'm late," I say, making my way to her. "The parking lot's a zoo."

"That's like *way* funny!" She laughs. "Are you Kai?"

I nod. She apparently thinks I'm a comedian.

"I'm Ashley." Her giddy green eyes and tiny freckles across her nose have *adorable* written all over them. "I brought my camera with the party photos." She turns down the corners of her sweet smile. *"So sad."*

"Should we go outside?" I ask.

"Totally," she replies. "It's my lunch break."

She heads for the store entrance and I follow. She's tall and wispy and sort of skips along. Her pink polka dot dress hangs on her and sways as she moves, continuing her carefree theme. She totes a handbag the size of a shopping cart, also pink. I'm hoping her camera is inside that cavernous thing—like she promised. I'm not optimistic.

Across from the store entrance, in the center of the open-air promenade, benches for weary shoppers surround a koi pond. Inside the pond the bright, patchy-colored ornamental carp swim lazily. I join Ashley on one of the benches.

I start off nice and easy. "How was your trip to Denver?"

"Kind of crazy," she says.

"Because you lost your cell phone?"

"Yeah, that . . ." She pauses. "But mostly 'cause I like found out when I landed about Heather and Lindsay. I was totally shocked, you know? And I felt *so* guilty. Like it was my fault. If I'd been there, Freddie wouldn't have driven them. He was *way* drunk."

"It's not your fault. The twins made the decision to ride with him. Those left behind often blame themselves."

"You're *way* cool, Kai. Thanks."

"If you don't mind my asking, who is Ethan and how did his phone number get into Fireball's—er, Freddie's—glove box?"

"Ethan?" she looks puzzled. "Oh, he's just a guy I stayed with in Denver. I wanted the twins to have his number, okay? But when I said goodbye to them I like forgot. So I wrote it on a receipt I found on the floor at the club and, you know, gave it to Freddie."

I nod and wonder again if she's telling or asking me.

"I really don't know how the number got into his glove box," she says. "Did he like put it there, or maybe they did? Whatever."

"Do you know whose receipt it was?"

She shakes her head. "The club was totally crowded. It could have been like anyone's."

"Probably doesn't matter now." I sigh. "But that reminds me. I've got something of yours." I pull from my pocket the bent Hawaiian bracelet with her name engraved on it.

"*Oh-my-god!*" Her mouth drops open as she takes the bracelet. "Where did you find it?"

"At the wreckage site—at the foot of the Pali."

"No way!"

I shrug. "Any idea how it got there?"

"I dunno," she says vaguely. "I was like showing it to some people at the club. I took it off and handed it around—okay?—and just sort of lost track of it. Later, on the airplane, I looked at my wrist and wondered, 'Where's my Hawaiian bracelet?' *Duh!*"

"Any idea why it might have been in Fireball's car?"

She looks puzzled again. "Maybe the twins found it and were like going to return it to me, or something?"

"Could be." Two potential pieces of evidence—the phone number and the Hawaiian bracelet—come to nothing. I'm wondering if the pics Ashley promises will turn out the same. I ask, "May I see your photos?"

"Totally!" She digs into that cavernous pink bag. Her fingers search like terriers. She pulls out her long-lost cell phone. "No, that's not it." Then she digs up a small leather purse. "No way." She continues digging. "I just know I put my camera in here this morning. *Really.*"

My hope is fading.

"Wait! Here it is!" She extracts a small digital camera of the point-and-shoot variety. She fiddles with the little buttons. "It's new—okay?—and I like really don't know how to use it yet."

"Take your time. No hurry."

She finally gets it turned on. An image appears. It's an ocean scene. I can see what looks like the Lindquist twins on a beach. More fumbling, and Ashley manages to scroll through the photos. One after another. More of the same. The twins on a beach. I'm getting impatient. And worried.

"*Oh, no!*" she says.

"What's wrong?" I'm fearing the worst.

"I put the wrong card in the camera. *I totally forgot!* The card with the party pics got filled, you know, so I put in another half-full card with a trip Heather and Lindsay and I took in February to Lāna'i. We stayed at Mānele Bay Resort. See?"

She shows me a photo of the three of them in bikinis on Lāna'i. Behind them dolphins frolic in bright blue Mānele Bay.

"You say there are photos of the party on this card?"

"I *think* so," she replies slowly, like she's unsure. "But most party pics are on the other one."

"Where's the other card?"

"In my apartment, I think." Then she scowls. "*Oh-my-god!* I hope I didn't leave that card in Denver!"

"Me too. Do you mind if I see the pics of the party that are on this card?"

"That's cool." She gives me the camera.

I rush along, hoping to find images of the twins' birthday party. One shot after another shows pretty much the same things. Beautiful bay. Beautiful bikinis. But none of the birthday party.

I'm about to give up. I'm about to quit when one photo freezes my attention. It's not from the party. It's another from Mānele Bay—dated in mid-February.

"Who's this?" I point to a couple—a man and a woman lying cozily together by the resort's swimming pool. The couple is in the background. One of the Lindquist twins poses in front of them.

"It's Lindsay," she says.

"No. I mean these two behind Lindsay."

"I don't know. But I remember them—he looked *way* younger than her. And they were like totally going at it. *Gross!* We felt like telling them to rent a room."

"I know the woman," I say. "She probably did rent a room. But I wouldn't have put her in it with this man. Whoever he is."

"Do they have anything to do with Heather and Lindsay?"

"I doubt it, but I'll follow up anyway. May I borrow the card?"

"Sure," she says. "Do you want to see the other one too, with the party pics? I'm totally sorry I didn't bring it. *Duh!*"

"Don't be too hard on yourself. Would you please call me when you find it?"

She agrees. "For now, here's this card." Ashley hands it to me, returns the camera to her pink handbag, and ambles back into Safari.

I clutch onto the card like it's solid gold. The woman in the photo is Donnie Ransom.

thirty

The photo poolside at Mānele Bay would have been taken a month before Donnie's husband died. I remember her telling me she spent a few days on the Pineapple Isle while her husband was undergoing tests at Wilcox Hospital. But she didn't mention she spent them with another man.

The photo calls into question everything she has told me. And the younger man she's lying with at Mānele Bay—longish dark blond hair, expressive eyes, and compact, muscular physique—gives her ample motive for not wanting her husband around.

Ashley's photo may be a game changer—though not in the game I had anticipated. The strawberry blonde who can't keep track of her own bracelet and cell phone and camera cards has come through like a queen.

Who is the man in the photo? How long has Donnie been seeing him? Did they scheme together to get her husband out of the way?

I'm mulling over these questions as I drive back to Maunakea Street, walk into the *lei* shop, and head for the stairs. Then I see Chastity and Joon and remember that I promised to talk with Blossom. She's not there.

"Went to lunch," Joon says.

"Latahs," I say and climb the stairs.

First thing I do in my office is to slip Ashley's photo card into the appropriate slot in my laptop, open the image of Donnie and the unknown young man, and print it on a full size sheet. It comes out well. Ashley apparently has been shooting with her new camera on highest resolution, though I doubt she knows it. It's a good thing. If I can find anybody who knows this guy, there will be no problem identifying him.

On a hunch I phone Caitlin. She answers on the first ring. I don't ask her to drive across town again from the university to my office. I offer to come to her. She says she's just seen her father's lawyer on Bishop Street and is now having a coffee at Starbucks on nearby Merchant Street—only a ten-minute walk from my office.

"Will you be there for a while?" I ask.

"Sure, I just ordered a latte. What's up?"

"I've got a photo of somebody to show you."

"A photo of whom?"

"That's what I hope you can tell me."

"And I've got something to share with you," she says. "Something my father's attorney said."

"Sounds promising," I say. "See you in ten."

I hang up and start out the door with the photo of Donnie and her new man. I stop and go back inside. I grab an old pair of scissors and carefully cut the photo. When I'm done, there's a hole in the sheet where Donnie used to be. I leave her on the desk. Then I pull from the top drawer the warning note Donnie told me she received moments before her husband died. I put both the note and the photo in a file folder and head for Starbucks.

I shuffle along through Fort Street Mall, feeling suddenly beat. It's only April and it must be eighty-five. Then I remember I awoke before dawn at the Volcano House, drove to Hilo, and flew home to Honolulu before breakfast. It's already been a long day. And it's only mid-afternoon. But I feel suddenly energized by the break in the case. I don't know where it will lead, but at least I'm getting somewhere.

My breath keeps time with my quickening pace. I cough. Vog. It just won't go away. I cover my nose and mouth with my handkerchief. Then I breathe easier.

Inside Starbucks, Caitlin is not hard to find. She stands out from the other patrons—well-dressed downtown types, on break from their office jobs. Caitlin appears more casual and nonchalant. Yet more elegant. As if looking good is easy.

I say hello and put the enlarged photo—minus Donnie— on Caitlin's table. I don't want her to see her father's second wife with the younger man. Not yet. No telling how she'd react if she suspected Donnie.

"Do you know this man?" I point to the boyish figure sunning by the pool at Mānele Bay.

"Yes, but what does he have to do with anything?" Caitlin sips her latte.

"I don't know yet," I say. "Who is he?"

"Jeff," she says matter-of-factly.

"Jeff who?" The name doesn't ring a bell.

"I guess most people call him Jeffrey. He's the guy who rents the suite over the garage at my dad's and Donnie's place on Kāua'i."

I put on my poker face. "Jeffrey Bywater? Donnie told me about him. He's a flight attendant and has a partner named Byron. Jeffrey's gay, right?"

"That was my impression," she says. "But why are you showing me his photo? Does he have anything to do with my father's death?"

"I don't know," I repeat. Then I ask her what she knows about Jeffrey.

Caitlin, it turns out, has met Jeffrey only once and knows little more than I do—though she recalls he acted recently in an amateur theatrical production on Kāuaʻi. She thinks he's been renting from her father for about one year, and before that he lived on Oʻahu.

"Did he know your father or Donnie before he moved in?"

"I don't think so," she replies.

"Thanks," I say. "Now I need you to promise me something, Caitlin. I need you to promise that you will not tell anyone I showed you this photo, and most of all you will not tell Donnie or Jeffrey. In fact, it would probably be best if you didn't speak to them at all. At least, for now. Okay?"

She nods. "I have no need to talk with Donnie anyway. And I don't really know Jeffrey."

"Mahalo," I say. "I better get working on these new leads." I rise from the table. "I hope to have some answers for you shortly."

"Wait," she says. "Don't you want to hear what my father's lawyer told me?"

"I do." I sit down again.

"His name is Sheldon Weller from Weller, Matsumoto, and Ching," she says. "He's an estate attorney and his office is in that big tower on Bishop Street right over there." She points skyward.

"So what did Mr. Weller say?"

"He said a few months ago my father phoned him about sending money gifts to my brothers and me and—"

"Do you think that's why you got the check?" I interrupt her. It's a bad habit.

"I think so," Caitlin says. "But more interesting, Mr. Weller said my father also talked about changing his will."

"Changing his will how?"

"Everything in the existing will—my dad's Hanalei home and his money—goes to Donnie, like I assumed. But my dad mentioned something to Mr. Weller about adding my two brothers and me as beneficiaries. Mr. Weller and he didn't discuss particulars, but they planned to talk again. My dad died before that could happen."

"That is interesting." I say. I don't mention it's even more interesting that his second wife was by then already hooked up with a new man.

* * *

On the way back to my office I stop at King Magazine in Fort Street Mall. It's a nondescript little red brick shop with dozens of magazines in its windows. You might just walk by without noticing, unless you're shopping for something to read. In which case, King Magazine is the place to go.

I step up to a rack containing newspapers from the various Hawaiian Islands—*Honolulu Star-Advertiser, Maui News, The Garden Island, Hawaii Tribune-Herald,* and so on. The *Honolulu Weekly*, a free newspaper, is outside in a stand by itself. From my folder I take the note Donnie said she received moments before Rex Ransom died. I have only a photocopy, but I remember the words were pasted on common white paper with no fancy threading or watermark.

A note like this seems a bizarre tactic in the digital age. But it makes sense. Hard copy is more difficult to trace. It leaves no electronic trail. The official investigation apparently found no usable prints on the paper or pasted letters. The maker obviously wore gloves.

I glance again at the note.

> as you value your health and your life
>
> keep away from Pele
>
> **Deadly**

The wording sounds quaint and bookish. Most people would say, "*if* you value your health" not "*as* you value . . ." Or was "as" simply handy and whoever made the note just slapped it down?

All the words appear to have been cut with scissors from a newspaper, except the word "Pele," which I recall from the original had the glossiness of a travel brochure. White correction fluid has been applied to cover glue smudges. Whoever made the note was a neat freak. And probably didn't make it on the fly—but with premeditation. I doubt the note originated at the Volcano House.

Four different fonts, of various sizes, make up the newsprint words. I check these fonts against those in the islands' newspapers. The *Hawaii Tribune-Herald,* the obvious choice, looks similar, but not really the same. *Hmmm.* Maybe the *Star-Advertiser?* It's available on all islands. The *Star-Advertiser* is close, but no cigar. I step outside and check the *Honolulu Weekly*. It doesn't work either.

Now it's anybody's guess. I come back into the shop. The *Maui News* looks like a prospect, but it too doesn't work. That leaves *The Garden Island*. I check its various fonts. They all match.

The Kāuaʻi newspaper.

I walk up Fort Street Mall to my Maunakea Street office, considering what I've learned. Donnie Ransom is not what she appears to be—devoted wife of her elderly, wealthy and now deceased husband. She's a cheater whose lover is the Ransom's own tenant, Jeffrey Bywater—though Bywater presents himself as gay. Maybe Ransom suspects his wife is unfaithful. Maybe his suspicion, coupled with his renewed closeness to his three children by his previous marriage, is his motivation for phoning his estate attorney and discussing listing them as beneficiaries. Changing his will means Donnie would get less—maybe a lot less.

I recall harsh words between Ransom and his wife at the Volcano House—so at odds with the public image of them as a loving couple.

"What about me? I'm your wife!" Donnie had exclaimed.

"You have nothing to worry about," the old man had replied.

Could this exchange have been provoked by Ransom's intention to change his will?

Back in my office I call Donnie Ransom.

"Kai?" She sounds surprised. Then she says perfunctorily: "How are you?"

"I'm fine," I say. "Thanks for the check and generous tip."

"You're welcome," she says.

"I wanted to convey my sympathy, again, and tell you how sorry I am about your husband."

"That's very thoughtful of you," she says. "Very thoughtful."

"And I also wanted to mention that I'll be on Kāua'i tomorrow and I wondered if you'd mind if I stopped by."

"Mind? No, I don't mind." She sounds puzzled. "What's up?"

"It's about your husband—a final detail I'd like to clear up for my records."

"Can we talk about it on the phone?" She's looking for a way out. I'm not giving it to her.

"We can, but in person is always better," I say. "What time is good for you?"

"Uh," she hesitates, "early afternoon."

"Thanks, I'll give you a call before I come. *Aloha*."

Donnie is cooperating with me—reluctantly. I expected she would.

I call Hawaiian Airlines and book a flight to Lihue on Saturday morning, returning later the same day. And I line up a rental car.

I'm about to do something unorthodox—*again*.

thirty-one

Saturday morning I fly to Lihue and drive the Garden Isle's meandering two-lane Kūhiō Highway to Hanalei. The home of the late Rex Ransom sits right on the pristine beach and has a commanding view of Hanalei Bay. The sprawling oceanfront residence is every bit as grand as I imagined it would be.

It's a little after noon when I arrive, so I grab a couple Spam *musubi* in the village, carry them down to the beach, and plant myself in the warm sand. As I bite into the grilled Spam and rice wrapped in *nori,* or dried seaweed, I watch the waves and remember why Hanalei is one of my favorite spots in the islands.

Hanalei must be other people's favorite spot too. Maybe that's why it's been featured in so many films. Millions who've never had the good fortune to set foot here have set eyes on images of this lovely little bay, covered pier, and lush mountain backdrop in *South Pacific, Lilo & Stitch, The Descendants,* and many more. Though the bay is small, it has several breaks: Waikoko on the west side, Hanalei Pier in the center, Hideaways on the east side beneath the cliffs by

Princeville Resort, and so on. I've got no board today, and a job to do, so I can only watch.

My Spam *musubi* gone, I phone Donnie and then walk up the beach to the Ransoms' home. It's not every day a private detective calls on a former client and accuses her of murder. I'm not going to do that, exactly. I plan to soft-pedal the thing.

Mainly, I want her to know that I know. My hunch is Donnie will say or do something hasty or desperate that will help the case along. Maybe not today. But soon. I still don't know how she and Jeffrey did it. I could use some assistance. It's a bit risky. But I'm betting the benefits outweigh the risks. If I'm right, I'll come off looking good. If I'm wrong, I may wipeout big time.

Why not let law enforcement take over from here? Simple. Given the circumstantial evidence against them—some of it sounding outright wacky—Donnie and Jeffrey could easily slip through legal loopholes. And if they were to stand trial, it's anybody's guess whether twelve jurors would convict. If not, the two would walk. And get away with Ransom's murder and his millions.

There's a FOR SALE sign in front of the house. Already. I check out the suite over the three-car garage where I assume Jeffrey lives. Or *lived*. I bet he's moved into the main residence by now. A pair of jogging shoes by the front doors, shoes too large for Donnie's delicate feet, seems to confirm this. But I'm not surprised when she meets me alone at the door.

I'd forgotten how attractive she is. Even greeting me casually in her own home, she maintains that beauty queen aura. Her lustrous black hair, her vivid brown eyes, and her inviting red lips make it easy to see why the late Rex Ransom and the late Mick London both fell hard for this island beauty. And at least one man before them. And one man after.

"Thanks for seeing me," I say.

"I'm curious," she says, as she leads me into the elegant home. "What are you doing on Kāuaʻi?"

"Working a case." I leave it at that and look around. More evidence of Jeffrey: A baseball cap embroidered *Pride of Aloha* on a chair. A half empty beer bottle on an end table that strikes me as male carelessness. I've never seen this home before, but I can tell at least two people reside here.

She leads me into a huge living room that looks out on the sunny beach where I've just been warming myself in the sand. All that blue water and blue sky in the windows reminds me of the late Rex Ransom's other home in Kona, now occupied by his first wife, Kathryn. *Two dream homes and he can't enjoy either.*

Donnie and I take matching leather chairs beside an inlaid *koa* table.

"Sad to see you're selling your home," I say.

"Yes," she replies. "Too many memories of Rex. I've got to move on."

"I understand."

"I miss that man," she goes on. "It's painful each day to live here without him."

"I'm sorry." I play along. "Where will you go?"

"I don't know," she says vaguely. "I haven't decided yet. One step at a time. First sell the house."

"I talked with your late husband's daughter recently," I say, getting to the point.

"Oh?" Donnie says.

"Caitlin asked me to investigate his death. She's not convinced it was an accident."

"Really?"

"Yes," I say. "I went back to the Big Island, interviewed people, and checked about everything I could check."

"And what did you find?"

"Nothing. Unless we can believe Pele did it."

Donnie gets a funny look. "So what do we have to talk about?"

"It turns out I'm working on another case. I told you about it—the Pali case."

She nods, but still looks confused.

"One witness in that case," I continue, "took photos in the Honolulu club where the twins and their driver were last served—probably over-served."

"Now I'm really lost," Donnie says. "What does this have to do with Rex?"

"Stay with me," I say. "So this witness brings the wrong photo card to our meeting. It's got no photos of the clubs, only an earlier trip to Mānele Bay on Lāna'i."

"So?" Donnie looks suspicious.

"One photo taken at the Mānele Bay Resort I thought you should see." I haul it out and she takes it.

When she recognizes herself lying by the pool with Jeffrey, Donnie's face freezes.

"The date," I say, "is February twentieth—about three weeks before your husband died. Was that when he was having the tests you told me about at Wilcox Hospital?"

I assume by the strained expression on her face that she's working fast to concoct a story.

She finally speaks. "Look, Kai, Jeffrey and I are friends, okay? He helped me cope with Rex's first heart attack. It changed everything."

"I'm sure it did." I sympathize.

"Jeffrey happened to be working a flight to Lāna'i when Rex was having those tests, and we sort of ran into each other at the hotel. That's all."

"I expected it was something simple like that," I say. "I'm glad you explained. I was concerned, you see, about the impression the photo might make if," I pause, "well, if the official investigation were reopened."

She strains again, but manages no reply.

"You can have the photo." I hand it to her, confident she'll show it to Jeffrey. "No worries," I say. "You were with me when your husband died. And Jeffrey was on a cruise ship, right?"

"That's right," she says. "You can check it out—and I wish you would. I don't like either of us being suspected."

"I'd be happy to do that, if it would make you feel better. And I'm sure I'll find it's just as you say."

"*Mahalo*, Kai," she says.

I'm walking along the beach to my rental car and turn around for one last look at the Ransoms' oceanfront palace. Through the sea-view glass I see Donnie already on the phone—probably talking to her partner in crime. I can almost read her lips: *"Jeffrey, he knows!"*

Suddenly I realize why the color of her lips looks so familiar.

Fiery red.

thirty-two

I'm back on Maunakea Street late on Saturday afternoon. Chinatown shops are already starting to close. Including Mrs. Fujiyama's. *Pau hana*. I'm about to close up shop myself. But not before I begin to check out Jeffrey's alibi.

The *Pride of Aloha*. I have no doubt Jeffrey was booked on the interisland cruise ship with his supposed partner, Byron Joslyn, just as Donnie claims. Why else would she have brought it up? So I don't need to see a passenger list. But it might be worth checking the cruise ship's schedule and ports of call.

I Google *Pride of Aloha*. I hit a site that gives a bunch of statistics about the ship. As a *keiki* I marveled at the immense size and grandeur of the ill-fated *Titanic*. The *Pride of Aloha* is even bigger—longer, wider, and heavier. The website shows a real-time satellite image of the liner and its position. From the heavens, where the satellite is perched, the huge white vessel looks like a toothpick in a puddle. But guess what? It's in port in Honolulu at this very moment. The *Pride of Aloha* is moored by the Aloha Tower. *Five minutes away.*

I get the brilliant idea to buzz over to the Aloha Tower and see if I can corral a real live person into talking to me about the ship. I drive down Bishop Street, wait for the long light at Ala Moana Boulevard, and then cross into the parking lot at the Aloha Tower Marketplace.

I can't miss the *Pride of Aloha*. It dwarfs the marketplace, rising nearly as high as the tower itself. A colossal white floating hotel. I crane my neck and gaze up at its countless decks with balconies and suites, and as many portholes below those decks. There's quite a crowd in the long covered concourse beside the ship. Passengers are milling around or in queues boarding the liner. By the huge doors and gangways swallowing them up, white-suited officers are checking documentation as one after another climbs aboard.

I know little about how the inter-island cruise operates, what schedule it follows, and how it accommodates passengers. I need to learn fast.

Another white uniform is roaming the concourse in what appears to be a hostess role. I approach her and say, "Aloha, would you please help me?"

"Did you complete your online check-in form?" she asks.

"I'm not boarding the ship tonight," I say. "I just have some questions."

"Would you like a brochure?" she asks. "It has the ship's schedule and frequently asked questions."

"Sure. That would be a good start."

She hands me the brochure. I step aside and scan it. On the front is a photo of the great white ship, cruising in dazzling teal waters between the islands. The *Pride of Aloha,* the brochure says, has over 660 balcony staterooms, eight restaurants, three pools, spacious public rooms and meeting facilities, a tennis court, and an art gallery. Plus a Hawai'i-themed Aloha Cafe and Waikīkī Bar.

Sign me up! I'm ready to sail. Except for the fare.

This kind of travel seems designed for those with a bank account like the late Rex Ransom's. Curious that a guy living in Ransom's garage could afford it.

The back of the brochure lists the ship's interisland cruise schedule. The schedule is unchanging. The liner departs from Honolulu on Saturday evening at 7:00 pm and follows the same itinerary, week after week. Sunday and Monday in Kahului, Maui. Tuesday in Hilo. Wednesday in Kona. Thursday and Friday in Nāwiliwili on Kāua'i. Saturday morning, back to Honolulu.

Interesting. The *Pride of Aloha* spends two nights each week, Tuesday and Wednesday, in Big Island ports. When Rex Ransom died on a Wednesday morning near the Volcano House, the ship was just arriving in Kona, after sailing overnight from Hilo. Jeffrey Bywater could have disembarked in Hilo on Tuesday and driven to the park, spent the night near the Volcano House, murdered Ransom on Wednesday morning, and then driven to Kona and re-boarded the ship.

The perfect crime and the perfect alibi. How he managed to pull it off is another question. But clearly Jeffrey had the opportunity.

I return to the hostess in white with a question: "If I take the interisland cruise, can I disembark in Hilo, explore the Big Island on my own, and then re-board in Kona?"

"Absolutely," she says. "As long as you re-board at least one hour before sailing time."

"Will I need to sign out when I leave the ship, and sign in when I return?"

"Yes," she says. "But it's very simple and quick. When you first board you'll receive an ID card, about the size of a credit card, with your photo and personal information in digital form. You'll use the card in many ways, from making onboard purchases to accessing your room. And also for boarding and disembarking the ship in ports of call. Whenever you disembark you simply swipe the card in a reader by the gangway, a crewmember double-checks that it's you swiping the card, and you're off. It takes all of about ten seconds."

"What about getting back on the ship?" I ask.

"Same procedure," she says. "You swipe your card again, the crew member double-checks, and you're in."

"Mahalo," I say. "Very helpful."

But I'm wondering: *How did he do it?* How could Jeffrey get off the ship at Hilo and then re-board the next day in Kona without being detected? I assume Donnie would not invite me to check out her lover's alibi unless it were ironclad. It's not easy to subvert digital ID cards, especially under watchful eyes. And I wouldn't think it's any easier to disembark other than by the gangway. A first-rate professional might pull it off, but could Donnie's lover?

"May I book your cruise?" She smiles and hands me her card with a gauzy image of the ship.

"Let me check with my better half," I say.

She glances at my left hand—without a ring—and looks dubious.

"For our honeymoon." I make tracks for the door.

As the *Pride of Aloha* readies to sail into the sunset, I head back to my office. The *lei* shop is closed, so I climb the outside stairs. First thing I do is send an email to Pualani at the Volcano House. I attach the photo of Jeffrey Bywater and Donnie Ransom.

"Evah see dis guy?" I ask in my email message. "He maybe stay in da Volcano House when Ransom *huli* inside da steam vent?" Then I close with *"Mahalo"* and leave her my cell phone number, in case she prefers to call.

I don't know if Pualani is working tonight, or how often she checks her email. I figure it may be Monday before I hear from her.

Almost instantly my cell phone dings. *Pualani? Already?*

No. It's a text from Maile. She wants to know if I'm taking Kula surfing this weekend. I haven't been in the water for days. Plus it's weekend and I just drooled over the rippling breaks at Hanalei Bay. I text back, "For sure."

"When?" she texts back.

"Tomorrow a.m.," I reply.

"Can u pick him up tonight?"

"OK."

"Kula in back yard," she replies.

That's it. While I'm stoked Maile texted me, I'm a little surprised at the arrangements. I've never picked up Kula at night before. Dogs are technically not allowed at the Waikīkī Edgewater. Maile knows the rules. That's part of the reason she adopted Kula and I didn't. So I'm a bit mystified. But I hop in my car and head up into Mānoa Valley.

My cousin Alika's thirteen-foot tandem board sits in Maile's carport—ready to go. I don't knock on the cottage door, even though there's a light on inside. I walk straight to her back yard, cursing Madison Highcamp under my breath, and call, "Kula."

He doesn't come.

It's dark. I can't see him. But I call him again. "Kula!"

Still no golden retriever.

Now I'm scratching my head. What's going on? She invites me to take the dog surfing, tells me he'll be in the yard, I come promptly as if called like a dog, but there's no Kula.

So finally I go around to the front door and knock. "Maile?"

"Come in," she says, as if she's expecting me.

I step into the cottage. Coconut, Peppah, and Lolo are lounging in their usual places. Kula's toys are scattered about the floor. But no dog.

Maile is sitting in her rattan loveseat in a strapless dress—rare for her. Her hair is down and shimmering.

"Maile?" I say. "Where's Kula?"

"Oh, Mrs. Lee asked if Kula could walk with her and her Labrador retriever. Kula goes crazy when he sees that lab," Maile says. "Do you mind waiting?"

"No, I don't mind," I say, glad for the opportunity to see her, whatever the excuse. My phone rings and I direct the call to voicemail.

"Would you like to sit?" She gestures to the rattan chair opposite her, occupied by Coconut.

"Sure." I move toward the chair. The Siamese jumps down and joins Maile on the loveseat.

"I was at the Waikīkī Canoe Club today with a client whose Siberian husky I recovered," Maile says, "and I ran into your paddling buddy, Nainoa."

"Nainoa? I haven't seen him since——" I stop midsentence. Nainoa introduced me to Madison Highcamp.

"Nainoa mentioned that drunken woman you knew who phoned me. I told him about the call and he said it was all a lie."

I'm about to say, *That's what I've been trying to tell you!* But instead I just make a mental note: *Buy Nainoa a six-pack.* My phone beeps indicating a new voicemail. I let it go.

Soon Maile and I are talking more like we used to—easy, comfortable, familiar. The animation and color return to her face.

When Mrs. Lee finally returns with Kula, he runs to me with that big goofy smile. I stroke his golden coat.

Maile pipes up, "What about that dinner you promised me, Kai Cooke?"

"Ah Fook okay?" It's the chop suey house in Chinatown where Maile stood me up after receiving Madison's drunken call.

"You're on." She feeds the animals and we go.

A few hours later we're back in her cottage, full and happy. I remind her that dogs aren't allowed at the Waikīkī Edgewater—and hope she'll get the hint.

"I'm feeling so much closer to you now, Kai," she says. "But we've been a long time apart. I'm not quite ready."

She's not quite ready, I'm thinking. *And I'm so ready.*

"But you can sleep here," she continues—and I perk up—"on the loveseat with Peppah. That way, you won't have to sneak Kula into your apartment."

"Thanks." I glance at the male Angora lounging on the loveseat and try not to show my disappointment. *Her feelings run deep,* I console myself. *It's going to take her a while.*

Maile disappears into her bedroom with Kula—*lucky dog*—but returns to the living room in her robe a minute later. I'm slipping off my aloha shirt.

"I missed that, you know." She fixes her eyes on my shark bite—the crescent of sixteen pink welts. "Funny, it makes you kind of—*vulnerable.*"

"I'll give you a private showing when you're ready." I wink.

"I'll look forward to that," Maile says and returns to her bedroom.

I climb onto the loveseat and curl around Peppah. Things could be worse. He's very soft. And at least I'm sleeping in Maile's cottage.

In the middle of the night I get up to use the bathroom and take my phone. There's that new voicemail—the one that came earlier in the evening. I listen.

"Hey, Kai," Pualani says. "Da guy in da picture—das da guy I wen tell you 'bout—Stapleton."

Stapleton? I wonder.

"Lars Stapleton from New Jersey." She sounds like she's reading the hotel register.

So Lars Stapleton equals Jeffrey Bywater.

Pualani goes on: "Stapleton da guy wen insist fo' crater view room numbah t'ree. Remembah?"

I remember. Next to room one—the Ransoms' room. With the connecting door between. Jeffrey—*Lars*—would have checked out before Ransom died and fled afterwards to re-board the *Pride of Aloha* at Kona. Just time enough to do the deed, but not enough—as he told Pualani—to view the eruption.

"Eh, Kai, what dis Stapleton guy doing in da picture by da pool wit' Mrs. Ransom? He her new boyfrien'? She no waste time, brah!"

Her boyfriend, yes. But not exactly *new*.

Pieces of the case start coming together. But the piece that still doesn't fit is that mystery woman. Donnie Ransom and her lover Jeffrey, a.k.a. Lars Stapleton, somehow manage to field a young Pele lookalike on the Crater Rim Trail, assisted possibly by Jeffrey's supposed partner Byron Joslyn. I don't know yet how they do this, or how Jeffrey disembarks the *Pride of Aloha* in Hilo and re-boards in Kona without being detected. But I hope I'll find out soon enough.

When I climb back onto the loveseat Peppah is gone and sleep doesn't come. It's not just Rex Ransom's murder I'm thinking about.

Donnie planned to make her husband's death look like the third in a string of deaths at Pele's hands. Three in a row is convincing. Four in a row, even more. *Mick London*. Did Donnie conspire to kill him, too?

Maybe Mick knew too much? He told me Donnie liked Ransom's money more than she liked him. Maybe he suspected his former boss's death was no accident. Jeffrey, an interisland flight attendant, could easily find himself in Kona with a few spare hours between flights. Donnie—presumably single again—could tag along and show up at Mick's place, have a few drinks with her former beau, and leave the rest to Jeffrey.

Two counts of murder instead of one?

thirty-three

Sunday morning after Maile and I breakfast together I take Kula surfing. We drive down Mānoa Valley, his head out the window, his fleecy fur glowing in the morning sun. He's wearing that goofy smile again. *Revved up to surf!*

Kula is beside himself when I turn *makai* off Ala Moana Boulevard into Kakaʻako Waterfront Park. The golden retriever hears the waves crashing beyond the dune and smells the salt spray. He wants to ride waves. Before we do, I power up my phone. It's been off since last night. There's a new voicemail.

"Easy, boy." I try to calm him. "Just a minute while I listen to this message." *Like he really understands?*

But he does. He sits quietly on the seat next to me. I dial my voicemail and hear Ashley's voice.

"*Way* stupid!" She chides herself. "I found that other photo card in my bag. It was there like the whole the time! *Duh!* Can you believe that?"

Yes I can.

She'll be working at the mall if I want to come by, 10 to 5. I'll return Ashley's call after I set up an interview with Jeffrey's friend, Byron Joslyn. First Byron, then Ashley.

Once Kula sees the phone call is over, he goes ballistic. I grab the tandem board and we hike over the dune to the water. In the break two surfers are sitting on their boards.

Kula jumps on the tandem and walks to the nose. I hop on behind the retriever and paddle to the break. The two surfers spot a set coming and paddle for it. When the first shoulder-high roller comes, they're on it. And ride it all the way in.

We watch a few more waves roll through. Then we go for one. I swing the board around and point the nose toward shore.

"Okay, Kula," I say. "Here we go."

The golden retriever hunches down, poised to ride. I paddle and Kula hangs his paws over the nose. Soon I feel the rush under the board of the cresting swell. I pop up and turn right, staying in front of the breaking wave. Kula balances himself and keeps in sync with me as I maneuver on the wave. It's like he has a knack, or something. I hear myself sounding like Ashley. *Gag me!*

While Kula and I wait for the next wave I worry about my vocabulary. And I think about Jeffrey's friend, Byron Joslyn. What might Joslyn's role be in Rex Ransom's murder? Was he a willing co-conspirator? Or an unsuspecting bystander—just along for the ride? It's hard to imagine him not being at least minimally aware and involved. You'd notice if your traveling companion went missing overnight. How much he was involved may determine his willingness to talk. I'm hoping he runs off at the mouth.

When I return Kula to her cottage after our session later that Sunday morning, Maile isn't home. I bathe the golden boy, dry him, give him food and water, and leave him in the yard. He's smiling at me when I close the gate and walk to my car.

On Sunday morning the *lei* shop is closed. I climb the outside stairs to my office and I Google Byron Joslyn. He has an address and phone number in Pauoa, the little valley along the town-side of the Pali Highway. I call the number and a woman answers. I ask for Byron. She tells me he's working a trip from Seattle and will be back this afternoon.

"He's still a flight attendant?" I ask, putting two and two together. "I haven't seen him for a while."

"Yes," she says. "Can I tell him who called?"

"An old friend," I say. "So did Byron finally tie the knot? Are you his lucky bride?"

"Me?" She laughs. "I'm not his type. We're housemates. We work for the same airline." She mentions the airline. It's the one Jeffrey works for too. That's all I need to know.

So I say, "You've been very helpful. I'll give Byron a call when I'm in town again. *Mahalo.*"

I hang up, go back on line, and check Sunday's flight schedule on Byron's airline from Seattle to Honolulu. Only one flight departs Seattle, at 12:50 pm, and arrives in Honolulu at 3:45 pm.

I check my watch. 11:30 am. I call Ashley. She doesn't answer. I leave her a message that I'll see her at noon at Safari.

Before driving to Ala Moana Shopping Center I burn a CD containing the images from her photo card. I put the card in a file folder for the Ransom case and take the CD with me. I'm feeling the Bishop Street attorney who represents the Lindquist twins' father breathing down my neck. Plus, racer-boys like Fireball who drive drunk, and the clubs that serve them when they're already drunk, need to be held accountable. I'm hoping this time Ashley comes through.

Parking is even worse on Sundays at Ala Moana Center than on weekdays. I finally find a spot, race across the mall to Safari, but step into Long's Drugs first. I buy a photo card identical to the one Ashley lent me and a lipstick that looks like the one I found on the Crater Rim Trail. Shoving the lipstick into my khakis for later, I cross the promenade to the gleaming hardwood floors of Safari. *Late again!*

Against the images of lions, giraffes and elephants that grace the pastel walls, I don't have to search long this time for the strawberry blonde. But she looks astonished. She says something to her gothic co-worker and then meets me in the middle of the store.

"Sorry I'm late again," I say. "The parking lot's a zoo, but this time no excuses."

"Late?" Ashley says. "Like for what?"

"Didn't you get my voicemail?" I'm incredulous.

"Um . . . no," she says. "I totally lost my cell phone again." Her giddy eyes turn a deeper green.

She lost her cell phone—again?

"I guess I just like left it, you know, somewhere," she explains. "I'm sure it'll turn up. I really haven't looked yet. Whatever."

"Good luck," I say.

"I found it last time," she says. "Well . . . uh . . . the airline found it. But I did find the other photo card. *Really!*"

"Great," I say. "Should we go outside?"

She nods and leads the way in her lanky carefree strides to the benches around the koi pond. She lugs her oversized pink handbag that I hope contains the photo card she's promised me. We sit by the pond.

"Before I forget," I say. "Here's a new photo card to replace yours, plus all your photos on this CD. I hand her both.

She doesn't question my keeping her own card. She just says: "Did that totally gross couple by the pool have anything to do with Heather and Lindsay?"

"I'm afraid not." I tell her the plain truth.

"Um . . . I didn't think so," she says. "I can still remember those two like really going at it. And I remember them saying some really weird stuff."

That gets my attention. "Like what?"

"She said this weird thing to him about Pele."

"Madame Pele, the goddess of volcanoes?"

"Bizarre . . . them lying there all wrapped up in each other—*Gag me!*—and talking about the volcano goddess."

"Can you remember what she said about Pele?"

"Something about revenge—like it was time for Pele to take revenge."

"What did he say—the guy?"

"He said, 'Anything you want, baby, you got it.'"

Hmmm. I scratch my chin.

"Baby?" Ashley says. "She was like twenty years older than him!"

I grab the spiral notebook I carry in the pocket of my aloha shirt. "Would you mind writing down what they said and how they were behaving?"

"Whatever," she says.

With the pen I also keep in that same pocket I write the date of the overheard conversation and the place at the top of the page. These will be corroborated by the dated photo Ashley gave me. I hand her the notebook. She records the conversation as she remembers it and describes Donnie and Jeffrey lying together poolside. I also have her state that she gave me the photo card, to establish chain of custody. She signs and dates her statement and returns the notebook to me.

"Mahalo," I say. "This could be a big help."

Ashley doesn't ask why. She just smiles and digs into her huge pink handbag. She digs and digs. Another puzzled look. Then she says, *"Oh, no!"*

"Oh, no?" I say, expecting the worst.

"The photo card." Ashley says. "It's like not here."

"I thought you said you found it last night?"

"I did," she says. "I found it and set it on my nightstand before I went to sleep, you know, just to make sure I would bring it today. I guess I like didn't put it back in my bag."

"So you don't have the card?"

"Yes . . . um . . . I do have the card." She frowns. "Just not with me."

I shake my head. But manage to hold my tongue.

"I'm totally sorry," she says. "Especially since, you know, I like forgot the card last time."

"It's okay," I hear myself say. "Could I meet you at your home maybe later today?"

"Oh, *barf!*" she says. "I can't. I'm going to Maui with some friends right after work. I'll be back on Tuesday."

"Tuesday?" I grab for some patience. It's hard to find. Finally I say: "Same place, same time on Tuesday."

I walk her back to Safari and she says, "No way I'll forget this time—*like I promise!*"

And I'm thinking: *Like I hope so.*

thirty-four

Back in my office I get on my computer again before driving to the airport to meet Byron Joslyn. I jot down the number of his flight from Seattle, the arrival gate, and baggage claim area. What I don't have, yet, is a mug shot.

I Google Byron Joslyn again. I get hits from ancestry. com and sites like that dealing with deceased and historical Byron Joslyns. *Who'd have known there were so many?* Why am I wasting time? I go to Facebook.

Two Byron Joslyns come up. Only one resides in Honolulu. And he has an uncanny resemblance to Jeffrey Bywater. The two look like brothers. There's a shot in Byron's photo gallery of the two of them arm-in-arm. Byron must be older. He's got features like Jeffrey's, but not his boyish looks. Byron's personal information says he's in a relationship. The implication of the photo is that the relationship is with Jeffrey. If so, it's not an exclusive one.

I look at Byron's list of friends. It includes Jeffrey, of course. And also Donnie Ransom. And checking his gallery again, I spot photos of all three of them arm-in-arm.

But what most impresses me is that uncanny resemblance of the two men. One could probably pass for the other. So I Google Jeffrey Bywater to see what I can find. I go to one of those public records sites that says it will supply dozens of records pertaining to Jeffrey Bywater if I pay $14.95. I don't usually pay for this kind of information, but I'm in a hurry and I'll take my chances. So I key in my credit card number and see what comes up.

There's quite a bit. Mostly addresses and previous addresses. A divorce about five years ago. I'm wondering if I've wasted my fifteen bucks. But then I see this: NAME CHANGE. Jeffrey Bywater is not his given name. He changed his name barely one year ago. And guess what? His given name is Joslyn. Jeffrey Bywater and Byron Joslyn don't just look like brothers. They *are* brothers.

On a hunch I Google Jeffrey Joslyn. The first hit is a review in *The Garden Island* of an amateur performance at the Pohu Theatre in Lihue of Oscar Wilde's *The Importance of Being Earnest*. I recall Caitlin's mentioning that Jeffrey acted in a play on Kāuaʻi. It appears he's kept his real name as his stage name. The review goes on and on about the controversial and daring move by director Nani Michaels of casting male actor Jeffrey Joslyn as a leading lady.

> Jeffrey Joslyn, in the role of the beautiful and pretentious Gwendolen Fairfax, who embodies the qualities of conventional Victorian Womanhood, is bound to raise eyebrows. The young Gwendolen—fixated on finding a husband named Earnest—played by a man? But Joslyn pulls it off swimmingly. He nails the

> speech, mannerisms, grace, and charm of the
> twenty-something Victorian beauty so com-
> pletely that you forget almost instantly he's
> cross-dressing and raising his voice an octave
> . . .

"You forget almost instantly he's cross-dressing." That line sticks in my mind. And suddenly it's so clear.

Jeffrey Bywater—a.k.a. Jeffrey Joslyn—is an accomplished amateur actor, especially accomplished at convincingly portraying young women. It was him I saw in his next role: the beautiful young *kinolau* of Pele on the Crater Rim Trail.

I don't bother with the other hits on Jeffrey Joslyn. I've found what I need. By now it's approaching three. Byron's flight arrives in forty-five minutes. I shut down my computer, take the business card of the *Pride of Aloha* staff who assisted me, and head for Honolulu International Airport.

I park near baggage claim area G, where passengers from Byron's Seattle flight will collect their luggage. And that's where the crew will most likely pass. I'm early, but I've never known a flight to arrive exactly on time. Often airplanes catch a tailwind to Hawai'i and arrive ahead of schedule. I can't risk missing Byron Joslyn.

I walk from the garage to baggage claim. The arrivals board says that Byron's Seattle flight has indeed landed early. Passengers begin streaming down an escalator and through sliding glass doors near where I'm standing. As bedraggled moms and dads with their yawning kids stumble in, I keep an eye out for the first sign of the flight crew.

As baggage claim fills, behind the throng the crew begins to emerge. Women flight attendants. Two pilots. More attendants. And finally a woman and a man walking together.

The man is Byron. He's put on weight since his Facebook photo, but Jeffrey's features still shine through. I follow Byron through baggage claim and out the glass doors to ground transportation and the parking garage. He and the woman part company. Then I walk up to him.

"You look familiar," I say. "Did you recently sail on the *Pride of Aloha?*"

"Yes," he says. "Were you on the cruise?"

"I work for the cruise line." I show him the *Pride of Aloha* business card, but pull it back before he can see the name "Margo" on it. "I'm waiting for some VIPs arriving on a flight from San Francisco."

"I don't remember seeing you on the ship," he says.

"I'm in customer relations," I say. "I don't very often sail."

"*Too bad.*" He sounds sincere.

"But I can't believe my luck." I deliberately perk up.

"What luck?"

"Well, I do the post cruise interviews after each sailing and it's often a pain to track down our customers after they disembark. But here you are!"

He looks at his watch. "How long will it take?"

"Only a few minutes," I say. "I have to meet that Frisco flight."

"Okay," he says. "Make it quick?"

"Quick it is." I point to a bench overlooking the endless stream of cars and cabs and buses gobbling up passengers and their belongings. We sit. I pull out my pen and spiral note-book, glance at his nametag, and write "Byron."

"Do you mind giving me your last name?" I ask.

"Joslyn," he says.

"Mahalo, Mr. Joslyn," I say. "So you took the cruise—when was it—the week of March 13?"

"Uh," he thinks for a moment, "that's right."

"And did you travel alone or with someone?"

"With someone. A friend of mine."

"Fantastic," I say in my best impression of a cruise con-sultant. "Did you both enjoy the cruise?"

"We did. Very much."

"Wonderful." I beam. "Did you take advantage of any on-shore activities at various ports?"

"Some," he says.

"How about on the Big Island, for instance? Did you and your friend disembark at Hilo or Kona?"

Byron hesitates. "Uh, I did," he says. "Both ports."

"And your friend?"

"Uh, no," Byron says. "He wasn't feeling well—a touch sea-sickness."

He's lying. But I know now how Jeffrey Bywater left and returned to the *Pride of Aloha* without a trace. Is Byron lying to hide his brother's relationship with a married woman, or to hide his brother's murder of her husband? The way Byron's blabbing, he's either stupid or he doesn't know everything.

"Where did you go on the Big Island?" I let him dig him-self deeper.

"Oh, the usual attractions," he says vaguely.

"Then you must have seen the eruption in the Halemaʻumaʻu Crater?" I throw him a curve. There was no eruption on those days.

"Yes, I sure did." He looks at his watch again. "Amazing."

I take the hint. "Thank you very much. *Pride of Aloha* is pleased you had a fun-filled cruise. And we hope to welcome you back again soon. You may receive a follow-up call asking you about our conversation. I'd appreciate if you'd give me positive feedback."

"I will." He taps me on the shoulder. "I know how it goes in the travel industry."

"Oh, could you tell me where I might find your friend to interview him?"

"He's also a flight attendant," Byron says. "And I happen to know he has Monday off. But he lives on Kāuaʻi."

"That's not in the budget, I'm afraid." I rise, say *"Mahalo,"* and walk away.

Now I can piece it all together.

Jeffrey Joslyn, a.k.a. Jeffrey Bywater, boards the *Pride of Aloha* on Saturday with his brother, Byron Joslyn. The ship calls at Hilo on Tuesday morning. Jeffrey disembarks using Byron's ID, rents a car probably as Joslyn, drives to the Volcano House, and stays in the room next to Rex and Donnie Ransom under the assumed name, Lars Stapleton. Donnie and Jeffry communicate through the rooms' common doors. Wednesday morning Jeffrey impersonates Pele on the Crater Rim Trail, approaches and startles Ransom, and then hurls him into the steam vent. Jeffrey ditches his costume, carelessly drops the red lipstick along the trail, drives to Kona, and re-boards the *Pride of Aloha* using Byron's ID.

Finally, to help sell Ransom's death as Pele's revenge, Jeffrey and Donnie return to the Big Island and kill Mick London, making it appear that he falls on rocks while fishing drunk.

This sounds convincing enough to me. But would it to a jury? There is little solid evidence. Though Jeffrey was identified by Pualani at the Volcano House, no trace of him or his costume turned up on the trail, except for the lipstick that lay in the sun, mist, and rain for several days. Not to mention that the key witness—who claims she saw the crime being committed—is an escaped mental patient.

Not enough to convict anyone of anything. Yet.

Back to Hanalei.

thirty-five

Monday morning before I fly to Kāuaʻi I gather all my notes and evidence for the Ransom case into a Manila envelope and slip it into my top desk drawer. Then I call Tommy. He's not in yet—he's probably sleeping off a late-night gig— so I leave him a message.

"Tommy, if you read about my untimely demise on the Garden Isle in tomorrow's paper, use your key to my office to recover an envelope in my desk pertaining to the Ransom case. You were right. Donnie has a new lover— Ransom's tenant, Jeffrey. She and the tenant killed the old man. Make sure you nail them. And make sure Ransom's kids get their rightful inheritance. If Donnie and Jeffrey really do go after me, that should clinch the case." I pause, wondering if I've forgotten anything. I give him Caitlin's phone number and then conclude, "Oh, yeah—if I don't come back you can have my '69 Impala."

Then I call Caitlin and also get her voicemail. "I'm wrapping up the investigation with one last neighbor-island trip," I tell her. "If I'm not in touch with you on Tuesday, please call my attorney, Tommy Woo." I give her his number and explain he will keep her posted in the unlikely event I am detained.

On the flight to Kāua'i I realize I've willed Tommy the one thing of value, besides my surfboard, I own. Imagine. Thirty-four years on this earth and my only possessions worth passing down are my board and a classic clunker that dates back to the moonshot.

From Lihue Airport I aim my rental car up the meandering Kūhiō Highway. Around Anahola I get behind a truck belonging to Oshiro Produce. On this narrow, winding road there's no chance of passing the big rig. So I follow the pineapple painted on the back until the truck finally turns off at the Princeville resorts. By then I'm on the even narrower and slower Highway 560 approaching Hanalei, and have to wait for oncoming traffic at the one-lane suspension bridge over the Hanalei River. The trip takes twice as long as it should, but no matter.

I park a few doors down from the Ransoms'. I'm back in Hanalei for the same reason I was here before. Last time I worked on Donnie. This time, Jeffrey. My hunch is he's not as smart as she is. And twice as arrogant. I'm not going to soft-pedal this time. And I'm betting he's going to do something desperate. Sooner rather than later.

Main thing: I don't want to see Donnie and Jeffrey walk. I don't want to see them get away with Ransom's murder and his millions—while his own children not only lose their father but also their inheritance. In the unlikely event anything happens to me, Tommy will follow through.

In the driveway are two new vehicles with temporary plates: a black Range Rover and an Audi convertible in the metallic red of Fireball's mangled Honda, but with more sparkle. Donnie and Jeffrey didn't waste time buying new toys. I knock on the door.

Jeffrey Bywater appears. We've never met, but instantly he knows who I am. And instantly I see why Donnie cozied up to him. He is—in person, as in his photo—a beautiful boy. His eyes are even more expressive than in the Mānele Bay pic. And his dark blond hair and trim muscular physique more striking. He's easily a dozen years junior to the widow of Rex Ransom. Now I can see how he passed for a young woman on stage and at Hawai'i Volcanoes National Park.

I don't expect him to invite me in, so I stand by the open door and say, "You dropped something on the Crater Rim Trail." I pull from my pocket the red lipstick I bought at Long's Drugs.

He glances at it. His eyes show a flash of recognition.

I toss him the lipstick.

He reaches for it. Then reconsiders and lets it drop. "You almost got me," he says. "You want my fingerprints—don't you?"

"I don't want your prints," I say. "That's not why I'm here."

He looks puzzled. Then he says, "Beat it, Sherlock, before you run into somebody more clever than you."

"Okay, but just one question before I go," I say. "I know you killed Rex Ransom . . ." I pause. "That's not my question. You had the old man believing you were gay, while you and his wife waited for him to die so you could collect his millions. But when you found out he planned to change his will, you hatched a plan for him to die mysteriously in Pele's domain, like two of his former executives. You arranged ironclad alibis. Donnie would be with me at the Volcano

House. And you would be on the *Pride of Aloha* with your brother, whose last name is different—since you changed yours."

"No shit, Sherlock." He smiles smugly. "Any moron can find name changes on the internet."

"You talked your way into the room at the Volcano House adjoining the Ransoms and made yourself up like Pele. So far, so good. You even fooled me."

"You're not much of a detective, Sherlock." The more he talks, the less I like him. And I didn't like him much to begin with.

"But you made some mistakes. Like lying poolside with Donnie at the Mānele Bay Resort. Like leaving this red lipstick," I gesture to it on the doormat, "along the Crater Rim Trail. Like pasting the warning note from newsprint in *The Garden Island*. And trusting your brother not to talk. There's more. But that's enough for now."

The first inklings of doubt cross his face. Will he call me Sherlock again? He doesn't.

So I say, "But my question isn't about Ransom. It's about Mick London." I pause again. "How did you and Donnie kill him?"

"Mick was drunk," Jeffrey says. "He slipped on a rock."

"I think he had help."

"You can't prove that," he says. But the way he shifts his weight from one foot to the other makes it seem like he's getting worried.

"She cast a spell over you, Jeffrey. She's a granite lady and you're a putty man. You wanted her so badly you'd do anything for her. Maybe that can be your plea deal."

The words barely get out of my mouth when Rex Ransom's widow strides to the door. Her beauty queen smile is gone. In its place is a dark, malicious grin. Her sparkling eyes now look like knives. She's scary.

"So long, Jeffrey." I step back. Enjoy your last days of freedom." Then I gesture to the red lipstick on the doormat. "So long, Donnie. You can keep the lipstick. It's your color."

Five minutes later I'm driving along the Hanalei River and the taro fields that border Kūhiō Highway doing forty-five—a good clip on this narrow, shoulder-less country road. As the hairpin turn and one-lane bridge approach, my rear view mirror is suddenly filled by a Range Rover—big and black and coming fast.

The Rover's motor roars. I feel a jolt from behind and hear metal grinding.

My car lurches forward and my speedometer climbs. *Fifty. Sixty.* I glance again at the mirror. Donnie is behind the wheel. Jeffrey is riding shotgun. Their faces show desperation. Looks like I got what I wanted. And it's not a pretty sight.

The hairpin and bridge are coming. No way I can make either at this speed.

But that's the idea. And that's the price I pay for taking a risk. They think I'm the only one who can put all the pieces together. They think I'm the only one standing between them and Ransom's millions. They don't know about Tommy.

My speedometer climbs. *Seventy.* That hairpin approaches. The push on my bumper suddenly eases. Donnie swings the big black Rover around on my left—against the flow of traffic. Lucky nobody's coming. She slams the Rover into the driver's side of my car. I hear another crunch of metal. She's trying to push me into the river.

I fight back. I crank my wheel to the left, against her. We careen down the highway—filling both lanes—locked in a battle that, odds are, I'll lose. My right wheels are already off the road.

The bridge arrives. But it's no longer empty. That Oshiro Produce truck I followed up from Anahola to Princeville crosses and turns onto the highway. The driver sees us coming. Doesn't matter. There's nowhere he can go—except head-on into the Rover. I slam on my brakes and hear the impact. Both the truck and Rover sweep behind me. My car slides sideways onto the bridge. It bangs the steel rails on either side. But makes it across.

I pull off the road and run back on foot. The wreckage lies on the Hanalei side of the bridge. A few cars have stopped and people are jumping out and hurrying to the scene. Some are talking excitedly on cell phones.

The Oshiro Produce truck looks okay from behind. Its dual wheels are still firmly under it. But the cab is crunched. Miraculously the driver is moving inside. He's talking to a bystander and pointing to his arm. The trucker apparently thinks it's broken. If that's all that happened, he's lucky.

Donnie and Jeffrey aren't so lucky. Through the Rover's shattered glass I see their unworn seatbelts hanging from the bent B-pillars. Inside the crushed cabin is a mess. Nobody is moving. Not even the bloodied and now deflated airbags could save them. Donnie is slumped over Jeffrey. They are locked in a last fatal embrace.

thirty-six

Tuesday I'm in my office reading the morning paper.

Two Dead in Kāua'i Head-on Collision

Lihue: A head-on collision yesterday on Kūhiō Highway claimed the lives of two Kāua'i residents and injured a third. According to Kāua'i police, a black Range Rover heading from Hanalei toward Princeville crossed the centerline when attempting to pass another vehicle near the one-lane bridge over the Hanalei River and collided head-on into a truck owned by Oshiro Produce. Both occupants of the Range Rover—driver Donnie Ransom, 47, and passenger Jeffrey Bywater, 29, of Hanalei—were killed. Neither was wearing a seat belt. The driver of the

> truck, Elton Yashima of Anahola, was admitted to Wilcox Hospital in serious condition, but has since been upgraded to fair.
>
> Excessive speed may have been a factor in the accident. Police estimate the Rover was traveling in excess of seventy miles per hour in a forty-five zone. Her Hanalei neighbors identified Donnie Ransom as the widow of the former CEO of Ransom Geothermal, who died recently at Hawai'i Volcanoes National Park. Jeffrey Bywater was a tenant in the Ransom home.

I was at the scene when Kāua'i police and EMS arrived. After the produce driver was taken to hospital and Donnie's and Jeffrey's bodies were removed, I gave a statement to police. My statement was corroborated by my badly damaged rental car and by the truck driver when he was interviewed later that day. There remained little doubt about Donnie and Jeffrey's desperate attempt to silence the only person who they believed could prove they murdered Rex Ransom.

Their violent deaths on Kūhiō Highway unfortunately won't bring him back, but at least Caitlin and her brothers should now be able to claim the inheritance their father intended for them.

The morning flies by. I'm pleased about closing the Ransom case. And I'm looking forward to seeing Maile.

She's stopping by this afternoon with Kula and later we're going out. I'm hoping she's finally ready.

Things are looking up. Except I still haven't closed the Pali case.

Just before noon I drive to Ala Moana Shopping Center again to see Ashley. She's promised to bring her photo card with the birthday pics that I hope may move the case along.

Soon we're sitting by the koi pond, Ashley reaches into her pink handbag and—miracles never cease—extracts the long-awaited photo card. She slips it into her camera.

Ashley turns on the camera and tries to scroll through the photos. "Oh, barf, I totally messed up!"

"Messed up?" I'm expecting the worst. *"Totally?"*

"Duh. I must have pushed the wrong button or something."

"So you've got no photos after all?" My hopes are fading.

"No photos," she says, "but I have this, you know, really long video instead. And look—*way* cool!—it's stamped with the date and time just before I left the party."

She's right. The date is early on Sunday, in the wee hours, about forty minutes before the estimated time of the fatal crash.

Ashley starts the video. She looks a little less perky as the images start to roll. One of the partyers is saying to a stumbling Fireball, "You're like really hammered, dude!" He gives her an odd look but seems incapable of a verbal reply. Then a woman appears in the frame with a tray of draft beers. It's Stormy, the same server who sold beer to my underage helper, Nicholas. Stormy hands a beer to Fireball and says, "That's the last one for you, pal." He takes the beer. Then she says, "You're not driving, right? He shakes his head. She replies, "You better not." She walks away.

I've seen enough.

"May I borrow your camera for a few days?" I ask. "I promise to return it."

"Whatever," Ashley says. "Is the video what you need?"

"It is."

I thank her, have her write another chain of custody statement in my notebook, and walk her back into Safari. Then I drive to Maunakea Street feeling relieved. Now I have a dated video that shows Fireball being served when he's obviously drunk, and the server, Stormy, appearing to acknowledge that fact. With this I've got something Mr. Lindquist's attorney should be able to use.

More than I could have hoped for.

Back in my office I call the attorney and he's pleased. It's turning out to be a good day. I phone Tommy with the news.

Tommy answers, "Howzit, Kai?"

"What—no joke?" I'm stunned.

"I'm not in a laughing mood." He sounds down. "The wedding's hit a glitch. Zahra may have to go back to Kenya."

"How come?"

"Long story," he says. "Meet you for dinner tonight? Same old place?"

"Sorry, I'm going out with Maile. How about tomorrow night?"

"Okay," he says.

"You don't sound good, Tommy. Sure you're alright?"

"I'll survive." He hangs up.

I'm feeling suddenly gloomy as I close up my office and walk down the shag stairs. The atmosphere inside the *lei* shop doesn't help. Blossom's ex-boyfriend, Junior, is back. He's shouting at her and Mrs. Fujiyama is picking up the phone. Junior rips the phone base cord from the wall, nearly knocking Mrs. Fujiyama down.

Then Blossom rises from her chair, defiantly looks him in the eye, and shouts, "Get outta here, Junior! Leave me alone!"

Junior lunges over the *lei* table at her, but I grab him from behind and hurl him down onto the floor. He rolls around on the linoleum, looking dazed. He glances up at his ex-girlfriend standing resolutely by the lei table, and then at me standing over him with fists clenched. No trash-talk this time. Junior pulls himself up, lumbers from the shop, and screeches away in his truck.

A post-traumatic silence descends on the shop. After her display of bravery, Blossom looks stunned. She clutches me and buries her suddenly tear-streamed face in my chest, darkening my aloha shirt.

At that moment Maile steps into the shop with Kula. When she sees Blossom wrapped around me, Maile's mouth drops open. The color drains from her face. She turns and stalks out of the shop, leaving the golden retriever behind.

I pry myself from the *lei* girl and run after Maile. "Wait!" I shout. "Maile, it's not what you think!"

"I don't want to hear it, Kai Cooke." She turns around. "You just burned your last bridge." She runs down Maunakea Street.

I chase after her. Kula pulls up beside me and then darts ahead after Maile. I grab his collar. Maile crosses the intersection at Pauahi Street. By the time we get there, the light turns red. Traffic whizzes by in both directions. I try to restrain the retriever, but he keeps pulling.

"Easy, Boy." I grip his collar with both hands.

When the light turns green, Maile is already half way down the next block and disappears in the crowded sidewalks around Hotel Street. There's no use trying to catch her in this traffic. Not with Kula off leash. If anything happens to him—I don't even want to think about it.

"C'mon, Kula." I turn around and start walking back to my office. He plants his paws. He wants Maile. *That makes two of us.*

"It's okay, boy." I stroke his warm fur. "We'll get her back. I promise."

I coax him to the *lei* shop. Before we get there I see Junior's truck pulled over on Maunakea Street behind two HPD cruisers. They're handcuffing him and putting him in one of the cruisers. *Got him!* I wish I could be happier about it. *No good deed goes unpunished.*

Inside the shop Blossom and Mrs. Fujiyama are sitting together at the *lei* table. Blossom isn't crying anymore.

"They arrested Junior," I say. "You're safe now, Blossom."

"Oh, *mahalo*, Kai!" She hugs me and pats Kula.

Then I have an inspiration, and switch to Pidgin. "You like do me one favah?"

She nods. "Shoots!"

I give her Maile's cell number and briefly explain what just happened.

"Okay, I gonna call right now!" Blossom says. "Fo' sure!"

She pulls her cell phone from her purse and dials. Before the conversation begins—I don't want to hear it—I turn to the retriever.

"C'mon, Kula," I say, "let's get some wheels and go fetch our favorite pet detective."

The dog looks up at me, wags his tail, and the two of us head for the parking garage.

About the Author

Chip Hughes earned a Ph.D. in English at Indiana University and taught American literature, film, writing, and popular fiction for nearly three decades at the University of Hawai'i at Mānoa. His non-fiction publications include two books and numerous essays on John Steinbeck.

An active member of the Private Eye Writers of America, Chip launched the Surfing Detective mystery series with *Murder on Moloka'i* (2004) and *Wipeout!* (2007), published by Island Heritage. The series is now published exclusively by Slate Ridge Press, whose volumes include *Kula* (2011), *Murder at Volcano House* (2014), *Hanging Ten in Paris Trilogy* (2017), and reissues of the first two novels.

Chip and his wife split their time between homes in Hawai'i and upstate New York.